Christian Responses to Issues of
Human Sexuality and Gender Diversity:
A Guide to the Churches in India

Christian Responses to Issues of Human Sexuality and Gender Diversity:
A Guide to the Churches in India

Editor
Philip Kuruvilla

National Council of Churches in India (NCCI)
2017

Christian Responses to Issues of Human Sexuality and Gender Diversity: A Guide to the Churches in India — jointly published by the Rev. Dr. Ashish Amos of the Indian Society for Promoting Christian Knowledge (ISPCK), Post Box 1585, 1654, Madarsa Road, Kashmere Gate, Delhi-110006 andNational Council of Churches in India (NCCI), Nagpur – 440 001.

ISBN: 978-81-8465-623-7

Front Cover Title:	Faces
Illustration and Artwork:	Varkey Parakkal
About the Artist:	Varkey Parakkal is a student of Journalism, a 'hobbyist designer', who has been designing for the LGBTI cause for several years.
Back Cover Title:	Breaking Binaries
Illustration and Artwork:	Angad Gummaraju
About the Artist:	Angad Gummaraju is a medical student at Manipal University. An artist, Angad describes surgery as the most noble form of art to exist. Angad identifies as a transgender, and often finds peace in the sanctum that is the operating room

Laser typeset at **ISPCK,** Post Box 1585, 1654, Madarsa Road, Kashmere Gate, Delhi-110006.

Tel: 23866323, Fax: 91-11-23865490

e-mail: ashish@ispck.org.in • ella@ispck.org.in

website: www.ispck.org.in

Disclaimer

This Guide or Handbook is meant to help readers understand same-sex sexual orientations and gender identities in order to help them know more about their own sexualities, help them with their interpersonal relationships and to deal with the complexities given by their own faith traditions. Even though it is intended primarily for Christians, Christian organizations, and the Church, it can also be used by parents and teachers, as well as family and friends of the sexual minorities. Anyone can read it, to gain better skills in interacting with people of diverse sexualities and gender identities, and to use the correct terminologies- not because they are 'politically correct', but because one needs to be sensitive with others walking in the same sacred space.

As you read, you will see that this book provides new theological and biblical insights. It also includes scientific and legal information from credible sources, but it is not to be confused for a medical or legal peer-reviewed journal, or to be used in place of psychotherapy in a clinical setting.

We have made every possible attempt to ensure the information in this book was correct at the time of going to press. However, the Editor and the Publisher do not assume - and hereby disclaim - any liability to any party caused by errors or omissions, whether such errors or omissions result from negligence, accident, or any other cause.

We pray this book will not hurt anyone's sensibilities, rather that it is able to shed light on the sensitive subject of human sexuality and gender diversity, help elucidate the complexities of the matter, and help the reader see that when it comes to personal struggles with sexuality, people are more similar than different, in reality as much as in God's eyes.

Contents

CHAPTER - 3
Unheard Voices, Insider Views:
Most-asked Q & A's, LGBTI Perspectives

CHAPTER - 5

Documents, Reports and Statements: Helpful NGO's and Suggested
Web Links/Books

Foreword

I am immensely happy to write a Foreword for a book that epitomizes NCCI's commitment to keep its member churches and institutions updated with the latest issues, however unpleasant they may seem. Sex and Sexuality are not words that usually appear in Church or Christian publications, yet it is evident that issues pertaining to human sexuality are finding their way into our daily lives in several forms, including through social media. The church cannot afford to turn a blind eye to this growing malaise.

NCCI took up such thorny issues as far back as 2001, in its First Study Institute on Human Sexuality. It continued to be linked with this crucial area and brought out an 'Ecumenical Document on Human Sexuality' in 2011. Let me give an excerpt from the 'Foreword' I wrote in the reprint of that publication, as it is still relevant today: *The purpose of this document is to invite and encourage churches to articulate mature responsible views on human sexuality and to enable Christians to live by such perspectives in their inter-personal relationships. We need to begin to teach the subject of sexuality with more positive and affirming messages about the biblical basis of sexuality, its compatibility with our spirituality, and God's desire for us to bring our sexuality and all its accompanying aspects into God's presence. Rather than avoid and ignore difficult issues associated with human sexuality, churches need to begin to engage in meaningful dialogue concerning biblical theology and ethics. In other words, it is important to recognise that human sexuality is a wonderful gift from our Creator; it is an integral part of our personalities. At the same time, since all human beings are created in the image of God, we need to discern this image in all, relate to all in justice and love, and thus include all of us in God's family.*

NCCI's work among the people living with HIV and AIDS [PLWA] brought us in direct contact with a group of people euphemistically called 'high risk groups'. When we went beyond the nomenclature, we touched the pain and anguish many of them felt on a day to day basis, and we felt the need to engage with them on a deeper and pastoral level. This we have been doing over the last 3 years, and we felt that such a publication as this would be useful to the churches. We are grateful to ICCO/Kirk en Actie for their loyalty, partnership and support in helping us to take our ideas forward into action through programs.

While dealing with this topic we realized that we need to move with a great deal of sensitivity, not only towards our Christian readers- this is a Handbook meant for the Churches- but also towards the representatives of the LGBTI communities that are focused upon in this book. We walk the fine line with trepidation, sensitivity and concern that no one should feel aggrieved or hurt at the contents of this book- which no doubt has explicitly sexual material which will not have appeared in any Christian publication before.

Fr Philip Kuruvilla is best suited as the Editor of this Handbook - he has worked with the NCCI in the fields of Human Rights, HIV and AIDS, and Human Sexuality, since 2000. In 2004, when the churches were struggling with the issues of HIV and AIDS, he brought out a similar Handbook for the Churches on HIV and AIDS. He has subsequently engaged churches and theological colleges in the arena of human sexuality, and challenged them to take their responses to a higher theological and pastoral level.

We expect bouquets and brickbats. There will be a fair bit of criticism over the contents- both in what it contains and about what it left out. At the end of the day, if it is useful to the reader, brings the rainbow hues of God's creation closer to understanding one another, and helps them to live out the differences peacefully, then this book will have achieved what it set out to do.

Rev. Dr. Roger Gaikwad
General Secretary,
National Council of Churches in India,
and Project Holder of NCCI's ESHA Program

The Editor's Choice

'To every thing there is a season, and a time to every purpose under the heaven' [Ecclesiastes 3:1]. The ancient Greeks had two words for time: *chronos* and *kairos*. While the former refers to chronological or sequential time, the latter signifies a proper or opportune time for action. A book such as this could not come out earlier than the perfect time – *kairos*. It would neither have been right nor acceptable. This book has been waiting for the right time, and that time is now. Although NCCI has been working in the field of Human Sexuality and Gender Diversity for over 15 years, it is in the last 3 years that the work has been taken to the churches and they have responded positively, which is starkly different from their response even 5 years ago. It could also be that it coincides with the heightened awareness coming from the NALSA judgment and the Rights of Transgender Bill of 2016 which the Government of India has been pursuing.

I preferred the title **'Editor's Choice'** to the standard 'Editorial', because I had to make several choices in the compiling of this Guide/Handbook, and not all of them have been easy ones.

I had to choose how deep to go into the world of sex and sexuality. Knowing this book would be read by good Christians, clergy, average church-goers, and men, women and youth who daily dabble with various areas of their own sexuality, often without realizing or acknowledging it, but whose sensibilities could easily be offended - the trick was to ensure that the Handbook contained a wealth of information and yet did not go into explicit sexual inputs which would possibly make titillating reading, but not be of much use to the genuine seeker. I am sure that there will be criticism about what it contains and about what it leaves out, but that is the result of the choices.

I had to choose how much information to put in- too little would make it irrelevant, and too much would make the book boring and insipid. Concerned parents looking for a way to deal with their effeminate son, debating religious and psychological responses, looking for NGO's who might make a difference. All are included here.

I had to choose as to who would write the articles representing the LGBTI communities, and who would answer the intriguing questions that most people ask, but no Christian book would answer. Some might say I should have used more Christians as authors/writers, but the fact is that there are not enough Christians who are well-versed with the subjects covered here. Rather than go on the internet and bring in umpteen 'foreign experts', I chose to rope in able members of the various LGBTI communities here in India. Deepak Kashyap and the Payana team had already created very informative material and were more than happy to allow us to use them.

I had to choose which authors to select to give us theological inputs. Seeing this book was mainly meant for readers not highly trained in theology, and yet knowing that the readers would like to understand how the scriptures deal with biblical texts about human sexuality and gender diversity, I chose four of India's renowned theologians from Marthoma, Church of South India, Presbytarian and Orthodox backgrounds to give new interpretations to traditional 'clobber texts' and seeming homophobic verses. Their theological articles are simple, readable and lucid, they allow the reader to see traditional texts and attitudes in a totally new light. The article by Prof George Zachariah, which has been seen in many *avatars* in articles, books and magazines, still remains the best article for an alternate look at traditional homophobic positions. Dr Aruna turns her exceptional feminist focii into an expose on gender issues . Prof John Lalnuntluanga from Mizoram has also offered an out- of-the-box article. The fourth article, by renowned Jacobite Syrian Orthodox theologian, Metropolitan Dr. Mor Coorilos, brings some fresh and unusual theological insights.

I had to choose, of all the wonderful rainbow community people I met on my journey, who to invite to tell their story in Unheard Voices. I chose four, but there are many others whose voices need to be heard as well, beautiful voices, hurt voices, suppressed voices.

For the Editor's Choice, I selected three pieces which tell the ups and downs of their journey much better than I ever can. They are presented here:

1. *"To those who are lesbian, gay, bisexual or transgender, let me say: You are not alone. Your struggle for an end to violence and discrimination is a shared struggle. Any attack on you is an attack on the universal values the United Nations and I have sworn to defend and uphold. Today, I stand with you and I call upon all countries and people to stand with you, too"* - United Nations Secretary-General Ban Ki-moon, March 2012.

The case for extending the same rights to lesbian, gay, bisexual and transgender (LGBT) persons as those enjoyed by everyone else is neither radical nor complicated. It rests on two fundamental principles that underpin international human rights law: equality and non-discrimination. The opening words of the Universal Declaration of Human Rights are unequivocal: "All human beings are born free and equal in dignity and rights."

Nevertheless, deeply embedded homophobic attitudes, often combined with a lack of adequate legal protection against discrimination on grounds of sexual orientation and gender identity, expose many LGBT people of all ages and in all regions of the world to egregious violations of their human rights. They are discriminated against in the labour market, in schools and in hospitals, and mistreated and disowned by their own families. On the streets of towns and cities around the world, they are singled out for physical attack – beaten, sexually assaulted, tortured and killed. [*From the Foreword to "Born free and equal": Booklet produced by UN: © 2012 United Nations]*

2. *"You pay a cost to assert your individuality and freedom"* [Deepak Kashyap, The Pink Booklet]

3. Hetero-normative ie., a world-view that promotes heterosexuality as the normal or preferred sexual orientation also leads to downgrading all

other kinds of sexual encounters. Society is so deeply rooted into hetero-normative bipolar genders that it does not recognize any kind of difference in expression or way of life. The mainstream morality guards the hetero-normative social fabric in such a way, that it either punishes severely or 'invisiblizes' any alternate expressions. The 'process of invisibalization' is an easy way of exclusion and marginalization. What is not to be seen is not recognized -and what is not recognized cannot get facilities, rights, and other entitlements. This invisibility of sexual minorities is one aspect. The opposite aspect is visible sexual minorities; people with alternate gender identities and sexual orientation who have accepted their identities even at the cost of losing facilities, rights, other entitlements and acceptance in the society. Within these community groups there is acceptance and comfort, and because of this comfort people have found it courageous to become visible. Many transgenders, hijras, and Kothis have formed their own community spaces which are visible groups in the society. These groups are not free of violence, violation of rights, discrimination, stigma and exploitation in the society. They are seen as challenge to social fabric of hetero-normative family and marriage systems.

Throughout history we have seen that when a section of society is stigmatized (Jews, Gypsies, Dalits), this leads to discrimination in the form of oppression, violence, harassment, poverty. Invariably groups rebel against the oppressor. The form of rebellion varies but the purpose of rebellion is to be part of the social fabric to change the beliefs and attitudes of the existing social structures. Similarly the movement that was initiated around homosexuality, bisexuality, trangenderism etc., took the form of people from these orientations or preferences coming out into the public sphere and expressing their right to freedom of expression and choice. This in turn led to the hetero-normative society posing a threat in the form of resistance, violence, denial of rights etc. Therefore the need to dialogue, debate, discourse on alternate genders and sexualities, so as to bring about a better understanding in the larger society for creating equality, respect and dignity. [*From 'To Be or Not to Be', by Payana*]

This Handbook attempts to bring many issues out of the closet and into the light. With social media, the internet and the ubiquitous cell phone now bringing pornography and sex into our homes unasked, seriously affecting our congregations, families and children, the National Council of Churches in India, [NCCI] has decided to share the learnings from its involvement with sexual minorities over the last several years - through this book it hopes to empower member churches and theological colleges to take up these issues and pro-actively respond to them, not only biblically and theologically, but also with psychological, medical and legal inputs, all of which are included here

Most faith leaders, I learnt from my decade long work in HIV, have to go through the classic responses —eg., denial, trivialization, judgmentalism - before accepting that the issue exists within their own communities, and that they have to take responsibility in dealing with them. Similarly Christian leaders have been equally guilty, of ignoring the LGBTI groups with traditional responses that 'they' do not exist in 'our church/society'; or that these issues are 'western' and not affecting Indians, or with downright homo and transphobic responses. Scripture and theology are then brought in to buttress positions. Meanwhile several groups of PDSO's [people with diverse sexual orientations] are clubbed together under acronyms like 'LGBTIQ's, and individually and/ or collectively made into objects of exclusion, ostracism, harassment and ridicule. The consequence of stigma for these communities has been repeatedly documented and often include social isolation, verbal and physical violence, lack of access to medical care, and loss of livelihood.

Here laid out is a smorgasbord – a veritable feast- for a genuine learner who seeks to understand. It has both variety and quality which will keep the reader occupied and enlightened. The question is, or rather the questions are, can the church of Jesus Christ go beyond highlighting 'sinful behavior' and God's punishment, and instead, tell of Christ's love - for the outcast, the marginalized, the diseased - the 'sinners' of his time? Can we focus on God's immense ability to include everyone, even as he forgives our sins? I believe this book will go a long way to bring about this change.

Philip Kuruvilla

Glossary

Sam Killerman

A. **A list of LGBTIQ+ Vocabulary Definitions**

B. **Glossary on Phobias [Fear] against Sexual Minorities**

This list is neither comprehensive nor inviolable, but it's a work in progress constantly honing and adjusting language. Identity terms are tricky, and trying to write a description that works *perfectly* for *everyone* using that label simply isn't possible. Some definitions here may include words you aren't familiar with, or have been taught a flawed or incomplete definition for.

A.   A list of LGBTQ+ Vocabulary Definitions

ally /"al-lie"/ – *noun* : a (typically straight and/or cisgender) person who supports and respects members of the LGBTQ community. We consider people to be active allies who take action on in support and respect.

androgyny/ous /"an-jrah-jun-ee"; "an-jrah-jun-uss"/ – *adj.* : **1.** a gender expression that has elements of both masculinity and femininity; **2.** occasionally used in place of "intersex" to describe a person with both female and male anatomy.

asexual – *adj.* : experiencing little or no sexual attraction to others and/ or a lack of interest in sexual relationships/behavior. Asexuality exists on a continuum from people who experience no sexual attraction or have any desire for sex, to those who experience low levels, or sexual attraction only under specific conditions, and many of these different places on the continuum have their own identity labels

*Asexuality is different from celibacy in that it is a sexual orientation whereas celibacy is an abstaining from a certain action.

biological sex – *noun* : a medical term used to refer to the chromosomal, hormonal and anatomical characteristics that are used to classify an individual as female or male or intersex. Often referred to as simply "sex," "physical sex," "anatomical sex," or specifically as "sex assigned at birth."

Often seen as a binary but as there are many combinations of chromosomes, hormones, and primary/secondary sex characteristics, it's more accurate to view this as a spectrum (which is more inclusive of intersex people as well as trans-identified people).* – Is commonly conflated with gender.

bisexual – *adj.* : **1** a person who is emotionally, physically, and/or sexually attracted to males/men and females/women. **2** a person who is emotionally, physically, and/or sexually attracted to people of their gender and another gender . This attraction does not have to be equally split or indicate a level of interest that is the same across the genders or sexes an individual may be attracted to.

*Can simply be shortened to "bi."

cisgender/"siss-jendur"/ – *adj.* : a person whose gender identity and biological sex assigned at birth align (e.g., man and assigned male at birth). A simple way to think about it is if a person is not transgender, they are cisgender. The word cisgender can also be shortened to "cis."

*"Cis" is a latin prefix that means "on the same side [as]" or "on this side [of]."

cisnormativity – *noun* : the assumption, in individuals or in institutions, that everyone is cisgender, and that cisgender identities are superior to trans* identities or people. Leads to invisibility of non-cisgender identities.

closeted – *adj.* : an individual who is not open to themselves or others about their (queer) sexuality or gender identity. This may be by choice and/or for other reasons such as fear for one's safety, peer or family rejection or disapproval and/or loss of housing, job, etc. Also known as being "in the closet." When someone chooses to break this silence they "come out" of the closet. (See coming out)

coming out – **1** the process by which one accepts and/or comes to identify one's own sexuality or gender identity (to "come out" to oneself). **2** The process by which one shares one's sexuality or gender identity with others (to "come out" to friends, etc.).

cross-dresser – *noun* : someone who wears clothes of another gender/ sex.

fluid(ity) – *adj.* : generally with another term attached, like gender-fluid or fluid-sexuality, fluid(ity) describes an identity that may change or shift over time between or within the mix of the options available (e.g., man and woman, bi and straight). **bigender** – *adj.* : a person who fluctuates between traditionally "woman" and "man" gender-based behavior and identities, identifying with both genders (and sometimes a third gender).

FtM / F2M; MtF / M2F – *abbreviation* : female-to-male transgender or transsexual person; male-to-female transgender or transsexual person.

gay – *adj.* **1** individuals who are primarily emotionally, physically, and/or sexually attracted to members of the same sex and/or gender. More commonly used when referring to men who are attracted to other men, but can be applied to women as well. **2** An umbrella term used to refer to the queer community as a whole, or as an individual identity label for anyone who does not identify as heterosexual.

*"Gay" is a word that's had many different meanings throughout time. In the 20th century it was meant to mean "happy"

gender binary – *noun* : the idea that there are only two genders and that every person is one of those two.

gender expression – *noun* : the external display of one's gender, through a combination of dress, demeanor, social behavior, and other factors, generally made sense of on scales of masculinity and femininity. Also referred to as "gender presentation."

gender fluid– *adj.* : : gender fluid is a gender identity best described as a dynamic mix of boy and girl. A person who is gender fluid may always feel like a mix of the two traditional genders, but may feel more man some days, and more woman other days.

gender identity – *noun* : the internal perception of an one's gender, and how they label themselves, based on how much they align or don't align with what they understand their options for gender to be. Common identity labels include man, woman, genderqueer, trans, and more. Often confused with biological sex, or sex assigned at birth.

heteronormativity – *noun* : the assumption, in individuals or in institutions, that everyone is heterosexual (e.g. asking a woman if she has a boyfriend) and that heterosexuality is superior to all other sexualities. Leads to invisibility and stigmatizing of other sexualities.

hermaphrodite – *noun* : an outdated medical term previously used to refer to someone who was born with some combination of typically-male and typically-female sex characteristics. It's considered stigmatizing and inaccurate. *See intersex.*

heterosexual – *adj.* : a person primarily emotionally, physically, and/or sexually attracted to members of the opposite sex. Also known as 'straight'.

homosexual – *adj.* & *noun* : a person primarily emotionally, physically, and/or sexually attracted to members of the same sex/gender. This [medical] term is considered stigmatizing (particularly as a noun) due to its history as a category of mental illness, and is discouraged for common use (use gay or lesbian instead).

intersex – *adj.* : term for a combination of chromosomes, gonads, hormones, internal sex organs, and genitals that differs from the two expected patterns of male or female. Formerly known as hermaphrodite (or hermaphroditic), but these terms are now outdated and derogatory.

lesbian – *noun* & *adj.* women who have the capacity to be attracted romantically, erotically, and/or emotionally to some other women.

LGBTQI +— *abbreviations* : shorthand or umbrella terms for all folks who have a non-normative (or queer) gender or sexuality, there are many different initialisms people prefer. LGBTQI is Lesbian Gay Bisexual Transgender Queer, and Intersex. Sometimes people put a + at the end in an effort to be more inclusive.

*There is no "correct" initialism or acronym — what is preferred varies by person, region, and often evolves over time.

metrosexual – *adj.* : a man with a strong aesthetic sense who spends more time, energy, or money on his appearance and grooming than is considered gender normative.

MSM / WSW – *abbreviations* : men who have sex with men or women who have sex with women, to distinguish sexual behaviors from sexual identities. Often used in the field of HIV/Aids education, prevention, and treatment.

Mx. / "mix" or "schwa" / – an honorific (e.g. Mr., Ms., Mrs., etc.) that is gender neutral. It is often the option of choice for folks who do not identify within the gender binary: *Mx. Smith is a great teacher.*

queer – *adj.* : used as an umbrella term to describe individuals who don't identify as straight. Also used to describe people who have a non-normative gender identity, or as a political affiliation. Due to its historical use as a derogatory term, it is not embraced or used by all members of the LGBTQ community. The term "queer" can often be use interchangeably with LGBTQ (e.g., "queer folks" instead of "LGBTQ folks").

- If a person tells you they are not comfortable with you referring to them as queer, don't. Always respect individual's preferences when it comes to identity labels, particularly contentious ones (or ones with troubled histories) like this.

- Use the word queer only if you are comfortable explaining to others what it means, because some people feel uncomfortable with the word, it is best to know/feel comfortable explaining why you choose to use it if someone inquires.

sexual orientation – *noun* : the type of sexual, romantic, emotional/ spiritual attraction one has; the capacity to feel for some others, generally labeled based on the gender relationship between the person and the people they are attracted to. Often confused with sexual preference.

sexual preference – *noun* : the types of sexual intercourse, stimulation, and gratification one likes to receive and participate in. Generally when this term is used, it is being mistakenly interchanged with "sexual orientation," creating an illusion that one has a choice (or "preference") in who they are attracted to.

sex reassignment surgery (SRS) – *noun* : used by some medical professionals to refer to a group of surgical options that alter a person's biological sex. "Gender confirmation surgery" is considered by many to be a more affirming term. In most cases, one or multiple surgeries are required to achieve legal recognition of gender variance. Some refer to different surgical procedures as "top" surgery and "bottom" surgery to discuss what type of surgery they are having without having to be more explicit.

third gender – *noun* : for a person who does not identify with either man or woman, but identifies with another gender. This gender category is used by societies that recognise three or more genders, both contemporary and historic, and is also a conceptual term meaning different things to different people who use it, as a way to move beyond the gender binary.

trans* – *adj.* : An umbrella term covering a range of identities that transgress socially defined gender norms. Trans with an asterisk is often used in written forms (not spoken) to indicate that you are referring to the larger group nature of the term, and specifically including non-binary identities, as well as transgender men (transmen) and transgender women (trans women).

transgender – *adj.* : A person who lives as a member of a gender other than that assigned at birth based on anatomical sex.

- Because sexuality labels (e.g., gay, straight, bi) are generally based on the relationship between the person's gender and the genders they are attracted to, trans* sexuality can be defined in a couple of ways. Some people may choose to self-identify as straight, gay, bi, lesbian, or pansexual (or others, using their gender identity as a basis), or they might describe their sexuality using other-focused terms like gynesexual, androsexual, or skoliosexual (see full list for definitions for these terms.

- A trans* person can be straight, gay, bisexual, queer, or any other sexual orientation.

transman; transwoman – *noun* : An identity label sometimes adopted by female-to-male transgender people or transsexuals to signify that they are men while still affirming their history as assigned female sex at birth. (sometimes referred to as transguy) **2** Identity label sometimes adopted by male-to-female transsexuals or transgender people to signify that they are women while still affirming their history as assigned male sex at birth.

transsexual – *noun and adj.* a person who identifies psychologically as a gender/sex other than the one to which they were assigned at birth. Transsexuals often wish to transform their bodies hormonally and surgically to match their inner sense of gender/sex.

transvestite – *noun* : a person who dresses as the binary opposite gender expression ("cross-dresses") for any one of many reasons, including relaxation, fun, and sexual gratification (often called a "cross-dresser," and should not be confused with transsexual).

B. Glossary on Phobias [Fear] against Sexual Minorities:

A **sexual minority** is a group whose sexual identity, orientation or practices differ from the majority of the surrounding society. It can also refer to transgender, genderqueer (including third gender) or intersex individuals. The term is primarily used to refer to LGB individuals, particularly gay people

biphobia – *noun* : a range of negative attitudes (e.g., fear, anger, intolerance, invisibility, resentment, erasure, or discomfort) that one may have or express towards bisexual individuals. Biphobia can come from and be seen within the LGBTQ community as well as straight society. Biphobic

— adj. : a word used to describe an individual who harbors some elements of this range of negative attitudes towards bisexual people.

homophobia *— noun* : an umbrella term for a range of negative attitudes (e.g., fear, anger, intolerance, resentment, erasure, or discomfort) that one may have towards members of LGBTQ community. The term can also connote a fear, disgust, or dislike of being perceived as LGBTQ. Homophobic *— adj.* : a word used to describe an individual who harbors some elements of this range of negative attitudes towards gay people.

*The term can be extended to bisexual and transgender people as well; however, the terms biphobia and transphobia are used to emphasize the specific biases against individuals of bisexual and transgender communities.

*May be experienced inwardly by someone who identifies as queer (internalized homophobia).

transphobia *— noun* : the fear of, discrimination against, or hatred of trans* people, the trans* community, or gender ambiguity. Transphobia can be seen within the queer community, as well as in general society. Transphobia is often manifested in violent and deadly means. While the exact numbers and percentages aren't incredibly solid on this, it's safe to say that trans* people are far more likely than their cisgender peers (including LGB people) to be the victims of violent crimes and murder. Transphobic *— adj.* : a word used to describe an individual who harbors some elements of this range of negative attitudes, thoughts, intents, towards trans* people.

CHAPTER - 1

Inclusive Theologies: Re-reading the Bible and Re-writing Worship

Inclusive Theologies

Church and Homophobia:
Envisioning an Inclusive Church

George Zachariah

For most of us, and for our Church traditions, homosexuality has always been a taboo topic, ignored altogether or condemned as "an intrinsic moral evil," as Pope Benedict XVI has put it. Even liberal minded Indian Christians opine that, "To think that such unnatural tendencies are God given or good is to give a wrong idea. For example, a man with criminal tendencies may be behaving like that because of genetic or hormonal problems. But no one would justify such criminal behavior. Society would try to correct him or keep him away from society. Similar is the case of an insane person. Society tries to give him opportunity for healing and make him a normal human being. Such an approach should be taken in the case of homosexuals also....There should be efforts to correct such behavior and bring them to normal life." Such liberal and patronizing approach emerges from the theological standpoint "love the sinner; but hate the sin." Such beliefs expose our obsession with legitimizing the dominant norms and morality, using

Bible and the teachings of the Church, as "normal" and "natural." This is the context in which we are invited by the NCCI and the CSI Synod to wrestle with the issue of homosexuality, theologically and biblically to help our faith communities to transform ourselves into inclusive communities.

Let me begin with the statements of two revered Christian leaders. "If someone is gay and he searches for the Lord and has good will, who am I to judge him?" This statement of Pope Francis is a historical shift from the Vatican position that homosexuality is "an intrinsic moral evil." Rev. Gary Hall, the Dean of the National Cathedral in Washington DC, in a sermon, condemned homophobia as sin. "We must have the courage to call homophobia and heterosexism what they are. They are sin. Homophobia is a sin. Heterosexism is a sin. Shaming people for whom they love is a sin." He further observed that "Only when all our churches say that clearly and boldly and courageously will our LGBT youth be free to grow up in a culture that totally embraces them fully as they are." Dean Hall concluded his sermon in an affirmative note: "It is not only just OK to be gay, straight, bisexual, or transgendered. It is good to be that way, because that is the way God has made you."

Let us clarify the meaning of some important terms that we are going to discuss in this consultation. *LGBT* is the acronym for lesbian, gay, bisexual, and transgender. It is an umbrella term for individuals who engage in same-sex acts and/or gender-variant behaviors. *Gay* is a man who is sexually attracted to other men. Gay is also sometimes used to refer to lesbians. *Lesbian* is a woman who is sexually attracted to other women. *Bisexual* is a person who is sexually attracted to both women and men. *Transgender* is a person who identifies with a gender that differs from that person's assigned sex at birth. *Intersex* refers to people who have physical characteristics, genital and/or chromosomal, of both male and female sexes. It is also known as disorders of sex development. *Queer* is an umbrella term for LGBT people. It also refers to an ethical norm of transgression and/or deconstructing false binaries such as female and male or homosexual and heterosexual.

Heterocentrism is the *ideology* and assumption that all people are essentially—by nature—heterosexual. *Heterosexism* is the *system* of oppression that gives privilege to heterosexual people to the disadvantage of those who are not. *Hetero-normativity* is the divinely destined and natural *norm* for human sexuality. Any deviance from this norm is immoral, abnormal, unnatural and hence a sin. *Homophobia* is the *fear*, discomfort, prejudice, or hatred of non-heterosexual people that is manifested at the individual and social levels.

Morality and Missiology of Hetero-normativity

In the arguments of the religious fundamentalists, homosexuality is perceived as a sinful and deviant behavior which is against our culture and tradition. They further argue that it is an immoral sexual practice imported from the West. But a deeper engagement with our history refutes this argument. The earliest known depiction of same-sex couples comes from 2400 BCE from Egypt. They were buried together in the same tomb. There are also evidences for Christian liturgical rites for same-sex unions from the Middle Ages. As in many other societies, homosexual practices have always been part of traditional Indian sexual practices. In ancient India, homosexual activity was either ignored or stigmatized as inferior but never condemned as sin and persecuted as a criminal act. *Kamasutra,* dwells on homosexual practices in sensual terms. The erotic sculptors that adorn temples like Khajuraho openly depict homosexual acts along with heterosexual acts.

As in other societies, in India also, the dominant prevailing order has always been perceived as the "natural order," and religion continues to play a vital role in legitimizing and perpetuating the status quo. But when it comes to sexuality, homosexual practices were tolerated as long as men and women fulfilled their responsibilities to heterosexual marriage, family, and procreation. A similar approach can be found in the Sufi mystics whose religious literature used homoerotic language to articulate their intimate relationship with God. So Islam also tolerated homosexual practices as long as they fulfilled their marital responsibilities. This is the context in which the British arrived in India with the mission of conquest and evangelization.

Inspired by the call of civilizing the heathens, with missionary zeal, the British colonial authorities started to identify the corrupt and immoral practices that were prevalent in the colonies. This had led to the imposition of Sodomy laws in all British colonies. The Christian colonizers found the prevailing culture of tolerance towards homosexual practices as against the normative Judeo-Christian understanding of sexual morality, and hence resolved to impose stringent rules that criminalize "unnatural" sexual practices, with a motif to save the colonized from their immoral and corrupt sexual practices. So in 1861, the British colonial administration in India imposed Sec. 377 on the colonized to "cure "and to "purify" them of their "primitive and deviant" sexual practices. Interestingly in 1967 the British Parliament passed the Sexual Offences Act 1967, which decriminalized homosexuality and acts of sodomy between consenting adults. But India and several other postcolonial nations still continue these inhumane and unjust laws.

This analysis of the imposition of Sodomy laws such as Sec. 377 exposes the theological and missiological motifs behind the imposition of the Victorian morality on the colonized. The orientalist attitude of the European colonizers constructed the communities in the colonies as uncivilized and their cultural practices as deviant and unnatural, to project themselves (the British colonial administration) as social reformers engaging in the noble act of civilizing the heathens. Colonial invasion and conquest thus got legitimized as a civilizing mission. They considered heterosexuality as the normative natural order given by the Creator God. Such a theological understanding of sexuality made it a missiological imperative to demonize and criminalize people and sexual practices that transgress hetero-normativity. So we need to understand Sec. 377 as the product of a particular understanding of Christian sexual ethics and the missionary zeal of the Christian colonizers to civilize the heathen world in the true spirit of evangelism.

Theories on the Origin of Homosexuality

Homosexuality as a matter of sexual orientation is still a contested issue. There are right wing Christian groups who earnestly believe that homosexuality is nothing but a satanic bondage, and Jesus has the power to redeem people from this bondage. Interestingly, all these groups use medical science and psychiatry to substantiate their respective cases. There are several myths about homosexuality which are used to enforce hetero-normativity. The most popular among them is the myth that homosexuality is a choice. Such a myth is a theological necessity for the Religious Right because if we accept homosexuality as orientation, it is an affirmation that different sexual orientations are part of God's plan. If God is the cause for homosexual orientation, we cannot condemn it as evil or sinful. But it has already been proved that homosexuality is not a matter of choice, which can be cured or changed. It is a matter of orientation. The second myth tends to reduce the definition of sexuality to what is done with the genitals, or to be precise, which gender one prefers to have sex with. Like heterosexuality, homosexuality is also essentially an issue of identity; not sexual activity. The third myth perceives homosexuality as an illness, a mental or emotional disorder, or a sin, probably caused during the childhood. The proponents of this myth believe that since homosexuality is an illness or disorder, it can be cured and corrected. But in reality homosexuality is a natural predisposition, just as some people are naturally predisposed toward left-handedness.

Recent scientific studies indicate biological causes for all forms of sexual orientation. Scholarship from medical and psychological fields informs us that chemical, hormonal and genetic conditions in the womb determine sexual orientation. So it is a futile attempt to cure homosexuality or change heterosexuality. There are "Christian" organizations such as Exodus and Refuge which are involved in helping young people to liberate themselves from the sin of homosexuality. But in reality through boot camps and other violent means these organizations force the young people to repress their identity to refrain from homosexual tendencies.

The fourth myth about homosexuality is our attempt to limit our discussions on sexual orientation to sexual organs. It is our sexual organ that determines our gender identity. But what happens when the sexual organs one possesses does not indicate ones gender? Intersexual people are born with a sexual anatomy which does not neatly fit the traditional ideas of male or female. Premature corrective surgery can upset their sexual orientation and force them to repress their desires. The fifth myth is that homosexuality can lead to pedophilia—the sexual abuse of adolescent boys.

But pedophilia is a form of predatory sex; and it has nothing to do with homo-eroticism.

All these myths are still popular in our communities and we develop our attitudes toward sexual minorities based on these myths. There are three different homophobic attitudes which are common in our communities: *Repulsion*: Homosexuality is perceived as a crime against nature. They are sick, crazy, immoral, sinful and wicked. All attempts to change or cure them—irrespective of the means used (imprisonment, shock therapy, hospitalization)—are hence justifiable. *Pity*: Heterosexuality is natural and more mature, and hence normative. Any possibility to become normal and straight should be reinforced. Those who seem to be born that way should be treated with pity. *Tolerance*: Homosexuality is just an adolescent phase and hence it is possible to grow out of it. They are less mature and hence they need our help and tolerance. Tolerance is needed to help them to gradually get out of it.

Up until the late 19th and early 20th century, homosexuality was predominantly understood as a religious category—as sinful acts. Things began to change with considering homosexuality as a pathological state which led to the emergence of a category of persons with the identity; the homosexual. This shift in the understanding from a behavior to an identity has got diverse consequences. Scientific researches established a high prevalence of same sex feelings not only among human beings from diverse ethnic background but also among other primate species. The researches further ruled out any psychological dysfunction or instability in homosexuals. As a result the American Psychiatric Association in 1973 and the World Health Organization in 1992 officially accepted homosexuality as a normal variant of human sexuality. This has led to the decriminalization of homosexuality in different countries, and many countries have recognized same-sex civil unions and marriages.

Theological and Ethical Responses: A Survey of Different Models

With the coming out of sexual minorities affirming their sexual differences a variety of theological and ethical responses emerged to address homosexuality and same-sex unions. James B. Nelson's classification of these responses into four categories is helpful for our understanding and consideration.

1. Rejective-Punitive Position unconditionally rejects homosexuality as sinful and immoral, and bears a punitive attitude towards homosexuals. In the western societies homosexuals have been rejected and severely punished by stoning, sexual mutilation, and death penalty. Church has always been supporting these civil persecutions through its silence. Rejective-punitive position ostracizes sexual minorities, and refuses them sacraments.

2. Rejective-Non-punitive Position also understands homosexuality as a physical, psychological, and social sickness. It is a phenomenon of immorality, perversion, decadence and decay. So homosexuality is nothing but idolatry seeking self satisfaction and self sufficiency. However, despite this theological position that homosexuality is unnatural as it violates God's command, this model does not advocate a punitive position because the Gospel is all about God's overwhelming grace in Christ. So homosexuality must be condemned; but not the homosexual person.

3. Qualified Acceptance of Homosexuality understands homosexual orientation as a choice and therefore is not an immutable characteristic worthy of civil rights legislation. So it is un-Christian to tell them that there is no hope for change. If the homosexual person can change his or her sexual orientation he/she should seek to change. It is a disorder like alcoholism—an addiction—that can be cured. By judging same-sex relations as a perversion of natural law, punitive attitude is reinforced in this approach.

4. Full Acceptance Position understands homosexual orientation as not a matter of free choice but it is given or socially constructed. Same sex relations are capable of expressing God's humanizing intentions. This model is founded on a sexual ethics of love which affirms commitment and trust, tenderness, respect for the other, and the desire for ongoing and responsible communion with the other.

Bible and Homosexuality: Queer Hermeneutics

"Homosexuality is sinful because the Bible says so" is the dominant Christian response to homosexuality. Our attempts to explore what the Bible says about homosexuality from the social location of heterosexism, is tainted by homophobia, and hence dangerous to the life and rights of LGBTs, because heterosexism is a reasoned system of bias holding heterosexuality as normative for judging all forms of human sexuality. The Bible has played a significant role in this violence inflicted upon sexual minorities. This experience of scriptural violence compelled many homosexual people to hate the Bible and to leave the Church. But the biblical abuse initiated by the heterosexist interpretations led to the emergence of queer interpretative communities who read the Bible from their standpoint to protect themselves from scripturally sanctioned violence and exclusion. Their attempt is to "take back the Word" not only to protect them, but also to celebrate their lives.

Robert E. Gross identifies three major reading strategies in queer interpretation. Deflecting textual violence is a 'negative' reading strategy used to critique the heterosexist interpretations of texts to deflect social violence. Outing the text and befriending the text are 'positive' reading strategies to challenge heterosexual erasures of homoeroticism from the text and discovering queer subjectivity within the text. The positive reading strategy of outing the text enables them to see them reflected in the stories of Ruth and Naomi, and David and Jonathan. Befriending the text is a deep spiritual experience for queer people because, it enables them to affirm that "we too have been graciously invited to God's inclusive table; our interpretative communities are spiritually maturing to produce their own readings of the scripture; and we are taking back the word as we take back our Christian practices."

To demonstrate how queer hermeneutics uses deflecting textual violence method to critique the heterosexist interpretations of text let us look at the story of Sodom (Gen. 19:1-29). What exactly is the sin of Sodom? For most of us the sin of Sodom is homosexuality. This is the text that has been used consistently to justify the condemnation of same-sex relationships. But Bible does not agree with this position. For prophet Ezekiel, Sodom's iniquity was the unwillingness of the people to share their abundance with those who were poor and marginalized (16:49). In Amos 4: 1, we see the prophesy of the destruction of Israel for following Sodom's example of "oppressing the needy and crushing the poor." Prophet Isaiah cries, "hear the word of Yahweh, O rulers of Sodom, listen to the law of our God, O people of Gomorrah!…Your palms are full of blood. Wash yourselves, purify yourselves, remove the evil of doings before my eyes. Cease doing evil…Seek justice, reprove the oppressor, be just to the orphan, contend for the widow" (1:10-17).

The biblical references to Sodom's wickedness do not list homosexuality as the cause for God's wrath. Rather it is the lack of justice done in the name of orphans and widows. The Apocryphal books also attest that Sodom's sin was the lack of demonstrating hospitality to strangers. The firsts to make a direct connection between homosexuality and Sodom's sin were Philo of Alexandria (BCE 25-CE50) and Josephus (CE 37-100). Sodom's sin does not refer to a loving relationship between two individuals, rather the unwillingness of the people to show hospitality to the visiting strangers, and their cruelty of raping the guests. It was a same-sex gang rape perpetrated by heterosexual men, which is different from same-sex relationships of people with homosexual orientation. Rape is not a sexual act; rather it is an act of domination in which pleasure is achieved through the humiliation and subjugation of the victim. "The sin of Sodom is not homosexuality, but unchecked heterosexuality in its attempt to dominate everything."

The Holiness Code in the book of Leviticus is another text that we normally use to condemn and demonize homosexuals. The Hebrew word for abomination used here does not indicate ethical prohibition. Rather it is a cultic term which denotes something ritually unclean due to crossing of boundaries. Other abominations included in the Hebrew Bible include the improper use of incense (Numbers 16:40), offering a blemished animal as sacrifice (Deut: 17:1), eating unclean animals such as shellfish (Lev: 11:10), dead carcasses (Lev: 11:11), and any part of the pig or other animals with cloven hoofs (Deut: 14:4-8), and having sex with a woman during her menstrual period (Lev: 20: 18-24). We need to further investigate why it is ritually unclean to "lie with a man like with a woman" (Lev: 18:22). The previous verse prohibits the offering of children as sacrifice. Sacred sex was practiced in the ancient world, particularly in many pagan religious institutions. Lying with a male prostitute was considered abomination because it followed the pagan ritual practices. Israel was instructed to avoid the ritualized sex that was part of the Canaanite religious practices. So what we find in Leviticus is not an attempt to condemn homosexual orientation as abomination; rather same-sex acts based on a power relationship that degrades and humiliates the vulnerable is indeed an abomination.

In the Pauline epistles also we find several texts that condemn homosexual acts. Here we need to make a distinction between homosexuality and homosexual acts. Paul was not aware of homosexuality as a matter of sexual orientation. For him heterosexism was normative, and hence any sexual act that violates hetero-normativity was sinful as it was against the natural order. So Paul was condemning the homosexual acts of heterosexual people. Further, in the Pauline context, young men were sexually abused and raped by men with political and military power. Whether it is homosexual or heterosexual, sexual violence and abuse using one's power and privilege is sinful. This is what we see in the Pauline instructions on homosexuality; not a condemnation of homosexuals or homosexuality as we understand it today.

Church and Homophobia: Envisioning an Inclusive Church

"Why don't Christians try to make me feel included? Why do you treat me like an outcast and not care about my feelings or want to relate to me in any way? You don't need to understand why I'm homosexual — but to understand me as a person and a fellow human being. Isn't that what Jesus would do?"

"I hope you never worship a God who makes you feel that He hates the person you have become. May you never grow up denying every feeling that comes from your heart. May you be able to visit your place of worship without fear that you will be rejected, judged, or have to listen to teachings that call your life wrong."

These statements coming from LGBT friends who experienced not only rejection and condemnation; but also violent attacks from the Church—the body of Christ—exposes the sin of homophobia that is prevalent in our churches today. Our sanctuaries which are expected to offer hospitality, comfort, and fellowship to all those who are weary and heavy-laden have become places that breed hatred, prejudice, and bigotry.

Homophobia is the irrational fear of people with homosexual orientation. The church becomes homophobic when it distorts the scripture and doctrines to condemn and demonize sexual minorities. As we tend to think, homophobia is not a "phobia" (fear) in a psychiatric sense. Rather, it signifies discrimination against sexual minorities, in the same way that the words "casteism" and "sexism" relate to discrimination based on caste and gender, respectively. Homophobic beliefs drive homophobic conduct that occurs in all domains of social life: at home, at school, in politics, in churches, in organizations, at work and on the streets.

Paul in his letter to the church in Ephesus (4:1-16) shares his vision of an inclusive church which celebrates diversity and differences. What are the theological reasons for imagining Church as an inclusive community? Is there a theological rationale to argue that the Church is essentially an inclusive community? For Paul, Christian faith that affirms one body, one spirit, one hope, one lord, one faith, one baptism, and one God is not a rejection of diversities; rather it is an affirmation of the reconciliation of all diversities in Christ. Plurality and diversity are not accidents or deformities that need to be cured and treated. The reconciled diversity that we find in the one Lord, one body, one spirit, and one baptism is not the imposition of a particular worldview or practice or sexual orientation as normative for all. Rather as members of the one body, sharing the same baptismal vow of allegiance to the one Lord, our differences are being reconciled in Christ Jesus. So inclusiveness is not a choice that the Church ought to make. Rather inclusiveness is the basic characteristic of the Church. A Church with fortified walls practicing untouchability towards people who share the same image of God and who are marked by the sign of cross in the sacrament of baptism cannot be considered as the Church of Christ. The Church of Christ is a Church without walls extending its fellowship to all those who are beloved by God in Christ Jesus. Said differently homophobia is a sin against God, and a homophobic church is a betrayal of the calling of the church as the body of Christ

Secondly, our calling as Christians is not to exclude but to practice the spirit of reconciliation for unity in the bond of love and peace. The author of the epistle reminds us that, "I therefore, beg you to lead a life worthy of the calling to which you have been called, with all humility and gentleness, with patience, bearing with one another in love, making every effort to maintain the unity of the spirit in the bond of peace." So if all our diversities are reconciled in Christ, then our calling is to lead a life worthy of this divine purpose of reconciliation for which God has called us. Often we exclude others out of our desire to become a holy people by condemning them as immoral and impure. But holiness is not something that we achieve by sanitizing and insulating ourselves from the sinful world; but holiness is an invitation to become holy in the way of Jesus, the Christ. Holiness for Jesus meant challenging the purity maps of his time which excluded people on the basis of their health, ethnicity, class, nature, and gender status. In that process he touched the leprosy affected people, he touched the ears and eyes of people with deformities, he touched human saliva, he dined with socially outcaste people, he protected notorious women, and he was crucified outside the city gates. Through touching the untouchables Jesus inaugurated God's reign in our midst. It is imperative on the Church to continue this mission of touching the untouchables. Christian mission of reconciliation presupposes the prophetic courage to touch the untouchables. Church becomes a first fruit of the reign of God only when we respond to this call in the bond of love and peace, and welcome into our midst those who are condemned by the world as untouchables.

Thirdly, the Church is called to speak the truth in love to grow into the fullness of Christ. Speaking the truth in love is a difficult task. Speaking the truth that in Christ we are all reconciled with one another is a dangerous proposition. Our homophobia against people with different sexual orientations, and our anger against people who are different from us expose our unwillingness to speak the truth in love. Speaking the truth in love demands from us the courage to expose the untruth of our dominant truth claims. Exposing our untruths is an invitation to a costly conversion: a conversion to transform our faith communities from our obsession with the prevailing dominant truth claims of our times to discover in love, new truths, truths that compel us to grow into the fullness of Christ. Growing into the fullness of Christ enables the Church to grow in love. From the fear of the unknown, the stranger, and the person who is different from us, we grow into the beauty of the rainbow where we celebrate the splendor of diversity without sacrificing our differences. Our reflections on Church and homophobia invite us to ask some foundational questions to ourselves and to our churches. Does our faith encourage an active and prophetic stance towards creating justice in this world; or does it explicitly or implicitly encourage complacency towards inequality here on earth? Does our faith affirm the fundamental dignity and worth of all people and reject any claims of superiority based on the dominant understanding of sexuality? Does our faith encourage critical examination of the context and deeper meanings of teachings and scriptures and is it open to continued revelation of eternal truths that come with new knowledge, instead of a fundamentalism that idolizes the past? Does our faith confront and reject any teachings that might cause anyone to act with bigotry or incite violence or hatred towards others? Is our faith grounded first and foremost in love, and do we believe that love, not dogma or condemnation, is the defining characteristic of God?

The Samaritan Church: A Church Called to be Socially Illegitimate

Gustavo Gutierrez, in a homily preached at a Vatican gathering challenged the Church to become a Samaritan Church. "The neighbor is not the person that we find on our way, but that person that we approach to the extent we leave our own way, our own path, managing to approach others. A Samaritan church is an open church, a church attentive to human needs. We don't need a church of the pure. We need a church of the compassionate, a church known more for the people we love than the sins we condemn." How do we become a Samaritan Church in India today in the context of homophobia, stigma and intimate violence? It requires the prophetic commitment to become illegitimate to the dominant norms and morality. Jesus' invitation to discipleship is to throw our social status and reputation, and to opt for an alternate existence without social legitimacy. "How different would Christianity look like if Christians understood that their basic vocation is to be illegitimate?" The illegitimacy to which Jesus calls us is founded on the gracious assurance that we are infinitely loved, just as we are, without merit. When we internalize that love we are liberated from the inhibitions that prevent us from loving unconditionally our bodies, ourselves and those are different from us. When we show the nerve to become illegitimate to the prevailing morality, we become a Samaritan Church. In our times, we need to be saved from the dominant expressions of Christianity to become a Samaritan Church.

The Extraordinary Synod of the Roman Catholic Church held last year, discussed in detail the Catholic approach to human sexuality. The document that was presented in the Synod proposed that, "Homosexuals have gifts and qualities to offer to the Christian community: are we capable of welcoming these people, guaranteeing to them a fraternal space in our communities? Often they wish to encounter a Church that offers them a welcoming home. Are our communities capable of providing that, accepting and valuing their sexual orientation, without compromising Catholic doctrine on the family and matrimony?" However, the Synod voted against the proposal. But it is important to note that, more than 50% of the participants voted in favor of the proposed change in the attitude of the church towards homosexuals. Before the commencement of the Synod, Pope Francis observed that, "Jesus did strange things, like walk with sinners, eat with tax collectors — things the scholars of the law did not like; doctrine was in danger, that doctrine of the law that they and the theologians had created over the centuries. The scholars were safeguarding the law out of love, to be faithful to God; but they were closed up right there, and forgot all the ways God has acted in history. The law teaches the way to Christ, and if the law does not lead to Jesus Christ, and if it doesn't get us closer to Jesus Christ, it is dead." But the Pontiff was not successful in converting the homophobic mindset of the majority. At the closing mass of the Synod, the Pope said, "God is not afraid of new things. That is why God is continuously surprising us, opening our hearts and guiding us in unexpected ways." This message from the Holy Father is a message of hope for the Indian Church as well. We need to have the audacity to patiently wait for God's surprises in the life of our churches so that we may become an inclusive community of hospitality, fellowship and solidarity.

The mission of the Church is not to protect or defend our heritage, liturgy, confessional doctrines, ecclesiastical offices or even the Bible. Rather, we are called to enable the process of making these means of grace and the rich resources of our faith to incarnate in the margins by exposing them to the challenges in the margins. Church happens in our constant leap of faith from our sanitized comfort zones of privilege to the margins. True repentance happens in our encounter with the margins, and it leads to transformation. The witness of the Church in the margins—our songs, our ministries of compassionate justice and care, our actions of solidarity, our struggles, our rituals—provides the community the foretaste of the eschatological banquet. Let us strive together and midwife the birth of that Church in our communities; a rainbow Church. From being defenders of lifeless dogmas, let us become the practitioners of the infectious love that destroys fear, privilege, and exclusion. "A prayer of lament" is a poem articulating the agony of a homosexual person: "Let me have a share of your peace without obsessing that my "lifestyle" is not Christian, without hating myself, my fate, my body, and my heart. Let me live a life of joy and peace, secure in the knowledge that your grace fills me, that nothing I have done or desired or worried about can erase your love for me that you bid me come "just as I am." This is the vision of a rainbow community of the beloved and equals. It is a historic moment for us to make a decision. We can either continue to remain as an inhospitable religious club; committing violence against sexual minorities, or we can become a just and inclusive rainbow community celebrating our God given diversities by welcoming those who are different from us into our midst to experience Christian fellowship in a deeper way. *God of love has called us as a community of friends and equals "to be filled with God's love; to share God's unconditional love; to demonstrate God's love to others—whoever they are, whatever their background be; to declare and show by our actions that God loves all, and has no pre-existing conditions for loving all of God's creations." May the God of love help us to become a Church to those who are demonized, criminalized, and excluded.*

[A Paper presented at NCCI's "Church Leaders and Key Affected People" Seminar : Chennai: April 23,2015]

Struggle to be Human:
A Reflection on
Human Sexuality in India

Aruna Gnanadason

Asian lesbian women participating in the regional consultation on violence against women, in Bali, Indonesia in 1994, challenged the women gathered to listen – with compassion and justice – to the struggles that they experience in a society that has systematically denied them their rights and even their existence. It was for the first time that I had heard Asian women articulate so clearly their conviction that we cannot any longer turn away from this issue and if we are to be serious about speaking of violence against women, then the violence that is perpetrated against lesbian women needs to be addressed. What the Bali meeting pointed to was the fact that sexual violence is rife in Asian societies. Women's sexuality has been commercialized and commoditized and this is often legitimized by religion. But within that scenario, violence against lesbian women needs particular attention. Compulsory heterosexuality is demanded in a context where women's fertility is controlled within a patriarchal system which places a glorified emphasis on motherhood. The final Declaration of the Bali Consultation acknowledged this complex reality:

The family along with the state today, has sought to control women through rigid definitions of sexuality and appropriate for itself reproductive rights and control over her body; violence and subjugation have been woven into institutionalized forms of religion whose patriarchal tenets have marginalized and domesticated the female and the feminine, shackling her and legitimizing violence against her. Social and legal codes of justice have either been blind to crimes against women like wife battering and prostitution that have in fact received tacit social approval; or have seen violations like sexual assault and rape as acts of individual aberration and deviance and have even rendered some totally invisible as in the case of homophobia.[1]

Lesbian women in Asia pointed out that homophobia is rampant even within feminist circles. Their struggle to assert their identity and claim their right to a life of security is not acknowledged even by progressive movements and groups, because issues relating to human sexuality are so often hidden from public discussions. However, there is some change in this situation as homosexual men and women get organized and articulate more clearly their demands for justice. Here, I will focus on the Indian reality though references will be made to other Asian contexts.

India's present: a hostile atmosphere for the homosexual community

That homosexuality is widespread in India is generally accepted – it is not unusual to see two men in close embrace or two women with arms around each other in public places. (In fact, it is often more difficult for heterosexual couples to publicly express their affection for each other!). But then, in the Indian context, there is a large percent of adults who would engage in both heterosexual and homosexual relationships. Unwritten family codes force most to hide their homosexual identity or express it only surreptitiously. A majority of homosexual men and women are content to lead a double life. They dutifully get married, as is demanded of them due to social pressure, and act out their parts as husband or wife – dropping their mask only when they are amidst people of their own sexual preference. They are expected to project a veneer of being "normal" – what happens outside of public eyes is ignored. In an article on Calcutta's homosexual men and women, Soumitra Das writes that:

Most homosexuals, however, feel there is no need to make a song and dance about an entirely personal matter. "Under no circumstances, do you discuss your sexual preferences with your family. So why should homosexuals do it?" asks a senior teacher of a public school. He is sure he won't lose his job if he chooses to 'come out', but a "stigma will be attached".[2]

It is this stigma that is attached to those who have the courage to 'come out' that forces many to pretend to be heterosexual. Frequently, when parents realize that their children have homosexual tendencies, they reject them or even worse try to get them "cured". Largely forced by such familial pressures a large number of the country's seemingly heterosexual population is in fact suppressing its true sexual identity. Tragically this has led to a life of misery and in some cases to suicide, in a society which prefers silence on this issue. Rather than telling a child who wishes to come out, a way in which he or she can cope with their sexual orientation, and be true to themselves, parents would dismiss it as a "passing phase" or would quickly get the young person married so as to avoid the "scandal" that this could involve. This often leads to a destructive heterosexual marriage. The fact that the married relationship is not working is ignored both by the couple and by the family, so as to keep up the façade.

A Delhi based doctor, whose research centers on homosexual men and women, says that prevalence of bisexuality is far greater in India than in the West. He attributes this to the lack of stigma attached to bisexuality before the British colonized India. Since according to him, "we are conditioned by Victorian mores". But in the lower rungs of society, he says, there is much greater acceptance of homosexuality.[3]

One of the best researched studies available on the issue is the Citizen's Report on the Status of Homosexuality in India, called 'Less Than Gay', prepared by the AIDS Bhedbhav Virodhi Andolan (ABVA) in 1991. This group of activists working against discrimination against AIDS victims discovered the need to focus attention on the rights of homosexual men and women because they saw that the "the emergence of AIDS as a major public health crisis has had a devastating effect on gay people in most parts of the world. It has become more necessary than ever before to understand the status of homosexuality in our society".[4]

Whether it is blackmail or physical violence, verbal abuse or police harassment, forced heterosexual marriage or denial of homosexual marriage, gay people live like second class citizens, unable to obtain fair treatment because of their 'wrong' sexuality. The question of the human rights of gay men and women is not about whether or not people approve of homosexuality or the concept of gay identities. Rather, it a question of equality under the law and under human rights covenants, like the International Covenant on Civil and Political Rights, to which India is a signatory.[5]

Organized voices of resistance and support

There have been some significant efforts by homosexual men and women to organize themselves and to raise their voices against the discrimination they experience. Most major cities in India have now got an organized group attempting to draw attention to the varied and rich forms of homosexual life that do exist in India, as they try to expose the forms of violence that exist by law and in the everyday life of people who choose to openly live their homosexuality. They have focused attention on providing a safe space for homosexual men and women to meet and discuss the multifaceted oppression they experience and to strategize for joint action.

Homosexuality: an accepted way of life in India's past

Perhaps the most important contribution these groups have made is to expose the fact that homosexuality is not a new phenomenon in India. There has been present, since ancient times, an acknowledgement of homosexual love and same sex contact. The Kamasutra is the first literary classic in the world on matters of sex. It was authored by the sage Vatsyayana in the 4th century A.D. The Kamasutra is not an original work – it is a compilation of the rules of love as written in the Kama Shastra, a treatise on life which dates back to the 4th century B.C. or earlier. According to Vatsyayana, the various works belonging to the Kama Shastra have become difficult to get access to. For this reason he undertook to collect them and summarize them in the Kamasutra, which became a classic in that genre.

In the Kamasutra, Lesbianism is described in detail, as well as the inversion of rules by a dominating female. Male homosexuality forms an integral part of sexual life and various homosexual practices are described in detail. Transvestite prostitutes play a role in public life, and their presence at weddings and religious ceremonies was considered a symbol of good luck down to our own times.[6]

The Kamasutra contains an entire chapter, Auparishtaka, on homosexual love. The Shushruta, a treatise of medicine some 2000 years old describes treatment of possible injuries incurred during homosexual love making. Eight century, A.D. temples dedicated to the Lord Shiva, in Bhubhaneshwar, Orissa and Khajuraho Temple, a 9th to 11th century masterpiece in Madhya Pradesh both, in instances explicitly carve in stone icons, homosexual love. Indian sculptures representing the various sexual positions, group sex, and homosexual practice are found in many temples, because according to legend, they protected temples from lightning. The Kamasutra teaches that "the final aim of sexual pleasure is spiritual", and that "like ethics and prosperity, sexuality is one of the bases of civilization". It also delinks sexual pleasure from procreation, emphasizing that procreation is not the aim of sexual love, "amorous ecstasy is assimilated to mystic experience, to the perception of the divine that is supreme enjoyment".[7]

According to A.A. Macdonell, Emeritus Professor of Sanskrit, in the University of Oxford, "the contents of this work (the Kamasutra), appear to us in the most part indecent, but it must be borne in mind that the Indian is much more outspoken on sexual matters, than we are". (India's past, A Survey of Her Literatures, Religions, Languages"). Quoting this passage, the ABVA Report, concludes that "it is a shame that a Westerner has to remind us about our traditional sexual openness whereas we continue to vigorously deny it".[8]

Another strand of India's ancient past that is referred to is found in the Puranas (pre-Aryan religious texts), which affirm the vision of sexual dualism. Giti Thadani, an independent researcher from New Delhi, elucidates this stream of philosophy where,

Importance was not attached to the 'male-female couple' but on the notion of the yoni which signifies "the womb, the infinite source", the symbol of which was the triangle. The triangle consists of two points of 'light' represented by female twins, symbols of fusion, and of a third point which is the earth. The notion of twins or jami also signifies, in various texts, 'homosexuality' ... Sexuality was based on pleasure and on fertility but not on progeny (the practice of passing over the children to the man). Phallic discourse only appeared with progenic sexuality. So the first notion of "heterosexuality" appeared later, under the terminology of a-jami, that which is not jami which is not paired, fused as it is in the notion of "homosexuality".[9]

Muslim Culture

There is a view often expressed that, homosexuality and particularly sodomy, was introduced into India by Muslims. But the texts quoted above, among others, indicate that the practice of homosexuality had existed as an accepted way of life for centuries before the Mughal invasions. Under Muslim rulers, however, homosexuality entered Indian court life. Harems of young boys were kept by Muslim Nawabs and Hindu Aristocrats in the 16th century. Babar, the Mughal ruler, wrote romantically about his famous love affair with a boy, Baburi. There are records of homosexual love in the culture of Delhi between 1739 and 1741.

In Islamic Sufi literature, homosexual eroticism was a major metaphysical expression of the spiritual relationship between god and man and much Persian fiction and poetry used gay relationships as examples of moral love. Although the Koran and early religious writings do make negative references towards homosexuality, Muslim cultures were in fact very tolerant. The classical works of Arabic poetry and prose, from Abu Nawas to the Thousand and One Nights, treat homosexual men and women and their sexuality with respect. The Arabic language contains a huge vocabulary of homosexual erotic terminology.

According to John Boswell, (Christianity, Social Tolerance and Homosexuality), the association of homosexual feelings with moral looseness appears to be a comparatively recent phenomenon.[10]

If Indian society had permitted same-sex eroticism for centuries, then when did the intolerance against homosexuality begin? The patriarchalisation

of Indian religions, which came several centuries after treatises such as the
Kama Shasthra were expounded, could be the origin of the intolerance.
Homosexual activists would claim that the hostility towards homosexuality
has its roots in patriarchal religions which would glorify marriage as the
only norm for family life. A personality is said to be incomplete without
a heterosexual relationship. In fact sex, according to religious teachers like
Manu, is purely for the procreation of a son. So in a rigid patriarchal system
there is no place for homosexuality. The pressure was placed particularly
on lesbians, as a woman's sexuality is to be kept under rigid control. Jaya
Ramanathan, in an article in The Pioneer writes:

> When sexuality, any kind of displayed sexuality, in Indian women, is an anathema
> to society and meant to be strictly under wraps, a total departure from 'normal'
> inclination is not only unacceptable, but is seen as an aberration, something to
> be treated, medically, psychologically or even violent.[11]

While a son's declaration of his homosexual tendencies is received with
consternation, the daughter's declaration is often suppressed because parents
would believe they could ignore her claim by getting her married. A
women's crisis centre in Madras has found that a large number of women
who come to them for intervention in failing marriages, seek help because
of the inability of the couple, (either of whom are homosexual in
orientation), to have a "normal" sexual relationship. Many homosexuals find
that the women they are forced to marry are no longer willing to silently
allow their "strange behavior" and this of course jeopardizes the marriage
relationship.

The legacy of British intolerance: unjust legal sanctions

The ABVA Report would trace it to the fact that the "erstwhile British
Rulers found it to be repugnant and declared it a crime in the Indian Penal
Code (IPC).[12]

Section 377 of the IPCV is interpreted as a sanction against
homosexuality, though the law does not clearly indicate it. Section 377
forbids "carnal intercourse against the order of nature", with man, woman
or animal and provides a jail term of ten years to a life time for a violator.
Lesbianism has been rarely brought before a court of law in India and this

is not covered by section 377. According to Jeffrey Weeks, lesbian acts are not outlawed because of *"the secondary position accorded to female sexuality in general. It is not so much lesbianism as female sexuality which society denies"*.[13] The ABVA Report quotes many examples of lesbians who have committed suicide because they were not permitted their relationships. The question we have to ask ourselves is whether we are going to remain silent as more and more women coming particularly from non-urban backgrounds die before Indian society will acknowledge that lesbianism exists in all sections of our society (Lesbians who have wished to get married have had to face legal prosecution at the behest of parents or not of family).

Ironically, the sodomy law is almost never enforced and not more than a few men have been prosecuted in all the years of India's independent history. But homosexual men and women would still want the law repealed because it makes them vulnerable to extortion and blackmail by both policemen and hustlers in public parks. Section 377 may not be enforced but it infuses fear among Indian homosexuals who feel insecure anyway, because they know that their sexual orientation arouses the loathing of the heterosexual majority.

The silent church – a theological response

The Asian church has been silent on this issue, as it is on all matters concerning human sexuality. Drawn into the vortex of Western patriarchal theology and inherited church structures, the Asian/Indian church has lost its cultural roots influenced strongly by its history as a minority among great religious faiths. Such a consciousness has rendered the church incapable of providing a holistic view of human sexuality, whatever form or expression it takes. In fact, in the Bali Asian Consultation, referred to earlier, violence against the lesbian women in the church was also spoken of. Women theologians in India, influenced by their Asian sisters are now beginning to speak out more clearly about sexuality. Asian women theologians have had to struggle not only against a patriarchal church and society, but have also had to contend with the fact that male liberation theologians have not themselves fully understood what patriarchal violence does to women. While almost all statements made by Asian theologians would refer to the oppression of women – it was only in passing as one would speak of one of the marginalized groups in a society. It is only very recently that Asian feminist theologians have been able to highlight the violence women experience in Asian society and how that violence is institutionalized in the family structure, in religion, in cultures and in all aspects of our societies. The docile, subservient image of Asian women persists in the minds of men and this has been the root of much of the oppression – in particular in the profits of the multi-national prostitution industry. Asian women now speak of an alternative theological paradigm drawn out of their experiences as Asian women in struggle. They affirm that sexuality has to be discussed as a theological concept if the church is to provide a word of comfort to Asian women:

> Sexuality is too often seen as the antithesis of spirituality. As a group we affirmed that human sexuality is part of spirituality and condemned the distorted view and practices which have led to the oppression, victimization and impoverishment of Asian women....What has liberation spirituality to say and do about sexuality in the Asian setting?[14]

Kwok Pui Lan urges us to go a step further. She writes:

> Many of us today would not be comfortable discussing sexuality and few would try to imagine what the gospel according to the prostitutes would be....while some lesbians are trying to break the taboo to talk about passionate love and relationships among women, many women have yet to find a language to speak about pleasure of the body, female sexuality and the power of the erotic because the yoke of "compulsory heterosexuality" is still heavy upon us.[15]

Conclusion

In the struggle to find justice and acceptance, homosexual activists demand that the legal and political climate be made free. They demand that civil rights legislation be enacted that will protect their life and liberty. They claim their right to safety and security and urge that the overt and covert forms of violence they experience be regarded as violations of human rights. But they also demand their right to live their lives in privacy, without the hostile and negative attitudes that follow them in their everyday lives. Can the church provide that space for an alternative life style and new forms of caring family life? Will the church express its commitment to create a sensitive and compassionate environment for understanding and open dialogue – this is the challenge before us.

End Notes

[1] The Bali Declaration of the Asian Regional Consultation on Violence Against Women, held in Bali, Indonesia, organized by the World Council of Churches, the Christian Conference of Asia and the Asian Women's Human Rights Commission, 1-6 August 1993. (Emphasis added).

[2] Das Soumitra, "Sad to be Gay", Miscellany Section, Sunday Times, 18 April 1993.

[3] Chaturvedi Swati and Sharma Navneet, "The Angry Young Men and Women", Miscellany Section, Sunday Times, 10 January 1993.

[4] Less Than Gay, A Citizen's Report on the Status of homosexuality in India, AIDS Bhedbhav Virodhi Andolan, (ABVA) New Delhi, India, November-December 1991, p.1. (Emphasis added). It was surprising to note that the word "gay" is often used in India to refer to both homosexual men and women. Perhaps it reflects the deep seated patriarchal attitudes in India, which have penetrated even movements for justice – such as that of the gay and lesbian movement.

[5] Ibid, p.67.

[6] Danielou Alain, Translator of the Complete Kamasutra, The First Modern Translation of the Classic Indian Text, Park Street Press, Vermont, 1994, p.10.

[7] Danielou Alain, ibid pp.34, 17, 10.

[8] Less Than Gay, ABVA Report, op cit, p.50.

[9] Quoted in Less Than Gay, ABVA Report, ibid, p.51.

[10] Quoted in Less Than Gay, ABVA Report, ibid, p.56.

[11] Ramanathan Jaya, Asian Homosexuals: No Longer in the Closet, The Pioneer, 22 November 1992, Delhi.

[12] Less Than Gay ABVA Report, op cit, p.31.

[13] Weeks Jeffrey, Against Nature, 1991, Quoted in Less Than Gay, ABVA Report, ibid, p.29.

[14] Ed. Fabella Virginia, Lee, Peter K. H., Suh David Kwang-sun, Final Statement of the Asian Theological Conference (ACT III), in Asian Christian Spirituality, Reclaiming Traditions, Orbis Books, 1992, p. 8.

[15] Kwok Pui Lan, The Future of Feminist Theology: An Asian Perspective", Voices from the Third World, Vol XV, No. 1, June 1992, p.157.

Biblical Perspectives on Human Sexuality

John Lalnuntluanga

Sexuality and the Bible

In early Old Testament times, adultery by a married woman was considered a sin and often incurred severe punishment. But practices such as concubinage (women as breeders) and polygyny (men being allowed to have many wives, but a woman only one husband) were considered acceptable. In times of war, capturing women in battle and forcing them to be wives seemed to be the norm. Levirate marriage (a younger brother marrying his dead sibling's widow so as to continue the deceased brother's bloodline) was an acceptable biblical practice.

In fact, concubinage was an official status in OT times. God rebuked Solomon not for polygyny (700 wives) and concubinage (300 concubines), but only because many of his wives were non-Hebrew who brought idols in for worship from their pagan cultures, which was contrary to God's teaching. Solomon's father David himself committed adultery, and that too only because Bathsheba was married and not one of his own women. The other 7 wives and 17 concubines of David were given by God as a 'blessing.' Hence, there was no issue of his committing immoral acts -either of adultery or concubinage.

Other OT men had many wives, but were never rebuked for their polygyny. There is no instance of God issuing condemnation against all the known instances of men having multiple wives and concubines in Hebrew history. The so-called 'Holiness Code' in Leviticus prohibits sex with granddaughters, but not daughters (Lev. 18:10; cf. Lot and his daughters in Gen.19). The New Testament treatment of sexuality is also wide-ranging. Though one may argue that Jesus disapproved of adultery, scriptural injunctions on sexuality and their interpretations are varied. Thus, it is practically impossible, even with a careful reading of the Bible, to gather a consistent biblical teaching on human sexuality that resonates with our modern way of thinking concerning the relationship between the sexes.

Homosexuality

In seeking to have a clearer understanding of a certain section of the "key affected people", namely the sexual minorities, it is imperative that we first strive to have a clear understanding of who and what they are. It was Karl-Maria Kertbeny, an Austrian-born Hungarian journalist, memoirist and human rights campaigner who coined the word 'homosexual'. In his attempt at classifying people according to differing sexual attraction and gratification, he argued that nature had divided humans into four sexual types: *monosexuals*, who masturbated, *heterogenits*, who had sex with animals, *heterosexuals*, who coupled with the opposite sex, and *homosexuals*, who preferred people of the same sex.

Kertbeny was the first to propose an argument that is now called the "medical model". Contrary to the dominant view of the time, that men committed "sodomy" out of mere wickedness, he argued that homosexuality is inborn and unchangeable. Homosexual men, he said, were not by nature effeminate, and pointed out that many of the great heroes of history were homosexual. The word homosexual now has widespread usage in pejorative sense. However, it initially started out as a non-judgmental neutral term to describe an orientation and/or an identity. Kertbeny first used it in 1868 in a private correspondence with Karl Heinrich Ulrichs, another champion of gay rights. 1869 marks the first usage of the term in the public realm, in a pamphlet entitled 'Paragraph 143 of the Prussian Penal Code of 14 April 1851 and its Reaffirmation as Paragraph 152 in the Proposed Penal Code for the Norddeutscher Bund. An Open and Professional Correspondence to His Excellency Dr.Leonhardt, Royal Prussian Minister of Justice.'

Richard von Kraft-Ebbing, a German sex researcher borrowed the terms homosexual and heterosexual in his *Psychopathia Sexualis* (1886). In his opinion, however, heterosexuality is the norm and to be heterosexual is to be normal while homosexuality and homosexuals are manifestations of sexual perversion.It is in the sense of von Kraft-Ebbing's usage that the term homosexual entered the English through C.G. Chaddock's translation of *Psychopathia Sexualis* in 1892.[1]

"Clobber Texts" Used Against Divergent Sexualities

There are a handful of biblical passages that are used to speak out against non-conventional sexualities. Gen. 18:20-21 deals with judgment on the sin of Sodom, while Gen. 19:4-9 deals with the Sodomites' attempt to defile the angelic beings who were to execute that judgment. Lev. 18:22 and Lev. 20:13 are injunctions against any sexual relation between two men, calling it an "abomination" which implies that any participant becomes ritually unclean. In the NT, we get passages such as Rom. 1:24-27, 1 Cor. 6:9-10 and 1 Tim. 1:9-10 which are also used in the same vein. However, it might be helpful for our purposes to try to understand what the Bible says in these passages, rather than simply using it uncritically to affirm whatever positions we might hold.

Sin of Sodom

Infamous for the abominable lifestyle of its citizens, the city of Sodom is the basis of the word 'sodomy', which is still a legal synonym for homosexual and non-procreative sexual acts, particularly anal or oral sex. Hence, in reading the story regarding Sodom's destruction as punishment from God, we immediately tend to project wanton immorality and homosexuality as the reasons for such punishment.

But the biblical writers did not see this as a denunciation of homosexuality. Jer. 23:13-14 lists Sodom's sin as adultery, lying, and encouraging evil. Isaiah, Amos and Zephaniah refer vaguely to the sin of Sodom without specifying what it is.Ezek. 16:49 went so far as to say, "This was the guilt of your sister Sodom: she and her daughters had pride, excess of food, and prosperous ease, but did not aid the poor and needy." Thus,

Christian theologians and philosophers including Origen, Jerome, and John Cassian also listed these as the sins of Sodom and never mention same-sex behaviour.

Elsewhere, a similar story in Judges 19 and the similar punishment in Judges 20-21 suggests that gang-rape is the real sexual problem. And when we come to the NT, the Epistle of Jude has a different view altogether. According to Jude 1:7, the sin of Sodom was "sexual immorality" and the pursuit of *sarkosheteras* (different/other flesh, probably that of angels).

Biblical Perspectives on Homosexuality

The Old Testament has nothing to say on homosexuals or homosexuality. Lev. 18:22 and Lev. 20:13, at best, speak out against male-male sex. Of course, we may concede with certain reservations that the passages speak out against fulfilment of male homoeroticism. However, the same passages cannot be asserted to have dealt with lesbianism or lesbian relationships in any sense.

The writings of Paul constitute a substantial part of the NT and may even be said to set the tone for the entire worldview of the NT. Hence, it is vital that we look at two terms Paul used that are in turn used as the scriptural basis for arguing against homosexuality.

Arsenokoites/ai and Malakos

Arsenokoites is a term that is now generally taken to mean 'homosexual'. The *Thesaurus Lingua Graecae* (TLG), a research centre at the University of California, Irvine, has identified 77 instances of its usage in the ancient world. It appears that Paul might have coined the term since his usage is the first that could be documented. It is often claimed that Paul combined the Greek words *arsenos* (man) and *koiten* (bed) from the Septuagint's rendering of Lev. 20:13, and used it to condemn male same-sex relationships. Of course, there is no documentary evidence to substantiate such a claim.

The English Bible has many differing translations for the word *arsenokoites*. Older versions were rather vague. The Wyclif Bible (1380), translated from the Vulgate, renders it as 'thei that don leccherie with men'. And it continued to be translated in the sense of 'abusars of them selves with the mankynde' till the 20th century,[2] while versions such as Douay-Rheims (1582) translate it as 'liers with mankinde'.

There was a gradual shift in translation from the second half of the 20th century onwards, with inputs from psychology relating to normalcy creeping in. While some versions used the older term 'sodomites,'[3] others used more modern terminologies such as 'sexual perverts,'[4] or 'homosexual offenders'.[5] In some versions, it is combined with *malakoi* from 1 Cor. 6:9 and collectively translated as 'homosexual perverts' or 'homosexual perversion'.[6]

Malakos is another term from Paul that is used in tandem with *arsenokoites* to clobber people with homoerotic feelings and inclination. In ordinary usage, it means soft or weak, but was often translated as referring to masturbation. However, in 1 Cor. 6:9, it is often taken to mean effeminate males who harbour sexual feelings other men.

Theology, Ideology and Biblical Sexuality

Theology coupled with ideology often clouds one's reading of the Scriptures. Widespread dislike for non-conventional sexualities, reinforced by a superficial reading of scriptural passages as injunctions, have often served as justification for discriminating against sexual minorities. However, acceptance of the fact that the Bible is an ancient text that deals with social issues in an ancient manner is a prerequisite for a proper understanding of the Bible's significance.

Moreover, the language of the ancients require proper translation even though the words themselves might not have changed. This is necessary not only in translating between languages but also with regard to usage of a word or words within the same language. A word takes on meaning in a particular context, but the context in which a word is used keeps changing. Hence, it is always a challenge to go beyond the dictionary definition or contemporary usage and seek to find out what any word or passage in the Bible means in its original setting. Related to that is the challenge of evaluating whether any rendering does justice when the Bible is translated into another language.

The world views expressed in the Bible also require proper interpretation, for they arose in a different culture in a different era. The worldview with which one approaches the text further complicates matters. Layer upon layer of meaning that are not necessarily part of the text are attached so that what one ultimately takes out from the Bible is often completely different altogether. Furthermore, sexual morality has varied greatly over time and between cultures. Sexual mores and customs that are prevalent today in a particular society are not necessarily the same as that in Biblical times. It is always tempting to assume that whatever is prevalent in one's particular setting is the definitive morality that the Bible itself advocates. But a careful reading of the text undergirded by the Biblical injunction to love one another would be of tremendous help to any diligent reader of the Bible.It would be of immense help in acquiring a deeper understanding of the phenomenon of non-conventional sexualities that is noticeable down the years across societies and cultures. It would help us as we strive to ensure justice for all.

End Notes

[1] The Oxford English Dictionary lists this translation as the first usage of homosexual in English.

[2] cf. Tyndale 1534; Coverdale 1535, Cranmer 1539, Geneva Bible 1557, KJV 1611, ASV 1901.

[3] OB 1966, NAB 1970, NRSV 1989, etc.

[4] RSV 1946, REB 1992.

[5] NIV 1973.

[6] TEV 1966, NEB 1970.

The Indian Church and the Sacred Cow of Human Sexuality

Bishop Geevarghese Mor Coorilos
[formerly George Mathew Nalunnakkal]

Introduction

Of all the issues that confront the Church today, sexuality, perhaps, is most sensitive and difficult. This is more so in Asia, particularly in the Indian context where there is an evident reluctance to address the issue. For most of the churches in India, it is still a taboo to talk about sexuality. There is a tendency in the South (also true of the Indian Church) to write on sexuality as too western and elitist. They would ever maintain that concerns such as homosexuality and HIV/AIDS are basically western 'imports'. Whilst the traditionalists would try to take false comfort in such unfounded claims, most of the liberals and progressives would want to sideline such issues as of less importance compared to much more serious concerns such as poverty, discrimination and human rights violations. For them, it would be a luxury to focus on those affected by sexuality issues at the expense of the majority of the poor and the outcasts. Having said that it should also be acknowledged that new voices are emerging both in the religious as well as secular circles, expressing concerns over sexuality related concerns. Perhaps, the continuing onslaught of globalization's compelling the South to wake up to these realities as it does lead to rapid decline in two-parent families and rise in teenage pregnancies and abortion, spread of homosexuality and HIV/AIDS. This article is an attempt to take a look at the issue of human sexuality from the Indian contextual perspective with particular focus on the response of the Indian Church.

Sexuality Defined

Sexuality is much more than sex, although of course it does include sex. Sexuality, essentially, is the human way of being in the world as male and female, and in some cases as neither or as both. According to James Nelson, human sexuality involves our affectionate orientation towards those of the opposite and/or same sex. It includes our attitudes about our own bodies and those of others. As far as the Indian attitude to sexuality issues, particularly that of the Indian church is concerned, not much has changed. The mainline churches in India, on the whole, have not made their stand clear on many of the issues related to sexuality. This, of course, excludes the Roman Catholic Church in India, which is bound to follow the official position of the Vatican anyway. Barring a few individual thinkers and theologians who have contributed to some extent to the debate on human sexuality, also challenging the Church in India to address these issues boldly, the Church in India as such is still reluctant to come to terms with this vexatious issue. One of the reasons for this neglect is the influence of the so-called traditional Indian (Hindu) culture and ethos.

The Indian Scenario

India's traditional silence on sexuality is nothing but a celebrated myth. In fact the Indian mind had always engaged sexuality in a very open and radical manner. It was in fact, the colonizers who had brought to India their 'values' and ethos, which suppressed the Indian tradition. What we encounter today in the rhetoric of 'Indian traditional values' is nothing but a glorified hypocrisy. Something that happened in India captures so well the spirit of this hypocrisy that surrounds any discourse on sexuality. When Deepa Mehta's controversial film "Fire" which depicted the story of two women who were forced into lesbian relationships was released (1998), a barrage of attack came from the Hindu right wing. According to lesbian critics, the film was "no attempt to take on the anarchic and threatening emotions that accompany sexual practices generally considered perverted, criminal and taboo". It still faced stiff opposition from various quarters. One of the right wing ministers of a State in Central India made this comment: "Lesbianism is a pseudo-feminist trend from the West and no part of Indian womanhood". Even progressive groups that addressed issues of oppression from a human rights perspective, did not find the issue of homosexuality worthy of being considered a justice issue because sexuality for them was all about 'personal choice'.

There is plenty of evidence to prove that homosexuality was prevalent in India from ancient times. World's first literary classic on sex and sexuality, Kamasutra, contains detailed references to and description of homosexuality. There is even a separate and exclusive chapter on homosexuality. One of the distinct features of India's old temples is the beautiful way in which sexuality including homosexuality is portrayed through sculptures. According to Sanjukta Ghosh, it was only in the post-Shaktic period that these traditions were subject to systematic destruction. During this period heterosexual determinism and the hegemony of masculine ideology took over. By the time of Manusmriti, lesbianism was made illegal. Ramayan and Mahabharat considered homosexuality as a degeneration of human behavior. Nevertheless, these references show that homosexuality did exist during these times. All this shows that human sexuality has not been a 'sacred cow' in the past in India. It was, arguably, the coming of Islam and later on British colonialism that had brought sweeping changes in the sexual ethic of India.

Indian Church and Human Sexuality

It is by no means an easy task to look at the Indian Church's response to the issue of human sexuality. The attempt is a problematic one because churches in India have not made any official pronouncements regarding most of the issues related to human sexuality. All that is available are some random statements on behalf of some churches or some ecumenical forums such as the National Council of Churches in India, on certain issues like marriage bills and divorce laws. However, individual theologians and church leaders have from time to time made reflections on such issues. Of course they do not enjoy the status of official position of the churches they represent. The burden of this section, therefore, is three-fold; to assess the responses made by the churches and various ecumenical bodies in India on sexuality issues; to survey the contributions of individual theologians in this regard; and to see why the Church in India keeps silence over the issue and why the Church should address this issue with seriousness.

Marriage and Family

Despite the overall coldness on the part of the Indian Church in responding to human sexuality issues, there have been attempts by ecumenical bodies like the National Council of Churches in India and the Christian Medical Association of India (hereafter referred to as NCCI and CMAI respectively) to address such issues in the past. One such intervention was a joint study project on sex, marriage and responsible parenthood, undertaken by the NCCI and the CMAI in the 1970's. The Report, entitled *Family in the Purpose of God: A Miscellany of Essays Relating to Parenthood in Indian Setting* provides a biblical, theological, ethical as well as psychological approach to sex, marriage and family planning. Questioning the traditional theological position of the Church on sexuality, itself heavily influenced by the Augustinian position that sex is intrinsically evil, the study made a fundamental theological affirmation that sexuality and its purpose have their origin in God as God created Humanity as male and female in relationships. It even challenges the association of 'original sin' with sexual intercourse, yet another Augustinian legacy. It alters the traditional position when it says that it was the disobedience of Adam and Eve that tainted their sex and vice versa.

In fact, the Bible (New Testament) identifies singleness and dedicated celibacy as Christ-like ways of leading life. The Lambeth document [1988], however, was not clear about certain practices such as cohabitation and some forms of traditional African marriage (where having children before marriage is a must). It did not want to call such practices as 'sinful' but may be as 'less than complete expressions' of the Christian way. There was consensus among the Indian churches about the 'un-Christianness of polygamy. J.R. Chandran, one of the most noted Indian ethicists and church leaders echoed this view when he says that the teachings of Jesus assume "monogamy as the pattern of Christian family".

Feminist theologians in India have made serious biblical and theological reflections on human sexuality issues, albeit from the perspective of women. Once again they are not to be seen as official church position, although of course, as theologians (some of them are even ordained ministers in various Indian churches) they do have certain intellectual impact in influencing the churches in taking decisions on such issues. *Lived Realities: Faith Reflections on Gender Justice,* deals with such concerns based on case studies from India. Each reflection also contains a challenge to the church in India to address the issues from a justice point of view.

Homosexuality

We have already seen that homosexuality has been in existence in India from time immemorial. Over the last decade or so, the gay and lesbian movements have gained momentum and gathered visibility with a proliferation of NGO's and publications on homosexuality issues. However, the stigma attached to homosexuality compels many homosexuals to pretend to be otherwise. They are forced to suppress their sexual identity and sexuality leading to such catastrophes as forced heterosexual marriages which eventually fail leading in some cases even to suicides. The British legacy of homophobia and criminalization of homosexuality lingers on with Section 377 of the Indian Penal Code still in operation.

Indian churches have generally speaking refused even to acknowledge the existence of homosexuality, although it is a reality even within the walls of the church, among clergy and even bishops. It is simply condemned as 'deviant' and 'sin'. As Ajit K. Abraham and K.C. Abraham put it: "As for the vast majority of the Christians in India, the very word 'homosexuality' seems to arouse more revulsion than almost any other word".

The reality, though, has to be faced by the Church in India, sooner rather than later. In most Indian cities, there are reported to be secret meeting places for homosexual people. Ajit Abraham's study of homosexuals in Marina beach in Chennai tells us how serious the situation actually is in India. According to him, because of the fear of discrimination and police torture, homosexuality continues to be a clandestine activity. However, except for a few individual voices, the churches in India have been largely judgmental in their approach towards homosexuality. It is time for the Church in India to wake up to the reality of the problem of homosexuality and treat it as a justice concern. One of the factors that can help this process of awakening is to concentrate on sex education both at home and in the church.

Sex Education

Absence of sex education at home and in educational institutions has tragic consequences for people, their marriage and family life. Monica Melanchton blames the Church as well for its reluctance to take up the issue of sexuality for education in the Church. She pleads for a positive approach to sexuality which, in fact, is compatible with a Christian biblical and theological perspective. Quoting passages like Gen 1 and Proverbs 5 and Song of Solomon, Melanchton argues that God intended sex to be pleasurable for both husband and wife. Sunil Raj Philip also argues that we should have the understanding of sexuality as divinely ordained nature. However, the issue of sexuality still remains by and large a taboo that is rarely addressed in religious and church circles. All this indicates that human sexuality is slowly becoming an area of public discourse in India today.

Indian Church and Human Sexuality: the Need for a new Approach

In a context where the Church continues to exhibit its lethargy and insensitivity towards issues of human sexuality, I try to argue here why the Church should address the issue seriously. One of the key reasons why the Church is still reluctant to talk about sexuality is because it still considers sex as a sensitive concern. As Gnanadason observes, the Indian Church "has been drawn into the vortex of western patriarchal theology and inherited church structures". The Augustinian legacy of treating sex as a 'Pandora's Box', and the view that sex is inherently evil, still dominates the Church. The 'original sin syndrome' still persists although quite a few theologians have challenged this idea. The Church Fathers tended to 'spiritualize' the sexual dimensions of the biblical faith. Origen's rather over-sensitive reading of the book of the Song of Solomon as a poem that talks about the symbolic love of God to humanity is a good example to illustrate this tendency. It was Carl Jung who said, "When people brought sexual questions to me, they invariably turned out be religious questions and when they brought religious questions to me, they always turned out to be sexual ones".

Sexuality: A Justice Concern

One of the main reasons why the Church in India must address sexuality issue is because it is indeed an issue of social justice particularly of Dalit and tribal women. The sweeping phenomenon of globalization and the emerging fascism in the form of Hindu revivalism (Hindutva) makes issues of sexuality increasingly a social justice and human rights concern. It is perhaps in the area of family and sexual relations that globalization poses the greatest moral and ethical challenge. Family break-ups are on the increase in India. Suddenly, the new 'freedom' and globalization and the 'open market' have given the Third World, especially its middle class and the elite, has given rise to rapid increase in teen-age pregnancies and abortion, promotion of tourism, sex-tourism that is, resulting in child abuse and prostitution and the spread of HIV/AIDS which in fact, is already affecting the whole population in Asia and Africa. The problem becomes more acute when its relation to child prostitution is also established. "Cyber cafes" are today centers of the youth to browse through pornographic materials, giving the young generation of today distorted views of sex. The globalised media also helps this process of corrupting the youth with distorted views of sex. Through 'beauty pageants', the female body is commercialized and commoditized, raising questions about the politics of sexuality, glamorization of sexuality being just one of the aspects of this project. Women, in particular are the worst victims of this enterprise of globalization which trivializes sex and sexuality into superficial pleasure through the institutions of rape and prostitution. Traditional family values are on the verge of a total collapse.

All this makes the issue of sexuality a justice concern. It is a justice concern because it has to do with women's right to own and control their own body and sexuality. Forced prostitution, "devadasi" system, rape both within and without marriage, wife beating and other forms of violence on women are all patriarchal political weapons with which men control the body of women. This is particularly true in India where even today, when

Dalit women continue to be the 'property' of the 'upper caste' men for their pleasure. Dalit women in many parts of India still do not enjoy the right to own their own body. They are raped almost every day by the upper caste men, thus get subjected to the most atrocious form of demeaning ones's sexuality.

Like land/nature, women too are considered here as the private property of men. It is this traditional India (Hindu) value system that the fascist Hindutva forces are trying to bring back. Sexuality and the exploitation of 'body' has always been a powerful tool in the hands of the fascists everywhere. The role of body feelings in Hitler's racist fascism was evidently strong. Hitler was apparently "preoccupied with the images of the Jews as people with dirty, grotesque and distorted bodies". One could see the same ideology of fascist hatred of 'the body of the other' in the emerging Hindutva brand of fascism in India. One of the reasons for the militant opposition of the right wing to homosexuality, particularly to lesbianism, could be the fear of the men folk of losing their control over women's body and their sexuality. The unholy alliance of hegemonic caste power and sexuality is becoming very clear. All this should give enough and strong reason for the Church in India to take up sexuality issues as social justice concerns.

Sexuality: An Identity Issue

One of the most widely discussed issues in the contemporary Indian academic and political circles is that of identity politics. The struggles of Dalits, tribals and women have given identity politics a much needed boost. Sexuality issues are also very much 'identity' issues and hence justice issues. When women are generally considered 'unclean' and 'polluting' during the period of menstruation and child birth, to affirm these natural sexual process, is to affirm the identity of women as dignified full human beings. Homosexuals are, perhaps, the most alienated lot of all of them. Because of the stigma attached and the fear of discrimination and torture, gays and lesbians are forced to hide and suppress their identity vis-à-vis their sexual orientation. Forced suppression of one's fundamental identity can cause serious psychological and mental problems leading to suicides. Another community which suffers from the agony and pain of identity crisis are the 'hijras' or eunuchs in India. Although there are a few hijaras coming out affirming their identity and rights, by and large, this community is also treated as 'untouchables'. The 'new minority', the community of homosexuals and hijras face the problem of identity crisis. Their alienation from the mainstream society as 'untouchables' should prompt the church to consider it as a social justice issue.

Sexuality: A Human Rights Issue

The facts and figures on sexuality problems in India illustrate the fact that the issues of sexuality are very much issues of human rights. In the Indian context where marriage and family occupy a central place, the denial of right to get married amounts to violation of a fundamental human right. Devadasis and homosexuals are denied of their right to marry. Because marriage between homosexuals is not legalized, they are also not legally entitled to be privileges like insurance, medical treatment, housing etc. [Article 377 of the Indian Penal Code is still used to discriminate against homosexuals]. Fear of revelation of homosexual orientation compels people to flee home, most of them ending up in poverty, unemployment, homelessness, isolation - and male prostitution in order to survive. All this makes sexuality problems very much a human rights concern. The Church need not look for a theological agreement on these issues to take them up as civil rights or human rights issues, although a new theology of sexuality also is an urgent challenge for the Church in India.

Conclusion: The Need for a New Political Theology of Sexuality

Just as environmental issues were originally considered as too elitist and primarily western concerns by the Third World liberation theologians for a long time - until recently when they began to see the connection between social justice and eco-justice, liberation theology should also be able to make the connection between social justice and sexual justice which is very clear. For this, however, the concept of 'body' and 'embodiment' should be taken seriously. An affirmation of the Word becoming flesh should be an affirmation of our own bodies and sexuality. Theology must be willing to be open to the possibility of encountering God's revelation of the Truth in new and fresh forms. This will help us not to be judgmental about sexuality issues, particularly homosexuality. After all, in the eschatological Kingdom what determines our identity, it will not be our sexuality (Luke:20), but our response to the loving and caring initiatives of God in whom sexuality is transcended.

Re-reading the Bible and Re-writing Worship

Realising a True Family of God

Joseph N. Goh

While he was still speaking to the crowds, his mother and his brothers were standing outside, wanting to speak to him. Someone told him, 'Look, your mother and your brothers are standing outside, wanting to speak to you.' But to the one who had told him this, Jesus replied, 'Who is my mother, and who are my brothers?' And pointing to his disciples, he said, 'Here are my mother and my brothers! For whoever does the will of my Father in heaven is my brother and sister and mother.'"(Matthew 12:46-50 RSV)

I begin this biblico-pastoral reflection with an imaginative reconstruction of an incident in Matthew 12:46-50, during which the author of the gospel paints Jesus as deeply engrossed in preaching. Jesus was probably so caught up in expressing the exuberance of his love for God and fighting for justice on behalf of the disenfranchised that he was oblivious to the arrival of his mother and relatives. Probably exhausted by the journey to see Jesus and eager to reconnect with him, they must have motioned to one of the disciples to tap him on his shoulder and draw his attention to their presence. "Your family is here," this disciple must have whispered to him. "They have been standing outside patiently for a long time, and they are exhausted from the journey to see you. They want to talk to you, especially your mother."

Being a brilliant, creative and resourceful preacher that he was, Jesus must have seen in this exchange a crucial opportunity to expound on what I offer as the aim of my reflection: to unpack ideas of realising—of making real—a true family of God. I imagine Jesus spinning around, smiling broadly and raising his voice saying "Well, if you do God's will, you are my mother and my brothers and my sisters" (Matthew 12:49-50). As a Jewish itinerant preacher who was steeped in his particular socio-cultural milieu, Jesus embodied and preached about God as his 'Abba'. True to the language of his time, the male and female siblings of Jesus are referred to as 'brothers'. I am certain that what Jesus said was not a dismissal of his family. I am even more certain that after he had made his point, he took a break from preaching, and rested and feasted with them.

It is very probable that Jesus was preaching on the loving fatherhood of God when his family arrived. I am fascinated by the idea that Jesus took advantage of their arrival to talk about family. Perhaps in saying what he said, Jesus was attempting to stretch the minds of people who lived 'in a society that placed a very high value on blood relationship' (Harrington 1992, 881). These were probably people who lived very exclusive, insular and close-knitted lives, who perpetuated the idea that blood relations were 'insiders' while non-blood relations were 'outsiders'. Jesus would have been very much against any ghettoisation, discrimination or exclusion of this sort.

Mujerista theologian Ada María Isasi-Díaz's thoughts are useful for thinking over this issue. She speaks of a 'kin-dom' rather than a kingdom of God. For Díaz (2008, 380), 'kingdom' implies 'a sexist and classist term that does not convey today what it did at the time of the gospels'. The notion of kingdom thus hints at oppressive power plays at the expense of the downtrodden. Conversely, it is the kin-dom of God that Jesus preached and sought to establish as a familial praxis of justice, care, truthfulness and liberation. In other words, kin-dom is a space in which 'family' is less a matter of blood ties than it is a matter of doing God's will.

The carrying out of God's will was concretely and substantially exemplified in the inclusive, non-judgemental and unconditionally loving attitudes, teachings and practices of Jesus. The preacher of Nazareth incarnated the face and gentle caress of God to the people who were the most ostracised in his day, notably the tax collectors, women, lepers and non-Jews. Hence, the 'true family of Jesus' consists of a 'spiritual family' (Harrington 1992, 881) that bursts the fixed kinship categories of conventional consanguinity. An introverted pride in resemblance gives way to a celebration of dissimilitude when there is a recognition and embrace of Jesus' vision that individuals and communities are eligible to claim kinship with Jesus—with God—based on the criterion of '[doing] the will of [his] Father in heaven' (Matthew 12:50).

This vision is one that is powerful and revolutionary, yet simultaneously arduous to personify, as the followers of Jesus need to emulate his vision of kin-dom that 'loyalty to justice and truth supersedes the traditional family' (Bohache 2006, 509). The journey of realising the true family of God requires a sincere and wholehearted embrace of both traditional and non-traditional spiritual family members, of 'insiders' and 'outsiders' who are invested in doing what is just, caring, truthful and liberating.

Who are traditional and non-traditional spiritual family members? I suggest that traditional members consist of people who are considered as 'insiders' because they adhere to social compliance and respectability in terms of gender and sexuality. These include people who are comfortable with, and express themselves according to the gender assigned to them at birth, or people in opposite-sex relationships who may also be parents. Who then, are non-traditional members? Here, my thoughts turn to 'outsiders, or gender variant and sexually diverse people. These are transgender men and women, and people who do not identify with a particular gender or live as two genders, or people who feel romantic and sexual attraction to people of the same sex like gay men and lesbian women, or people who feel that they can love men and women, like bisexual people. Such people often feel excluded from the true family of God due to accusations of deviance and sinfulness by Christian individuals, communities and churches that are struggling to understand them.

Yet these gender variant and sexually diverse people may be devoted to living out the kin-dom of God in various ways. They may be fighting for justice and the right to live without fear of persecution. They may be involved in caring for partners, children, the ecology and the underprivileged. In many cases, they are struggling to be truthful to themselves after years of self-loathing and trying to conform to mainstream gender and sexual norms, roles and expectations. They are people who attempt to experience true liberation in societies and religious communities that desire only to 'repair and reform' them before they can be accepted. They are well aware of their status of 'outsider' simply on the basis of their gender and sexual identities. Nevertheless, if their actual lives reflect the kin-dom that Jesus preached despite being non-traditional, they must then still be part of the family. To exclude them as family members is to go against the inclusive spirit of Jesus. It is vital to remember that the loving and unconditional acceptance of God, who is 'not merely God *for* the world, but also God *with* us and the world' (Athappilly 2014, 88; original emphasis), is the entitlement of each and every human person.

How can we as Christian individuals, communities and churches in any part of the world realise a true family of God that has room for everyone? How can we establish again and again the kin-dom that Jesus envisioned? Despite doctrinal and theological differences, how can we create spaces where gender variant and sexually diverse people can breathe in a genuine air of welcome, acceptance and non-judgement?

There are neither simple nor singular solutions to these questions. Nevertheless, the words ascribed to Jesus in Matthew 12:46-50 can hold meaningful guidelines that can be translated into concrete action for us. Jesus always spoke as someone who lived and practised what I refer to as a methodology of 'love seeking understanding' and 'listening from the heart' (Goh 2016, 17). As followers of Jesus, it is incumbent on us at all times to imitate Jesus by preserving an acute awareness that the kin-dom which Jesus believed in, abided by and died for points to a mandate to realise a sense of family that goes beyond conventional boundaries of identity and expression. The proclamation that whoever does the will of God is part of Jesus' family cannot be taken as a sole reference to people who are aligned to mainstream expectations of gender and sexuality. Such an understanding does not reflect the values and hopes that Jesus harbours for human persons who have always demonstrated, and will always demonstrate untold diversity. We know from our experiences that family members are often very different, but they are still family.

As followers of Jesus, we need to dismantle insider/outsider binary, and an 'us-versus-them' mentality. We need to recognise that the ultimate criterion for being a member of the true family of God is the desire and the commitment to execute the will of God according to one's circumstances and location in life by being as inclusive, non-judgemental and unconditionally loving as Jesus was. God calls all people to live by God's will regardless of gender or sexual identity. If we extend this vision in an impartial way to each and every human person, including those who are gender variant and sexually diverse, we are participating in realising a true family of God.

Bibliography

Athappilly, Sebastian. 2014. *Theology of the Heart: Towards an Affective Theology*. Bangalore, India: Dharmaram Publications.

Bohache, Thomas. 2006. 'Matthew'. In *The Queer Bible Commentary*, edited by Deryn Guest, Robert E. Goss, Mona West, and Thomas Bohache, 487–516. London: SCM Press.

Goh, Joseph N. 2016. 'Christianity, Sexual Diversity and Access to Health Services'. APCOM. https://apcom.org/wp-content/uploads/2016/11/DiscussionPaper_Christianiy-2016.11.25.pdf.

Harrington, Daniel J. 1992. 'Matthew'. In *The Collegeville Bible Commentary: Based on the New American Bible with Revised New Testament*, edited by Robert J. Karris and Dianne Bergant, 861–902. Collegeville, MN: Liturgical Press.

Isasi-Díaz, Ada María. 2008. 'Se Hace Camino Al Andar—The Road Is Made by Walking: What the Future Demands of Women-Centered Theologies'. *Feminist Theology* 16 (3): 379–82. doi:10.1177/0966735008091404.

Special Worship Orders

Order of Worship during Dialogue
'Church Leaders and Key Affected People'
On June 2nd, 2015: Organised by
Kerala Council of Churches (KCC) and NCCI

Invocation song

Call to Worship

Leader : We come into God's presence naked, as we are

All : God come into us

Leader : We crave to feel God's fondling and caressing in our lives

All : God spread in us

Leader : We are committed in long lasting working relationships

All : God partner with us

Prayer of Adoration

Leader: God, the gardener of loving relationships, we are enjoying your stimulating presence amidst us. We adore and praise your arousing presence in all the walks of our life. We thank you for your everlasting love towards us amidst our unfaithfulness. Seal our lips with kisses of understanding and multiply in us the attraction to one another that we may authentically celebrate your loving witness among us. Amen

Confession

All: O God, our companion and mate, as we trace back our memories we confess that we have failed to realize and acknowledge the diversities that have risen from your womb of creation. As Sexual Beings we crave for your breath of life that forgives our disabilities to appreciate the beauties of human sexualities. Touch and heal our minds that we may explore and discover the uniqueness in our fellow companions. Embrace us as we comfort each other with our hugs and arouse in us the desire to blossom in all that you created us to be.

Absolution

(Let us observe a moment of silence for introspection. Let us hold hands of those beside us to ensure God's forgiveness and our companionship in path ahead. Let us absolve each other by saying the absolution together.)

All: Let the God who communes in the needs of our body and mind, make us bold enough to express our diverse desires truly and fully. The God will make us vulnerable enough that we could not hold ourselves from being appealed by the beauties she created. Hereafter we will not just blossom but the spring itself will sprout from us as we the lovers come in union. Amen

Affirmation of Faith

Leader: We, believe in the God who mated with the deserted chaos, giving birth to lives, in assorted forms. These offspring of God, in heaven and earth are fond of carnal knowledge, and in this urge they re-create as their parent do.

All: We, believe in Christ Jesus the son, whom Mary bore for God. He dared to relish all those beautiful things which appealed Him, let it be the amorous chat of a prostitute, the perfume of an ardent woman or the warm embracement of His beloved disciple. His endless privation for earnest love, led him to the cross, where He was killed by and for those whom He loved. But death couldn't restrain His passion to men, women and creation, and hence He returned to where He met His loved ones.

We, believe in the Spirit of God, who hastens us closer to our mates and keeps us united in desires, will and commitment.

We, believe in the association of devout ones where the fete of erotic love befalls.

We, believe and long for the day when we could express our perpetual cravings for love, intimacy and sensual union with liberty. Amen

Intercession

Leader: Let us remember those who have not had the space to celebrate the beauties of their body and their sexuality, those who have not been able to feel the pleasure of sex, and those who have become objects of ridicule because of their sexual orientation.

Pray in silence: God make us also agitated about the silence imposed on your people. Help us to obey our conscience and your Spirit.

Leader: Let us remember those whose rights, dignity and respect have been ripped because of their different sexual orientations, those who have to live with society-moulded frameworks of masculinity, femininity and relationships.

Pray in silence: God make us also agitated about the silence imposed on your people. Help us to obey our conscience and your Spirit.

Leader: Let us remember those who are estranged by the sin of hypocrisy to be framed as polluted and immoral by the dominant norms. Those who are exploited, commercialised and made commodities in the flesh market because of their sex, colour or caste.

Pray in silence: God make us also agitated about the silence imposed on your people. Help us to obey our conscience and your Spirit.

Concluding Prayer

Disturb us O Lord disturb us, when we are too pleased with ourselves... Disturb us O Lord, when our dreams have come true, because we have dreamt too little... Disturb us O Lord, when we reached the shore safely, because we have sailed too close, to the shore, Disturb us O Lord, disturb us... Amen

Benediction (Let us say the benediction together)

Let us remain here now, for the peace we enjoy still needs to be justified.

God be with us when we attend the unattended struggle for justice

Christ be with us when we disobey the dominant norms in our unmasking

The spirit be with us guiding in the truths unknown to us. Amen

- Collected and Arranged by **Rev Georvin Joseph,**
Clergy, Mar Thoma Sabha Office, Tiruvalla

Worship Service

Worship Orders created by Rev Juswantori Ichwan of Indonesia and Rev Miak Siew of Singapore, NCCI's Asian Consultation in Bangalore, February, 2017

Leader: In the name of God, the beneficent, the merciful. Praise be to the Lord of the Universe, who has created each of us beautiful in diversity,

All: That we may know each other, not that we may despise each other.

Leader: Praise be to the Lord of the Universe, who has shown us His love and tender care,

All: That we may share His love to those we meet, not that we may spread hatred and live in disunity.

Leader: Praise be to the Lord of the Universe, who has inclined his ears to hear our cries for help,

All: That we may also listen to the cries of the world, not that we may neglect those in trouble.

PRAYER SONG: 'PRAISE THE SOURCE OF ALL CREATION'

[Sung to the tune of "WHAT A FRIEND WE HAVE IN JESUS"]

1. Praise the Source of all creation,
   giving life throughout the Earth,
   blessing every love relation,

filling all with sacred worth.

Celebrate all forms and colors,

varied beauty everywhere.

Streams of goodness overflowing,

wondrous gifts for all to share.

2. Many genders, many races,

all reflect Divinity;

many gifts and many graces

help us be all we can be.

Partners on this path of freedom,

taking down each stifling wall.

We will open doors of welcome,

bringing hope and joy to all.

3. Long have many been excluded,

judged and scorned by custom's norms;

everyone will be included,

as we work to bring reforms.

Let us end abuse and violence,

bringing justice everywhere,

joining Holy Wisdom's mission,

helping all be free and fair.

4. Equal marriage, healing, freeing,

nurtures body, mind and soul,

reaffirming every being,

all created good and whole.

Come, rejoice and sing together,

celebrating life and love;

praise the great Creative Spirit,

living in us and above.

ANY PRAYER - FOLLOWED BY THE LORD'S PRAYER

SCRIPTURE READING: 1 John 4 : 7-11 [or any other suitable passage]

HOMILY/SERMON

RESPONSIVE READING: 1 Cor: 13

Leader: What if I could speak all languages of humans and even of angels?

All: If I did not love others, I would be nothing more than a noisy gong or a clanging cymbal.

Leader: What if I could prophesy and understand all mysteries and all knowledge? And what if I had faith that moved mountains?

All: I would be nothing, unless I loved others.

Leader: What if I gave away all that I owned and let myself be burned alive?

All: I would gain nothing, unless I loved others.

Leader: Love is patient and kind, never jealous, boastful, proud, or rude. Love isn't selfish or quick tempered.

All: It doesn't keep a record of wrongs that others do.

Leader: Love rejoices in the truth, but not in evil.

All: Love is always supportive, loyal, hopeful, and trusting. Love never fails!

Leader: Everyone who prophesies will stop, and unknown languages will no longer be spoken.

All: All that we know will be forgotten.

Leader: We don't know everything,

All: And our prophecies are not complete.

Leader: But what is perfect will someday appear,

All: And what isn't perfect will then disappear.

Leader: When we were children, we thought and reasoned as children do.

All: But when we grew up, we quit our childish ways.

Leader: Now all we can see of God is like a cloudy picture in a mirror.

All: Later we will see him face to face.

Leader: We don't know everything, but then we will,

All: Just as God completely understands us.

Leader: For now there are faith, hope, and love.

All: But of these three, the greatest is love.

Song: LET LOVE BE REAL [Sung to the tune of "DANNY BOY") Or any other Hymn

1.   Let love be real, in giving and receiving,
      without the need to manage and to own;
      A haven free from posing and pretending,
      where every weakness may be safely known.
      Give me your hand, along the desert pathway,
      give me your love, wherever we may go:
      as God loves us, so let us love each other,
      with no demands, just open hands
      and space to grow

2.   Let love be real, with no manipulation,
      no secret wish to harness or control;
      let us accept each other's incompleteness,
      and share the joy of learning to be whole.
      Give me your hope
      through dreams and disappointments,
      give me your trust, when all my failings show:
      as God loves us, so let us love each other,
      with no demands, just open hands
      and space to grow.

3.   Let love be real, not grasping or confining,
      that strange embrace that holds yet sets us free;

that helps us face the risk of truly living,

and makes us brave to be what we might be.

Give me your strength

when all my words are weakness,

give me your love, in spite of all you know:

as God loves us, so let us love each other,

with no demands, just open hands

and space to grow.

[The following portion was created by Rev Miak Siew of Singapore]

Communion

Leader: As grains of wheat once scattered on the hill are gathered into one to become our bread, so may all your people from all the ends of the world be gathered into one in You.

All: Amen.

Reading: 'God of Moon and Stars'

1.   God of the moon and stars

God of the gay- and singles bars

God of the fragile hearts we are, **I come to you**

God of our history,

God of the future that will be,

What will you make of me, **I come to you**

2.   God of the meek and mild,

God of the reckless and the wild

God of the un-reconciled, **I come to you**

God of our life and death

God of secrets un-confessed

God of our every breath, **I come to you**

3.   God of the rich and poor
      God of the princess and the whore
      God of the ever open door, **I come to you**
      God of the unborn child
      God of the pure and undefiled,
      God of the pimp and paedophile**, I come to you**

CLOSING BENEDICTION

- Created by **Rev Juswantori Ichwan** of Indonesia - conducted at NCCI's Asian Consultation: Bangalore: February, 2017

CHAPTER - 2

Body – Mind – Justice: Medical, Psychological and Legal Responses

Transgender Status:
Biology and Psychology

Varghese Punnoose

The first designation given to a new-born baby is its status as male or female. This status is usually assigned at birth based on the appearance of external genitalia. It is an either-or situation. There is no in-between status. This dichotomy regarding sex is the general rule within the animal kingdom especially among the higher species. The assigned sexual identity at birth later transforms as gender identity, which is more of a psychological entity of being masculine or feminine. The general rule of dichotomy regarding sex is carried forward and applied to gender also - that is, the expectation that a child assigned to male sex should grow up as a boy and the child assigned to female sex should develop as a girl. The general rule expects a fine matching between sex and gender, but there are some situations, though rare, where this perfect match does not occur. This is an ill-understood area. When understanding is poor, it becomes a fertile breeding ground for prejudice, stigma and discrimination. Thus exceptions to the general rule of dichotomy of sex and gender have becomes objects of ridicule and stigma.

Transgender status is a rare situation where the psychological gender does not match with biological sex or the assigned gender at birth.

Basic Biology of Sexual Identity

The term 'sex' is used to refer to the biological characteristics which defines an animal or person as male or female. This identity is based on the primary sexual organ possessed by the animal/person. The primary sex organ of the male is a pair of testes and that of female is a pair of ovaries. These organs are formed within the first few weeks of pregnancy. Whether the infant develops testes or ovaries is determined by the way in which chromosomes get paired at the time of union between the egg (from the mother) and sperm (from the father). The eggs always carry one X chromosome in its core. The sperms may carry either X or Y chromosome. If the egg happens to be fertilised by a sperm which carries Y, the combination is XY and it results in the development of testes. If the egg is fertilised by a sperm which carries X chromosome, the combination will be XX and the developing foetus will be possessing ovaries. During the course of development of the foetus within the uterus, there occurs a sprinkling of male hormones (androgens- testosterone) in those with XY pattern. This results in the development of male external genitalia - the penis and the scrotum (the bag of skin in which testes are located). In those with XX pattern, the male-hormone rush does not occur and the external genitalia will remain in the female pattern.

The above is a description of what happens in normal sexual development. But rarely some abnormalities of this sexual differentiation can happen during intra-uterine life (period of pregnancy) and this can result in intersex conditions (hermaphroditism).

The second phase of sexual development happens during adolescence. The male hormone surge results in male pattern of body hair growth, increase in size of penis and testes, voice changes and skeletal growth. The female hormone surge (oestrogens and progesterones) brings in breast development, onset of menses, skin changes and hair growth in female pattern. By the end of this sexual development, the body is ready for reproduction.

Gender Development

Biological factors

We have already seen that the maleness and masculinity depends on exposure to male sex hormones even when the baby is inside the mother's womb. Neurones (brain cells) in areas such as hypothalamus are programmed by male sex hormones like testosterone to express masculine behaviour. If for some reason this testosterone exposure is not adequate or hypothalamus does not respond in the expected manner, the expression of masculine behaviour may not occur even though the sex is male. Sex hormones also influence sexual behaviour later in life, but this effect is less pronounced in humans than in lower animals.

Psychosocial factors

Children usually develop a gender identity consistent with their assigned sex. The formation of gender identity is influenced by child's temperament and parental – cultural attitudes. Cultural stereotypes may expect that girls should be more sensitive and delicate and boys should be aggressive and active. However, greater tolerance for cross-gender activity in children has emerged in the last few decades. Learning theory postulates that children may be rewarded or punished by parents and teachers on the basis of gendered behaviour, thus influencing the way in which they express their gender identities. Psychoanalytical view points put forward by Sigmund Freud that, [a]the quality of mother-child relationship early in life and [b] unresolved Oedipus - Electra Complex leads to gender identity disturbance later in life, do not find much acceptance in the scientific community nowadays. To sum up, biological and psychosocial factors may operate together towards the development of transgender status.

Is Transgender status a psychiatric disorder?

Transgender status is not a psychiatric disorder. Just because a person's (psychological) gender does not match with his/ her (biological) sex, he/ she cannot be considered mentally ill. At the same time this is a condition which requires help and intervention from the medical profession including psychiatrists. It is because of this fact both the International Classification of Diseases (ICD-10) by World Health Organization and Diagnostic and Statistical Manual (DSM-5) of American Psychiatric Association have included transgender statistics in their listings. Various terminologies like 'transsexualism' (term used in ICD 10), 'gender identity disorder'(DSM –IV) and 'gender dysphoria' (DSM-5) are used .

The DSM-5 uses the term 'Gender Dysphoria' and specifies that it is a condition characterised by a marked incongruence between ones experienced/expressed gender and gender assigned at birth. These persons may have strong desire to get rid of his/her primary or secondary sex characteristics and to acquire the primary and secondary sex characteristics of the other gender. They have a strong conviction that they have the typical psychological makeup of the other gender and have a strong desire to be treated as the other gender.

Are all transgenders [TG] the same ?

Majority of transgenders are born in male sex, assigned as male gender at birth and desirous of assuming the gender status of female. Female to male trangender status are relatively less.

Transgender people are diverse. There are a group of TG's who want to have the body of another sex- they are described as transsexuals. Then there are those who feel that they are 'between' 2 genders, or have both genders, or have neither genders- they are called (gender fluid or gender queer). Those who wear clothing of the opposite gender for sexual excitement alone are not transgenders – the term used to describe this cross-dressing is transvesticism.

There is a lot of confusion regarding the sexual orientation of transgender individuals. They have diverse sexual orientations. For example, a transgender female assigned as male at birth may identify as straight (attracted to men) or lesbian (attracted to other women) or bisexual (attracted to both men and women)

What should be the medico-scientific approach to persons with transgender status?

Children and adolescents are brought by parents to psychiatric services with a hope that the psychiatrist will do counselling or some therapies (like hypnosis) to get rid of their 'undesirable' tomboyish or effeminate behaviour and 'unacceptable wish' to change over to the opposite gender. Adult persons may approach mental health professionals when they undergo crisis situations like pressure from the family to get married in the conventional manner. Sometimes they may approach medical professionals like dermatologists (skin specialists) with a request for cosmetic procedures like hair removal, or endocrinologists with a request for hormone treatment for breast enlargement, or plastic surgeons requesting a sex change surgery.

The first step is to do a comprehensive assessment of the problem. This requires a team effort by a group of professionals like general physicians, psychiatrists, dermatologists, endocrinologists, plastic surgeons, social workers, etc.

The next step is to educate the person and his family members about the nature of the problem and the realistic options available for its management. Unrealistic expectations by family that it can be "cured by" counselling or psychiatric treatment should be dealt with in a sensitive manner. The family members expect the affected person to change his/her mind according to the body, while the transgender person expects medical help to change his/her body in tune with his/her mind! The psychiatrist has to negotiate this conflict in a skilful manner. The unrealistic expectations by the transgender person about the effects of hormone treatment or an immediate surgery for sex change also should be addressed.

The third step is the psychological counselling to equip the person to accept and anticipate problems in the course of treatment and adaptations thereafter. Issues like depression, anxiety, substance use, sexual orientation, relationships, occupation, rehabilitation and getting financial support for the treatment are addressed. The lived experience in transgender community and in the society for at least one year is desirable before proceeding to permanent surgical corrections.

Fourth step is the initiation of cosmetic measurers like laser treatment for hair removal and hormonal treatment for breast enlargement. Close medical supervision and follow up is needed for hormonal therapy. There should be a good financial planning before initiating these, as tests and therapies are expensive.

The last step is the surgical intervention – Sex Reassignment Surgery [SRS]. It is a multi-step procedure done in several settings. It includes castration (removal of testes or ovaries), top surgery (for breast augmentation and implantation) and bottom surgery (for reshaping of the external genitalia). The bottom surgery may require a joint effort by urologist, gynaecologist and plastic surgeon. The fact that, though surgery may provide the chance for sexual intercourse in a limited way, the chances of bearing children does not exist, has to be emphasised before resorting to this final step.

Even after the surgery, the person may require continued medical and psychological help. The guidelines for this treatment generally follow those laid down by World Professional Association for Transgender Health (WPATH) Standards of Care.

The Kottayam Initiative: The First Transgender [TG] Clinic

The District Legal Service Society in Kottayam (Kerala) took an initiative to address the problems of the transgender people by organising a medical camp in February 2017. In the discussions which followed, it became evident that the needs of this gender minority has to be addressed with priority. It was in this background that a Transgender Clinic with multidisciplinary involvement was inaugurated in Kottayam Medical College in May 2017, perhaps the first of such initiative by the Government sector in India. The TG Clinic is held on the first Tuesday of every month attended by a general physician, psychiatrist, endocrinologist , dermatologist and plastic surgeon. Paralegal volunteers deputed by the DLSA co-ordinate the running of the clinic. Infrastructure limitations, man power limitations and the lack of funds for providing costly interventions are major roadblocks. However, the initial response from the civil society, medical professionals and media are encouraging.

Much still needs to be done for public awareness regarding the issue of this gender minority. Only scientific knowledge can bring in attitudinal changes, thereby reducing the stigma and discrimination.

Understanding Health Issues, Access to Services and Challenges in Sexual Health

Ronald Lalthanmawia

Introduction

The topics of sex and sexuality have always been taboo in India. And so the discussions around them go into a unhealthy, unhygienic environment. Speaking about sexuality and sexual pleasure in a healthy way is a topic everyone prefers to shy away from. This often leads to myths and misconceptions about sex and sexuality and leads to unhealthy practices in many ways. Sexual health is usually tied up with Reproductive Health and Human Immunodeficiency Virus (HIV)/Sexually Transmitted Infections (STI), focusing only on certain issues like child birth, contraception, HIV/STI transmission etc. The topic, "Reproductive Health" does not cover all the issues of sexual life of humans, which is vibrant and diverse for different purposes, whether it is for sex work, sexual pleasure, sexual needs, etc. In this process the reproductive health or HIV/STI discourse does not cover sexual hygiene, or safe and happy sexual interactions.

According to the American Sexual Health Society,[1] sexual health is the ability to embrace and enjoy our sexuality throughout our lives. It is an important part of our physical and emotional health. Being sexually healthy means:

- Understanding that sexuality is a natural part of life and involves more than sexual behavior.

- Recognizing and respecting the sexual rights we all share.

- Having access to sexual health information, education, and care.

- Making an effort to prevent unintended pregnancies and STIs and seek care and treatment when needed.

- Being able to experience sexual pleasure, satisfaction, and intimacy when desired.

- Being able to communicate about sexual health with others including sexual partners and healthcare providers.

Whether transgender, cisgender or intersex, the attitudes towards sex being taboo, shameful and 'sinful', they nurture a feeling to ignore the health of sexual organs because of the inbuilt fear. People with different sexual orientations and gender identities face health care risks that are often not addressed because of lack of knowledge of the patient's sexual orientation, ignorance of specific health care issues, or because the patient feels that the health care professional is homophobic or transphobic. Access to health services, acceptability of health programmes and prevalence of multiple health issues have always been a challenge among persons with different sexual orientations and gender identities. It is important to understand and address various factors contributing towards the incidence of Sexually Transmitted Infections (STIs), HIV infection, and other psychosocial health conditions.

Access to health services, acceptability of health programmes and prevalence of multiple health issues has always been a challenge among persons with different sexual orientations and gender identities. It is important to understand and address various factors contributing towards the incidence of Sexually Transmitted Infections (STIs) and HIV infection and other psychosocial health conditions.

Prevalence of diseases

According to Chakrapani V et al, the prevalence of the number of psychosocial health conditions among Men who have Sex with Men (MSM) were: none = 31.3%, one = 43%, two = 20%, and three = 5.7%; and among Transgender (TG) women: none = 9%; one = 35.33%, two = 38.33%, and three = 17.33%.[2] In addition to the number of syndemic conditions, resilient coping and social support were significant predictors of sexual risk among MSM and transgender women.

HIV Infection levels in men who have sex with men [MSM] are very high in many cities in Asia, with levels between 13% and 32% (China, India, Myanmar and Vietnam). Across the region it has been found that men who have sex with men are becoming infected by HIV at a young age. HIV prevention and testing services were reaching fewer young MSM's and they reported lower condom use than their older counterparts.[3] In India, particularly high HIV prevalence rates have been found among transgender populations in cities such as Delhi (49%) and Mumbai (42%) in India.[4]

Additionally, because of social discrimination and stigma, most transgender people in India have no opportunity for schooling or access to higher education, eventually leading to poor health literacy. Even though transgender people in India have been given their civic identity, they are still vulnerable to verbal and psychological abuse by others.

Factors contributing towards health issues, health seeking behaviors

Anatomical vulnerability

Common sexually transmitted bacterial organisms may affect the ano-rectum and peri-anal skin. While some of these infections are a result of contiguous spread from genital infection, most result from receptive anal intercourse. The HIV virus is more easily transmitted through unprotected anal intercourse than through unprotected vaginal intercourse, and men, women and transgender persons who engage in receptive anal intercourses are at increased risk of contracting the HIV virus.[5] Generally, the receptive partner is at greater risk of contracting the HIV virus because the lining of the rectum is thin and may allow the virus to enter the body through semen exchange. The insertive partner is also at risk, in the context of unprotected sex, because STIs can enter through the urethra or through small cuts, abrasions, or open sores on the penis. Also, condoms are more likely to break during anal sex than during vaginal sex, unless sufficient lubrication is ensured. Thus, even with a condom, anal sex can be risky.[6]

Criminalization and lack of laws for protection

In the Asian context, 23 of the 48 countries in the region criminalize male to male sex.[7] They are often subjected to police abuses, extortion, harassment, assault, detention and human rights violations. Most Asian countries do not have specific anti-discrimination laws relating to discrimination on the grounds of sexual orientation or transgender status.

Transgender persons who identified as neither men nor women were included in India's census survey of 2011 for the first time. A landmark judgment in 2014 at India's Supreme Court ruled that transgender people had equal rights under the law, and granted legal status to the third gender. However, absence of protection from police means ruffians find Hijras/ Transgender [TG] people as easy targets for extorting money, and as sexual objects. A 2007 study[8] documented that in the past one year, the percentage of those men who have sex with men –MSM - and Hijras who reported forced sex is 46%; physical abuse is 44%; verbal abuse is 56%; blackmail for money is 31%; and threat to life is 24%.

Transgender people have very limited employment opportunities, and they have no access to bathrooms/toilets and public spaces. The lack of access to bathrooms and public spaces access is illustrative of the discrimination faced by transgender people in availing each facilities and amenities. They face similar problems in prisons, hospitals and schools.

Stigma and Discrimination

Research has found that more than 80% of people living with HIV in the South Asia region have experienced some form of discrimination whether that is in the work force, community or among family members.

The need to be accepted, respected, loved and protected drives people into desperation. This often puts people into situations that could be harmful to them and lead to other psychosocial conditions like depression, drug and alcohol dependency, multiple-sexual partnerships and many have gone to an extent to commit suicide.

High risk behaviors

Factors associated with increased rates of STIs include the loss of fear regarding human immunodeficiency virus (HIV) transmission because of the increased manageability of the infection, the use of the Internet as an efficient way to find sex partners, increasing use of erectile dysfunction agents, and possibly the expanding role of oral sex in STI transmission.[9] One of the major factors facilitating the increased risk-taking behavior by MSM is the use of disinhibiting substances, including alcohol, crystal methamphetamine, and other recreational drugs.[10]

The reasons for risk-taking behavior are complex. In many cases, psychosocial health concerns, such as depression, may predispose MSM to increased STD risk-taking.[11] Frequently, these behaviors are in response to stigma, discrimination, homophobia or transphobia. Younger MSM, particularly those who do not discuss their sexual orientation with their partners, friends, or health care providers, are at increased risk for HIV and other STIs. Miscommunication and misperceptions about HIV serostatus and the visual absence of STIs may enable some MSM to feel comfortable engaging in unprotected sex.[12]

Access to Health Services and Treatment

Only a limited amount of information is available on health care risks within the lesbian, gay, bisexual, or transgender population. Most studies do not address sexual orientation, behavior and identity. Fear of stigmatization prevents many people from identifying themselves as lesbian, gay, bisexual, or transgender. In addition, many do not seek health care because of prior negative experience. As many as two thirds of physicians never ask their patients about their sexual orientation.[13] Some health care professionals assume that their patients are heterosexual. Others may be homophobic and hostile and prefer to avoid the issue.

According to a study conducted,[14] it revealed that the main implications of homosexuality towards access to health service are

- Differences in health care between heterosexual and homosexual individuals, particularly for the female homosexual population

- Communication difficulties as a accessibility barrier to the gay population to health services

- Prejudicial conduct adopted by health professionals

- Breach of confidentiality during consultations

- Disclosure of sexual orientation in health services

- Pursuit of health services in major conditions situations, because of institutional homophobia

- Internalized homophobia

- Aging and homosexual orientation as access barriers

- Need for holistic care beyond the sexual issues of the homosexual population

- Higher performance of professional services towards the care of LGBT youth

Conclusion

The LGBTIQ community experiences difficulties communicating with health professionals when expressing their homosexuality/bisexuality [this is apart from the fear of assumptions about their sexual orientation, and such embarrassing situations], often due to the homo and trans-phobic conduct of the health professional. Being excluded from various health services and programmes has led to the reduction in this community's attendance for healthcare services. It is therefore necessary to provide qualified and equipped health services free of discrimination in order to ensure there is improved access for all. These should be able to analyze the health status of their clients, taking into consideration the health, social, and cultural context in which they are placed, because lesbian, gay, bisexual, and transgender persons face unique health care risks. Reducing stigma and discrimination, providing an enabling environment, and empowering people of different sexual orientations and gender identities will go a long way in preventing health issues among the community.

End Notes

[1] *http://www.ashasexualhealth.org/sexual-health/.*

[2] Chakrapani, V., Newman, P. A., Shunmugam, M., Logie, C. H., & Samuel, M. (2017). Syndemics of depression, alcohol use, and victimisation, and their association with HIV-related sexual risk among men who have sex with men and transgender women in India. Global Public Health, 12(2), 250-265. doi:10.1080/17441692.2015.1091024 View BMC Public Health.

[3] UNAIDS Prevention Gap Report 2016.

[4] *http://apcom.org/sites/default/files/PolicyBrief-TG%289%29.pdf.*

[5] *http://www.avert.org/men-sex-men.htm.*

[6] Center for Disease Control; "Can I get HIV from anal sex?

[7] "State Sponsored Homophobia 2016: A world survey of sexual orientation laws: criminalisation, protection and recognition" (PDF). International Lesbian, Gay, Bisexual, Trans and Intersex Association. 17 May 2016. Retrieved 19 May 2016.

[8] *http://www.unaids.org/sites/default/files/media_asset/20110829_PLHIV StigmaIndex_en_0.pdf*

[9] Illa L, Brickman A, Saint-Jean G, et al. Sexual risk behaviors in late middle age and older HIV seropositive adults, AIDS Behav, 2008, vol. 12 (pg. 935-42).

[10] Mansergh G, Flores S, Koblin B, Hudson S, McKirnan D, Colfax GN. Alcohol and drug use in the context of anal sex and other factors associated with sexually transmitted infections: results from a multi-city study of high-risk men who have sex with men in the USA, Sex Transm Infect, 2008, vol. 84 (pg. 509-11).

[11] Centers for Disease Control and Prevention. HIV/STD risks in young men who have sex with men who do not disclose their sexual orientation—six U.S. cities, 1994–2000, MMWR Morb Mortal Wkly Rep, 2003, vol. 52 (pg. 81-6)

[12] MacKellar DA, Valleroy LA, Behel S, et al. Unintentional HIV exposures from young men who have sex with men who disclose being HIV-negative, AIDS, 2006, vol. 20 (pg. 1637-44).

[13] Allen LB, Glicken AD, Beach RK, et al. Adolescent health care experience of gay, lesbian, and bisexual young adults. J Adolesc Health 1998;23: 212-220. [PubMed]

[14] Alencar Albuquerque G, de Lima Garcia C, da Silva Quirino G, et al. Access to health services by lesbian, gay, bisexual, and transgender persons: systematic literature review. BMC International Health and Human Rights. 2016;16:2. doi:10.1186/s12914-015-0072-9. Unintentional HIV exposures from young men who have sex with men who disclose being HIV-negative, AIDS, 2006, vol. 20 (pg. 1637-44).

Psychological

Homosexuality in India

T.S. Sathyanarayana Rao and K.S. Jacob

The shift in the understanding of homosexuality from sin, crime and pathology to a normal variant of human sexuality occurred in the late 20th century. The American Psychiatric Association, in 1973, and the World Health Organisation, in 1992, officially accepted its normal variant status. Many countries have since decriminalised homosexual behavior and some have recognised same-sex civil unions and marriage. The new understanding was based on studies that documented a high prevalence of same-sex feelings and behavior in men and women, its prevalence across cultures and among almost all non-human primate species. Investigations using psychological tests could not differentiate heterosexual from homosexual orientation. Research also demonstrated that people with homosexual orientation did not have any objective psychological dysfunction or impairments in judgement, stability and vocational capabilities. Psychiatric, psychoanalytic, medical and mental health professionals now consider homosexuality as a normal variation of human sexuality.

Human sexuality is complex. The acceptance of the distinction between desire, behavior and identity acknowledges the multidimensional nature of sexuality. The fact that these dimensions may not always be congruent in individuals suggests complexity of the issues. Bisexuality, both sequential and concurrent, and discordance between biological sex and gender role and identity add to the issues. Medicine and psychiatry employ terms like homosexuality, heterosexuality, bisexuality and trans-sexuality to encompass all related issues, while current social usage argues for lesbian, gay, bisexual and transgender (LGBT), which focuses on identities.

The prevalence of homosexuality is difficult to estimate for many reasons, including the associated stigma and social repression, the unrepresentative samples surveyed and the failure to distinguish desire, behavior and identity. The figures vary between age groups, regions and cultures. Medicine and science continue to debate the relative contributions of nature and nurture, biological and psychosocial factors, to sexuality. Essentialist constructs argue for biology and dismiss personal and social meanings of sexual desire and relationships. On the other hand, constructivists support the role of culture and history. While essentialism and constructionism, on the surface appear contradictory, they may mediate orientation and identity, respectively.

Anthropologists have documented significant variations in the organisation and meaning of same-sex practices across cultures and changes within particular societies over time. The universality of same-sex expression coexists with variations in its meaning and practice across culture. Cross-cultural studies highlight the limits of any single explanation of homosexuality within a particular society. Classical theories of psychological development hypothesize the origins of adult sexual orientation in childhood experience. However, recent research argues that psychological and interpersonal events throughout the life cycle explain sexual orientation. It is unlikely that a unique set of characteristics or a single pathway will explain all adult homosexuality. The argument that homosexuality is a stable phenomenon is based on the consistency of same-sex attractions, the failure of attempts to change and the lack of success with treatments to alter orientation. There is a growing realisation that homosexuality is not a single phenomenon and that there may be multiple phenomena within the construct of homosexuality.

Anti-homosexual attitudes, once considered the norm, have changed over time in many social and institutional settings in the west. However, heterosexism, which idealises heterosexuality, considers it the norm, denigrates and stigmatises all non-heterosexual forms of behavior, identity, relationships and communities, is also common. In addition to the challenges of living in a predominantly heterosexual world, the diversity within people with homosexual orientation results in many different kinds of issues. Sex, gender, age, ethnicity and religion add to the complexity of issues faced. The stages of the life cycle (childhood, adolescence, middle and old age), family and relationships present diverse concerns. In most circumstances, the psychiatric issues facing gay, lesbian and bisexual people are similar to those of the general population. However, the complexities in these identities require tolerance, respect and a nuanced understanding of sexual matters. Clinical assessments should be detailed and go beyond routine labelling and assess different issues related to lifestyle choices, identity, relationships and social supports. Helping people understand their sexuality and providing support for living in a predominantly heterosexual world is mandatory. People with homosexual orientation face many hurdles including the conflicts in acknowledging their homosexual feelings, the meaning of disclosure and the problems faced in coming out.

Gay-affirmative psychotherapies have been developed, which help people cope with the awareness of being same-sex oriented and with social stigmatization. There is no evidence for the effectiveness of sexual conversion therapies. Such treatments also raise ethical questions. In fact, there is evidence that such attempts may cause more harm than good, including inducing depression and sexual dysfunction. However, faith-based groups and counsellors pursue such attempts at conversion using yardsticks, which do not meet scientific standards. Clinicians should keep the dictum "first do no harm" in mind. Physicians should provide medical service with compassion and respect for human dignity for all people irrespective of their sexual orientation.

The landmark judgement of the Delhi High Court, [2009] which declared that Section 377 of the Indian Penal Code violates fundamental rights guaranteed by the constitution, was in keeping with international, human rights and secular and legal trends. However, the anti-homosexual attitudes of many religious and community leaders reflect the existence of widespread prejudice in India. Prejudice against different lifestyles is part of many cultures, incorporated into most religions, and is a source of conflict in Indian society.

There are few small case series in psychiatric literature detailing homosexuality in males and its treatment with aversion therapy. Heterosexim and anti-homosexual attitudes among psychiatrists and mental health professionals have been documented. The international classification of diseases-10 category (F66) employed to code ego dystonic sexuality seems to be only employed in clinical practice only for homosexuality, suggesting continued pathologization. It places the responsibility on the individual without critically examining the social context, which is stigmatising and repressing. The medicalization of sexuality and the political impact of labelling and its role in social control are often discounted. The ubiquitous use of disease models for mental disorders is rarely questioned.

There is a dearth of Indian psychiatric literature that has systematically investigated issues related to homosexuality. Data on prevalence, emotional problems faced and support groups and clinical services available are sparse. Research into these issues is crucial for increasing our understanding of the local and regional context related to sexual behavior, orientation and identity in India. Despite medicine and psychiatry arguing that homosexual orientation is a normal variant of human sexuality, mental health fraternity and the government in India are yet to take a clear stand on the issues to change widely prevalent prejudice in society. The fraternity needs to acknowledge the need for research into the context-specific issues facing LGBT people in India. The teaching of sexuality to medical and mental health professionals need to be perceptive to the issues faced by people with different sexual orientations and identities. Clinical services for people with such issues and concerns needs to be sensitive to providing holistic care. A positive and a non-judgemental attitude will go a long way in relieving distress. Professional societies need to increase awareness of these issues, transfer knowledge and skill and provide opportunities to increase the confidence and competence of mental health workers in helping people with different sexual orientations and identity. Psychiatrists and mental health professionals need to be educated about the human rights issues and possible abuses. The emphasis should not just be on education but also on a change of attitude. The development and dissemination of clinical practice guidelines is also essential. Human sexuality is complex and diverse. As with all complex behaviors and personality characteristics, biological and environmental influences combine to produce particular sexual orientation and identity. We need to focus on people's humanity rather than on their sexual orientation.

[This is taken from the Editorial, Indian Journal of Psychiatry: 54 [1]: Jan-March 2012]

References

Sadock VA. Normal Human Sexuality and Sexual Dysfunctions. Kaplan and Sadock's Comprehensive Textbook of Psychiatry 9th ed. (In: Sadock BJ, Sadock VA, Ruiz P, Editors) Philadelphia: Lippincott Williams & Wilkins; 2009. p. 2027-59.

Drescher J, Byne WM. Homosexuality, Gay and Lesbian Identities and Homosexual Behaviour. Kaplan and Sadock's Comprehensive Textbook of Psychiatry 9th ed. (In: Sadock BJ, Sadock VA, Ruiz P, Editors) Philadelphia: Lippincott Williams & Wilkins; 2009. p. 2060-89.

Forstein M. The pseudoscience of sexual orientation change therapy. BMJ 2004;328:E287-8.

Kumar N. Delhi High Court strikes down Section 377 of IPC.

Available form: *http://www.hindu.com/2009/07/03/stories/2009070358010 100.htm* [Last Accessed on 2011 Sep 13].

Kalra G, Gupta S, Bhugra D. Sexual variation in India: A view from the west. Indian J Psychiatry 2010;52:264-8.

Narrain A, Chandran V. Medicalisation of sexual orientation and gender identity: A human rights resource book, New Delhi: Yoda Press; 2012.

Sakthivel LM, Rangaswami K, Jayaraman TN. Treatment of homosexuality by anticipatory avoidance conditioning technique. Indian J Psychiatry 1979;21:146-8.

Pradhan PV, Ayyar KS, Bagadia VN. Homosexuality: Treatment by behaviour modification. Indian J Psychiatry 1982;24:80-3.

Pradhan PV, Ayyar KS, Bagadia VN. Male homosexuality: A psychiatric study of thirteen cases. Indian J Psychiatry 1982;24:182-6.

Mehta, M, Nimgaonkar S. Homosexuality-A study of treatment and outcome. Indian J Psychiatry 1983;25:235-8.

The reversal on Gay Rights in India

T.S. Sathyanarayana Rao and K.S. Jacob

India's Supreme Court recently issued a ruling against human rights by reinstating a law that bans gay sex. The Court restored Section 377 of the Indian Penal Code, a 19th century law, barring "carnal intercourse against the order of nature". The judgment has caused great dismay among liberal and progressive people and amongst activists and advocacy groups, which use judicial intervention to redress grievances against minorities of all shades in India. It has also been criticized from legal and human rights perspectives.

The police use the law in question to threaten and blackmail gays, lesbians and transgender people. Violation of the law is punishable by a fine and imprisonment. Following the recent ruling, India's crimes bureau has stated that it will compile crime statistics under Section 377.

The British colonial Government enacted Section 377 of the *Indian Penal Code, based on Victorian* morality, to criminalize non-procreative sex. The Naz Foundation, a non-Governmental Organization working in the field of human immunodeficiency virus/acquired immunodeficiency syndrome (HIV/AIDS) and sexual health, challenged the constitutional validity of Section 377 because it violated the rights to privacy, to dignity and health, to equality and non-discrimination and to freedom of expression. It also argued that the law prevented public health efforts at reducing the risk of transmission of HIV/AIDS as the fear of prosecution prevented people from discussing their sexuality and life style. The Delhi High Court on 2nd July 2009, in a landmark judgment, held Section 377 to be violative of Articles 21, 14 and 15 of the Constitution, as it criminalized consensual sexual acts of adults in private.

Individuals and faith-based groups appealed the High Court verdict. The Supreme Court of India, on 11th December 2013, upheld Section 377 and overturned the judgment of the Delhi High Court that had decriminalized adult consensual same-sex conduct. National and International Human rights groups condemned the Supreme Court decision.

The Naz Foundation and the Government of India have since filed a petition seeking review of the judgment. They argue that there are a number of grave errors of law that need to be corrected.

The judgment goes against the grain of the Supreme Court's own jurisprudence on advancement of fundamental rights and freedoms of all people, especially those who face marginalization in society. The Court's reliance on the principle of judicial restraint and Parliament's prerogative to change laws is misplaced, particularly when the law has been challenged for violation of fundamental rights of citizens. The judgment raises significant constitutional issues with far reaching public importance. There is a need to seek an interim stay on the operation of the judgment, as the judgment has caused immense prejudice to all adult persons who engage in consensual sex. This is particularly true for those from the Lesbian, Gay, Bisexual and Transgender (LGBT) community who had become open about their sexual identity since the High Court judgment and are now at risk of prosecution under criminal law. Historical records document the presence of homosexuality from time immemorial, even in our culture. The universality of same-sex expression coexists with variations in its meaning and practice across culture. Medicine and psychiatry, since the 1970's, abandoned pathologizing same-sex orientation, behavior and LGBT life-style choices. The new understanding was based on studies that documented a high prevalence of same-sex feelings and behavior in men and women, its prevalence across cultures and among almost all non-human primate species. Investigations using psychological tests could not differentiate heterosexual from homosexual orientation. Research also demonstrated that people with homosexual orientation did not have any objective psychological dysfunction or impairments in judgment, stability and vocational capabilities. Psychiatric, psychoanalytic, medical and mental health professionals now consider homosexuality as a normal variation of human sexuality. It suggested that much of the distress faced by people with same-sex orientation is due to difficulties they face living in our predominantly heterosexual world.

Many countries have decriminalized same-sex orientation and behavior. Several liberal and progressive nations recognize LGBT rights to include human, civil and political rights. Many countries have also legally recognized same-sex civil partnerships, whereas some have even legalized same-sex marriages (e.g., Brazil, Canada, England, France, South Africa, Spain, Sweden and in some states in USA). LGBT rights laws include government recognition of same-sex relationships, civil unions and marriage, adoption and parenting. They also include anti-bullying legislation, anti-discrimination student, employment and housing laws, immigration equality, equal age of consent law and hate crime laws providing enhanced criminal penalties for prejudice-motivated violence against LGBT people. The United Nations Human Rights Council recognizes LGBT rights.

The Supreme Court judgment dismissed jurisprudence from around the globe related to LGBT rights, which have struck down such discriminatory laws on grounds of violation of privacy, dignity and autonomy of individuals. It also rejected international human rights law on sexual orientation and gender identity.

The distinction between justice and law is crucial, particularly when a 19th century law is interpreted in the 21st century context. The demand for justice brings a case before the law; this demand puts the law at issue. The law requires an extension or a reinterpretation when the demand for justice exceeds the law or brings new issues before it. Justice, then, renews the law - makes it new; extends its hold. The law can never escape from this demand for justice since it is a demand that can never be finally met. The law-justice couple gives us a sense of how the demands of a context, the call of justice, demands a creative citing of the law in relation to the questions that present before it. Judges may opt to close off the call of justice and renew the rule of the law in relation to the new question that is presented. Alternatively, they may take up the challenge and rethink/

remake/cite the law as best as they can in ways that measure up to the call of justice.

The Supreme Court judgment, which upheld Section 377, is value-laden and seemingly allowed personal ideological views to determine the interpretation of statutory law. The ruling has disregarded the constitutional vision of an equal and inclusive society and has violated the fundamental tenets of India's Constitution. The suggestion that that Parliament is "free to consider the desirability and propriety of deleting Section 377 I.P.C. from the statute book or amend the same" is disingenuous, given the fractious nature of India's current Parliament, the conservative views of many of its members and the political stakes in the run-up to 2014 general elections.

Humanity in general needs to become more tolerant of diversity. Majorities within democracies need to view minority groups and those who differ from them with respect. We need to focus on other people's humanity rather than on their sexuality. We should voice our concerns against the Supreme Court verdict. It is also time for social groups and professional associations to clearly state their positions and demand a review of the flawed verdict. The Indian government and its Parliament now have an opportunity to leave a lasting legacy of progress and should act immediately to seek a repeal of Section 377. The 19th century law has no place in a 21st century democracy.

[This is taken from the Editorial, Indian Journal of Psychiatry: 56 [1]: Jan-March 2014]

Bibliography

Koushal SK and another versus NAZ Foundation and others. Civil Appeal NO. 10972 of 2013. Available from: *http://www.judis.nic.in/supremecourt/imgs1.aspx?filename=41070*. [Last accessed on 2013 Dec 30].

Lawyers Collective. LGBT and Section 377. Lawyers Collective. 23.11.2010. Available from: *http://www.lawyerscollective.org/vulnerable-communities/lgbt/section-377.html*. [Last accessed on 2013 Dec 29].

Sengupta A. The wrongness of deference. The Hindu 16.12.2013. Available from: *http://www.thehindu.com/opinion/lead/the-wrongness-of-deference/article5463126.ece*. [Last accessed on 2013 Dec 29].

Amnesty International. India re-criminalizes homosexuality. Available from: *http://www.amnesty.org.au/news/comments/33598/*. [Last accessed on 2013 Dec 30].

Naz Foundation versus Government of NCT of Delhi and Others WP(C) No.7455/2001. Available from: *http://www.lobis.nic.in/dhc/APS/judgement/02-07-2009/APS02072009CW74552001.pdf*. [Last accessed on 2013 Dec 30].

Anon. Centre moves apex court for review of Section 377 ruling. The Hindu. 20.12.2013. Available from: *http://www.thehindu.com/news/national/centre-moves-apex-court-for-review-of-section-377-ruling/article5482511.ece*. [Last accessed on 2013 Dec 29].

Lawyers Collective. Naz Foundation files review petition against the Supreme Court judgment on Section 377. Lawyers Collective 24.12.2013. Available from: *http://www.lawyerscollective.org/updates/naz-foundation-...judgment-section-377.html*. [Last accessed on 2013 Dec 29].

Rao TS, Jacob KS. Homosexuality and India. Indian J Psychiatry 2012;54:1-3.

Drescher J, Byne WM. Homosexuality, gay and lesbian identities and homosexual behaviour. In: Sadock BJ, Sadock VA, Ruiz P, editors. Kaplan and Sadock2 s Comprehensive Textbook of Psychiatry. 9th ed. Philadelphia: Lippincott Williams & Wilkins; 2009. p. 2060-89.

United Nations Human Rights Office of the High Commissioner. Born Free and Equal: Sexual Orientation and Gender identity in International Human Rights Law. New York and Geneva: Office of the High Commissioner United Nations Human Rights; 2012. Available from: *http://www.ohchr.org/Documents/.....EqualLowRes.pdf*. [Last accessed on 2013 Dec 31].

Jacob KS. Reclaiming Primary Care: Managing depression and anxiety in a different framework. In: Zachariah A, Srivats R. Tharu S, editors. Towards a Critical Medical Practice: Reflections on the Dilemmas of Medical Culture Today. New Delhi: Orient Blackswan; 2010. p. 311-9

Legal: International

United Nations Fact Sheet: Combating discrimination based on sexual orientation and gender identity UN Free and Equal Campaign: Human Rights of LGBT persons

Frequently Asked Questions

What kind of human rights violations are LGBT people exposed to?

LGBT people of all ages and in all regions of the world suffer from violations of their human rights. They are physically attacked, kidnapped, raped and murdered. In more than a third of the world's countries, people may be arrested and jailed (and in at least five countries executed) for engaging in private, consensual, same-sex relationships. States often fail to adequately protect LGBT people from discriminatory treatment in the private sphere, including in the workplace, housing and healthcare. LGBT children and adolescents face bullying in school and may be thrown out of their homes by their parents, forced into psychiatric institutions or forced to marry. Transgender people are often denied identity papers that reflect their preferred gender, without which they cannot work, travel, open a bank account or access services. Intersex children may be subjected to surgical and other interventions without their or often their parents' informed consent, and as adults are also vulnerable to violence and discrimination.

Is there any reason to criminalize homosexuality?

No. Criminalizing private sexual relationships between consenting adults, whether the relationships are same sex or different-sex, is a violation of the right to privacy. Laws criminalizing consensual same-sex relationships are also discriminatory, and where enforced, violate rights to freedom from arbitrary arrest and detention. At least 76 countries have laws in effect that criminalize private, consensual same-sex relationships, and in at least five countries conviction may carry the death penalty. In addition to violating basic rights, this criminalization serves to legitimize hostile attitudes towards LGBT people, feeding violence and discrimination. It also hampers efforts to halt the spread of HIV by deterring LGBT people from coming forward for testing and treatment for fear of revealing criminal activity.

Are there LGBT people only in Western countries?

No. LGBT people exist everywhere, in all countries, among all ethnic groups, at all socio-economic levels and in all communities. Claims that same-sex attraction is a western practice are false. However, many of the criminal laws used today to punish LGBT people are western in origin. In most cases, they were imposed on the countries concerned in the 19th century by the colonial powers of the day.

Have LGBT people always existed?

Yes. LGBT people have always been a part of our communities. There are examples from every locality and time-period, from prehistoric rock paintings in South Africa and Egypt to ancient Indian medical texts and early Ottoman literature. Many societies have traditionally been open towards LGBT people, including several Asian societies that have traditionally recognized a third gender.

Is it possible to change a person's sexual orientation and gender identity?

No. A person's sexual orientation and/or gender identity cannot be changed. What must change are the negative social attitudes that stigmatize LGBT people and contribute to violence and discrimination against them. Attempts to change someone's sexual orientation often involve human rights violations and can cause severe trauma. Examples include forced psychiatric therapies intended to "cure" (sic) individuals of their same-sex attraction, as well as the so-called "corrective" rape of lesbians perpetrated with the declared aim of "turning them straight."

Does being around LGBT people or having access to information on homosexuality endanger the wellbeing of children?

No. Learning about or spending time with people who are LGBT does not influence the sexual orientation or gender identity of minors nor can it harm their well-being. Rather, it is vital that all youth have access to age-appropriate sexuality education to ensure that they have healthy, respectful physical relationships and can protect themselves from sexually transmitted infections. Denial of this kind of information contributes to stigma and can cause young LGBT people to feel isolated, depressed, forcing some to drop out of school and contributing to higher rates of suicide.

Are gay, lesbian, bisexual or transgender people dangerous to children?

No. There is no link between homosexuality and child abuse of any kind. LGBT people all over the world can be good parents, teachers and role models for young people. Portraying LGBT people as "paedophiles" or dangerous to children is wholly inaccurate, offensive and a distraction from the need for serious and appropriate measures to protect all children, including those coming to terms with their sexual orientation and gender identity.

Does international human rights law apply to LGBT people?

Yes, it applies to every person. International human rights law establishes legal obligations on States to make sure that everyone, without distinction, can enjoy their human rights. A person's sexual orientation and gender identity is a status, like race, sex, colour or religion. United Nations human rights experts have confirmed that international law prohibits discrimination based on sexual orientation or gender identity.

Can depriving LGBT people of their human rights be justified on grounds of religion, culture or tradition?

No. Human rights are universal: every human being is entitled to the same rights, no matter who they are or where they live. While history, culture and religion are contextually important, all States, regardless of their political, economic and cultural systems, have a legal duty to promote and protect the human rights of all.

[*http://www.ohchr.org/Documents/Issues/Discrimination/LGBT/FactSheets/unfe-28-UN_Fact_Sheets_English.pdf*]

United Nations:
Five core legal obligations of States with respect to protecting the human rights of *LGBT* persons – Summary of Recommendations

1. Protect people from homophobic and transphobic violence. Include sexual orientation and gender identity as protected characteristics in hate-crime laws. Establish effective systems to record and report hate-motivated acts of violence. Ensure effective investigation and prosecution of perpetrators and redress for victims of such violence. Asylum laws and policies should recognize that persecution on account of one's sexual orientation or gender identity may be a valid basis for an asylum claim.

2. Prevent the torture and cruel, inhuman and degrading treatment of LGBT persons in detention by prohibiting and punishing such acts and ensuring that victims are provided with redress. Investigate all acts of mis-treatment by State agents and bring those responsible to justice. Provide appropriate training to law enforcement officers and ensure effective monitoring of places of detention.

3. Repeal laws criminalizing homosexuality, including all laws that prohibit private sexual conduct between consenting adults of the same sex. Ensure that individuals are not arrested or detained on the basis of their sexual orientation or gender identity, and are not subjected to baseless and degrading physical examinations intended to determine their sexual orientation.

4. Prohibit discrimination on the basis of sexual orientation and gender
    identity. Enact comprehensive laws that include sexual orientation and
    gender identity as prohibited grounds of discrimination. In particular,
    ensure non-discriminatory access to basic services, including in the
    context of employment and health care. Provide education and training
    to prevent discrimination and stigmatization of LGBT and intersex
    people.

5. Safeguard freedom of expression, association and peaceful assembly for
    LGBT and intersex people. Any limitations on these rights must be
    compatible with international law and must not be discriminatory.
    Protect individuals who exercise their rights to freedom of expression,
    association and freedom of assembly from acts of violence and
    intimidation by private parties.

[From 'BORN FREE AND EQUAL': Booklet produced by UN: © 2012
United Nations]

Legal: Indian

Indian Law and People with Different Sexual Orientations and Gender Identities

Sanchit Saluja

The Indian Penal Code, which was introduced in India in 1861, during the regime of Queen Victoria, lays down some acts that are punishable as crimes. Section 377 of the Code reads, 'Whoever voluntarily has carnal intercourse against the order of nature with any man, woman or animal, shall be punished with imprisonment for life, or with imprisonment of either description for a term which may extend to 10 years, and shall also be liable to fine'.[1] The law is commonly understood to criminalize homosexuality. Section 377 is seen to apply exclusively to sexual minorities in light of their image as 'sexual deviants' who would perform intercourse 'against the order of nature'. Further, it is interesting to note that under the section, there is no difference between forced and consensual sex, hence, even if two men are having any kind of sex with each other's consent, it will still be considered a crime under this law. In practice, even though the law targets *only* sexual intercourse, it has been used as a tool by State authorities to harass and persecute homosexual persons (as well as others who identify as LGBT).[2]

In 2009, the High Court at Delhi decided that §377 was against the very basic rights of homosexual persons to their dignity, their privacy and equality,[3] which are very basic guarantees under our Constitution. Therefore, the High Court held that §377 no longer criminalized consensual sexual intercourse between any two persons.[4] However, on appeal, the Supreme Court of India overturned the decision and held that any change whatsoever to the law must be made by the legislature (India's law making body).[5] Such a decision led to an increase in blackmailing, intimidation and harassment of LGBT individuals, both by the police as well as organised gangs.[6] Currently, a petition is pending before the Supreme Court to reassess its decision.

Unfortunately, whatever little attention has been given by India's legislature to the issue of sexual orientation has not been positive. Member of Parliament Shashi Tharoor sought to introduce two private member bills in the Lok Sabha to repeal §377, only to have both his motions defeated.[7] In law, homosexual relationships do not get any recognition in the context of defining 'family' for the purpose of insurance claims, claims for compensation,[8] gratuity benefits etc.[9] Same-sex marriage is also not officially recognized in India. Various legal provisions, such as the offence of 'obscenity' as well as the concept of 'moral turpitude' as a ground for dismissal from service may be used to target homosexual individuals as well.[10] Further, the Surrogacy (Regulation) Bill, 2016, which has been introduced in the Lok Sabha on November 21, 2016, denies homosexuals the right to have children through surrogacy.[11] Hence, as is evident, the reality today is that LGBT identity faces immense stigma on account of multiple factors influenced by the law as it stands.

Law and Gender Identity

Historically, transgender persons have faced intense suspicion and surveillance under the eyes of the law, for being suspected of kidnapping or castrating children, or committing unnatural offences under §377.[12] Even today, there are laws that exist, which criminalize transgender persons. For instance, the Karnataka Police Act allows the Commissioner of Police to regulate *eunuchs* by maintaining a register recording their names and places of residence and to pass orders prohibiting such registered eunuchs from doing any such activity as they may specify.[13] Further, other laws such as §377 of the Indian Penal Code as well as the Immoral Traffic Prevention Act, 1956 are used by the State authorities to persecute and intimidate transgender persons, who are often especially vulnerable because of their generally distinct and visible gender identity.[14] Transgender persons, who generally have to resort to begging or sex work to make ends meet, face immense violence and abuse because of these draconian laws, which stigmatize them further in the eyes of society, hence preventing much change in the way they are perceived in society.

NALSA Judgment

On April 15th, 2014, the Supreme Court of India delivered a landmark judgment (*National Legal Services Authority v. Union of India*),[15] where it provided legal recognition to transgender persons as the 'third gender' and held that they were entitled to legal protection in all spheres including employment, healthcare, education as well as civil and citizenship rights, which are enjoyed by other citizens in the country.[16] In granting this recognition, the Supreme Court held that 'transgender' was an umbrella term, which includes individuals who have undergone surgery to change their gender identity, who intend to do so and who may not have any such intention, but still identify so. Hence, the focus is on how the individuals identify themselves, and not on whether they have or intend to utilize medical procedures on their body.[17] Further, the right to speech and expression, which is available to all citizens in India, includes the right of a transgender person to express themselves through words, dress, action or behavior.[18]

The Supreme Court lay down certain directives for the State, whereby it was bound to take affirmative action for advancement of the transgender community which would include the formation of various welfare schemes as well as steps to ensure their civil, political, social and economic rights.[19]

The Transgender Persons (Protection of Rights) Bill, 2016

For a Bill to be recognized as Law, it must be passed by both Houses of Parliament, namely the Lok Sabha and the Rajya Sabha. On April 24th, 2015, The Rights of Transgender Persons Bill, 2014 was passed by the Rajya Sabha and is currently pending before the Lok Sabha. Meanwhile, the Government has introduced a competing bill, namely The Transgender Persons (Protection of Rights) Bill, 2016 before the Lok Sabha. The bills seek to adopt the ethos of the Supreme Court *NALSA* judgment as discussed above.[20] It seeks to embody equality, dignity, reasonable accommodation, freedom of expression as well as protection from violence, harassment, abuse and violence for transgender persons. It also mandates that the Government provide social security measures to aid transgender persons, including socio-economic rights, unemployment allowance, food, shelter vocational training and counseling centres. Further, it seeks to introduce a 2% reservation for transgender students in all primary, secondary and higher educational institutions belonging to the Government or receiving aid from the Government, and to ensure that transgender students receive an inclusive education and they are accommodated in such institutions.[21]

Various states, (without waiting for a central law to be passed on the issue) to initiate reform based on the guidelines laid down in the Supreme Court judgment, have adopted policies concerning transgender persons. As an illustration, the State Policy for Transgenders in Kerala, 2015 seeks to provide free legal aid, self-employment grants to transgender persons as well as to mandate sensitization and anti-discrimination policies at workplaces, and schemes for healthcare and education.[22] Further, in pursuance of this positive outlook, the Kochi Metro in Kerala (which is a Government owned company) has employed 23 transgender persons to push for their welfare in the State.[23] Other States have also come out with policies for transgender persons, or are in the process of initiating reforms.

Reforms in Education

The University Grants Commission has issued various notifications to Universities concerning transgender students, the failure to comply with which may result in a withdrawal of funding from the UGC. In a notification dated October 28th, 2016, the UGC directed Universities to take various steps to reasonably accommodate transgender students, by including columns for transgender students under the gender category in various forms, and to work towards creating infrastructure such as washrooms and restrooms in the campuses.[24] This is a positive move which will make education in general including the institutions and the admission process much more accessible to transgender students. The UGC has also held that any bullying based on the gender identity of the student (including transgender identity) would be considered as 'Ragging' and punishable as the same.[25] This will further protect transgender students from unwarranted harassment, teasing and intimidation in educational institutions. Further, the UGC, in a notification dated May 2nd, 2016 also introduced guidelines governing sexual harassment whereby they allowed not just women but also men and transgender students to complain against sexual harassment. The UGC mandated that the Higher Institutions act against such violence, which though primarily may target women, but also affected some men and transgender students.[26] Unfortunately, the current law governing sexual harassment at the workplace only allows women to complain against sexual harassment and thereby leaves men and transgender persons unprotected.[27]

Conclusion

Hence, the legal landscape in India leaves LGBT persons in India vulnerable and marginalised, and there is much to be done to help ensure them an existence which is dignified and free from stigma and violence, as is the right of every Indian citizen.

End Notes

[1] §377, Indian Penal Code, 1861.

[2] 'Rights for All: Ending Discrimination against Queer Desire under Section 377', Report compiled by 'Voices Against 377' (2004) available online @ *http://www.voicesagainst377.org/reports/*

[3] *Naz Foundation v. Government of NCT*160 Delhi Law Times 277.

[4] *Ibid.*

[5] *Suresh Kumar Koushal & Ors. v. Naz Foundation* Civil Appeal No. 10972 of 2013.

[6] Hairish V Nair, *'The last rainbow of hope: Supreme Court will hear a curative petition against ban on homosexual acts, as gay community suffers rise in rape and harassment'*, THE DAILY MAIL, 28 January 2016 available online @ *http://www.dailymail.co.uk/indiahome/indianews/article-3421574/The-rainbow-hope-Supreme-Court-hear-curative-petition-against-ban-homosexual-acts-gay-community-suffers-rise-rape-harassment.html.*

[7] *'Lok Sabha votes against Shashi Tharoor's bill to decriminalise homosexuality. Again.'*, THE INDIAN EXPRESS, 12 March 2016 available online @ *http://indianexpress.com/article/india/india-news-india/decriminalising-homosexuality-lok-sabha-votes-against-shashi-tharoors-bill-again/.*

[8] People's Union for Civil Liberties-Karnataka, *Human rights violations against sexual minorities in India* (February 2001) p. 12 available online @ *http://www.pucl.org/Topics/Gender/2003/sexual-minorities.pdf.*

[9] *Ibid.*

[10] *Ibid.*

[11] The Surrogacy (Regulation) Bill, 2016; *See also,* Hansa Malhotra, *'Surrogacy for Gay Couples is Against our Ethos: Sushma Swaraj'*, The Quint, 25 August 2016 available online @ *https://www.thequint.com/india/2016/08/24/union-cabinet-surrogacy-regulation-bill-2016-sushma-swaraj-against-our-ethos-commercial-surrogacy.*

[12] Criminal Tribes Act, 1871 [The Act was repealed in 1949].

[13] §36A, The Karnataka Police Act, 1963.

[14] People's Union for Civil Liberties, *Human Rights Violations against the Transgender Community: A PUCL Report* (September 2003) available online @ *http://www.pucl.org/Topics/Gender/2004/transgender.htm; NALSA v. UOI* WP (Civil) No. 604 of 2013¶18.

[15] WP (Civil) No. 604 of 2013.

[16] *NALSA* at ¶128.

[17] *NALSA* at ¶11.

[18] *NALSA* at ¶62.

[19] *NALSA* at ¶129 [These were directions to the appropriate Governments].

[20] As of today, the bills have not been passed by the Lok Sabha.

[21] Transgender Persons (Protection of Rights) Bill, 2016.

[22] State Policy for Transgenders in Kerala (2015) available online @ *https://kerala.gov.in/documents/10180/46696/State%20Policy%20for%20Transgenders%20in%20Kerala%202015.*

[23] *'Kerala: In a first, Kochi Metro to employ 23 transgenders'*, HINDUSTAN TIMES, 15 May 2017 available online @ *http://www.hindustantimes.com/india-news/kerala-in-a-first-kochi-metro-to-employ-23-transgenders/story-52WRY2ees5fo6hEnk VsukI.html.*

[24] UGC Notification dated 28th October 2014 [D.O. 14-8/2014 (CPP[II)]

[25] Notification dated 29th June 2016 Amended the University Grants Commission Regulations on Curbing the menace of Ragging in Higher Educational Institutions, 2009 available online @ *http://www.ugc.ac.in/pdfnews/ 7823260_Anti-Ragging-3rd-Amendment.pdf.*

[26] University Grants Commission (Prevention, prohibition and redressal of sexual harassment of women employees and students in higher educational institutions) Regulations, 2015 [Notified on 2nd May 2016]

[27] The Sexual Harassment of Women at Workplace (Prevention, Prohibition and Redressal) Act, 2013.

A summary of the Supreme Court verdict on Section 377

Anjali Gopalan

Brief Background

Section 377 of the Indian Penal Code, 1860, makes certain acts illegal. It is an archaic colonial law that was brought in by the British. The section seems neutral in that it criminalizes certain sexual acts and not people and their identities. However, it has never been used against consenting heterosexual persons and has been misused against homosexual persons. The primary problem with the provision of law is that it does not take into consideration age or consent. Therefore, it criminalizes adult consensual same sex acts.

The fight against section 377 has been going on since 2001 before the courts. It started with the petition by Naz Foundation before the High Court of Delhi. Subsequently Naz Foundation was joined by other petitioners (Details of the parties and proceedings before the courts are available at *www.377.orinam.net*). The Delhi High court gave its judgment in *Naz Foundation* v *NCT of Delhi* wherein section 377 of the IPC was read down to not apply to consenting adult consensual acts in private. The Delhi High Court held that section 377 is against constitutional values embedded in Article 14 (Right to Equality), Article 15 (Non Discrimination) and Article 21 (Right to Life).

However, immediately after the verdict of the High Court, Suresh Kumar Koushal appealed before the Supreme Court against the Naz decision. He was followed by 13 other Appellants in the appeal. It is pertinent to note that the Government of India agreed with the decision of the high Court and did not appeal. Naz Foundation, Voices Against 377, Parents of LGBT persons, Teachers, Law Academics and Shyam Benegal opposed the appeal to the Supreme Court and supported the High Court decision. The Apex court gave its verdict on 11th December, 2013 and reversed the judgment of the Delhi High Court and upheld the constitutional validity of section 377. This means that section 377 IPC is valid law and the Delhi High court decision is no longer applicable.

Delhi High Court

The High Court of Delhi declared that "section 377 IPC, insofar as it criminalises consensual sexual acts of adults in private, is violative of Article 21, 14 and 15 of the Constitution". The High Court relied on affdavits, FIRs, Judgments and Orders to illustrate misuse of S.377; they also place reliance on academic literature, scientifc and medical literature, international law, constituent assembly debates, comparative jurisdictions and judgments of superior courts in India.

The High Court held that the right to life cannot be restricted by what the majority thinks and that section 377 violates the right to dignity and privacy guaranteed under Article 21. The court further held that no one can be discriminated on the basis of their sexual orientation and that the provision is in violation of right to equality.

The High Court decision was legally sound and was humane in its approach.

Supreme Court

The Supreme Court reversed the judgment of the Delhi High Court and held that section 377 does not violate the constitution and is therefore valid.

The Supreme Court reasoned its judgment on several grounds. First, it held that all laws enacted by Parliament are presumed to be valid under the Constitution. This means that in order to hold a law to be invalid, it must be shown, through evidence, that the law is violating the Constitution.

The Supreme Court held that there is not enough evidence to show that S.377 IPC is invalid under the Constitution. The Court held that there is very little evidence to show that the provision is being misused by the police. Also, just because the police may be misusing a law, does not automatically mean that the law is invalid. There must be something in the nature of the law itself that is unconstitutional. According to the Supreme Court, the law can be implemented without misuse.

It was also argued before the Supreme Court that because S.377 applies to certain sexual conduct, it essentially means that all forms of sexual expression by LGBT people would be unnatural. This would mean that any sexual conduct by such people would be illegal. Therefore, S.377 prohibits all sexual expression of LGBT persons. The Supreme Court disagreed with this argument and held that S.377 speaks only of sexual acts and does not speak about sexual orientation or gender identity. This would mean that even heterosexuals indulging in acts covered under S.377 would be punished. Therefore, the section does not target LGBT persons as a class.

Further, the Supreme Court held that the Delhi High Court in its anxiety to uphold the so called rights of LGBT persons had relied on cases from other countries. They are of the opinion that cases from other countries cannot be directly used in the context of India. Therefore, important cases from South Africa, Fiji, Nepal, USA etc., where homosexuality was decriminalized was not taken into account by the Supreme Court.

Laws are presumed to be valid therefore the responsibility of changing laws is with the parliament. In this case also parliament is free to consider deleting or changing S.377. The Supreme Court also said that despite so many years the Parliament has not changed the law in spite of having ample opportunities to do so.

In light of the above factors considered, the Supreme Court reversed the decision of the Delhi High Court and upheld section 377.

Reaction

The decision of the Supreme Court was received by a wave of protests spanning across the country. People across a spectrum of sexuality and gender identity were shocked and felt betrayed by the guardian of fundamental rights. The decision of the Supreme Court is wrong because of several reasons. These are summarized as follows:

The Supreme Court held that the LGBT community is an extremely tiny and insignifcant minority. This is wrong on the basis of data as well. However, even if the population of LGBT people is in fact tiny, it does not affect the question of harassment or constitutional rights. The violation of the right of one person is as serious as that of millions of people.

The Supreme Court has failed in its decision to understand the scale of misuse of S.377 by the police against people of the LGBT persons. The Supreme Court held that there have been less than 200 cases of prosecution under the Section since 1860. However, this is wrong because it does not include the number of police complaints, arrests or harassment on the basis of this Section. There are several well-known instances of abuse and harassment by the police which the Supreme Court fails to consider.

The Supreme Court has held that the law applies to heterosexuals as well as homosexuals and therefore, there is no discrimination against members of the LGBT community. However, the truth remains that the law is used against the LGBT people and not against heterosexual couples.

The Supreme Court is wrong in its application of laws from other countries. It does not consider the fact that same-sex acts have been decriminalized in a lot of countries, including the UK and the USA. The Supreme Court should have considered the decisions from other countries as it always has been doing. In this case, the Supreme Court ignored foreign decisions.

The Supreme Court held that the law applies only to certain acts and not to the identities of people. However, this is wrong because it means that for members of the LGBT community, any way in which they could express themselves sexually becomes a criminal act. This is not so for heterosexual people who can have sexual intercourse without violating the law.

The Supreme Court held that the law should be changed by Parliament and not the Court. However, the Supreme Court was never asked to change the law! It is the duty of the Court to restrict or strike down a law which is against the Constitution. The Supreme Court had to do that in this case, which it failed to do.

Way Forward

Though the decision of the Supreme Court is extremely unfortunate and goes against the basic rights of the LGBT community, the struggle for equal rights and dignity does not end here. There are several ways forward for the community against the decision of the Supreme Court. These are outlined as follows:

Review Petition

A review petition is filed before the same judges who have decided the case. A review petition asks the judges to have a re-look at the case because they may have made an error in the decision. This has to be done within 30 days of the decision. In the present case, a review petition will be filed. Since Justice Singhvi has retired, the review petition may be heard by another judge along with Justice Mukhopadhyay (who decided the original case with Justice Singhvi).

Curative Petition

A curative petition may be filed if the review petition does not succeed. This will be filed before the Chief Justice of India and decided by a five judge bench of the Court.

Legislative Amendment

The decision of the Supreme Court has been criticized by every part of civil society. Political parties, journalists, academics, activists, lawyers and citizens have criticized the decision. Ministers in the government, including Kapil Sibal, P. Chidambaram and others have stated that they would bring an amendment and consider all options to ensure that the High Court verdict is restored and the Supreme Court decision is set aside. The Supreme Court has itself stated that Parliament might consider amending S.377. Parliament might amend S.377 to ensure that same-sex consensual conduct between adults in private is no longer a crime.

Ordinance

An ordinance is a temporary piece of law which can be enacted when Parliament is not in session to pass a law and because the law is urgently required, it can be done through an ordinance. In this case, the government can choose to bring an ordinance into effect which would restore the High court decision and reverse the Supreme Court. This will have to be finally converted into a regular law after Parliament comes into session.

Legal Issues of Sexual Minorities

Rebina Subba

Lesbian, gay, bisexual and transgender (LGBT) people in India face certain legal and social difficulties not experienced by non-LGBT persons. Sexual activity between people of the same gender is illegal, and same-sex couples cannot legally marry or obtain a civil partnership. India does, however, legally recognize Hijras as a gender separate from men or women.

Law regarding same-sex activity

Homosexual intercourse was made a criminal offense under *Section 377 of the Indian Penal Code*, 1860. This made it an offence for a person to voluntarily have "carnal intercourse against the order of nature." In 2009, the Delhi High Court decision in **Naz Foundation v. Govt. of NCT of Delhi** found Section 377 and other legal prohibitions against private, adult, consensual, and non-commercial same-sex conduct to be in direct violation of fundamental rights provided by the Indian Constitution. On 23 February 2012, the *Ministry of Home Affairs* expressed its opposition to the decriminalisation of homosexual activity, stating that in India, homosexuality is seen as being immoral. The Central Government reversed its stand on 28 February 2012, asserting that there was no legal error in decriminalising homosexual activity. This resulted in two judges of the Supreme Court reprimanding the central government for frequently changing its stand on the issue. "Don't make a mockery of the system and don't waste the court's time," an apex court judge told the government.

On 11 December 2013, the Supreme Court set aside the 2009 Delhi High Court order de-criminalising consensual homosexual activity within its jurisdiction. The bench of justices *G. S. Singhvi* and *S. J. Mukhopadh*aya however noted that Parliament should debate and decide on the matter. On January 28, 2014 *Supreme Court* dismissed the review Petition filed by Central Government, NGO *Naz Foundation* and several others, against its December 11 verdict on Section 377 of IPC. On December 18, 2015, *Shashi Tharoor*, a member of the *Indian National Congres*s party, introduced the bill for the decriminalisation of *Section 377*, but the bill was rejected by the house by a vote of 71-24. Human rights groups expressed worries that this would render homosexual couples vulnerable to police harassment, saying: "The Supreme Court's ruling is a disappointing setback to human dignity, and the basic rights to privacy and non-discrimination." The *Naz Foundation (India) Trust* stated that it would file a *petition for review* of the court's decision. On February 2, 2016, the Supreme Court decided to review criminalisation of homosexual activity. In 2016, Kerala mooted free sex-reassignment surgeries in Government hospitals after it introduced the first State government policy on transgender people.

LGBT Rights in India

Lesbian, gay, bisexual and transgender (LGBT) people in India face certain legal and social difficulties not experienced by non-LGBT persons. Sexual activity between people of the same gender is illegal, and same-sex couples cannot legally marry or obtain a civil partnership. India does, however, legally recognize Hijras as a gender separate from men or women, alongside neighboring Pakistan, to legally recognize a third gender.

Indian Penal Code On Homosexuality

Section 377, *Indian Penal Code*, 1860 (herein after 'IPC') was enacted by the British colonial regime to criminalize 'carnal intercourse against the order of nature'. It was rooted in the Judeo-Christian religious morality that abhorred non-procreative sex. Lacking precise definition, Section 377 became subject to varied judicial interpretation over the years. Initially covering only anal sex, it later included oral sex and still later, read to cover penile penetration of other artificial orifices like between the thighs or folded palms. The law made consent and age of the person irrelevant by imposing a blanket prohibition on all penile and non-vaginal sexual acts under the vague rubric of 'unnatural offences'. Section 377 was used as a tool by the police to harass, extort and blackmail homosexual men and prevented them from seeking legal protection from violence, for fear that they would themselves be penalized for sodomy. The stigma and prejudice created and perpetuated a culture of silence around homosexuality and resulted in denial and rejection at home along with discrimination in workplaces and public spaces. This led to depression and suicidal tendencies among the communities.

Law and Morality

Those against legalizing homosexuality argue that it is against the moral values of the society. What is forbidden in religion need not be prohibited in law. Morality cannot be a ground to restrict the fundamental rights of citizens. A legal wrong is necessarily a moral wrong but vice versa is not correct. A moral wrong becomes a legal wrong only when its consequences are for society and not just the person/s committing it.

Transgender

Globally most legal jurisdictions recognises the two traditional gender identities and social roles, man and woman, but tend to exclude any other gender identities, and expressions. However, there are some countries which recognize, by law, a third gender. There is now a greater understanding of the breadth of variation outside the typical categories of "man" and "woman", and many self-descriptions are now entering the literature.

This raises many legal issues and aspects of transgenderism. Most of these issues are generally considered a part of family law, especially the issues of marriage and the question of a transsexual person benefiting from a partner's insurance or social security.

The degree of legal recognition provided to transgenderism varies widely throughout the world. Many countries now legally recognize sex reassignments by permitting a change of legal gender on an individual's birth certificate.

Transgender in Indian Law and Society

The states Tamil Nadu and Kerala in India were the first states to introduce a transgender (hijra/ aravani) welfare policy. According to the transgender welfare policy transgender people can access free Sex Reassignment Surgery (SRS) in the Government Hospital (only for MTF); free housing program; various citizenship documents; admission in government colleges with full scholarship for higher studies; alternative sources of livelihood through formation of self-help groups (for savings) and initiating income-generation programmes (IGP). Tamil Nadu was also the first state to form a Transgender Welfare Board with representatives from the transgender community. In 2016, Kerala started implementing free SRS through government hospitals.

On 15 April 2014, with the NALSA Judgment, the Supreme Court of India declared transgender people as a socially and economically backward class entitled to reservations in Education and Jobs, and also directed the Union and State governments to frame welfare schemes for them. According to the court decision, state and federal governments will now allow transgender to identify themselves on official documents, such as birth certificates, passports and driving licenses, as a third gender along with males and females. Any person who has undergone surgery to change his or her sex will be recognized as belonging to the gender of their choice said the court, adding that transgender people would have the same right to adopt children as other Indians. Transgenders will also be included in welfare schemes offered to other minority groups, and the government will provide public sector jobs, places in schools and colleges and medical care.

Conclusion

We cannot predict how long it will take before the global mindset about homosexuality will change to have greater acceptance to them. However, in India, the TG community has gained some powerful supporters over the past few years, but there's much more to be done before they can truly feel equal to the heterosexual community.

Update
Non-implementation of the NALSA Judgment [2014] and the weak points in the Transgender Persons (Protection of Rights) Bill, 2016

Thomas Ninan

The Independent People's Tribunal [IPT] was constituted in 1993 as an alternative system of justice—a "people's court"—whose aim has been to provide an alternative redressal mechanism for people faced with human rights violations. The Tribunal, an unofficial body, is led by retired judges who form a panel that conducts public inquiries into human rights abuses on a specific issue. In doing so, it provides a platform for affected communities, grassroot organisations, networks and movements to voice their grievances and a mechanism for seeking redressal and policy change.

IPT's People's Inquiry into the Status of the Implementation of the NALSA Judgment and the National Consultation on Transgender Persons (Protection of Rights) Bill, 2016, and Allied Legislations was held from November 2-4, 2016, in New Delhi. This was supported by the Center for Social Discrimination & Exclusion, and Women's Studies Department, both from Jawaharlal Nehru University, other Partnering Organizations & Collectives, including Human Rights Law Network.

Background
On April 15 2014, the Supreme Court of India passed a landmark judgment in the case of *National Legal Services Authority vs. Union of India & Others* (hereafter referred to as NALSA) that not only laid down the principle of

a right to self-determination of gender and recognition thereof in the law, but also placed various obligations on the Central and State Government with the aim of creating a political and legal environment that would enable trans persons to reach their full potential. Two and a half years since the passage of the landmark judgment, very little has been done to uphold the spirit of NALSA on the part of the Central and State Governments. As a result, trans Persons continue to be denied the right of self determination, access to documentation, education, healthcare, housing, livelihood and in effect dignity. With the exception of a handful of pioneering steps by a few State Governments, the conduct of the Central Government actually demonstrates an indisputable resistance to effecting the mandates of the NALSA judgment. The Central Government first sought to modify and erode the enabling provisions of the NALSA judgment through an application for clarification/modification in the Supreme Court in July 2014,[which the Apex Court later decided in June 2016.]

Thereafter in December 2014 Tiruchi Siva introduced a Private Member's Bill whichsought to get the Governments to effect the directives of the NALSA Judgment. The Central Government, however, brought out its own version of what it proposed should be the law called the Transgender Person's Bill, 2015. Following recommendations on the proposed legislation from civil society actors and the community, what was later passed by the cabinet and introduced in the Lok Sabha on August 2nd, 2016—The Transgender Persons (Protection of Rights) Bill, 2016, IPT and allies feel is express resistance to the spirit of the NALSA judgment.

Earlier, members of 'Sangama' and 'Reach Law', two Bangalore-based minority rights group, had presented a chapter wise review of 'The Transgender Persons (Protection of Rights) Bill', 2016, introduced in Lok Sabha on August 2, to bring to notice the Bill's flaws and gaps with respect to transgenders' abuse, rehabilitation, education, and equal status in the society. Among its many shortcomings discussed, they strongly opposed the use of 'biological test' to pronounce a person as transgender as proposed in the draft bill and advocated for the use of 'psychological test' instead. They also recommended to the ministry to extend reservation in educational institutes and for public appointments to transgender persons. They also demanded removal of the derogatory words such as "chakka, ombotthu, gandu etc." and the removal of the term 'Third gender' to refer to transgenders as they were discriminatory.

The Independent People's Tribunal [IPT] feels the current bill is problematic on several fronts: Firstly, it eliminates the option of identifying as male or female, undermining the right to self-determination of gender. Secondly, it creates an onerous bureaucratic procedure for the recognition of transgender identities, which allows the Government to act as gatekeepers in deciding who can or cannot identify as transgender and strips agency from transgender persons of the same. Thirdly, the proposed legislation fails to provide a concrete definition of what constitutes discrimination, and lacks enforcement mechanisms for invoking criminal sanctions when discriminatory behavior occurs. Fourthly, it deprives transgender person's right of residence by failing to take cognizance of the fact that the home is often a site of violence for trans children. And fifthly, nowhere in the bill does it grapple with inheritance, property, adoption, or marriage rights, nor with reservations or anti-discrimination provisions, all critical components for enabling transgender persons to reach their fullest potential and live with dignity. This assessment is further strengthened by a reading of the Surrogacy (Regulation) Bill, 2016.

A Rights Bill Gone Wrong:
The Transgender Persons (Protection of Rights) Bill, 2016

Shruti Ambast and Namrata Mukherjee

A disturbing facet of lawmaking in India is that laws are often drafted without in-depth research, as a result of which they are misinformed and remain paper tigers. Another is that a culture of tokenism prevails regarding pressing social issues, seen most recently in **The Transgender Persons (Protection of Rights) Bill, 2016.**

In April 2014, the Supreme Court delivered the landmark judgment of NALSA v. Union of India, which affirmed the fundamental rights of transgender persons. The court gave a series of directives to the government to institute welfare measures for transgender persons, including affirmative action. It also directed that the Expert Committee Report prepared by the Ministry of Social Justice and Empowerment (MSJE) be implemented. In December 2014, Tiruchi Siva, a Dravida Munnetra Kazhagam Rajya Sabha MP, introduced the Rights of Transgender Persons Bill, 2014 as a Private Member's Bill. On April 24, 2015, in a rare instance, the Rajya Sabha unanimously passed the Bill. However, it never made it to the Lok Sabha. Instead, the government decided to get its own Bill- *The Rights of Transgender Persons Bill, 2015*- drafted, which was put up for public comments in December. The 2015 Bill was largely based on the 2014 Bill, but it did away with provisions on Transgender Rights Courts and the National and State Commissions. The Ministry also consulted civil society and activists.

In April 2016, the 2015 draft Bill was sent to the Law Ministry, in July the Cabinet approved it, and in August it was introduced in the Lok Sabha. It is unclear at which point the drafting changed, for the Bill introduced in the Lok Sabha was drastically different from the 2015. Not only was it shorn of many critical features of the previous two Bills, it also completely disregarded all existing discourse and resources — the NALSA judgment, the Expert Committee Report, and public comments. The 2016 Bill has now been referred to a Standing Committee.

Not a rights based approach

While the NALSA judgment is couched in rights language, locating the fundamental rights of transgender persons in the golden trinity of Articles 14, 19 and 21 of the Constitution, the 2016 Bill, though it uses the word "rights" in its title, deviates from a rights-based approach and leaves transgender persons at the mercy of the "benevolent" state. This is puzzling considering that the 2014 and 2015 Bills, and even other recent laws like the Rights of Persons with Disabilities Act, 2016, and the Mental Healthcare Bill, 2016, are framed in 'rights' language. Further, the Bill is completely silent on how its content will impact the operation of existing laws. Most laws, including of marriage, adoption and succession, continue to be based on the binary of male and female. Criminal laws, especially those dealing with sexual offences, also continue to be gendered. The cisnormative (the assumption that everyone has a gender identity that matches the sex the person was assigned at birth) foundation of the law remains a significant barrier to access to legal justice for transgender persons. Jurisdictions like the U.K., Ireland, Argentina and Malta, which have legislated on transgender rights, clarify in their laws the impact gender change will have on existing legal institutions that are inaccessible to persons with non-conforming genders.

The NALSA judgment too recognises the need for making civil rights accessible to transgender persons. However, the Bill fails to take this into account. Finally, none of the Bills have addressed the issue of Section 377, which is frequently used to harass transgender persons, specifically transgender women. The conventional understanding of Section 377 is that it criminalises all sex that is not between people of opposite genders. But recognising trans-rights means recognising that there are more than the "opposite" genders of male and female. Embracing rights of persons with non-conforming genders while criminalising persons with non-conforming sexual orientations is thus absurd. The 2016 Bill is the product of an uninterested and insincere attempt at lawmaking. India is within touching distance of enabling the legal empowerment of a hitherto marginalised community and it would be a shame if it squandered the opportunity by passing a bad law.

[This article is taken from The Hindu newspaper, dated January 10, 2017.]

CHAPTER - 3

Unheard Voices, Insider Views: Most-asked Q & A's, LGBTI Perspectives

Unheard Voices

Being Maya

Maya Ann Joseph

It was on 20th August, 2016, that Maya Ann Joseph, a transgender woman, stepped into the CSI Christ Church, Elamkulam, in Kochi, and been just herself. Maya, who had earlier stopped going to churches owing to stigma against transgender people in religious spaces, not only disseminated warmth among the audience, comprising of laity [parents, youth], Bishops and clergy men, but also could absolutely tune into the empathy seeking experience. Many words regarding her aspirations for life were conveyed during the dialogue on 'Envisioning an Inclusive Church', organised by National Council of Churches India. In this interview, Maya, speaks about her journey as a transgender woman, with adolescence, love and the conflict her family had in accepting her identity, to Dr Jijo Kuriakose, the Founder of Queerala, an NGO in Kerala.

Q: *How warm was the experience for you being at the session organised by NCCI and what was the response from your family regarding the program?*

A: As a transgender woman who is from a Christian family, I felt extremely glad to speak at such a gathering. I felt so relieved to realise that collectives like NCCI are striving to balance harmony on the matter of Gender Identity through such hopeful initiatives and I am sincerely thankful to ESHA project team for giving me the unique opportunity. If we look at nations, like Ireland, which is Christian dominated, human rights are given utmost importance and citizens are treated with equal dignity; something which our social system can learn and practise. I feel, Christian groups can contribute well to catalyse such a change in the state I dwell in, and across India. My family was also amused, post the program, over the involvement of priests to extend humanitarian solidarity for transgender persons. Any Christian family, which stays as constant pedestals of opposition in name of faith and holy texts, would be enthralled to know about these practical forms of support for the sexual minorities. Moreover, they did not debate quoting faith and the 'sin' aspect of not being fixed to the binary form of gender.

Q: *How contrasting was your childhood and teenage years- and what possible changes do you expect from educational spaces?*

A: Being brought up in a suburban space, my difference in body language and soft gestures during adolescent conversations were found apprehensive by my friends. I was neither interested in leisure time activities like sports nor keen after usual phrases like 'Boys would be Boys'. My childhood stint being in a boy's only school was too frightful; the mandatory engagement in drill periods is the worst memory I hold with regard to my schooldays. Hardly any day passed, without being tormented for being effeminate. At times, I felt to run away from home and my home state, because as a teenager I wasn't equipped myself to declare my gender identity (Tears broke out as Maya narrates this). I feel that educational spaces need to be immediately sensitized on gender diversity and bring in inclusive and anti-bullying policies; for it's the positive and bad experiences during those days which mould a major facet of our personality. Worse still, family is on a neutral stand for they are not so OK with me being me. I could come out to my family only after the Red Lotus Saree campaign, for which I was a model. It's still too hard for them to grasp the fact that being transgender doesn't only mean surgical transition but a state of being, which is absolutely natural and normal. I think sensitisation across the educational arena in India is one key area that Church led groups can focus on.

Q: *Considering the contemporary solidarity campaigns and attempts to implement a Kerala State TG Policy across various departments, what further strategic actions do you suggest for recognition of Equal Rights?*

A: I feel it's quite vital to have some sort of reservation for Transgender-identified individuals in colleges and workplaces. Both these are spaces where a young person spends most of the time outside the house, hence, certain actions by society to let this community complete their education and get employed is very essential. Not many among my circle know the struggle I pass through for I am not able to be myself in my everyday life. I might not fit in a group of people who strictly pursue gender roles at workplaces, in terms of dress code and gender expressions. Personally I do an independent job of a yoga instructor, where not many preach me how to behave or pass subtle 'be a man' comments. Only if more workplaces adopt and implement non-discriminatory policies, people like me can end up in respectable jobs, which would also let co-workers understand us and be empathetic. People often hide something if they happen to do anything wrong- which may cause harm to them. In our case, we had to hide ourselves for a decade or more, for we had not committed any wrong deed- only intolerance by the rest made us hide. I wish the next generation of transpeople don't pass through this. Awareness is the key; which can unlock states of confused notions and inhumane approaches; the key which can let loose the narrow minds, specially pertaining to less supportive cross sections like teaching, family, church parishes and all social spaces.

Q: *How do you look at your future, living in Kerala?*

A: Being into yoga instruction I dream to be known as a national icon in the area, where people from across various religious groups and cross sections come together to share harmony of peace. This field actually penetrates through various age groups also. If I can sustain myself in this, I can not only represent my community but also can train more beings like me to be professionals in this area. For people like me, such individual and independent jobs help a lot. Meanwhile, am not satisfied for not being able to lead a contended 'family life' of my own. I am of a dignity no less nor more than others, yet I am not given my right to live together with a loving life-partner, like all others. I have a partner, but he isn't yet ready to reveal the same, for he fears discrimination and loss of bond with his own family. I truly wish I can survive in Kerala, witnessing the change, the results of which can be enjoyed by next generation of rainbow minds, who need not stay socially isolated and discriminated from their kith and kin.

Q: Do you wish to pass a message to parents and families?

A: Yes, I do! Being Transgender isn't an odd case nor a curious case to be sympathised with-but one like any other human being. Being a [sexual] minority let this be considered as a training ground of societal acceptance versus visibility. Change starts from within each one among us. The worst scenario can be when a person like me isn't able to accept myself and stay connected with the community. Family, being one of the base units of the society we dwell in, can be taught about our human rights. Let no transgender person be disowned by families and let them not be in mental struggle due to the religious beliefs or related customs that some families follow. I believe that everyone is born for a reason and has some purpose for life, and it is only through loving one another can each of us be purposeful and socially responsible. Let parents not stay blind to Jesus's commandment 'Love one another'.

Daniel's Choice

Daniel Francies Mary Mendonca

"*Yes, I am a half male and a half female*". To say these words to the world - and make myself comfortable with the statement - has taken me long years. It has never been easy to come 'out of the closet' and explain myself to the world, but my coming out has filled me with happiness and joy. Through this life's journey there was only one person who was next to my heart, which was none other than my friend, my savior, my love "Jesus". Today with faith and convection I say to the world "I am in love with a man whose name is Jesus". I am happy that I am what I am. Looking at my past reminds me of all pain, discrimination, hatred and all forms of violence that I have faced being an "Intersex" person. It was never been easy to face this so called normal world.

I was born as a conjoined twin. My sister and I shared one body, with two heads. Difficult to digest the fact, but the work of nature and the hands of gods created this wonder. During our birth, my sister was born dead, so the doctors took the decision of separating my sister from me. From outside I looked like a male, but the doctors knew that though I looked like a male, I had a woman's organs inside this body [this term basically called as 'hermaphrodite' [Greek] or more commonly today, "Intersex"]. The doctors then told my parents that I was a 'eunuch'. My father, when he came to know this, rejected me. As a child who had just come into this world, didn't even know who his parents were, I was rejected for who I was, rejected because of my sexuality, rejected because my father's child was a eunuch. Thank God, at that very moment, my aunt — that is my father's sister - adopted me as her own child. She saw me differently. She said that if this child is born the way he is born, there must be God's plan in creating him. And so, in spite of having parents I was given to someone one else, having parents, but still I was an orphan.

Life continued. Right from the time I was small I knew that I was different, and the world around me did not leave a single chance of abusing me and making me feel out of this world - as if I was an alien that was born in another planet. I never received fatherly attention, my relatives always ignored me, and I was always kept behind from attending any religious or family function. Everyday became a questioning day, "Why Lord?', and not single day of my childhood was a happy day. Children my age enjoyed childhood and I was made to enjoy the loneliness around me. The silence of fear, the silence of voices, the silence of "being who you are", was all around me.

The time came for me to go to school, the biggest mistake that my family made was putting me in all Boys high school. As I was growing up, I always felt I was the only girl in the school. My teachers and my school friends often used to taunt me, tease me and insult me for being who I am. Whenever I used to go to the toilet or washroom my seniors would always pull down my pants to see what organ I would have down below. I have been abused so often, several seniors had tried to rape me, but with God's grace I had been lucky enough to be saved. It was just not the situation at school, even at home, my own cousin tried to rape me. When I shared that incident with my parents, I still remember the words my father told me, "It's okay if people use you for sex, because people like you are born to serve the society". When people enjoyed their childhood I enjoyed the silence within me. When other children played, I played with my questions, asking myself, "Who am I?"

The time came that the truth was revealed to me, the answers to my questions, but in a way I never expected. I was in class 4, about ten and a half years old. It was a usual day and I went to school- but before I left for school from home I told mom that my stomach was hurting. She thought I was just making excuses and forced me to go to school. After the lunch break, suddenly I felt a strong pain in my stomach. I ran to the loo, like never before, and I had just removed my pants when I felt something coming out of my stomach. My anus felt like it had torn into two parts, and something like the intestine came out – along with a lot of blood. It was my first menstrual period, but I didn't know. I fainted- when I opened my eyes after 3 days I found myself in a hospital in London! It was possible to admit me in London because my aunt who had adopted me told her boss about me, and he took me there for treatment, so that I could be saved. I asked the doctor what happened, he said there was no orifice for your menstrual blood to come out. He also told me "You are different and unique, and you are just here for your treatment".

The treatment went on for a long eight years, and I have spent in the hospital 8 years of my life. During this time I went through 29 major operations and 19 minor operations and it was only to see how my body was responding. Only my aunt was there with me -my father never bothered to ask how I was, and I was too far from my mother. It in this hospital where I came to know about myself. I tried to commit suicide thrice but saved with God's grace. The doctors took a decision that they will give me some religious counselling. That was the time when things changed. This was the time when I met my best friend Jesus through the holy Bible. I was very keen to know if there were other people like me, and to have God speak about people like me. I had always cursed myself and God for who I was created to be. But then I came to the verses which changed my whole life - Isaiah 56:4-5 and Jeremiah 1:5-7.

Slowly, as days passed Jesus became closer to me and I become close to him. A personal relationship started to develop with him and I become more comfortable with myself. I decided the sooner I accepted myself the way I was, the better I would feel about myself. Days passed and I was happier than ever. It was declared by the doctors that I now had a female organ inside my body so it would be better to change my sex and become a full fledged woman. I was ready for the surgery, but just few hours before it I decided not to go in for this surgery – I wanted to stay in this world with my original identity, and not come out in this world as someone I am not. Finally it was time to decide whether to continue in London or return. It was not easy for me to take a decision but yet I chose to come down to

India, the only reason being is I wanted to show my parents - specially my father - that an intersex child can also take care of the parents and have a dignified life.

When I returned to India, it was difficult for me at the start and very stressful to be with family, but my mother was always there with me to support me. I wanted to study and with the help of my mother and aunt I was able to study. I had never even touched my books before and never done formal schooling but with the help of teacher I was able to complete my SSC board exam privately, and even passed the examination. I wanted to study further, so I joined college. It was again a challenge, because everyone in the college teased me, I had no friends. One day, out of the blue, I stood up in the college and shared my life story to each and everyone in the class. I started saying that "I am happy to be who I am and I am proud of my sexuality". After sharing my story things changed - I had friends who now understood me and I began to get respect in the college for who I was. It was then I got the biggest opportunity of my life I was selected to represent the UN from India on the issues of LGBTIQ+ .

With the help of my mother, aunt and friends, life continued. I topped the 12th grade and went for further studies, taking up a Bachelor of Social Work. The reason was that I wanted to contribute to the issues of LGBTIQ+ in Indian society. My dream was and is to make society inclusive for gender minority communities. It was not easy again to survive in the college and in the society, but I made my way, proving my existence, and fought for my rights at every stage of my life.

There was a special moment in my life when NCCI played a major role in my life. My first journey with them began in Anand (Gujarat) where I was invited to share my story. After that NCCI took me all over India to make people and churches realize the diversity of gender, and that people like me existed. I realized that God was using me for this work and to bring a new revolution that will definitely create a history in days to come. The journey with NCCI has not only made me grow up mentally but also spiritually. Today the same world looks at me differently. Today I am working in YUVA in Mumbai as a Community organizer. As a good child of God, I believe I am a living testimony of Christ. Today I volunteer to work in the church and take Sunday school classes, and I am part of the Church's youth group. This was only possible because I have accepted to be myself and the world around me accepted me the way I am. The only difference was I had to prove my existence every day of my life- and it was really very different. Today life is much happier but the struggle goes on. The day will come when people will accept gender minorities, and there will be no discrimination against them in this society. People will accept the diversity of God and justice will prevail in the Kingdom of God.

My Saviour helped me to accept my sexuality

Romal M. Singh

I have always been someone who wanted to learn; someone driven solely by an unquenchable desire for knowledge. But, let's begin where this should begin. I was born in Saikot, a small provincial valley town in Churachndpur, Manipur. The fourth of four boys. Being Manipuri (Meitei) on my paternal side and Tamil and Malayali on my maternal side... I was destined to be a polyglot, but my mixed parentage wasn't a part of my reality, just yet.

My childhood was several thousand kilometres away from where I was born, 3,700 kms to be precise, in a small provincial hill town called Kotagiri in the Nilgiris, Tamil Nadu. From valley to hill, north east India to southern India, country bumpkin to South Indian snob; my life was already facing its ups and downs. But, let me be fair... my childhood was idyllic. The hills, the clean air, the greenery stretching into the horizon, the great weather... I'd often assume I'd grow up to be a poet of sorts. And, maybe, I did.

Childhood passed by swiftly and the next thing I knew I was a young man. My body changed, though at a much lazier pace than most friends around me, and life seemed perfect. Nothing could go wrong. Then fate, that friend-you-wish-you-never-had-but-just-can't-avoid... still had a few tricks up his sleeve. Half way through secondary school, I was pulled out of Kotagiri and flung back into Manipur. I loved and hated this move equally, but I am thankful to my father for doing so, because this is where the discovery of 'I' began.

Forced into an isolation, removed from friends and in the midst of a population that largely spoke an unfamiliar language – the focus went from the outside, to the within. Chance readings of references to gay people in magazines and newspapers and faint memories from Church-driven 'terror texts' against the gay community… drove me into a heady mix of genuine interest, lust for the forbidden and academic pursuit, that led me to discover that I was indeed what I feared all along: a raging homosexual 'man-boy'.

The inability to digest this unquestionable truth plagued me for years. Confiding in my faith and belief in prayer, I struggled on, till several years later… I found love. But I digress. Fate, my frenemy dearest, catapulted me back to the South a few years later, and I studied well and made my parents proud… and blah, blah, blah. But, yes, I found love. It didn't last very long, but it cemented who I was, for me.

Years later, many arguments won, many friends and relatives lost… I stand today as an open, 30-year old, media professional—proud about his sexuality and unapologetic for the lifestyle he has chosen. My family, friends and community (that I have chosen as inhabitants of my microcosm) play a huge role in allowing me to be who I am, and I am eternally grateful. Most importantly, however, I am thankful to Jesus my Saviour, who stood by me steadfast, and taught me to accept and love myself.

I am Romal. I am Gay. I am Proud.

[This excerpt is taken from the 18 November, 2016 issue of DNA]

Here I am

Lifter Tua Marbun

I kept asking myself many years ago: Did I become a homosexual because I had been sexually abused by men – first by a person who was close to my family, and then by a neighbour during my childhood? Honestly speaking, I do not know the answer to this question. In fact, I never actually felt traumatized by this childhood event. When I reached high school, I experienced my first sexual contact with men. After some time, I did not feel good about it. I was in agony for long periods. I felt that, in having sex with men, I was not normal. I felt disgusted and I feared God would punish me by giving me a terrible disease that I would die of. I was not happy at school and I felt hopeless and scared. Several times I developed an intention to kill myself. There was no-one I knew to whom I could turn for help and to whom I could talk to about this feeling. I felt ashamed and unworthy. I also lost any sense of trust and intimacy for my own body, because I thought that it was also sinful to seek intimacy and pleasure through your own body. I was also very frustrated when I met a guy from high school and I felt very close and connected with him, but I had to suppress my loving feelings and affection because I thought these feelings were sinful too and could break my new relationship with God.

I began attending Jakarta Theological Seminary in 1999. I hoped that studying theology and bringing myself into such a close relationship with God would make me feel better and could 'cure' my homosexual feeling. I studied hard and took on a lot of church activities near the seminary. The more I wanted to be healed, the more I got sick and depressed. I was tortured by my own feelings. As time went by, studying in the context of a very open minded seminary, I was challenged to accept my sexuality. I was open about it to my class mates. From that moment, I believed that God is Almighty, but I did not believe that God wanted me to be 'healed' and to convert me to become a heterosexual. This is who I am. God loves me and God wants me to be happy.

Early in my quest towards accepting my own sexuality, I created images in my own mind of homosexuality, which most of us do whether we are homosexual or not. What became obvious through my story is that at the beginning is that I had images of brokenness, sin, sickness, and being authentic when I looked at my homosexual feelings. Through the image of brokenness, I saw myself as a broken person. My sexual orientation was something bad. But then, how can be being loved and loving someone be seen as broken and bad? Aren't to love and to be loved good things, and give strong meaning toward the wholeness, self-fulfilment and self-acceptance? Therefore, I do not think being a homosexual means I am broken. Because when I love a person so dearly and feel connected with them, I feel happy and fulfilled.

When I told my sister that I was a homosexual person, and later when I asked some of the respondents whom I interviewed for the book I wrote together with my former professor, what their thoughts about homosexuality were, their reaction was very clear: that homosexuality is a sin. It is a sin, they thought, because it is against the law of creation. That is what they said and I also felt the same many years ago. The conversation with my sister two years ago was very emotional. She cried and she thought that I had chosen a sinful life. The most pitiful but sweet thing she said was that she would never be an aunt and that I would be alone when I am old.

I am a Batak man. Bataks are a tribe from North Sumatra, Indonesia. Having children, especially boys, is important in our ethnic community. And we are also family-oriented people. Family is number one, wherever you go. Therefore, you must get married and have children to continue your offspring who will take care of you when you get old. This is the most common issue in Indonesia, and is the basis of the pressure that is put on you if you live as a single person.

I met and talked with many men who have sex with men in Indonesia. Their sexual identities and their sexual activities are completely opposite. For them, having sex with a person of the same sex does not make them gay. Men who consider themselves as homosexual, and even those who act in a very feminine manner still want to get married with women and have children. For them, being a homosexual is a lonely "life style" and "choice". Men should get married, not have ongoing relationships with men. Having a relationship and getting married with another man is not considered normal, but having male sexual partners is acceptable, because they think they cannot stop that feeling and they also like men's bodies. To be sure, when we talk about human sexuality there is no black and white, because human sexuality is very complex. But are these men homosexual or bisexual? I do not want to put label on it. However, when they are asked, they also cannot describe their own sexuality.

For me, what is sinful is denying yourself and letting yourself being unhappy for the rest of your life. In my point of view, creation is not only about reproduction, but also about recreation, about being happy with your life and accepting what God has given you. I want to establish an equal and mutual loving relationship with my partner. Is it sinful to love someone, to spend your life with him to and to take care of each other for the rest of your life? I do not think so.

It is easy for us to stigmatize something beyond our beliefs and vision, especially when we see homosexual people. This attitude just brings condemnation to the people who are different than us and makes homosexual people unable to live with dignity and pride as their own feelings would normally direct them to do. Churches often condemn and stigmatize homosexuals as having a sickness; as being paedophiles; or as those who are the victims of sexual abuse and domestic violence. Most homosexuals are not victims of sexual abuse and domestic violence, and even for those who are, there is no evidence at all that this is what has determined that they are homosexual. And how can homosexuals or relationships be condemned as paedophiles? The kind of relationship that the great majority of homosexuals have, or aspire to, is one of equality and respect; whereas paedophilia is based on inequality and exploitation. Further, statistics show clearly that the great majority of sexual abuse of children is done by men to girls. Homosexual men have been a convenient and fictitious scapegoat.

I used to hear a lot when I lived in Indonesia that people, even among homosexual people, referred to themselves and each other as "sick" or "the sick". I find this is very hurtful and I often objected to my friends when they spoke this way. When I read the Gospel of John 9: 1-4, I find it very comforting, when it tells: "Now as *Jesus* passed by, He saw a man who was blind from birth. And His disciples asked Him, saying, "Rabbi, who sinned, this man or his parents, that he was born blind? "Jesus answered, "Neither this man nor his parents sinned, but that the works of God should be revealed in him.I must work the works of Him who sent Me while it is day; *the* night is coming when no one can work." I remember what Henri J. Nouwen reflected about this verse. He said that in this part from the Gospel of John talks about "Theology of Reversed Mission", where the wounded and the sick become the healer. Jesus does not talk about and does not care about who is to be blamed for the man being blind. His concern is how the glory of the Father can be manifested in them so we can do something for them and how this blind man can show the work of God for us.

Although Nouwen was talking about people who were infected and dying from HIV/AIDS when he expounded this theology, the same theology can be applied when we consider the condition of homosexual people. Homosexual people are not the object for a mission as we have usually understood it. On this 'mission' model, churches condemn their orientation and try to 'cure' and to save them as if they are cursed from this world. But homosexual people are not sinful and not sick. Instead of judging and looking for a way to 'heal' homosexual people, churches should reach out and help to bring them closer to God and the church, for many of them have left their faith and their trust in loving God because they are tired of being condemned and judged. The church's proper role is to show love and compassion towards homosexual people, and how they can stand strong amidst condemnation and hate, but still showing love. There are many examples of gay men and lesbian women who have continued to live out

Christian values in their lives and relationships, despite being condemned and rejected by the church.

The encounter with homosexual people is part of the church's prophetic dimension, because it can be an invitation to revalue the church establishment. The *missio dei* concept challenges us to see mission from the perspective of God, not our own preconceptions, so all His children, whatever their sexualities, can bring the truest values of His kingdom to all people. Therefore, the Theology of Reverse Mission means that the homosexual people can come and speak freely about their faith, about their love and about their difficulties in life, with their brothers and sisters in the church. Through the life experiences of homosexual people, the church can learn something, be more open and more compassionate in reaching people from different backgrounds and situations.

I see many homosexual people around me and in this world who contribute a lot of good things to their community and the wider world. They are very dedicated and devoted people. My homosexuality is a gift from God, in which I can be useful for the work of God. My sexuality does not limit me to do the work of God and to bring the Kingdom of God to people. In fact, it opens new ways for me to do this. I also do not want to use my experience of being sexually abused to get mercy and be excused for my sexual orientation. First, I do not believe the experience of abuse shaped my sexuality. Secondly, I do not believe that either being a survivor of abuse, or a homosexual, means I am lost from God and His love; but I am found and shaped better.

My acceptance of myself as a homosexual person brings me to the last image of homosexuality, which is being authentic or being who you are, as God knows you. I do not ask God to change me to be a heterosexual anymore and I do not want to. To be yourself means also to be honest to yourself. That is very important. If I cannot be honest with myself, how can I be honest to God? To be yourself means also not feeling ashamed for being who you are, and as God created you and loves you. Many families who have children who are homosexual and have come out to them, are ashamed to introduce their homosexual children to people. I have found this in many cultures. I remember how my ex-boyfriend in the Netherlands introduced me to his family as a student who was renting room in his house, because he was ashamed to have a very young Asian boyfriend. And it was not until the age of 51 years that my partner told his family that he was gay and that I had been his partner for 3 years.

In his life, Jesus was very faithful to himself and to his calling. Jesus was very faithful to be himself when people condemned him for befriending the sinners. He was not ashamed to talk with tax collectors, prostitutes, the outcast, and sick people. He touched them with compassion and love, because that's the way he was. People, including homosexuals, should act like Jesus, to be true with their calling and themselves.

In this journey, as Martin Luther ever said in defending what he believed: "Here I stand. I can do no other. God help me!" Therefore, I can say as well "Here I am. I cannot be someone or something else. May God help me in my quest."

An Insider's View

[Excerpted from "*To Be or Not to Be*" with permission.
Co-authored by Members of Payana]

Explaining
Alternative Sexuality Issues

Payana Team

1.   About 'Sex'

Sex has two connotations; one being the biological sex – the sex that one is born with based on the physical characteristics (penis/vagina); the physical organs that defines whether male or female. This is easy to define at the time of birth and based on this an identity of male or female is given; where the penis or the vagina is clearly a defined or visible, it is easy to decide on the biological sex. There may be rare cases of infants born with both the sexual organs, which are differently defined. In such cases it is difficult to make an exact identity, as male or female. Invariably the decision is made based on the more prominent sexual organ. Such cases are defined by us as inter sexed. The situation of being born as inter sexed sometimes leads to a wrong decision being taken by the concerned medical practitioners. Due to the decision being based on the visible characteristics, corrective surgeries may be undertaken, so that the body will fit into male or female. This identification of male body and female body is again based on reproductive system and in this process the two sex system excludes differently defined bodies like that of intersex people.

Since most of these corrective surgeries are done during the infant stage, this could lead to problems for the concerned person during the process of physical development, where the body may not develop characteristics that are in sync with the mind and sex that has been assigned. For example if the decision was taken and corrective surgery was done to denote a person as female, while growing up the individual may start showing characteristics such as growth of facial hair, changing of voice, etc. so the individual ends having female body along with male characteristics, similarly male bodies with female characteristics. It is often misinterpreted or misconstrued that people who are born inter sexed become Hijras. All males do not grow up to be men and all females do not grow up to be women (refer gender).

Let us begin with the example of a person who was born biologically male, though identified as male due to the physical characteristics, during the process of growing up this person started displaying more feminity due to a natural in born inclination. The person was uncomfortable with the male body due to there being a strong motivation from within the mentality of the person to take on more female roles in everyday life. This person's behavior portrayed a very confusing image, where on the one hand the person was forced to wear the attire, engage in activities that are designated for males and on the other hand the person was engaging in activities that society has assigned to female born people. This created a mental trauma within that person. At that stage the person was like a cat on the wall. The person was unable to understand whether the person should change the body or change the mind; having a physique of a male and constantly thinking and behaving as a female. Because the person was more inclined to portraying female attributes the person was constantly under pressure from family and society outside to conform to the body that the person was born with. This further increased the person's anxiety. After the person's adolescence when the person was in a position to think clearly for herself, the person decided that the person needed to synchronize the mind and body by changing the male body into a female body through sex reassignment process. This is an example that we are using so as to bring about an understanding as to how sometimes people are uncomfortable with their biological sex due to the mind, feeling and telling them that, that the body is not what they need to conform with with their biological sex due to the mind, feeling and telling them that, that the body is not what they need to conform with.

This process of reassigning one's sex could be from male to female or female to male. This is process through which a person has transitioned from one body type to another giving importance to the mind and feelings. This is trans (changing) sexual. The process of reassigning of the right sex to synchronize with the mind, whereby you make the person comfortable and remove the trauma that was constantly faced by them, is widely accepted in many countries.

Legally sex reassignment surgery [SRS] is possible only if the approved legal process is followed. The traditional method of removing the testicle and penis is illegal especially if the person is minor according to section 320, 325 and 326 of the IPC. It amounts to grievous harm. This is particularly for the male to female trans surgery. This does not apply to the female to male trans surgery, moreover female to male trans surgery is not done in traditional methods (refer to Hijra Culture). The law does not conceptually envision that a female born person would want to change the sex to male and also the reasoning that in the process no physical part of the anatomy is being removed. So for both male to female and female to male a certificate of a psychiatrist stating that the person is gender dystonic or not comfortable in sex that they are born in is necessary for the surgery to take place.

2.   About Sexual Acts

In general when we hear the word 'sex', it brings to mind images of sexual attraction, stimulation, intercourse, etc. This indicates that we very often are referring to the act of having sex, which is the second connotation of the word sex. What are the reasons why people have sex? The belief or the strong notion that having sex is for procreation- and only this reason- is accepted and sanctioned by the social norm, and is strongly rooted in the minds of most people, but this is not true. Still, any form of sexual engagement, which does not lead to procreation, and/or is outside the sanction of marriage is seen as sinful and immoral.

It is widely known that people engage in sexual acts outside the bond of marriage which does not result in procreation. It is also accepted that within the institution of marriage people engage in regular sexual acts which do not lead to procreation. This makes us wonder why people engage in sexual acts, if it is not for procreation. Being born as human beings, we have sexual desires, preferences, attractions, cravings, and these are natural. (Refer I Cor. 7:1-9 which indicates the sexual desires are natural to humans, and therefore the advice to get married) In restricting the sexual acts to mere reproduction we are oppressing the natural desire for sexual gratification.

Through the points given above, it is understood that among all sexually active human beings, sex is pleasurable, sex is a gift of God given for pleasure, given to all nature - and sex is not dirty, perverted, sinful or immoral, as is generally portrayed. These come out of the double standards of the society, where personally most people engage in sex for sexual gratification - but are reluctant to acknowledge this in public.

3. About Gender

Gender is a socially constructed definition of the performance that is expected by the society that we live in of a certain biological sex. It is not the same as sex (biological characteristics of male and female). Gender is defined by the concepts of tasks, functions, roles and behavior attributed to women and men in public and private life as part of the social fabric. Throughout life except at the time of birth male or female is normally referred to by the gender identity (man and woman). This creates confusion as to what is 'sex' and what is 'gender'.

Gender is what we grow with. Social barriers/restrictions on a particular sex is the basis of gender definition. Perceptions of these norms have evolved with the passage of time, during this time religion, and culture have played an important role in the construction of gender. Gender has also been defined by biological performance, where the child bearer becomes the care giver and the impregnator becomes the bread winner or protector. There are many theories about the evolution of gender, one among them being that mankind used to cover themselves from weather conditions that slowly lead to social attitudes of safety, protection, ownership and gradually oppression. The way male and female have separate forms of dress code are a means by which a person's gender is externally expressed mostly.

An individual explores a gender identity that they have understood from observing. This makes an individual to take on a specific existing gender identity in order to fit into the social fabric. Individuals observe and imbibe what is already pre existing with limited space for questioning or developing alternate form of gender expression. Gender is a belief, governed by the majority who conform to the existing denominators. It is a thought process that adheres to morals and cultures that exist from time to time. It evolves as history progresses, making limited changes that conform to the existing patriarchy. In this journey of gender, different people express their gender differently or even break the norms or rigidity, according to their needs.

At the same time one can also recognize that hetero-patriarchy at its convenience has loosened the norms of gender around the economic sphere but without separating the sex-gender associated roles and traits. From the time of birth, gender has an overbearing influence in an individual's life. At the time of birth gender does not play a very major role. In the process of growing up the gender norms come into play more specifically during mid childhood. This is the time where it is differentiated between boy and girl gradually gaining importance during adolescence through creation of strict guidelines and behaviors for male and female. Ultimately during adulthood society governs the gender role that an individual is forced to perform. On the contrary life offers diversity and multiplicity in all spheres and gender is one of the many expression modes and a major part of a person's individuality. The hetero-patriarchal system makes this journey of gender so rigid that many times, this could be one of the reasons for the shift in gender. Gender is not a physical condition. Most men having facial hair, muscular body and deep voices, and most women having soft body, developing breasts and soft voices are biological conditions of male and female sexes. In the definition of gender identity these are sometimes used as forms of gender identity, while they are just physical characteristics that are natural part of the sex that one is born with. Human beings are born with a sex. Gender is something that becomes part of life through the growing up process and continues to be a requirement for social, legal, political, cultural and economic acceptance all through life.

A historical view: Initially both man and woman shared equal responsibility to fetch food (hunt) and protect the tribe. Slowly these tasks were distributed and divided. What began as work and tasks gradually grew to be more gendered roles like child bearing and child rearing, for females and role of bread winner or a protector for males. Through ownership patterns, patriarchy grew and eventually led to gender oppression. The gender category with time has become a water tight compartment of man and woman with specific conditions or norms for each in regard to behavior, dress code, roles, responsibilities, freedom, mobility and hierarchy, which allows hardly any flexibility to shift between the two rigidly defined genders. During the times of the hunter gatherer nomadic society, the division of labor was more equal, when males and female shared equal responsibilities in hunting, gathering, sharing, protecting and caring. It was a time of communal living. Once the ability to cultivate food was discovered, it led to process of identifying cultivable lands, in turn bringing about a process of ownership. This progressed to a state of possessiveness, possession of physical property (land, housing etc). The desire for continuity of ownership within the family lineage led to possession over offspring, therefore ownership of the child bearer.

Through this process, the need to cover the sexual parts of female and male anatomy, as a form of not making opportunity available to others who may desire to do so, became symbolic to state the ownership over the female body. Over a period of time this led to dress code as a form of gender expression, which was also an agency of gender suppression. Women were restricted to child bearing and child rearing along with other labour which was restricted to within the owned premises and that which was not means for independent livelihood. The male being the provider had the freedom of movement beyond the possessed boundaries, whereas the female was restricted to operate within the given boundary. Gradually with economic onus on women they were able to move out of these boundaries, but even till today are still controlled to a large extent.

In the present gender scenario though many drastic changes have evolved due to various influences (religion, culture, economy, education, politics, etc), the gender norms and the roles that pertain to these norms have not widened the scope to explore and adopt gender expressions that are beyond the existing male-man, female-woman gender identities.

Gender being seen as an important aspect of the society that we exist in, leads to one trying to adhere to the specified norms, so as to gain acceptance, protection, importance recognition, dignity, in the larger society. This sometimes leads to many individuals not being free to express their gender outside of the given bipolarity. The present society has built its beliefs and provides the political, legal, economic, cultural sanction only to those who conform to the gender expectations. In this context there are a large number of individuals who are uncomfortable living up to this framework. Due to this, these individuals are faced with complexity of trying to become part of the society, even though their gender does not conform to the given norms.

These individuals go through life performing different gender acts in different spaces and times. When individuals like this venture to assert their right to express themselves in ways that make them comfortable, this is seen as rebellion against social order. It is also looked at as a threat to the fabric of an assumed decent and regulated society. Due to this the society rejects people like this. Rejection leads to loss of status in society, no legal sanction, and discrimination, physical and mental violence. With this as the platform on which people of alternate gender expression are expected to survive, it becomes inevitable for such people to become invisible to the eyes of society or are put in a situation where society closes its eyes to people with alternate gender expressions.

Again this leads to fitting into the gendered norms given by society, where you are accepted in the full form of gender change, but when there isn't a complete change and individuals opt to change a certain aspect or characteristics of their gender then this is seen as breaking away from the box and a threat to security of those within the box. There are many individuals who want the right to express their gender in a manner which has meaning to them and allows them to define their own gender outside of the given socially accepted norms.

The concept of "Trans" is a journey from the assigned gender or sex to a comfortable, aspired gender or sex. It is the individual's choice to complete the journey or not. Many times the individual might not want to stay in a particular phase which is neither of the extremes of the "two points". The problem is – this journey is visualized or understood as a horizontal single layered straight journey from point one to point two being male to female or visa versa – this is the binary that is fixed by the society. If this perspective can be changed to understand and visualize a circle of gender expressions, which could be according to the individual's understanding or choice the fluidity can be retained. Retaining of fluidity makes space for freedom of expression and also growth of the individual in multi-spheres more comfortably than that of restricted fixtures of positions becoming life's inevitability.

Any sort of difference is hard to accept. Diverse gender expression has existed from time immemorial, whilst forming the bipolar gender structures this has been ignored conveniently and many a times suppressed and pushed below the carpet.

Throughout history gender diversity has never manifested itself in the form of breaking or destroying societal norms. It has always co-existed in spite of exclusion, marginalization, and disempowerment. So the perceived threat is based on no evidence and incidents. In today's society there is very little space for inclusion of people whose gender expression is contrary to the accepted bipolarity. To bring about a change in the attitude that only patriarchy can have control over society, there is a strong movement among the people whose gender expression is diverse and different to move away from the patriarchal norms and create a society that is more inclusive of diversity.

Due to the fixed prevalent gender structure, that has been pre existing from before, a gender choice is denied. Existing pressures from society which is shaped by socio economic factors, rules and regulations set by a society for a particular gender makes gender fixed and bipolar. The Third gender was formed due to the lack of flexibility in the existing model of man and woman. Hence the third gender carved a unique identity for themselves and this third gender has since evolved as initial Hijra community to various sub sects like Kothis etc. Some people have stuck to different identities during this journey making a space for themselves and creating new identities in spaces that they can create and call their own. There is a constant questioning in self expression of gender.

The concept of there being a difference between the sex that one is born with and the gender that is imposed upon a particular sex by society is sometimes confusing and conveniently overlooked. The influence of culture religion politics in framing legal systems and processes further confuses by not using clear identities, when legalizing or criminalizing certain acts that are accepted or considered to be harmful to the society. This non-clarity leaves room for both advantage and disadvantage. The question that needs to be answered in today's world of gender, is whether people who identify as male -but are not Men, or as female - but are not Women, will be recognized as transgender, third gender, inter-gender, alternate gender or choose any other gender identity? And will this be understood, accepted and treated with equal rights and given equal dignity and respect.

4.   About Sexuality

Conversations, debates, dialogues, discourses around having sex, which include feelings, expressions, behavior, politics, economy, culture, orientation, attraction, choice, material produced based on having sex, etc is sexuality. Anything that pertains to having sex, etc are all issues around sexuality. Usually it is restricted to orientation of same sex attraction or opposite sex attraction. Sexuality is a wider domain, when we restrict it to the mere act of sex, it narrows down the scope and limits its understanding. Most often sexuality is understood as one's attraction, preference, choice and orientation towards whom one wants to engage in any act or form of having sex. In this limited sphere of the understanding of sexuality, sexuality identity has been divided into the three given terms - *homosexual, bisexual and heterosexual*. Sexual orientation to us defines the mental location of one's inclination towards who one is attracted to and wishes to engage in a sexual relationship. In the spectrum of sexuality the orientation clubbed with attraction is often seen as the main denominator for one's sexuality identification.

Sexuality is an individual choice but it is invariably regulated by hetero-normative expectations of society. Usually influences of the hetero-normative society give little space to realize that it is an individual choice. Also the journey of one's sexuality is diverse. The individual decides how much fluidity or space that one would want. The lack of understanding of one's sexual choice restricts the opportunity to explore one's own desires /preferences /Orientation. The journey of one's sexuality begins at a stage in life when one starts feeling the desire for sexual pleasure. This happens quite early in life for most people during puberty. This desire manifests itself for each individual in different ways. Due to the upbringing and the beliefs that are ingrained in people by those around, it is perceived that the right sexual attraction, preference, choice or orientation is only when the individual's desire is for the opposite sex/gender. This leaves no room for exploration of one's natural inclination/orientation. Choosing one's sexuality after giving thought to fulfill the natural inclination should be the most desirable way.

'Sexual Identity' or 'Sexuality Identity,' is based on biological sex (male or female). The term sexuality itself denotes the involvement of an act of sex between two people of a biological sex (sex that they are born with). Looking at sexuality from this narrow perspective restricts the scope to include role of gender in sexuality. The way we identify people of different sexes is purely based on the external, visible characteristics. The immediate visible identity is a gender identity. The mannerisms, roles, and appearance is what one visualizes when identifying a biological sex. This is an indication that biological sex and gender have an important role in sexuality identity.

Nature in its bounty has created huge diversity, in the process also uniqueness to each and every naturally created species. Within a particular species nature has further diversified the uniqueness with individuality. Each individual is unique in their own way. Sexuality comes as part of the uniqueness of the individual and is imbibed within the individual by nature. If the commonly accepted normative sexuality is termed natural and the acceptability being based on an assumed conformation from nature, one needs to define the conformation of nature. Usually the confirmation of nature is defined based on reproductive possibility. Even within the commonly accepted sexuality, the part that 'pleasure' is a dominant requirement for people engaging in sexual activity, is often overlooked, giving reason for the belief that alternate sexuality is not natural, when most times people engage in sex for pleasure, the question of alternate sexuality not being natural is baseless. Because of the possibility of reproduction and the dominant nature of the commonly accepted sexuality it gains the sanction as natural by law, religion, and morals. It is in this context and not on the role of nature that alternate sexuality is termed 'illegal', 'immoral', 'abnormal' and 'unnatural'.

Unfortunately in certain cultures, which have been influenced by religion, class, caste, economy, education, this right to choose one's sexuality is being denied by the boundaries that are imposed on individuals depending on which society, country, religion, caste, class, race, etc., that they belong to. For example inter-caste, inter-religious, class-difference marriages are not part of the accepted norm. The family values of dignity, respect, status in society also act as a barrier to one having the freedom to choose their sexual partners. The belief that sex between two people gains social and legal sanction only through the institution of marriage, further impedes the right of the individual to choose sexual partner. In this situation, most of the time when people have same-sex or gender attractions, the space to express and fulfil these preferences does not exist. This forces people to perform an accepted role in society and to express their sexual preferences in very secret, hidden and threatening environments, leading to various forms of vulnerability for those indulging.

Sexuality is expressed when the person feels a natural inclination towards another person. The attraction is expressed to gain attention of the person(s) with certain behavioral patterns for example flirting. Flirting encompasses providing overt attention, pre-empting the needs and likes of the person(s) one is attracted to and acting accordingly in given situations. This is done with the intention to project oneself in a certain way to the person(s) one is sexually interested in. It is also important to note expression of sexuality through an appropriate dress sense for example, a man using tight fitting clothing could be seen as an expression of gender with the intention of attracting somebody sexually may be interpreted as an expression of sexuality.

People find it hard to express themselves differently due to the prevailing fixation. Though naturally the desire to perform multiple roles in sexual acts exists, it is restricted due the fear of deviating from the accepted or approved forms of conduct/performance. The sexual roles that are played conform to hetero-normativity. All sexual acts which are consensual are natural. There is a fear to deviate from it due to pressure of power, relationships, acceptance, based on the gender restrictions. Sexual roles are guarded by social conditions based on procreation leading to hetero-normativity.

As per the attitude that has evolved, based on the belief that women are the vessel that receives fulfilment from the man, the woman is groomed to believe that she has to play the submissive passive role in order to satisfy the need or desire of the man. This attitude has led to women to not to express their sexual desires and wants or initiate the sexual act.

When women initiate or express their sexual need in a form which is not in sync with beliefs or attitudes, this situation portray the woman as someone with loose moral values. This in turn restricts women from gaining sexual freedom and the right to fulfill the natural urge, desire, stimulation and inclination.

On the other hand men are given the freedom to fulfil their urge, desire, stimulation and inclination through various avenues that are available, though some of these may be hypocritically ignored in the public sphere yet accepted in the private domain. Many a times the desire for a man to adhere to morally accepted attitude invariably does not sexually gratify the man and woman, who are in a hetero-normative marital relationship. This situation leads to many men and women seeking sexual gratification outside of the institution of marriage. The sexual role that one adapts to is purely based on the institution of marriage between a man and a woman. Outside of the institution of marriage, whether pre- or post- marital, any desire to perform a role that is sexual, is seen as 'deviant' from the accepted, expected role that society sanctions. Sexual desire, urge, inclination and stimulation are natural. Sexual roles are fixed and certain forms of sexual acts are not encouraged due to hetero-normativity. There are various identities to human beings; profession, religion, caste, class, roles, gender, sexuality etc.

It is made problematic to see human beings only in the context of sex or sexuality. Sexual activity was considered to be pleasurable in various cultures and societies, before the control of religious influences came upon sexual activity. It is during the period when religion began to play a major role in the construction of society, that sexual activity became restricted to procreation, and the pleasure derived out of sexual activity was seen as sinful. Moreover the assumption that homosexuality revolves around sexual pleasure and not procreation, there is a bias that most of the homosexuals and bisexuals are preoccupied with sexual acts- which is simply not true. It is important that this society recognizes the role of sex and sexuality and to respect identities based on sex and sexuality.

5.   About Stigma, Discrimination and Phobia

Homosexuals and sexual minorities are no way different except for their sexual preference. If bones, blood, muscle, brain and body parts are similar then why does mere sexual preference make an entire community [who do not conform to the procreative sex] just sexual beings. All human beings are sexual beings and all human beings seek sexual gratification. When we describe a heterosexual we call him or her an engineer/doctor or good at dancing/writing, or one who has passion for sports or culture. No one ever mentions that a heterosexual man/woman enjoys having sex with a man/woman but when it comes to describing a homosexual then the first point of description is that he has sex with men or she is attracted to women. There is no other point of identification besides their preference and hence this differentiation of sexual preference has been over played. In this scenario it is perceived that homosexuals are more interested in sexual pleasure and exploring different forms with different individuals. The notion that they cannot get sexual satisfaction with one partner therefore to fulfil their immense sexual drive they need to engage in sex with multiple partners. This is basically a belief which is not the truth. Utility of sex is connected mainly to procreation anybody who does not procreate is branded 'impotent' and/or 'infertile'. Homosexuals are not impotent and infertile. They have all the biological requirements for procreation. They have the capability to reproduce as much as heterosexuals. Impotency/ infertility is a condition that has nothing to do with the sexual orientation. It can affect anyone. A person can be impotent and infertile and yet can be oriented as 'hetero, homo or bisexual'. These are contradicting assumptions about homosexuality, viz., it is for people who are impotent and infertile *and* it is pleasure driven.

There is a huge resistance to decriminalize consensual homosexuality due to the assumption that everyone will become homosexuals. This assumption is based on a fear that homosexuality would lead to the destruction of the values and beliefs that male and female have been created to ensure the continuation of the human race. Excessive fear becomes Phobia. Just as it is impossible for heterosexuals to become homosexuals, homosexuals cannot become heterosexuals. Homosexual relationships challenge hereditary, property inheritance, family ties, religion, politics of body; politics of economy, politics of power, hence becomes a threat to the existing family and heterosexual marriage system.

Hetero-normativity has been propelled by the culture we live in today. A deviation from the prevalent norm could be seen as an opposition to existing customs and traditions. Culture is a collective of people, customs, traditions and practices. It evolves over time and gets shaped into phenomena. Evolution is conveniently ignored by the rest. Gender/Sexual diversity has been recorded in form of mythological stories, folk fables, literature and politics, art and culture. The diversity has influenced numerous expression of art like sculpture, poetry and dance. The Ajanta Ellora, Khajurao, Belur are proof to it. After centuries of existence, how is it being a threat to culture? It is not a threat but a challenge as it does not fall in line with the structure of family and procreation (hetero-normativity). Some people feel that gender/sexual diversity is an alien influence that will destroy the existing culture- but it is not. The fear that the oppressed or disadvantaged group will gain prime importance, gain more supporters and power, which might pose a threat to the larger society, is the reason for their suppression. There has always been a point wherein the majorities try to influence the minority and oppress them by being large numbers and power. This oppression leads to exploitation, violation of human rights, discontentment, marginalization and disempowerment. Hence a multi gender and multi sexuality system is seen as a threat to the existing heteronormativity of society. An institution such as religion or faith does not sanction gender and sexuality diversity, but a closer look one would find numerous instances of stories from the religious texts that highlight the lives of gender and sexually diverse followers. When it has been so back then, how is a threat now? Yet it is being perceived as a danger now, as the gap between fundamentalism and religion is narrowing.

Who are Hijras?
Is there a special 'Hijra Culture?

Payana Team

There are many communities that are not recognized in India and one such community is the Hijra community. Across India this community identifies themselves with respect as hijras. The general public usually refers to them in insults translating to incompleteness, impotent people. For many centuries hijras were respected and accepted as blessed people. This was more predominant in north of India. The accepted forms of livelihood for this community were and are receiving alms in appreciation of their giving blessings, usually to newly married couples and new born babies. Due to these beliefs gradually deteriorating, the income generated through these means decreased. As a result of loss in income and having no other form of employment because of the social marginalization and legal unacceptability, the hijras were forced to engage in begging and sex work for their livelihood.

Though we live in a democratic country under whose constitution all citizens are guaranteed rights, hijras are denied of fundamental rights, citizenship rights and undergo severe human rights violation. Hijras due to the desire to conform to an alternate gender lose all the support and protection that is automatically granted to a person who conforms to the two gendered system. With no other option for support and protection a system has evolved from within the hijra community whereby the protection is provided through certain cultures and systems that have been set up by the hijras themselves. This system is based on matrilineal relationships. To become a hijra it is necessary that you express your desire and willingness to do so. On confirmation of this desire by seniors who are already part of the hijra community one may be initiated into the community by a process of adoption, where a senior member of the community adopts the new member creating a relationship of guru (mother) and Chela (daughter). The matriarchal lineage continues to extend both ways. The new entrant when adopted by the guru automatically becomes the chela, natichela, santi chela and sadak chela meaning that she has a mother, grandmother, great grandmother, great great grandmother. In turn the newly initiated chela is free to adopt chelas of her own. Her chelas may also adopt chelas, chela's chelas, could again adopt their own chelas meaning the person that we are referring to as the newly initiated community member can have daughters, granddaughters, great grand daughters and great great granddaughters.

The initial adoption is done through a special ceremony where all the seniors and leaders of each Gharana (home) are present and the new comer is taken under the protection of the immediate guru, which also automatically extends to all the seniors. On adoption the person inherits the protection of all the seniors. When the present new comer starts to adopt her own chelas, the process of initiation has to be repeated for each one.

The system of Gharanas (homes) has been in existence for many centuries. The gharana system exists in the entire South Asian region almost. There are seven gharanas in this system. Each gharana is headed by a Nayak, who is the senior most person in the hierarchy of that gharana. Each Nayak acts as the sole ruler of the gharana. All decisions, problems, adoptions, financial transactions and occupations are controlled by the Nayak. The Nayak has the ultimate power for that gharana and those belonging to that gharana. In situations where decisions or rules and regulations need to be discussed all the Nayaks from the seven gharanas participate in this process. The Nayaks financial support comes from all members of that particular gharana.

All hijras need to go through a process after adoption. This process builds their skills to earn either through Basti or Badhayee. They are taught by the Gurus how to dance and perform at various auspicious occasions.

They are also taught how to ask for and receive alms. During this process the hijra takes the form of a woman. She begins to grow her hair and wear female attire. Through this the individual would learn to become comfortable living as a female and as part of the hijra community. Since all hijras are born biologically male. When the individual expresses the desire to become a transsexual and with consent from the guru it is decided to go for sex reassignment which is referred to as Nirvan, meaning that the person has achieved ultimate fulfilment of desire to live in society as a female. There may be people who do not wish to have their male genetilia removed but may continue to adapt the role and mannerisms of a woman. This is also accepted within the community but people who have attained Nirvan are considered superior. The process of attaining Nirvan may be done through a medical procedure by selected doctors who are friendly to the community's needs or through a process where her senior within the community who has sufficient experience in the process may perform the role of a surgeon and conduct the operation. These two forms of Nirvan are commonly referred to within the community as Doctor Nirvan or Dayamma Nirvan. Individuals who opt for the Dayamma process are treated with more dignity and respect within the community.

Before the invasion by the British and India being colonized transgenders and Hijras were part of the society and treated with dignity and reverence. They were given ample opportunity to express themselves and enjoy positions of power based on their capabilities. Due to India becoming a colony of the British Empire and being influenced by the invader's religion a process of marginalization started. Marginalization led to the community being stigmatized and branded as criminal tribe which in turn led to the community facing various forms of discrimination having no locus standi constant verbal ridicule physical and sexual abuse by various power structures. The community bore this for many years assuming that they were to blame for their situation and whatever was being done to them was their fate and needed to be accepted. In the early 1990s people from the community started getting exposure to various human rights forums. This led to the community realizing that they had the power to assert their rights. Community members across India started mobilizing themselves into groups and organizing debates and discussions in the public sphere around their pathetic situation. Community initiated various forms of revolt against the atrocities that was perpetuated against them over the many past centuries. The forms of protest varied from situation to situation such as public protests, rallies demanding rights, speaking in public platforms, addressing the media, taking Political initiative in contesting various elections, demanding from the government inclusion in various schemes, privileges, etc. Today there is an effort to include hijras and the transgenders as the 'other' in legal systems and administrative systems. For example Tamilnadu has been the frontrunner in initiating inclusion and provision of special privileges such as sex reassignment surgery, allocation of housing, etc through setting up of a special welfare board. In Karnataka the recent development where the Bangalore University has declared that special emphasis would be given and facilities provided to those from the community who wish to pursue higher education. Changes have been initiated and put in place this is the beginning of the means to the end of a long struggle that needs to continue.

The community's vision is to see all hurdles removed from their path to achieving the status of a respected productive and worthy human being.

[Excerpted from "*To Be or Not to Be*" with permission. Co-authored by Members of Payana.]

Who goes through a Sex Re-assignment Surgery [SRS], and for what purpose?

Payana Team

⚬

Reassigning through surgery is more in the context of synchronizing the body and the mind, while sex change is mostly just removal of genitals that defines a particular sex. It is part of the reassigning procedure to synchronize the body to the desire of the mind for transgender/ transsexual. It may also be performed on intersex people. Sex reassignment surgery (initialized as SRS; also known as genital reconstruction surgery, sex affirmation surgery) is a term for the surgical procedures by which a person's physical appearance and function of their existing sexual characteristics are altered to resemble that of the sex with which the person is comfortable and more mentally suited to continue their life. In medical terms initially Trans persons were looked at as people with gender identity disorder/gender dysphoria. In today's world, in a society that is more scientifically in tune with advanced understanding of diversity this belief has ceased to exist. The term 'sex change operation', though commonly used by the educationally disempowered people does not bring out the full meaning of sex reassignment.

The process of Sex Reassignment Surgery goes through many stages. Initially mental health is important to ascertain the true location of the person's mental status, an assessment needs to be undertaken by competent psychologist/psychiatrist to certify the person has true transsexualism and that he or she is strongly motivated not only to undergo surgery but also for the long journey to complete transition. Physically and mentally the person should be prepared and fit to undergo the rigors of anaesthesia and surgery. This requires many sessions over a period of time which would vary from individual to individual. The person should also be stable and must not be the type who might change his/her minds after operation, because the operation is irreversible.

One should also understand that we are dealing here with a situation that is not usual and is predominantly psycho-emotional rather than physical. Operation is only one of the steps. The person should be prepared to adapt to a lifestyle that will lead to many barriers in being accepted in the new form socially. This could further traumatize and create exclusion from being accepted in the new form in spaces that are socially reserved for the biological identities. The individual may also have personal barriers stemming from the belief that they would face ridicule and marginalization in these spaces.

Hormonal therapy is an important part of treatment. These are administered to help develop secondary sexual characteristics. Operation provides only primary sexual characteristics. Many people have voices, bodies, muscle structure, body and facial hair, which are natural physical characteristics that are part of the sex that one is born with.

Administration of hormones helps to bring about changes which would depict the sex that the person intends to transition to. Administration of hormones is done to seriously motivate people and will vary from individual to individual based on the biology of the person. Hormonal treatment must be undertaken with strict supervision by qualified endocrinologist.

On completion of the mental assessment and with the process of hormone therapy surgery will be performed to remove the biological sex and reconstruct the desired sex. The results of the surgery are usually successful yet there may be some limitations like the following:

Male to Female

For male to female transsexualism menstruation is not possible because there is no uterus and no ovaries. Orgasm is possible because there is erogenous sensation and the mental component is also intact. Breast-feeding is generally not possible.

Most adult transsexuals confess to having experienced a hatred for their body right from early life - well before puberty. Many remember puberty with abhorrence, because of the hormone-induced changes in body characteristics which they perceived as totally alien to their sexual identity. Often, it is around the pubertal period that most transsexuals reinforce their determination to rid themselves of their primary and secondary sexual characteristics. In some cases, hatred for one's body is seen at a very young age. It may manifest, for example, in a young boy as a natural desire to display more female oriented characteristics.

Female to Male

For female to male transsexualism, a satisfactory erection of the surgically constructed penis is possible with inflatable prostheses. Semi-rigid ones will give rigidity. Ejaculation is not possible. Remember, there is no spermatic fluid in these persons. Testes, seminal vesicles and the prostate gland are absent. Sex with a female is possible. Satisfaction is in the penis and mind of the copulator. With good operative results, they can be happy. Impregnation is not possible because there is no sperm production.

Sex Reassignment Surgery from female to male includes surgical procedures that will reshape a female body into a body with a male appearance. Many transmen considering the surgical option which are very unaffordable and not available in India easily do not opt for genital reassignment surgery, though some do undergo a bilateral mastectomy, the removal of breast and shaping of a masculine chest and hysterectomy, (the removal of internal female reproductive organs), along with hormone treatment with testosterone. In India the option to undergo phalloplasty though available restricts the individual's choice to opt for it due to the exorbitant financial implications.

Sex reassignment surgery from male to female involves reshaping the male genitals into a form with the appearance of and, as far as possible, the function of female genitalia. Prior to any surgeries, transwomen usually undergo hormonal therapy to enhance breast development or may opt for breast implants. Other surgeries undergone by transwomen may include facial feminization surgery and various other procedures.

The purpose of SRS is so that the body and mind are synchronized leading to the individual living at peace within themselves. The trauma that one goes through where the body and the mind is not in agreement is taken care off through this procedure leaving individuals at a stage where they are comfortable with themselves and this builds emotional strength.

Most-Asked Questions About Homosexuality

Deepak Kashyap

A.   About Homosexuality

1.   What does my child mean when he/she says he/she is a homosexual person, i.e. he or she is gay/lesbian?

When your child tells you that he/she is a homosexual person or 'comes out' to you as gay/lesbian, they are telling you that they find themselves attracted towards a person of their own sex; a man who is attracted towards a man, or a woman who is attracted towards a woman. This is not just sexual attraction; this attraction is romantic and emotional as well. Don't worry, it's not a disease or disorder. It simply means that your child has different emotional and romantic needs than the vast majority of children that you see around yourself. You must understand that when your child 'comes out' to you, he is trying to reach out to you and asking for your support on three levels:

- Personal
- Interpersonal
- Social

On a personal front, your child is conveying to you the fact that he is someone different than what you understand about sexuality, that he/she is gay or a homosexual person. You must understand that it requires great courage for your child to tell you that he is homosexual and for him to share with you what he/she has gone through, as a person of an unusual sexuality. In doing so, he is asking for your love and support as parents or guardians.

On an interpersonal level, your child is asking you to invoke every bit of love that you have for him because he is going to present to you an idea of himself that you may not fully understand or support. And although you may not find yourself at peace with this newly discovered side of him, he is asking you if you can find the strength to educate yourself on the matter instead of dismissing it outright as abnormal.

Then, on a social level, your child is asking you to stand by them and support him/her when he/she is ready to face the society as a gay or lesbian person resisting pressures of marriage and other societal norms that apply to heterosexuals. They are also asking you if you are ready to defend them in front of others if the same pressures also confront you as a parent/guardian of a homosexual person.

To understand this further, look around you or outside the window or think of all the different people you have met in and outside of your family. None of them look like each other; even identical twins have some differences in them. Our faces, heights, hair, eyes and many more things are very unique to us. We, somehow, seem to be fine with these differences because they are very evidently and unavoidably physical in nature and we come face to face with this physical variety of life almost on a daily basis and thus get used to the fact that there are a large variety of people in the world around us.

In the same way, we as humans are very different from each other in our sexual desires, orientations, fantasies and our understanding of our gender. In simpler words, just like we all look and behave differently, we all have a unique sexual nature. However, this difference seems more threatening to us than the above mentioned ones because we don't know much about these differences and the moral cloud around sexuality is filled with ambiguity and irrational judgments. Ask yourself a question: how can we all have same sexual natures? Since we expect our sexual natures to be a certain way for everyone, we thereby choose to club some people as abnormal or unnatural, if their sexual nature seems to not conform to our understanding of it. In reality, we all are very complex and unique.

2. Is homosexuality a choice? Can he/she choose to be straight again?

No, homosexuality is not a conscious choice. A child did not wake up one day and decide that he or she wants to be someone who has a sexual and romantic attraction towards a same sex person. Ask yourself, did you ever sit down and select your own sexual attraction towards the opposite sex person? Or would you be able to now choose to be homosexual, if you so desired? So, if as a heterosexual person you did not choose your own orientation, how could a homosexual person be able to choose theirs? As humans we don't and we can't choose whom we get attracted towards. Most gay people report to have been aware of their homosexual feelings quite early on in life or during their adolescence. In fact, it is reasonable to imagine that it was equally, if not more of a traumatic and confusing experience for them to gradually discover this side of themselves, as it might be for you now. It is important to understand that at such an emotional time, one could take a moment to ask your child or friend: "Are you okay?" "I hope you did not go through too much of a tough time accepting yourself." Sometimes acknowledging other people's pain can give you the strength to deal with your own.

So the question of whether they can choose to be straight again doesn't arise, when sexual orientation is not a matter of choice in the first place. A lot of people might erroneously think that one can choose their sexual orientation, however, it is quite clear from the scientific data that is available that sexual orientation and attraction is beyond human choice.

Also one needs to understand the difference between behavior and orientation.

Behaviour is: what you do in actions.

Orientation is: what you are inclined towards and what you want.

So even if a gay man or lesbian woman has been able to perform behaviourally in bed with the opposite sex, their orientation in terms of desirability and attraction towards same-sex doesn't change. Even the studies that report some religious therapy having successfully worked in "reorienting" people have statistically negligible rate of any success. Even when the so-called successful individual cases are looked at in these largely self-reported studies, one finds that the researchers didn't differentiate between bisexual and homosexual individuals and no attention was paid to the distinction between behaviour and orientation.

In fact, most of the ex-gay movements are criticized for having instilled self-damning guilt and shame in their clients, during the unsuccessful attempts at trying to change sexual orientation of gay and lesbian individuals.

3. What makes some people homosexual?

Sexuality is an extremely complex subject, making it very hard to find one specific cause for homosexuality in human beings. But some theories are supported by more evidence than others, which makes them more likely explanations of unusual human sexuality than the conjectures prevalent in the socio-religious schools of thoughts.

Epigenetic theory: All human characteristics are encoded in the form of genes on human DNA. Everything from the colour of their eyes to their sexual interest develops in the pre-natal stages of human development. Epigenetic markers are chemicals that control to what degree a certain gene is expressed. Think of it as a switch that turns a gene on or off. The researchers found that a particular kind of epi-marks that are wrapped tightly around the DNA sequence, affect sexual preference in individuals without altering genitalia or sexual identity.[1] This research gives support to the hypothesis that homosexuality stems from the expression of certain genes on the DNA sequence connected with sexual preferences, as against earlier theories that pointed towards an independent gay gene.

Brain Structure theory: This is a somewhat inconclusive research aimed at studying the brains of heterosexuals and homosexuals. The research found that the structure of the brain of a gay man was very similar to that of a straight woman and vice versa for straight men and lesbians. Though, it is still to be conclusively proved if the structure of the brain affects sexuality or if the brain development follows sexual orientation which may have been decided on the genetic level.[2]

Hormone theory: This is another popular theory also related to prenatal development. Research suggests that during the sexual development phase in the womb, the child is subjected to androgens or male hormones like testosterone that influence the sexuality of the child. A male child exposed to less testosterone during development may stand chances of being gay. Conversely, a female fetus exposed to more than normal testosterone may become a lesbian.[3]

Despite the many researches, no serious scientist today suggests that a simple cause-effect relationship applies to sexuality.[4] It is also probable that all of the above factors, in part, help influence the sexuality of a child. However, the bottom line is that the common denominator of all of these studies is that sexual orientation cannot be chosen and is not a mental or genetic disease; nor can one become homosexual by being molested by a member of the same sex as it is popularly believed. It is important for scientific purposes that the cause of homosexuality is understood, but it is more important that we treat people of less common orientations with dignity and respect.

4. Is homosexuality natural; is it seen anywhere else aside from human beings?

We need to first look at the definition of 'natural' itself. We tend to believe that whatever is the "norm" is natural, or what we are accustomed to seeing as common and usual is natural. One must understand that everything that exists in nature is natural. For instance, a person who has grown up in a cultural setting seeing only brown eyes, may find blue eyes unnatural because he/she hasn't seen them before. We must understand that 'unfamiliar' is different from 'unnatural'. Rig-Veda, one of the four canonical sacred texts of Hinduism, says 'Vikriti Evam Prakriti' which means that even anomalies that exist in nature are a part of nature.

Homosexual behaviour has been observed in 1500 animal species other than human beings and is not just limited to homosexual sexual behaviour but also pair bonding, where animals pair up for companionship for extended periods of time as mates. No species has been found in which homosexual behaviour has not been shown to exist, with the exception of species that never have sex at all, such as sea urchins and aphis. Moreover, a part of the animal kingdom is hermaphroditic, truly bisexual. For them, homosexuality is a redundant matter.[5]

Homosexuality has also been a part of ancient cultures worldwide, including India, and has never been held in a negative light. In fact, there are ancient temples with explicit carvings of homosexual sexual behaviour among similar depictions of heterosexual sex. Construction of Hindu temples in stone began around the sixth century of the Common Era. Construction reached a climax between the twelfth and the fourteenth century when the grand pagodas of eastern and southern India such as Puri and Tanjore came into being. On the walls and gateways of these magnificent structures we find a variety of images: gods, goddesses, demons, nymphs, sages, warriors, lovers, priests, monsters, dragons, plants and animals. Amongst scenes from epics and legends, one invariably finds erotic images including those that modern law deems unnatural and society considers obscene. Curiously enough, similar images also embellish prayer halls and cave temples of monastic orders such as Buddhism and Jainism built around the same time.[6] References to homosexuality and complex gender identities have also been part of our mythology and legends. Arguably, homosexuality was held in the same regard as heterosexuality in our culture during pre-British times.

But even if someone were to disagree with that notion, in any case, the modern man doesn't necessarily have to look at the behaviours of his ancestors as a moral sanction for his actions today. For example, regardless of the length of time and the social reasons at the time, the tradition of Sati cannot and should not be followed today, as it stands in clear violation of our modern values of gender equality and freedom.

It is fundamental that an idea ought to be considered valid not because of its time frame and how many people support it, but because it is in consonance with physical reality and human nature.

B.   Parent Related Queries

5.   Do parents play a role in the development of their child's sexual preference? Did we (parents) make some mistake in his/her childhood?   OR

6.   Had he told us when he was younger, could we have done something about it?

This question stems from another popular Freudian myth about homosexuality - that it's environmental and that an absent or overbearing parent can affect the child's orientation. Homosexuality is largely a result of natural predisposition of a person that cannot be altered or influenced by childhood experiences or acts. There are many case studies that have proved that even if the childhood environment is in support of or against homosexuality, it does not change the innate nature of the child.

A notable example of this is a tribe in New Guinea in which boys are removed from female company at a young age and encouraged to engage in homosexual acts with older boys as a rite of passage. These boys spend a good portion of their teens fellating (giving oral sex to) older boys and ingesting their semen as a means to make themselves 'virile' and to prepare themselves for adulthood, much like the ancient Greco-Roman practice. After entering adulthood, almost all of these men except about 5% continue to lead completely heterosexual lives despite the prolonged past experience of homosexual sex with other boys in the tribe. 5% - the percentage of men who continue to have same sex sexual encounters even into adulthood - is the general percentage of gay men in most populations. Another similar example of nature versus nurture is that of David Reimer, who was a Canadian man, born as a healthy male, but was sexually reassigned and raised as female after his penis was accidentally damaged during circumcision. Psychologist John Money oversaw the case and reported the reassignment as successful, and as evidence that gender identity is primarily learned. Academic sexologist Milton Diamond later reported that Reimer failed to identify as female since the age of 9 to 11, and that he began living as male at age 15. Reimer later went public with his story to discourage similar medical practices. He later committed suicide, owing to suffering years of severe depression, financial instability, and a troubled marriage.[7] As a parent, rather than dwelling on what you may have done wrong in the past, it might be better to focus on the present and how you can help your child lead a good life regardless of his orientation or gender identity and how you can be a better parent to them now, when they really need the affection and support from you.

7.   Is it because the child was molested in childhood?

There is no substantial evidence to link CSA i.e. **Child Sexual Abuse** and homosexuality in adults and all studies that have claimed this to be true have been discredited as anecdotal evidence by experts in the field of sexual research. As we have previously addressed, likely causes of homosexuality in humans are largely biological in nature, at the genetic level, which is probably why sexual orientation has been shown to not be influenced or changed at any later point in a person's life.

In 2007, the Ministry of Women and Child Development published the "Study on Child Abuse: India 2007." This study, that included more than 15,000 participants including children, young adults and stakeholders across 13 Indian states, found that 53.22% of children reported having faced sexual abuse. Among them, 52.94% were boys and 47.06% girls.[8] Now, if claims that child sexual abuse survivors end up becoming homosexual adults, we should have a homosexual population of more than 50% in both sexes, however, this is not the case. Percentage of homosexuals in any given population is not more than 5-10% of the entire population.

There are, of course, co-relations that exist between the two, but that does not mean that CSA is a cause for homosexuality. It may just be that children that are apparently homosexual may be easier targets for abuse. Also, since statistically 1 out of every 2 children in India are sexually abused, it is only logical that half of the homosexual population would have been exposed to sexual abuse of some sort as a child leading to this myth. Going back to the example of the New Guinea tribe given in the previous answer, we can further conclude that homosexual experiences in formative years, whether positive or negative, do not influence the innate sexual orientation of a person in his/her adult life.[9]

The American Psychiatric Association noted in a 2000 fact sheet on gay, lesbian and bisexual issues that "no specific psychosocial or family dynamic cause for homosexuality has been identified, including histories of childhood sexual abuse." The fact sheet goes on to say that sexual abuse does not appear to be any more prevalent among children who grow up and identify as gay, lesbian or bisexual than in children who grow up and identify as heterosexual.

This, however, does not mean that CSA does not affect the victim at all. CSA survivors have been known to struggle with issues of self-esteem, confidence in dealing with challenges of life and many other psychological issues but homosexual tendencies are not one of them. Such childhood experiences may give rise to a lot of fears and doubts, or influence the way we express our attraction and love, but not whom we love or who we get attracted towards.

8. Has the child's friends influenced him into being gay?

To quote the American gay-rights activist Harvey Milk, "How do you teach homosexuality? Is it like French? I was born of heterosexual parents, taught by heterosexual teachers, in a fiercely heterosexual society. So why then am I homosexual?"

This is true for most children, even yours. Most homosexual people grow up in mostly heterosexual environments at home, at schools and at workplaces. We are surrounded, largely, by heterosexual friends and family. Heterosexuality is implicit in our day-to-day interactions with everyone. For example, when anybody talks about their spouse or kids, it's simply meant to be understood that they are straight. Their heterosexuality is implicitly stated. Even popular culture like films and television, which is purported to be one of the most influential factors in our lives, is driven by heterosexual themes. So, how is it that homosexuals are not influenced by heterosexuality as easily? The truth is that you are as likely to become homosexual in homosexual company as you are to becoming tall just because you make friends with tall people! You may aspire to being taller but that will not change who you are at the biological level. It cannot be transferred as behaviour to another person simply by introducing them to it.

It is, in fact, much later in life and with their own evolution as gay and lesbian individuals, that people seek out other gay and lesbian friends. As social animals, it is important for us to find like-minded individuals and form groups. We see this all the time with religious groups or people sharing common interests. This is even more likely to happen when a person feels threatened, less accepted or disapproved of in their existing social circles, as is generally the case with gay people, since most cultures do not look kindly upon homosexuality. We have an inherent need to feel accepted by our peers and when this need is not fulfilled, we invariably seek out people who share our lifestyles or understand our struggles. It is no different than people with similar interests in music or books coming together and becoming friends. It is the inclination that affects the choice of friends one has, and not the other way around.

C.   Measure of Certainty

9.   How can one be so sure? Is it just in his or her mind (state of mind)? OR

10.   Is it a trick that your mind plays to feel different/special from the rest of the people?

For one to understand sexuality as a trick that the mind plays, one needs to first understand the mind. The mind is a dynamic process that arises from the brain. There needs to be a basis for a thing in the biology of the brain for the mind to act a certain way and specifically in sexuality. This is because we do not decide who we get attracted to, or for that matter what we get attracted to or like, be it art, people or the food we like. We may not particularly know the reason why, but our bodies know when we like something.

An example of a mind trick would be a mirage in a desert. Your brain fools you into believing that there is water where there is none, but when you reach that place, you do not continue to think that the water exists. You will automatically realise that it was a trick since the brain has a built-in mechanism to correct its own misinterpretation of the facts of reality. Calling homosexuality a trick of the mind does not serve any purpose in understanding it, since a lot of people across countries and cultures do experience this sexual orientation. Are they all being afflicted by this trick? Sexuality first arises at the biological level and is experienced at the mind level later. We first experience it as a biological desire, like for food or shelter, and then understand it at the cognitive level, which is why homosexuality can't be a trick of the mind.

The second belief that your child is acting out to seem special or rebellious is also not an adequate causation. Human beings wish to be special or noticed as a survival instinct since being noticed or considered special means that they would be provided for. If their providers -like parents-believe that their child is special, they will be more invested in their happiness. Human beings do have the desire to be perceived as special or different but only for the right reasons, homosexuality on the other hand is rarely considered an acceptable thing. So why would anyone decide to pretend to be homosexual and invite prejudice and hate into their lives, thereby reducing their chances at having a healthy social life? The reason why homosexual people want to come out is not to be considered special or stand out, but because they can't help doing so. They do so as a way to reach out and seek emotional support, because they are homosexual and the best thing one can do in such times is to provide them the support and love they need without judging their motives for doing so or being sceptical of their homosexual nature.

11. Is it because they have never had sex with the partner of the opposite sex? OR

12. Do you think you are gay because there are no women around to relieve you sexually? Do you think you can have sex with a woman if we arrange a prostitute?

Let us tackle this by first asking ourselves, 'Are we straight because we have not had sex with the same sex?' Of course, that's not the case. We know ourselves to be heterosexual from the time we hit puberty - our bodies changed and we started developing an attraction towards the opposite sex. No one had to tell us that, we experienced it by ourselves because our hearts, bodies, minds and genitals all told us what we like and desire. This process is no different for homosexuals. They've also had the same automatic sexual responses but only to the same sex. Pioneering researchers Masters and Johnson have conducted numerous studies on sexual orientation with huge sample sizes. In their book 'Sex and Human Loving' their research has found that a person with no sexual experience whatever may still consider himself or herself homosexual; also, many homosexuals are able to be aroused by heterosexual partners or heterosexual fantasies.

They do not develop these feelings in the absence of the opposite sex. You can understand this better with the example of situational homosexuality, where sometimes men and women do seek sex with the same sex in a temporary situation when they don't or can't meet the opposite sex for extended periods of time, like prisons, hostels, military etc. Many people change their sexual behaviour temporarily, depending on the situation or at different points in their life.[10] This is not the case with most homosexuals; their desire for the same sex remains unchanged, even with the choice of the opposite sex being available.

As for having sex with a prostitute of the opposite sex, you have to understand that if they had wanted it for themselves, they would've sought it on their own without you having to arrange it for them. The other argument that one presents is that perhaps after trying sex with the opposite sex, they would lose interest in same sex sexual acts and become heterosexuals. There are a lot of gay men who have been forced into marriage by their parents with this same logic and most married gay people continue to seek sex with the same sex after they're married, or at least still feel attraction even if they suppress the urges to act on them. You cannot change what they desire by giving them something that they never had a desire for in the first place. The fact that they may or may not be able to perform sexually within the marriage does not change their innate orientation.

This also does a great deal of damage to their self-esteem when you repeatedly tell them that they are so unacceptable to you that you would go to any lengths to change their orientation instead of trying to understand or accept it. If you have doubts about what your child desires, you only have to ask them to find out. Talk to your child and try to understand what they feel about the same sex or opposite sex, you are bound to realise that there is nothing different about what your child experiences in sex, love and attraction than you do, with the exception of the gender or sex of whom they desire.

D.   Is change possible?

13.   Do we know of any therapy that can change sexual orientation?

In 1990, the American Psychological Association [APA] stated that scientific evidence shows that reparative therapy does not work and that it can do more harm than good.[11] Changing one's orientation does not correspond with changing one's behaviour. To change one's orientation would require altering one's emotional, romantic and sexual feelings, and reconstructing one's self-concept and self-identity. Furthermore, the APA pointed out that therapists who undertake this kind of therapy usually come from organisations with an ideological perspective against homosexuality. The APA has specifically stated that "orientation reparative therapy" (conversion therapy) is not recognized as a valid form of therapy.

Many of the claims made by ex-gay organisations of having successfully 'converted' gay and lesbian people into heterosexuals have been found to be short-lived as most of the people going through such traumatic forms of therapy have reverted to a homosexual lifestyle after suppressing their innate desires for a brief period of time where they may have become behaviourally heterosexual, but remained attracted to the same sex.

We must understand that you cannot cure something that is not an illness to begin with. Can one be 'cured' of the colour of their eyes? Or can they be 'treated' for their race? Invariably, every credible psychologist, psychiatrist and mental health professional has agreed that homosexuality is not an illness, mental disorder or emotional problem.

Wellbeing and emotional stability are defined as an individual's ability to live a fully functional life. Homosexuality, by itself, does not cause a person to stop functioning as a productive human being, but the abuse and rejection by peers or family, that comes with being a homosexual person, can cause a great deal of emotional trauma and suffering. There is ample evidence that societal prejudice causes significant medical, psychological and other harms to LGBT people.

There is plenty of empirical evidence to say that more than not having a cure, homosexuality does not 'need' a cure. And the best thing that parents and guardians of homosexual children can do to ensure the mental and physical well-being of their children is to ensure the child is not made to feel unaccepted or rejected for his sexual orientation.

E.   Religion

14.   Can my son believe in God and still be gay?

There is absolutely no connection between belief in God and being gay, or for that matter, being a good human being. There are just as many atheists who are straight, and many fundamental terrorist groups are also known for their belief in their God. Would you consider terrorists as pillars of morally upright behaviour merely on the basis of their religious beliefs?

The belief in God is an extremely personal experience in a human being's life. If one defines their God as someone who judges them on the basis of what they eat or who they love, then perhaps one might not be able to reconcile themselves with their beliefs; but if one defines their God as an internal driving force or a source of strength that one finds within themselves, then it wouldn't be a challenge for one to be a homosexual and still believe in God.

15. Wouldn't human society end if everyone were gay? Isn't sex meant for procreation?

This is a very common fear that many people have but you must understand that homosexuality is not chosen. It is a natural disposition that has been shown to occur in 5 to 10 % of any human population and also in the animal kingdom. The remaining population is heterosexual and will continue to be so. And even if a majority of the population were to be homosexual, it doesn't have to mean that the human population has to end. Many homosexual couples today have the option of choosing surrogacy or artificial insemination to have children. You also have gay and lesbian couples coming together and having children together.

The acceptance of homosexuals in society will not cause the rest of the population to change their orientation; it would only make lives of homosexuals easier. In fact, if homosexuals were given adoption rights after due process, it would help them start their own families, giving caring homes to many orphans in the process.

As for sex as a means for procreation, do we really believe that human beings have sex solely to produce offspring? Yes, that is a major reason why sex is important to human beings, but sex is also a means of being physically intimate with a person one loves, as well as for recreation. If sex was solely a means to reproduce, then why would we need inventions like condoms and birth control pills? Do heterosexuals only have sex when the intention is to produce children?

Having kids is an extremely personal choice that an individual or a couple makes after careful deliberation, and many may choose to not have a child. If impotent people or straight couples that do not wish to have children are not forbidden from having sex, then there is no reason why homosexuals should not have the liberty of doing the same.

F.   Homosexuality and Society

16.   Is homosexuality a threat to social and moral fabric of a country?

We first need to analyse the word 'threat'. A threat is a menace that may restrain a person's freedom, or compromise the political security of a country. The social and moral fabric of a country may only be under threat if the acceptance of homosexuality would take from you, your freedom to choose or act the way you desire. This is not the case; in fact, acceptance of homosexuality by society only allows homosexuals to experience the same sort of freedom that heterosexuals have been enjoying. The freedom to choose to be with the one they love and to act on those feelings.

If gay people had the right to marry, it would only mean that they would not be stopped from marrying someone they love, it does not mean the rest of the population would be forced into homosexual marriages.

Imagine, if tomorrow the government were to take away your right to practice your religion and not others'. Would you not feel that the moral or social fabric is under threat? So, it is precisely the taking away of equal rights from the people, that is a threat to the country and its social and moral fabric.

17.   Are most Paedophile [a person who is sexually attracted to children] men gay?

Members of disliked minority groups are often stereotyped as representing a danger to the most vulnerable members of the society. For example, Jews in the Middle Ages were accused of murdering Christian babies in ritual sacrifices. Many black men in the United States were often lynched after being falsely accused of raping white women. In a similar fashion, gay people have often been portrayed as a threat to children. Back in 1977 in America, when Anita Bryant campaigned successfully to repeal a Dade County ordinance prohibiting anti-gay discrimination, she named her organization "Save Our Children," and warned, "A particularly deviant-minded teacher could sexually molest children".[12]

The fact, however, is that Paedophilia has absolutely nothing to do with sexuality. Paedophiles can be both heterosexual as well as homosexual. It is a psychiatric disorder in adults, typically characterized by a primary or exclusive sexual interest toward prepubescent children; this interest can be either towards young boys or girls and generally has little to do with the orientation of the perpetrator. According to research, in most cases of child sexual abuse, the perpetrator is most likely to be a man and 90% of convicted paedophiles have generally no interest in adult males and identify as heterosexuals; molestation of young girls by adult women is next to none.

Another problem arises because of terminology; sexual abuse of male children by adult men is often referred to as "homosexual molestation." The adjective "homosexual" (or "heterosexual" when a man abuses a female child) refers to the victim's gender in relation to that of the perpetrator. Unfortunately, people sometimes mistakenly interpret it as referring to the perpetrator's sexual orientation. It is often found that paedophiles generally don't care about the gender of the victim as much as they care about their age. Sexual abuse isn't about sexual attraction; the perpetrators are motivated more by power and control, not by sexual desire. Paedophilia isn't about gay or straight or bisexual. Abusers abuse those they have access to. A high number of boys are molested, not because molesters are disproportionately gay or bi, but because arguably, men typically have more access to boys than to girls.

We must understand that co-relating paedophilia to homosexuality because most victims are boys, is the same as perhaps co-relating heterosexuality and rape of women.

[From 'The Pink Booklet']

References

[1] "National Geographic Explains the Biology of Homosexuality." YouTube. YouTube, 04 Feb. 2009. Web. 13 Apr. 2013.

[2] Simon LeVay. Salk Institute for Biological Studies, San Diego, CA 92186. Web. *http://www.sciencemag.org/content/253/5023/1034*. 30 August 1991.

[3] Brook, Charles, Gerard S. Conway, and Melissa Hines. "Androgen and Psychosexual Development: Core Gender Identity, Sexual Orientation, and Recalled Childhood Gender Role Behavior in Women and Men with Congenital Adrenal Hyperplasia (CAH)." Journal of Sex Research 41.1 (2004): 75-81. Online.

[4] 'Homosexuality and Bisexuality'. Sex and Human Loving. William Masters, Virginia Johnson, Robert Kolodny. Book. ISBN 81-7224-041-4.

[5] '1,500 animal species practice homosexuality'. October 23, 2006 at 4:28 PM *http://www.news-medical.net/news/2006/10/23/20718.aspx.*

[6] Devdutt Patnaik. Mythologist and Historian. *http://devdutt.com/blog/did-homosexuality-exist-in-ancient-india.html.* June 30, 2009.

[7] Colapinto, J (2001). As Nature Made Him: The Boy Who Was Raised as a Girl. Harper Perennial. ISBN 0-06-092959-6. Revised in 2006.

[8] "Study on Child Abuse: India 2007" (PDF). Published by the Government of India, (Ministry of Women and Child Development). *http://wcd.nic.in/childabuse.pdf.*

[9] The Sambia: ritual, sexuality, and change in Papua New Guinea. Gilbert H. Herdt. Book.

[10] Rosario, M., Schrimshaw, E., Hunter, J., & Braun, L. (2006, February). Sexual identity development among lesbian, gay, and bisexual youths: Consistency and change over time. Journal of Sex Research, 43(1), 46–58. Retrieved February 8, 2011.

[11] Facts Regarding "Reparative Therapy". Web. http://community.pflag.org/page.aspx?pid=503.

[12] "Facts About Homosexuality and Child Molestation". Web. *http://psychology.ucdavis.edu/rainbow/html/facts_molestation.html.*

LGBTI Perspectives: Defamatory Language and Terms to Avoid

Defamatory Language:

"fag," "faggot," "dyke," "homo," "sodomite," and similar epithets

The criteria for using these derogatory terms should be the same as those applied to vulgar epithets used to target other groups: they should not be used except in a direct quote that reveals the bias of the person quoted.

"deviant," "disordered," "dysfunctional," "diseased," "perverted," "destructive" and similar descriptions

The notion that being LGBTQ is a psychological disorder was discredited by the American Psychological Association and the American Psychiatric Association in the 1970s. Today, words such as "deviant," "diseased" and "disordered" often are used to portray LGBTQ people as less than human, mentally ill, or as a danger to society. Words such as these should be avoided in stories about the LGBTQ community. If they must be used, they should be quoted directly in a way that clearly reveals the bias of the person being quoted.

Associating LGBTQ people with pedophilia, child abuse, sexual abuse, bestiality, bigamy, polygamy, adultery and/or incest

Being LGBTQ is neither synonymous with, nor indicative of, any tendency toward pedophilia, child abuse, sexual abuse, bestiality, bigamy, polygamy, adultery and/or incest. Such claims, innuendoes and associations often are used to insinuate that LGBTQ people pose a threat to society, to families, and to children in particular. Such assertions and insinuations are defamatory and should be avoided.

Terms to Avoid

Terms To Avoid (Deemed Offensive)[1]	Terms To Use (Preferred)
"homosexual"	"gay" (adj.); "gay man" or "lesbian" (n.); "gay person/people"
"homosexual relations/relationship," "homosexual couple," "homosexual sex,"etc.	"relationship," "couple" (or, if necessary, "gay couple"), "sex,"etc.
"sexual preference"	"sexual orientation" or "orientation"
"special rights"	"equal rights" or "equal protection"
"transgenders," "a transgender"	"transgender people", "a transgender person"
"transgendered"	"transgender"
"sex change," "pre-operative," "post-operative	"transition"
"biologically male," "biologically female," "genetically male," "genetically female," "born a man," "born a woman" Defamatory: "tranny," "she-male," "he/she," "it,""shim"	"assigned male at birth," "assigned female at birth" or "designated male at birth," "designated female at birth"
"transgenderism"	"being transgender"
Referring all Transgender people as Kinnar, Aravani and Hijras etc.	Not All Transgender people are Hijras, Transgender is a gender identity whereas Indigenous Gender Minorities identities refers to the sociocultural communities.
Hermaphrodite people (Highly offensive)	Intersex person or people
Intersex people are transgender people	Intersex people are not transgender people

End Notes

[1] Excerpted Resources from GLAAD Media Website: *https://www.glaad.org/ reference/lgbtq*

CHAPTER - 4

Ecumenical Milestones, Inclusive Churches: The Christian Response

Ecumenical Milestones, Inclusive Churches: The Christian Response

Documenting Christian Perspectives and Initiatives on Human Sexuality and Gender Diversity

Philip Kuruvilla

Introduction

Never before have the sexual ethics of our culture been faced with such a confusing array of material. Divorce is increasing; co-habitation before – or instead of – marriage, is fast becoming the norm in Indian metros; new technologies have made pornography immediately accessible to young adolescents through the ubiquitous cell phone and the internet; consensual sex between two heterosexual adults is common, while consensual sex between two homosexuals was [temporarily] decriminalized. The once inconceivable notion of same-sex "marriage" is now recognized by law in a growing number of [albeit, western] countries. What should be our response to the LGBTIQ Communities and the issues that trouble them? The need for a clear voice from the 'Mother' Church in the areas of human sexuality and gender diversity is critical, both for the health of our own faith communities, and for our faithful witness to the world. This voice must not be homophobic or transphobic, but rather must use Jesus' responses to the 'sinners' of his day as its touchstone.

In India, the NCCI has been in the vanguard of the Church's response to critical issues. NCCI took up the mantle of guiding the Churches through the HIV-AIDS pandemic, making Member Churches aware of the issues involved, as far back as 2003. Today the NCCI's ESHA program is exclusively meant for bringing Member Churches to a better understanding of a topic they have stayed clear from so far, viz., human sexuality and gender diversity. This article attempts to document the history of both the WCC and the NCCI's contributions to assist churches to focus on these issues, in the hope that they will go beyond the traditional ideas of mission to a place where the wellbeing of *all* humans on this earth become important enough; where the issues around human sexuality and the LGBTI are re-examined in the light of the latest scientific, medical and empirical discoveries in the field. To ask whether, instead of homophobic or transphobic responses, we could deal with them with understanding, with tolerance? Could we give them 'space' to be part of God's community - without judgment, without stigma, without discrimination? Could we remove them from the 'other' category, and instead realize 'they' are part of 'us'?

A.   The International Christian Community's Response to the issues of the LGBTI

The World Council of Churches' [WCC] response- a chronological journey

It would be correct to start with the 'fountainhead' - the WCC- and its thrust on this area. **From New Delhi to Canberra**: The survey carried out by Birgitta Larsson[1] best explains how the WCC dealt with issues of human sexuality in the period between the New Delhi Assembly (1961) and the Canberra Assembly (1991). The New Delhi Assembly stated: '*The churches have to discover what positions and actions to take in regard to sex relations* *before and after marriage; illegitimacy; in some cultures polygamy or concubinage as a social system sanctioned by law and customs. All this, and much else, forces the churches to re-examine their teaching, preaching and pastoral care and their witness and service to society'.*

From Canberra to Harare,[2] **(1991-1998),** the issue of homosexuality progressively took centre stage. A small consultation in 1997 in Geneva underlined that issues of human sexuality were already on the agenda of many of the member churches, and that the different approaches and positions taken posed serious new challenges to the quest for the visible unity of the church. At the Harare Assembly, the Programme Guidelines Committee recommended to the Assembly a shift of focus -from sexual orientation to human sexuality - that would address issues of personal and interpersonal ethics. The Assembly further urged the WCC *"to engage in a study of human sexuality in all of its diversity, to be made available for member churches".* The mandate of the Assembly was not to start a programme, but to "provide space" through which the member churches were enabled to discuss the difficult issues related to human sexuality.

The **Assembly in Porto Alegre**[3] **[2006]** was devoid of direct references to the issues of sexuality – though the issues of HIV and AIDS and Gender did make their mark. **Busan** [4]**[2013]** also held much promise but did not take any bold decisions or steps. Even now WCC keeps the issue on low key as it has proved to be an emotional and divisive subject. However, a more recent publication from them is a book titled: *"Created in God's Image: From Hegemony to Partnership"*[5]. It is a church manual on Men as Partners, and has a creative 'Module' on Sexuality, that 'invites participants to consciously examine the processes of socialisation' of males.

The Churches' Response to Human Sexuality

Within Christianity there are a variety of views on the issues around human sexuality, ranging from acceptance to outright condemnation or labeling some people as 'sinful'. However, within any particular denomination it will be seen that individuals and groups hold differing views, and not all members of that denomination necessarily support their church's stand on the matter -if there is one. To get a better picture, we can examine the responses of some churches on this issue, while accepting that they may not be truly representative.

Internationally, the Churches' Response

I.   Anglican

The second official response to this issue was from the **Lambeth Conference[6] in 1988**, where they resolved: *This Conference: 1. Reaffirms the statement of the Lambeth Conference of 1978 on homosexuality, recognising the continuing need in the next decade for "deep and dispassionate study of the question of homosexuality, which would take seriously both the teaching of Scripture and the results of scientific and medical research." 2. Urges such study and reflection to take account of biological, genetic and psychological research being undertaken by other agencies, and the socio-cultural factors that lead to the different attitudes in the provinces of our Communion. 3. Calls each province to reassess, in the light of such study and because of our concern for human rights, its care for and attitude towards persons of homosexual orientation.*

In the 1998 Synod[7] they also stated that: This Conference:

- *recognises that there are among us persons who experience themselves as having a homosexual orientation. Many of these are members of the Church and are seeking the pastoral care, moral direction of the Church, and God's transforming power for the living of their lives and the ordering of relationships. We commit ourselves to listen to the experience of homosexual persons and we wish to assure them that they are loved by God and that all baptised, believing and faithful persons, regardless of sexual orientation, are full members of the Body of Christ;*

- *while rejecting homosexual practice as incompatible with Scripture, calls on all our people to minister pastorally and sensitively to all irrespective of sexual orientation and to condemn irrational fear of homosexuals, violence within marriage and any trivialisation and commercialisation of sex;*

- *cannot advise the legitimising or blessing of same sex unions nor ordaining those involved in same gender unions;*

In February 2007 a change is noted- the Anglican General Synod[8] debated on Lesbian and Gay Christians and amended the motion, and carried in the last part, *(d)* that this Synod:

> *affirms that homosexual orientation in itself is no bar to a faithful Christian life or to full participation in lay and ordained ministry in the Church and acknowledge the importance of lesbian and gay members of the Church of England participating in the listening process as full members of the Church.'*

In July 2017, the Church of England's ruling body voted overwhelming in favour of welcoming transgender people in parish churches. The vote came after bishops overwhelmingly backed a motion calling for a ban on unethical 'conversion therapy' for gays.[9]

II. Evangelical Christians

Although traditionally Evangelical Christians have been very clear in their non-acceptance of the LGTB community, more recently there are some signs of a softer stance. [See the study, "How the Messy Middle Finds a Voice: Evangelicals and Structured Ambivalence towards Gays and Lesbians,"[10] which analyzed national data from the 2010 Baylor Religion Survey, conducted by Gallup.]. In 2015, *Time* [11] published a piece entitled, "How Evangelicals Are Changing Their Minds on Gay Marriage."The article alleges: *'In public, so many churches and pastors are afraid to talk about the generational and societal shifts happening. But behind the scenes, it's a whole different game. Support for gay marriage across all age groups of white evangelicals has increased by double digits over the past decade, according to the Public Religion Research Institute, and the fastest change can be found among younger evangelicals — their support for gay marriage jumped from 20% in 2003 to 42% in 2014'.*

On August 30, 2017, 150 prominent evangelical figures joined together to sign a document taking direct aim at the lesbian, gay, bisexual, transgender and queer (LGTBQ) communities. They affirmed what signatories saw as traditional, "biblical" marriage and sexual ethics: between one married man and one married woman.The 14-article document, dubbed the "Nashville Statement,"[12] was released by the Council on Biblical Manhood and Womanhood (CBMW), focusing primarily on issues of gender and same-sex marriage. The document followed the Southern Baptist

Conference's Ethics and Religious Liberty Commission's (ERLC) Annual Conference in Nashville.

A theologically liberal coalition quickly issued a counter-statement to the Nashville document. Going under the name "Christians United," [13] the leftist response reverses the historic Christian understanding of homosexuality as a sin and replaces it with the "sin of exclusion," of which it calls on the Church of Jesus Christ" to repent. The leftist "Christians United" statement is being promoted by a host of pro-LGBT groups, including the well-funded LGBTQ lobby Human Rights Campaign, which slammed the evangelical Nashville Statement as a "vicious attack on LGBTQ people."

III.   The Roman Catholic

One sees fluctuations in the Roman Catholic Church position. Gossip was swirling around the Vatican at the time of Pope Benedict's abdication[14] that he was resigning because a "gay scandal" was about to break which would implicate high ranking members of the curia. The present Pope Francis had spoken openly about a "gay lobby." The Huffington Post[15] reports his comments in a meeting with members of the Latin American Caribbean Confederation of Religious Men and Women:*"Yes, it is difficult. In the curia there are holy people, truly holy people. But there is also a current of corruption, also there is… they speak of a 'Gay Lobby' and that is true, it is there… we will have to see what we can do…".* However, the Vatican Synod of Bishops in October 2014 approved a final document *'Relatio Synodi"*[16] which gives greater acceptance to gays: *'men and women with homosexual tendencies must be accepted with respect and delicacy'*. A statement by Pope Francis[17], in July 2014, in which he said: *"If someone is gay and seeks the Lord and has good will, who am I to judge?"* is being widely discussed and even appreciated.

IV.   NCCI's Intervention in India in the field of Human Sexuality and Gender Identity

When looking at the Indian Church's response in these fields, it would be necessary to look at NCCI's involvement and interventions. NCCI has been working in the field of human sexuality since the early 2000's. After the first intervention came the Statement of the 1st Study Institute on human sexuality in June, 2001, in Ooty, TN. Here the small gathering made some affirmations and a Statement was published. The second intervention was at the 2nd Study Institute on human sexuality, which took place in September, 2003, co-organized by Student Christian Movement of India (SCMI), in Bangalore. Here the delegates brought forth 'An Epistle on Human Sexuality to the Churches in India'[18][see Chapter 5 for full details].

On 18th July, 2009, NCCI organized an interfaith response to the Delhi High Court Judgment of 2nd July, 2009, by which Article 377 was struck down and consensual homosexual activities were decriminalized. The Indian Express[19] report, 'Indian Faith-Based Organisation's Response to Human Sexuality' on 18th July, 2009 in New Delhi said, 'Among those who spoke on the issue were Mujtaba Farooq, secretary of the Jamaat-e-Islami Hind, Very Rev M.S. Skaria, Orthodox Church, Sd Bhupinder Singh, Delhi Sikh Gurudwara Prabhandak Committee, and Anuradha Mukherji of NAZ India, [the petitioners who fought against the almost 150-year-old Article 377 in the Delhi High Court]. Although the participants showed more of an accommodative attitude, the discussion brought to the fore friction between the ideologies of the panelists as far as homosexuality was concerned'.

Then NCCI organized a Study and Public Debate: 'Indian Church and Repealing of Sec.377 of IPC' on 28th July, 2009. This was held at ICSA, Chennai. 110 participants from several member churches, related agencies, theological seminaries and the LGBT community came together for a one-day study and reflection. Although there was no uniform consensus, it was the first time all spectrums of the church came together to have an open discussion on this topic.

The fifth meeting – the third to be held in the same year - was the 'Theological Roundtable on the Churches' Response to Human Sexuality', in Kolkata, on 5th and 6th December, 2009. Here, the National Council of Churches in India, in collaboration with the Presbyterian Church of India, the Student Christian Movement of India and the Senate Centre for Extension for Pastoral Theological Research (SCEPTRE) organized in Kolkata a Theological Roundtable on the theme 'Churches' Response to Human Sexuality'. In their "Message to the Indian Christian Communities"[20], they boldly called on the NCCI member churches to initiate an in-depth study of human sexuality, and on theological colleges to integrate issues of human sexuality into theological and ministerial formation. They affirmed:

- *We recognize that there are people with different sexual orientations....We consider the Delhi High Court verdict to "decriminalize consensual sexual acts of adults in private" upholding the fundamental constitutional and human rights to privacy and the life of dignity and non-discrimination of all citizens as a positive step.*

- *We believe that the Church as 'Just and Inclusive Community' is called to become a community without walls to reach out to people who are stigmatized and demonized, and be a listening community to understand their pains, desires, and hopes.*

- *We envision Church as a sanctuary to the ostracized who thirst for understanding, friendship, love, compassion and solidarity, and to join in their struggles to live out their God given lives. So we appeal to the Christian communities to sojourn with sexual minorities and their families without prejudice and discrimination, to provide them ministries of love, compassionate care, and justice.*

The *Commission on Justice, Peace and Creation* of NCCI was mandated in September 2009 to study the issues related to Human Sexuality in the light of Delhi High Court's verdict to repeal the IPC Sec.377. It came up with "*An Ecumenical Document on Human Sexuality*"[21] which passed through many turbulent stages – including where member churches threatened to withdraw their membership if NCCI pursued this course - and was finally adopted by the General Assembly of the NCCI on 16th September, 2011, as a 'Document', and not a "Policy on Human Sexuality," as was originally intended [see Chapter 5 for full details of the Document]. This was followed by an NCCI Bible Study Workshop in 2011, themed "*Daring to study scriptures publically and sensually*", and attended by about 40 young men and women, some of whom were theological students. The result was a publication by NCCI, "*Public and Sensual: Exploring Solution: Bible Studies on Human Sexuality.*"[22] Subsequently, during the Centenary celebrations of the NCCI in Nagpur, in 2014, a National Ecumenical Forum of Gender and Sexual

Minorities was created by NCCI to voice the pains and needs of the LGBTI communities in India.

It is important to know the background. The Indian churches awakened to the issue of homosexuality in 2009 when a Bench of Delhi High Court struck down the provision of Section 377 of the IPC which criminalized consensual sexual acts of adults in private. It declared in a 105-page judgment on July 2, 2009: *"In our view, Indian constitutional law does not permit the statutory criminal law to be held captive by the popular misconception of who LGBTs are. It cannot be forgotten that discrimination is the antithesis of equality and that it is the recognition of equality which will foster dignity of every individual"* [23]. With this declaration a 148-year old law that inclined many people in the country to regard same-sex relationships as illegitimate came to an end - under the old law homosexual acts were punishable by a 10-year prison sentence. This judgment had a wide range of responses, for and against, and the majority of those who opposed it were faith leaders. On 11 December, 2013, however, the Supreme Court of India set aside the 2009 judgment given by the Delhi High Court, thus ruling homosexuality once again to be a criminal offence. It is in this backdrop that the ESHA programs took place.

NCCI's ESHA Program

NCCI started its work among People Living with HIV and AIDS [PLWA's] from 2003, when the 'India Watch Desk' began its journey, with this writer as its Executive Secretary. However the *'Ecumenical Solidarity on HIV and AIDS'* [**ESHA**] program of NCCI only began among NCCI's member churches in 2009, and went on till 2015. In the process it brought out several supportive publications, including a 'HIV/AIDS: a *Handbook for the Church in India'[2004],* a *'Policy on HIV/AIDS: a Guide to the Churches in India'* [2010], and *"Positive Readings: Biblical Reflections"* [2011]. In 2015, '**ESHA**' – now a name and not an acronym - having come face to face with the issues of human sexuality and gender diversity, decided to focus on sexual minorities, and the Indian Churches and Theological Colleges were brought into the ambit of the programs of ESHA. This perfectly coincided with the Government of India's focus on justice issues faced by the LGBTI community, and the Transgender Persons (Protection of Rights) Bill 2016, which gave

ESHA a chance to offer even the recalcitrant churches, a new message of greater inclusivity.

The Indian Churches' Response

Traditionally, Indian culture does not exude homo or trans-phobia. Roots of sexuality issues go back to ancient Hindu scriptural writings and can be seen in the carvings of some ancient temples. However, from the modern faith leader's 'non- response' in India, it would seem that the issue was a 'western' one- and not affecting the Indian faith communities. NGO's and Gay Rights activists in this country have made it evident that the issue cannot be glossed over- it is touching our homes and communities, with no barrier of faith. Earlier, after an initial hesitation, the Indian Churches, spearheaded by NCCI, stepped in to deal boldly with HIV and AIDS, and since 2004, they gave leadership even to other faiths on how to remove stigma and discrimination towards PLHIV through their Faith Communities. This work among 'high- risk' communities and Key Affected Populations [KAP]'s automatically led them face to face with the LGBTIQ people and the issues that divided *them* from the various faith communities, but Christianity in particular. Some Churches had already started working with these issues, but ESHA's support over the last 3 years has taken them to a deeper level of engagement. [For a more detailed response of the Indian Churches and the Theological Colleges, see Chapter 4].

Conclusion

The Churches —both internationally and in India - are still not clear on their stand, and diverse voices are being heard, some of them more shrill and homophobic than others. However a welcome emerging trend sees more inclusive language, a greater acceptance of the LGTBI community, and a call for a more humane response. In India, starting with the Theological Colleges, this is finding its echo in the Churches, and the NCCI's ESHA program has played a stellar role in bringing this about. It is more and more evident that this issue is not a 'western' or 'foreign' malaise - one that will go away if we ignore it - but one very deeply embedded within the Indian ethos, and therefore in the Indian Church's psyche as well, which is probably why there are such highly emotional responses. We have come a long way from 2001, and it is evident that it is the *kairos* moment for Christians to bring these issues 'out of the closet', to re-read the Bible and look within each church's traditions for more Christ-like responses. Those with diverse sexual orientations [PDSO's] are human beings who need some 'sacred space' and a greater degree of pastoral understanding. In the midst of all the phobia and confusion, Christians and Churches have to listen to the voices of pain and anguish, understand the issues, and respond, while enlightened Church Leaders need to speak out. The need of the hour is for a loving, more inclusive response. Christ would expect no less.

End Notes

[1] Birgitta Larsson, "A Quest for Clarity". *The Ecumenical Review*, Vol. 50/1, (WCC Publications, Geneva. 1998).

[2] WCC Archives: GEN 14: Aide Memoire, World Council of Churches and Human Sexuality

[3] WCC Archives

[4] Ibid

[5] *"Created in God's Image: From Hegemony to Partnership"*:Edited by Philip Peacock and Patricia Sheerattan-Bisnauth [WCRC and WCC: 2010:Geneva]

[6] Lambeth Conference Resolutions Archive: Index of Resolutions from 1988: Resolution 64-Human Rights for Those of Homosexual Orientation

[7] Lambeth Conference Resolutions Archive: Index of Resolutions from 1998: Section I.10 - Human Sexuality

[8] https://www.churchofengland.org/our-views/marriage,-family-and-sexuality-issues/human-sexuality/lesbian-and-gay-christians,-general-synod-debate-2007.asp

[9] http://www.independent.co.uk/news/uk/home-news/church-of-england-bishops-ban-gay-conversion-therapy-pride-2016-lgbt-ri

[10] https://www.baylor.edu/mediacommunications/news.php?action=story&story=131931

[11] http://time.com/3669024/evangelicals-gay-marriage/

[12] https://www.vox.com/identities/2017/8/31/16226088/evangelical-leaders-signed-sexuality-church-nashville-statement

[13] https://www.lifesitenews.com/news/pro-gay-religious-left-condemns-toxic-evangelical-nashville-statement-defen

14 https://www.theguardian.com/world/2013/feb/21/pope-retired-amid-gay-bishop-blackmail-inquiry

15 http://www.huffingtonpost.com/2013/06/11/pope-francis-gay-lobby_n_3420244.html

16 http://www.sify.com/news/vatican-approves-document-accepting-gays-divorced-news-others-oktfueggidjja.html

17 http://www.catholicherald.co.uk/news/2013/07/29/if-a-gay-person-seeks-god-who-am-i-to-judge-him-says-pope/

18 The only extant copy of the 'Epistle' remains available with NCCI only in a draft form. It is reprinted in NCCI Review, June, 2015

19 'Church Panel organises discussion on Sec 377': Sukalp Sharma :Indian Express: New Delhi: July 19th, 2009

20 'An Ecumenical Document on Human Sexuality :NCCI: Nagpur: 2012. P. 6-8

21 *An Ecumenical Document on Human Sexuality: NCCI: Nagpur: 2012. P. 1-4*

22 *"Public and Sensual: Exploring Solution: Bible Studies on Human Sexuality"* Editor: Christopher Rajkumar. [NCCI: Nagpur: 2012].

23 http://www.infochangeindia.org/environment/37-human-rights/news/7817-gay-sex-not-criminal-delhi-high-court

Christianity, Sexual Diversity and Access to Health Services [In Asia-Pacific countries]

Joseph N. Goh

Abrahamic religions such as Islam and Christianity often condemn same-sex behaviour and gender non-conformity. This kind of stigma can and does create a sense of low self-esteem among men who have sex with men (MSM) and transgender people (TG). This, in turn, can prevent them from protecting themselves from the risks related to unsafe sexual behaviour as well as accessing available health services. APCOM took up the responsibility of coordinating an empowering response to such faith-based stigma and discrimination that is head-on and strategic. A Faith in Action Working Group was formed in 2010. The Working Group organised a satellite session at the 10th ICAAP in Busan, South Korea, in 2011, comprising MSM and transgender activists working with faith issues from the region and various key experts to discuss issues of faith, sexual diversity, impact on stigma and discrimination, and access to health. The session also formulated strategies to overcome such problems.

Mainstream, traditional and conservative forms of institutional and popular Christianity in Asia-Pacific countries such as Singapore, the Philippines, India, Hong Kong and Tonga are often disapproving of sexual diversity and gender variance. People who attempt to access HIV preventive measures are often held in suspicion and regarded as indulging in 'sin' (Wanje 2012). This becomes particularly problematic for gender variant and sexually diverse people who are often automatically connected to HIV and AIDS. Furthermore, People Living with HIV (PLHIV) are frequently perceived as being punished for their 'sin' (Pieters 1994).

To make the situation worse, sex between men is criminalised under specific state laws in countries such as Singapore (Government of Singapore 2008) and Tonga (Bureau of Democracy, Human Rights, and Labor 2011). India is in the process of reconsidering its sodomy laws (The Times of India: 2016). Countries such as Sri Lanka have reported a strong correlation between the criminalisation of MSM and the spread of HIV (Cooper 2016). While such laws do not, or no longer, exist in countries such as the Philippines or Hong Kong (P. C. W. Chan 2008; Mosbergen 2015), political, socio-cultural and religious forms of discrimination, exclusion and violence towards gender variant and sexually diverse people continue to exist. Christianity finds convenient allies through such policies and attitudes.

This article examines the attitudes of institutional and popular Christianity towards MSM, TG and HIV, the impact of such attitudes towards MSM and TG in relation to HIV prevention and treatment, and Christian teachings and strategies that affirm MSM, TG and PLHIV.

Although many institutional and popular forms of Christianity condemn the sexual identities and behaviours of MSM, TG and PLHIV (ABC News 2003; Tan 2014), it is inaccurate to say that Christianity is their enemy as a whole. Recent history shows the efforts of numerous Christian clergypersons and laity who challenge specific representations of Christianity. They offer alternative ways of understanding Christianity that can offer crucial support and affirmation to MSM, TG, and those living with

HIV. This brief web and literature review considers these complex issues from four perspectives: (i) singular interpretations of biblical passages; (ii) 'spiritualistic dualism' (the separation of body from soul); (iii) heteronormative theologies and ethics; and (iv) divine punishment.

i.   Singular Interpretations of Biblical Passages

The Bible is often used against sexually diverse and gender variant people based on specific interpretations of biblical passages. Hence, the Bible becomes 'proof' of the 'sinfulness' of sexual diversity and gender variance. Furthermore, HIV is regarded as the consequence of such 'abnormalities'. The act of using the Bible for this purpose is called 'textual harassment' (Tolbert 2000, vii) or 'bible bashing' (West 2010a). The parts of the Bible that are used for this purpose are called 'clobber passages' (West 2010b). These interpretations create feelings of guilt among many MSM and TG. This, in turn, sends them 'underground' with feelings of deep shame. These interpretations also foster a feeling among MSM and TG that they are going against God and the Bible. They feel that being tested for HIV further compounds their 'sinfulness' and that they 'deserve' to be infected with HIV because of their gender and sexual identities. In response, some Christians have come up with alternative ways of understanding and interpreting the Bible. For instance, scripture scholars suggest that Genesis 19:1-28 can be interpreted as pederasty (the initiation of younger men by older men which includes sexual activity between them), sexual violence, pride and lack of hospitality to strangers (Boswell 1981; Scroggs 1983). Leviticus 18:22 and 20:13 may be discussing ritual (im) purity, or maintaining bodily cleanliness for worship, rather than same-sex behaviour (Boswell 1981). The insistence that Romans 1:26-27, 1 Corinthians 6:9-10, 1 Timothy 1:9-10 and Jude 1:7 are referring to same-sex behaviour is challenged by various alternative ideas. One such idea is the claim that the original texts have been inaccurately or erroneously translated into English. Other alternative ideas are that these biblical passages point to an overindulgence in genital pleasure as an end in itself, infidelity to God, going against one's usual sexual attractions, sexual violence, and the reinforcement of heteronormative ideas of sex (Brooten 1998; Martin 2008). The question of what really lay in the mind of the biblical authors as they wrote these passages remains a mystery. Scripture scholars also argue that gender variance and sexual diversity exist among the various personages of the bible. In the Hebrew Scriptures (Old Testament), the relationships between David and Saul (1 Samuel 16:21), David and Jonathan (1 Samuel 18:1, 3-4), and Ruth and Naomi (Ruth 1:16-17; 2:1011) are sometimes viewed as having same-sex romantic and/or sexual overtones

ii.   'Spiritualistic Dualism' (the separation of body from soul)

'Spiritualistic dualism' (Nelson 1992, 30) refers to a traditional Christian understanding of separating the body from the soul. Consequently, the body is considered less important than the soul, spirit or mind. A person's body is considered a site of sinfulness that is responsible for 'misleading' and 'contaminating' his or her soul. The soul is therefore much more important, as it must 'rise above' the body and strive towards eternal salvation in the afterlife. Spiritualistic dualism creates the feeling that the soul (church, God) and the body (sex, being MSM, TG, and PLHIV, HIV testing) have little to do with each other. This idea leads to the perception that the soul should be taken care of more than the body (Smith 1992). The body's worth is therefore limited to heteronormative marriages and procreation. Conversely, gender variant and sexually diverse people need to 'repent' and have a 'normal' way of life in order to get to heaven when they die. On the other hand, there is an increasing pool of work that deals with affirming theologies and spiritualities of sexual diversity and gender variance. These include feminist, body, sexual, lesbian, gay, bisexual, transgender, intersex and queer theologies and spiritualities. Such theologies and spiritualities often emphasise the doctrine of the incarnation, or the teaching that Jesus Christ is both God and a human being, as proof of the sacredness of all human bodies, regardless of their gender or sexual identities (Cheng 2013; Hero 2012; Hunt 1994). Therefore, these theologies and spiritualities highlight the fact that all bodies are good and worthy in God's sight, and need to be cared for in the present life.

iii.   Heteronormative Theologies and Ethics

Institutional and popular forms of Christianity that disapprove of MSM and TG often refer to heteronormative theological ethics that are based on the teachings of the fourth century theologian Augustine of Hippo and the thirteenth century theologian Thomas Aquinas. As someone who struggled with sex, Augustine supported the idea that to abstain from sex and remain unmarried were ideal for Christians. Nevertheless, he thought that marriage could have a 'redeeming factor' because it provided a legitimate means for men and women to express their lust and produce children (Augustine 1887). Aquinas saw sex as legitimate only between a man and a woman within marriage, and for producing children. For him, homosexuality goes against the idea of marriage and children, which is part of divine law (Aquinas 2013, Q. 154, 11). These two theologians have influenced Christianity through history into determining 'right' and 'wrong' sex. For them, either sex within marriage or total sexual abstinence is the sole, legitimate form of sexual expression. It is very likely that many Christian churches and communities in Asia-Pacific countries are influenced by Augustine's and Aquinas' ideas of theology and ethics. Many churches adopt a 'love the sinner, hate the sin' attitude towards sexually diverse and gender variant people, see their efforts to fight for equal rights as evil (Tan 2014), encourage them to seek 'counselling' and embrace chastity (understood as celibacy) (W. Goh 2014). Consequently, they oppose same-sex behaviours (Catholic Bishops Conference of the Philippines 2013; New Zealand Kaniva Pacific 2015), invalidate procedures that can prevent the spread of HIV as sinful, and consider HIV infection as the result of gender and sexual 'deviation'. Nonetheless, theologies and ethics that value and include the experiences, knowledge and activities of sexually diverse and gender variant people are increasing (Farley 2008; J. N. Goh 2016). These theologies and ethics appreciate the ways in which such people see their sexuality and faith as compatible (Bong 2009; Luk 2015; Yip 2012). In these theologies and ethics, MSM and TG are considered as part of the diversity of creation (Hero 2012). Furthermore, thee theologies and ethics challenge heteronormative ideas of God, church, scripture, doctrine, human-divine relationships and non-heteronormative people (Long 2012; Meneses 2014; Siew 2015; Wong 2015). There are also numerous Christian leaders, groups and organisations that demonstrate greater affirmation and inclusivity towards all people, including sexually diverse and gender variant people through church services, and faith-building and social justice programmes (Free Community

Church 2013; National Council of Churches in the Philippines 2016; Sriram 2015; United Church of Christ in the Philippines 2016).

iv.   Divine Punishment

There are some Christian communities that see HIV and AIDS as God's way to punish and educate human beings for sexual 'misconduct' (Longchar 2011), including for MSM and TG. Nevertheless, many Christian institutions disagree with such a view. For instance, the Primates of the Anglican Communion made a definitive theological stand that HIV and AIDS are not consequences of divine punishment (Primates of the Anglican Communion 2002). In response, affirming theologies of HIV and AIDS hold the idea that the body of Christ consists of the living and breathing bodies of all Christians. This is based on the logic that Christ is the head of his body, which are his followers (Colossians 1:18). Therefore, he takes on the hopes and sufferings of his followers. Such theologies believe that Christian churches and communities everywhere are all interconnected and are bound to assist one another (Nalini 2012; Van Wyngaard 2006). These theologies are emphasise compassion and solidarity for all people, which reinforces the idea that to reach out to those who have HIV and AIDS is to reflect the mercy and loving acceptance of Christ and God (Dube 2002; A. S. van Klinken 2010). Moreover, the theological idea of the body of Christ provides a way to see PLHIV as created in God's image (van Klinken and Phiri 2015), and who act as missionaries to other PLHIV and those who are HIV-negative (Senturias 1994). Through their meaning-making and appreciation of life, PLHIV are members of the body of Christ who demonstrate the gift of life more deeply and purposefully.

This article also suggests the following practical steps: a]. Provide more opportunities for 'balanced' and non-discriminatory education in issues on gender and sexuality, especially on sexual diversity, gender variance and HIV, in Christian churches and communities. b]. Create spaces where Christian churches and communities can dialogue with MSM [Men who have Sex with Men], TG [Transgenders] and PLHIV [People Living with HIV] Christians as equal partners in a spirit of honesty and mutual respect. c]. Foster a spirit of listening to the stories of MSM, TG and PLHIV in churches without suspicion, discrimination or condemnation. d]. Take up the challenge of journeying with and supporting MSM, TG and PLHIV as part of church outreach without any ulterior motives. e]. Increase official church statements that denounce discrimination and violence towards MSM, TG and PLHIV. f]. Collaborate with schools, colleges and universities on issues of physical and cyber bullying of gender variant and sexually diverse children, teenagers and young adults as part of church outreach. g]. Include more MSM, TG and PLHIV in church ministries and leadership positions. h]. Encourage greater collaborations between Christian churches and MSM, TG and PLHIV in human rights and social justice initiatives. i]. Promote greater collaboration between Christian churches and MSM, TG and PLHIV in HIV awareness, care and treatment. j]. Identify experts who can facilitate discussions on alternative biblical and theological interpretations that support and affirm MSM, TG and PLHIV.

[Excerpts are taken from APCOM's Discussion Paper: "Christianity, Sexual Diversity and Access to Health Services" with due permission © APCOM 2016].

A Birds-Eye View of South and South-East Asian Countries

Douglas Sanders

Introduction

The UN 'region' that is the most divided on these issues is Asia. The region includes five states that still have the death penalty on the books for male-male sexual acts (Afghanistan, Iran, Saudi Arabia, the UAE and Yemen). As well, there are recent stories of the extra-judicial executions of males accused of homosexuality in areas controlled by the so-called Islamic State or ISIS. In other parts of Asia, in sharp contrast, there are large LGBTI 'pride' parades, or similar public celebratory events (Hong Kong, India, Israel, Japan, Singapore, South Korea, Philippines, Taiwan, Thailand).

Criminal Laws

Criminal laws against same-sex sexual acts in South and Southeast Asia date back to periods of British colonialism. Those laws have religious origins (tracing back to Leviticus). The wording of Article 377 of the 1860 Indian Penal Code, which avoids explicitly religious references, was copied for other British colonies in Asia, Africa, the Caribbean and the Pacific. In South and Southeast Asia only former British colonies have these laws. The criminal laws in Sri Lanka and Malaysia have been extended to cover lesbian acts. Repeal occurred in Hong Kong before reversion to China. The constitutional validity of the law in India is back before the Supreme Court. Usually there are no active campaigns to enforce these laws. The Singapore Prime Minister has pledged "no proactive enforcement." Over the years, these laws have served to keep LGBT individuals (and their issues) out of sight, 'in the closet'. But that doesn't work very effectively anymore. There have been two criminal prosecutions of Anwar Ibrahim, the leading opposition politician in Malaysia. He is currently serving a five year jail sentence. The allegations against him were for consensual acts between two adults in private. If there are prosecutions, they are more likely to be for minor offences of vagrancy, solicitation, public nuisance, or public scandal. China used to charge gays hanging around in parks with hooliganism, but those days are long gone. Even the offence of 'hooliganism' has been chucked. Islamic Sharia (Shariah, Syariah) criminal laws against same-sex sexual acts and transgender practices exist in the various individual states within Malaysia, as well as in Brunei and in the autonomous province of Aceh in Indonesia. The introduction of the death penalty for sodomy has been promised in Brunei, but delayed and delayed.

Confucian Influenced Areas

Confucian traditions and beliefs strongly support heterosexual marriage and procreation. One judge, upholding a criminal prohibition in Singapore, quoted a Confucian adage that the greatest infidelity on the part of a son was the failure to produce a male heir. This was quoted in defense of a law which criminalized only male-male homosexual acts, ignoring lesbians. Over and over again, we hear stories of the pressure on gay sons to marry. Fidelity in marriage, it is often said in Confucian influenced areas, is far less important than producing heirs. Family and societal pressure on individuals to marry and procreate is the major burden gay men and lesbian women face. Most do not 'come out' to their parents – or to the heterosexual partners that they may reluctantly marry. But now we see some change. PFLAG groups – Parents and Friends of Lesbians and Gays – are now publicly active, in China and Vietnam, supporting their LGBT children. What is the future of the focus on procreation? In all of the Confucian influenced areas we see a drop in procreation, a drop in marriage rates, the postponement of marriage and a sharp rise in divorces. China, Japan, Singapore, South Korea and Taiwan all face possible declines in population. The decline has begun in Japan. China has eased its one child policy, but with little effect.

Islamic Areas

A majority of Muslims, world-wide, live in Asia. Bangladesh, India, Indonesia and Pakistan have very large Muslim populations. In South and Southeast Asia Sharia courts with criminal jurisdiction only exist in Malaysia, Brunei and Aceh. Only a few voices can be heard arguing from within Islam that the faith is compatible with LGBT lives. Voices in Indonesia speak of 'Islam Nusantara', that is Islam as it has developed in the archipelago. Prime Minister Badawi in Malaysia, spoke of 'civilizational Islam' and the current prime minister speaks of the importance of moderation in religious and social views (while regularly condemning homosexuality). Many saw Islam in Indonesia as compatible with the acceptance of diversity, human rights and democracy. But in the first half of 2016, political, educational, medical and religious elites spoke out in active opposition to any tolerance of sex and gender diversity. They often called for new criminal laws and compulsory treatment. The minister responsible for higher education said that gays and lesbians should be barred from any colleges and universities, sparking the flood of hostile statements from other major figures in Indonesian society. The president and vice president only said the police should ensure that there was no discrimination or violence against LGBT individuals. Otherwise silence.

Christianity in Asia

In Asia there are older or well-established Christian groupings in some areas. In looking at attitudes to sex and gender diversity, attention is captured by the relatively limited evangelical groupings, which have arisen in the post-war period, often with links to the United States. Active opposition to law reform on issues of decriminalization, anti-discrimination laws and legal recognition of relationships is associated with evangelical Christian activism in Hong Kong, Singapore, South Korea and Taiwan.

Buddhism

Buddhism does not have the focus on marriage and procreation that we find in other major religions. Young people in Thailand (where this author lives) do not report pressure on them from the religion, but an inability to be 'out' to their parents. There is not the very strong pressure to marry that is reported in other areas, except for Sino-Thai young people.

Hinduism

Justice Shah wrote the judgment of the Delhi High Court striking down the colonial era 'carnal intercourse' law. He comments on traditions recognizing sex and gender diversity:

> There is enough evidence to show that homosexuality has been prevalent and recognized in all its forms during ancient and medieval Indian history. Temple imagery, sacred narrative and religious scripture do suggest that homosexual activities – in some form – did exist in ancient India. Kamasutra devotes an entire chapter to Auparistaka – homosexual intercourse. In Hinduism some of the divinities are androgynous and some change gender to participate in homoerotic behavior.[1]

LGBTI Visibility

It is said that there is only one gay bar in India, and it is gay only one night a week. There are no openly gay, lesbian, bisexual or transgender politicians at the national level in South Asia or Southeast Asia. One exception. A transgender woman was elected to the Philippine Congress in the last national election, a person effectively inheriting the seat of a family fiefdom. There was high 'name recognition'. There are elected gay, lesbian and transgender individuals in Hong Kong and Japan at local government levels. In the past, one Hijra in Madhya Pradesh served at the state level.

Public 'pride' parades are held in Hong Kong, India, Japan, the Philippines, Taiwan and Thailand. Singapore pioneered a static event, in which individuals gathered in the one park where public free speech is allowed, all wearing pink. The country liked the label of being the "Red Dot" – a tiny spot on maps, colored red as British colonies had been traditionally identified. So the protest gathering was a "Pink Dot", and a tradition developed of thousands gathering, wearing pink, and at dusk, holding candles or flashlights or mobile phones that showed as much pink as possible. This resulted in a dramatic photo opportunity from a nearby high rise hotel, of the illuminated thousands in the park, with the lights of the central business district in the distance. Parades are not possible in Singapore, but the Pink Dot has entertainment and speakers. Pink Dots now occur in Japan and Hong Kong as well. Individuals or corporate sponsors that are not Singaporean by nationality or permanent resident status are barred from participation.

A bicycle rally is now held annually in Hanoi, with flags and matching t-shirts. While it traverses public streets, it is not a 'parade' and has no permit. Police do not interfere. In other places, where parades and near-parades cannot be held, indoor events are now common. LGBTI film festivals are increasing in number, now occurring in Cambodia, Hong Kong, India, Indonesia, Japan, Myanmar, Taiwan and Thailand.

There are nationally famous transgender media figures in Indonesia, China and South Korea. Dorcee Gamalama in Indonesia and Jin Xing in China have both been dubbed the 'Oprah' of their countries as very popular hosts of talk shows (citing the model of Oprah Winfrey of the United States, who is not transgender). Harisu in South Korea is a singer and actress with ten music albums and ten films or television series. These are very exceptional figures. Similar transgender media hosts have been active in India and Pakistan.

In non-Confucian parts of South and Southeast Asia there are named transgender communities or identities that are known to everyone: Hijra in India, Kathoey in Thailand, Waria in Indonesia, Bakla in the Philippines, Mak Nyah in Malaysia, Metis in Nepal. These individuals present as women, but may assert distinct collective identities. In other parts of Asia the dominant pattern seems to be that transgender individuals identify either as men or women, not as a 'third sex' or a distinct identity category.

State attitudes towards Hijra or Aravani in India have notably changed over the last twenty years, pioneered by reforms in Tamil Nadu, now copied in other parts of the country. The groupings are seen as socially and economically marginalized, and affirmative action programs have been extended to them. Reforms in programs and attitudes have also occurred in Pakistan, Bangladesh and Nepal. Attacks on gay and lesbian events in Indonesia, however, are usually attacks on transgender or Waria events.

The Asia Pacific Transgender Network, with offices in Bangkok, was established by transwomen (including Kathoey and Hijra). It now includes transmen, and more recently gender diverse or gender neutral individuals as well. Intersex organizations have started in parts of the region.

Recognition of Relationships

The Ministry of Justice in Vietnam supported legal recognition of same-sex relationships for purposes of resolving legal issues relating to property and children. That was rejected by the national legislature. The earlier provision in Vietnamese law that made it illegal to hold an event and call it a same-sex "wedding" was finally repealed. Such events are now fairly common.

Court cases seeking the opening of marriage to same-sex couples have occurred in China, South Korea and Taiwan. The South Korea case is currently under appeal to the supreme court.

In May, 2017, the constitutional court in Taiwan held that denying same sex couples the right to marry violated constitutional equality rights. Opening marriage has been publicly debated in Taiwan for twenty years, and a bill was being considered by the legislative branch even before the ruling of the constitutional court. The president elected in 2016 had pledged her support for opening marriage during her election campaign. The court gave the legislature two years to amend the law.

Taiwan was already the leading jurisdiction in Asia in terms of LGBT rights. It has no criminal prohibitions. It bars discrimination on grounds of sexual orientation and gender identity in employment and in education. It permits document change for transgender individuals without the requirement of genital surgery. Some local governments allow individuals to register same-sex relationships (which can be useful in joint rentals, employment benefits or hospital visitations). Taiwan has the largest 'pride' parade in Asia. 80,000 people participated in the event in 2016. Taiwan

LGBTI organizations organized the Asian Regional Conference of the International Lesbian and Gay Association in 2015, without incident or problems.

Overview

In this analysis, modern 'conservative' attitudes to sex and gender diversity, are the product of colonialism, not indigenous tradition. Asia is a huge and diverse region. LGBT rights face strong opposition in parts of the region – and growing support in other places. Twenty years ago it would have been inconceivable that India would host a dozen pride parades and film festivals. When the Delhi High Court struck down Section 377, the national BJP government shrugged its shoulders and did nothing, saying it would not appeal the decision. Others forced an appeal, and the matter remains unresolved at the moment. As noted, 2016 saw an unexpected and very harsh backlash over a period of six months from leading political, educational, medical and religious figures in Indonesia, but attention there has shifted to other issues. Hong Kong is fighting over an anti-discrimination law. Six or more local anti-discrimination laws are now in place in the Philippines at local levels. Some reforms are occurring in Thailand and Vietnam. Taiwan is the brightest spot, but not the only leader.

Endnotes

[1] Honourable Ajit Prakash Shah, India and Section 377, UN Development Programme, Punitive Laws, Human Rights and HIV prevention among men who have sex with men in Asia Pacific: High Level Dialogue Report, May 17, 2010, 30. His decision on 377 is to be reargued before the Supreme Court (after a considerable delay). In China, Japan and Korea, as well, it is possible to document pre-colonial era patterns of the acceptance of sex and gender diversity in particular periods.

An Introduction to
Queer Theology Academy

Pearl Wong

Background

Founded in 2009 by a group of queer theologians and church leaders, Queer Theology Academy (QTA) develops and practices queer theologies and gender justice in the context of Hong Kong. QTA promotes sexual rights for people of different gender identities and sexual orientations through publication and education. We also work in partnership with sexual minority groups to provide them with appropriate pastoral counseling and spiritual formation.

Our Projects include: Publication/Theological Education/Pastoral Care for LGBT/ Outreach/ Partnership with LGBTIQ Groups

Publication

We have published two books in Chinese, the English title for the first one is, ***Who isn't Queer? Exploring Queer Theology in the context of Hong Kong.*** We published the second book last year, the Chinese edition of ***Radical Love: An Introduction to Queer Theology*** written by Rev. Dr. Patrick S. Cheng. Our third book is *work in progress*, and will be published this year. The working title is, ***Queer Reading of the Bible***, authors are LGBTIQ Christians from Hong Kong, Taiwan and China; the articles feature their critical responses to the scriptures from the perspective of the marginalized.

Theological Education

Queer Theology Academy Asia Project (Summer 2014): We organized a Queer Theology Academy Asia Project in Summer 2014, total of 25 key LGBTIQ Christian leaders and twelve instructors from Hong Kong, Taiwan, China and the United States attended a week long workshop in Hong Kong. The course provided key LGBTIQ Christian leaders with the resources to counter fundamentalist Christians who are opposed to the equal rights of LGBTIQ people in Chinese-speaking countries.

Seminars in China and Taiwan

We have also run seminars on issues concerning sexuality, disability and queer theologies in LGBT-affirming churches and seminaries in Taiwan and China.

Ecumenical Summer Students' Internship Program

QTA is one of the participating associations in the Ecumenical Summer Students' Internship program organized by Hong Kong Christian Council and Hong Kong Christian Institute, and we are the only association in this program working with LGBTIQ.

Pastoral Care for LGBTI

We have been running a program for three years called *CCQ: Caring Community for the Queers,* we render Emotion-Focus Therapy training for counselors, social workers, psychologists and pastors working with LGBTI people. We invite pastors who have experiences in counseling LGBT Christians to share their knowledge and resources. Partnership with LGBTIQ Groups

Queer Theology Academy is one of the founding members of Covenant of the Rainbow - Campaign for a Truly Inclusive Church and we advocate for justice and inclusivity for LGBTIQ both in the churches and the society. We have participated in the annual Pride Parade in Hong Kong and Taiwan, we participate every year at IDAHOTI and Pink Dot HK to show our support for LGBTIQ rights.

Interfaith Dialogue

We also run public forums and invite LGBT friendly religious leaders from other religions to promote together an inclusive environment for LGBTIQ people.

[website: *www.queertheo.com*: Facebook page: queertheologyacademy]

The Indian Christian Response: Responses by Churches

Arcot Lutheran Church
Department of Transgenders

The Lutherans

The UELCI which represents the Lutheran Churches in India has made great strides since its meeting of doctors, theologians, laity etc., back in September 2009, where it sympathetically discussed the issue of TGs in relation to the Delhi High Court Judgment. Detailed modules, brochures, pamphlets, posters and study materials were developed and distributed to the participants. Gurukul Lutheran Theological Seminary held several Seminars on the issues of sexual minorities, same sex marriage etc. Since then, Training of Trainers (ToT) programs on prevention, care and support among transgenders had also taken place in Salem, Tricoillur, Tiruvanamallai, Ulundurpet and in Ambur districts, between 2009 and 2015, according to a report from UELCI. NCCI then connected with the ALC Bishop and clergy of this church in 2015-2016. It was wonderful to know that the church already had a pastor working among the TG's of the district, especially since the temple of the Transgender God was situated in Koovagam, in the

Church's jurisdiction. Three meetings were held in 2016 with clergy and laity of the ALC under the partnership of the NCCI's ESHA program. Below is the follow up by the ALC as reported:

The Department of Transgender was inaugurated by Bishop Raja Socrates, of ALC. As a result, a consultation on "The Issues of Transgender" was organized by the Transgender Department of the Arcot Lutheran Church on November 16, 2016, at the ALC Office, Cuddalore. The invitation was extended to the members of the Transgender committee and the ALC Cuddalore region Pastors. The Meeting was enriched by the participation of Fr. Thomas Ninan, NCCI, and Rev. Esther Bharathi, a Transwoman who is a Pastor turned freelance writer and Gospel speaker.

The Bishop explained the involvement and commitment of the Arcot Lutheran Church for the welfare of the Transgendered. Mr. P. Franklin Joseph, Secretary CB, urged that the department should be taken forward to the next step and that it involves the community at large. Rev. Dr. Peter Paul Thomas, Central Manager greeted the gathering. Rev. Esther Bharathi (A Transwoman and an ordained Pastor) placed the challenges in front of the Church in accommodating the Transgender in the ministry of the Church and Society. The issues and problems faced by the Transgender community such as verbal abuse, dress code acceptance in schools and acceptance in the Church were some of the crucial needs which have to be addressed and taken care of at the moment, told Rev. Esther.

Apart from the above programme, a One-day seminar was organized by the Transgender Department of the ALC in Tiruvannamalai on June 5, 2017. The programme was enriched by the participation of 10 Transwomen from Tiruvannamalai region. A few members of the women's fellowship from Tiruvannamalai region were also invited for the same. The meeting started with a devotion led by Rev. V. Murali Christian. The Transwomen from Tiruvannamalai expressed collectively their struggles and sufferings that they undergo everyday for their livelihood. The way they were being stigmatized and ill-treated by the society and the existing challenges to recover their human dignity was brought out by them. They did express their aspiration to adore a God who would care for them. Caring is something that most of the Transgender (Men and Women) could not attain neither from their own family nor from the members of the society. They gave a call to treat them just as they are and not to discriminate.

The following concerns were brought out at the end of the seminar:

- Create employment opportunity and provide technical skills training for economic development.

- Create awareness among the public about the sensitive nature and problems of transgender and make the people to accept them as normal human being.

- Promote and provide formal and non-formal education.

- Emphasize the Christian value through various human development activities and spread the word of Gospel to heal the pain of transgender.

Apart from the above said programmes, then and there local level programmes were organized to highlight the issues to the congregation members. The department is planning for a higher level of consultation in order to bring in a kind of acceptance in the families, society and the Church at large. The department also will stress the need to be more inclusive and that the trans-people do find a space. Let us adopt the ministerial model of our Lord Jesus if at all we aspire for a change.

The Church of North India

A 2004 consultation on homosexuality at CNI Bhavan in New Delhi brought together nearly 40 delegates, including bishops, physicians, pastors, social activists, women's leaders, youth leaders and children's coordinators. The group concluded that homosexuality as an orientation is not sin and one cannot be blamed for it. Among other things, the consultation recommended that scriptures historically related to the sexuality issue should be re-examined with regard to their socio-cultural context. Although the CNI Health Services Board worked successfully with HIV issues for many years and came in contact with many people from the sexual minorities, there was little follow-up on the 2004 report. However, in 2015, the Moderator of CNI, Rt. Rev. P.K. Samantaroy, and Rt. Rev. P.C. Singh, President of NCCI, were both present at NCCI's National level meeting with Key Affected People and the LGBT community in Delhi in August. They subsequently encouraged partnership with NCCI-ESHA, and supported joint programs in Amritsar, Shimla, Delhi and Bhopal in 2016-17.

Rev Dr Paul Swarup, Pastor of the Cathedral Church of Redemption in Delhi, and Dr Alma Ram from Tarn Tarn, were deputed by the General Secretary, CNI Synod, Mr Alwan Masih, to represent the CNI in the NCCI's Pre-Assembly Conference, which was held on April 19-20, 2016, in UTC Bangalore. Subsequently, on July 7th, 2016, in Amritsar [Punjab] there was a program where delegates from Khem Karan, Batala, Taran Taran also came. The resource persons were Ms Mohini (a TG from Jalandhar), and Mr Manoj Benjwal (a gay from Chandigarh], and Fr Philip Kuruvilla from NCCI. Bp Samantaroy inaugurated the program and specifically mentioned that Transgender children would be welcomed in CNI church schools. On July 9th the same team went to Shimla in the Christ Church Cathedral.

Both these programs we organized by Bishop Samantaroy and coordinated by Dr Alma Ram of CNI, together with the local pastors. In both cases the format was the same-after NCCI introduced the need for the churches to enter into this field, the theological inputs were given by a theologian, and the voices of the sexual minorities spoke, showing their deep hurt and grief at the often inhuman treatment they were meted out by the general public. Then the floor was open to the delegates for their discussions. The following are some of the points that emerged [as reported by Dr Alma Ram]:

- We need to be more open-minded, patient and take the first step to reach out, to accept the TGs in our churches.

- The churches can play a key role in finding greater acceptance for the LGBTI, within their families , the society and with government agencies.

- We welcome a re-reading of the Bible through appropriate Bible Study groups and its re-interpretation in the perspective of the LGBTI.

On November 22nd, 2016, in Delhi, a Workshop was conducted by ESHA with CNI Delhi Diocese with the blessings and initiative of Bp Waris Masih. Also present, together with sexual minorities, as resource people, were Rev Mohit Hitter, Rev Philip V Peacock of Bishops College, Kolkata and Fr Thomas Ninan of NCCI.

A one day workshop on theme "*Towards an inclusive church facing transphobia and homophobia*" was organised by NCCI-ESHA with the consent of the Bishop Rt Rev PC Singh, Bishop of the CNI Diocese of Bhopal, at Masihi Kanya School, Indore on 22nd March, 2017. Rev. Deepak Yohan, CNI, reported that *It was great challenge to talk on such issues in the open. Personally, it was a privilege to be part of this programme. All the presentations were good and made clear statement to the audience and served food for thought. It is essential that the church should have dialogue with its members and extend a hand of love and affection empathetically.*

Trans-accompaniment
A trans–experience of the Church of South India

Transgenders as a group of persons have been at the core of the ministries of the Church since long. The Church of South India has pioneered in the accompaniment of Transgenders in different ways:

1. The ministry among transgenders

The Diocese of Madras has had a Ministry among Transgenders for over 25 years. A pastor has been working all these years dedicated to the task. He has met almost every transgendered person in the city of Chennai and their contacts till Mumbai.

Through this ministry many have experienced the love of Christ and now live with dignity and hope; some have even come into full time ministry. The diocese supported the theological education of Pastor Bharathi who now ministers extensively in different parts of Tamilnadu including with the Transgendered communities. Two others are now working as evangelists supported by the CSI Diocese of Madras.

The Church has extended the celebration of Christmas in sharing with the Transgendered people in different dioceses – Thoothukudi-Nazareth, Madras, Vellore, Madurai and Coimbatore.

Healing ministry services are extended where required. One person is being helped for her dialysis through contributions from different churches in the Madras diocese.

2. Integration

In the Thoothukudi Nazareth Diocese the Social Welfare Department and the Women's fellowship have been instrumental in integrating the Transgendered persons along with women in a local church. In a special program, the seating was arranged in such a way that the women of the church and the transgendered persons were seated alternatively to sensitise and familiarise each other.

The Madras diocese has accepted Noori into the full membership of the CSI Wesley Church Perambur, one of the suburbs in the City of Chennai. Noori also attended the Diocesan Council as a voting delegate nominated by the Chairperson of the Diocesan Council the Bishop in Madras.

In one of the recent pride parades in the city of Thiruvananthapuram Rev. Dr. Prakash Juswil a priest of the South Kerala Diocese marched alongside Transgenders and others with his cassock on. This bold act in the heartland of Christian orthodoxy went a long way in helping the church learn to integrate with the concerns of the LGBTQI+ communities and their assertion of rights and dignity.

3. Sensitisation

The Dioceses have planned and implementedsensitisation programs. In the Thoothukudi Nazareth Diocese of the CSI orientations are given to local congregations through the Diocesan department of Social Welfare.

Periodic sensitisation programs are conducted in the Churches in Madras, particularly among the youth of the diocese.

The NCCI-ESHA has been instrumental in organising training for Pastors on LGBTQI+ and the issues and concerns relating to these groups of people.

The CSI-SEVA, the diaconal concerns division of the CSI has partnered with the Trans Resource Centre in producing a music album *'vaanam thaandi'* (beyond the skies) in Tamil showcasing the different fields in which transgendered persons are employed – from business, to news reading, to driving autos and cabs, to serving in the police force, in music, drama and theatre, field of literature, research, and so on.

4.   Income Generation Skills

Several attempts have been made to train the transgendered persons in income generating skills. A bakery training was organised in the Thoothukudi Nazareth Diocese. In the Madras Diocese trainings were organised as per their request and in making different handicrafts.

Recently during Chennai Pride 2017 a training on jewellery making was arranged for twenty persons along with DORCAS Research Centre for Education, Art and Culture. This training course will continue as a joint venture between CSI and the Dorcas Research Centre.

CSI will also support the skills trainings organised by the other outfits of transgenders in Chennai. In Madurai negotiations are going on to support a group of transgendered persons who are involved in catering business.

The Trans Resource Centre in Madurai and Coimbatore are negotiating with CSI for support to income-generating activities.

Self-employment and Entrepreneurship Development trainings are given through the Ecumenical Church Loan Fund (ECLOF)

5.   Networking

The Church of South India has networked with different groups of Transgenders in different places. It supported a part of the expenses of the participation of Transgenders in Chennai Pride 2017.

Trans Resource Centre in Madurai and Coimbatore, *Thozhi* and *Snehidi* in Chennai are some of the Community Based Organisations of Transgenders that Church works with.

The Dorcas Research Centre for Education Art and Culture and the Bravo Movement are also associated in CSI's ministries among Transgenders.

The CSI networks with the East West Centre for Counselling in seeking to address the concerns of the transmen – a course on Psychodrama is planned to address needs of transmen and their families.

The CSI will collaborate with a CBO of transgenders in undertaking a census of transgenders in the city of Chennai. The Loyola College, Chennai will provide technical support to the census.

Challenges

No good work is without its share of challenges. CSI's pioneering and pathbreaking work with transgenders is growing by the day. The challenges mentioned below need to be addressed in due course.

1. The interventions have not gone beyond trans-women. A lot need to be done to understand the world of Transgenders – the transmen etc.

2. Most interventions have only been a ministerial experience with 'them' as the objects of mission. We need to learn to work with them as persons with dignity and rights.

3. Most discourses on transgendered people are in the realm of TGs spoken of in the human sexuality realm and not in the people realm – as people with dignity and rights

Despite the challenges the joy in the heart and smiles on the faces of the transgendered persons amidst whom the Church locates itself and serves urges the Church to press on. There is no looking back. With the rights that the recent legislation gives them and the openness with which the public receive them the Church cannot lag. The Church will continue to journey with the transgendered friends and will seek to be taught by them on its courses of action.

The Mar Thoma Church:
Navodaya Movement
(A Project of the Mumbai Diocese
of the Mar Thoma Church)

Navodaya Movement, a project of the Mumbai diocese of the Mar Thoma Church, is a social platform for justice striving to reach out to the margins, collaborating with them to attain the fulfillment of their basic human rights, and empowering them to experience and enjoy life in its fullness through capacity building initiatives and programmes of both the individual and the community. One of the projects taken up is the Transgenders' Reintegration Programme which started its ministry among the sexual minority community of transgenders in Mumbai since 2014.

As per the 2011 Census, India has approximately 490,000 transgenders with a literacy rate of about 56%. Although transgenders have always been part of the society, they have been only recently recognized as the third gender in a landmark Supreme Court ruling in April 2014. However, there is still a long way to go as transgenders continue to face discrimination and denial of rights and opportunities in social life, particularly in the areas of education, health, and employment.

In addition to providing fellowship and solidarity to the members of the community, Navodaya engages with the transgenders through the following programmes:

Documentation

A good majority of the TG community have either been kicked out of their own homes or have fled themselves. In these situation most of them leave behind any sort of documents they had with them. Thus they find themselves in a new place like Mumbai devoid of any identity documents or educational certificates. This prevents them not only from entering into any employment opportunities but also from being the beneficiary of any government related scheme or project.

Navodaya Movement, in association with the Community Based Organizations of the TGs, has started creating databases of the members in the community. Documentation includes the provision of voter identity cards, Aadhar cards, PAN cards, etc. Through the help and support of local authorities like the MLA, Tahsildar, Corporator, Navodaya is thus engaged in the process of officially registering the identities of transgenders. In addition, name change is facilitated for those who do have some kind of old documentation butwish to be known by their new name. Navodaya also facilitates the opening of bank accounts for the transgenders while inculcating the habit of financial saving, a practice quite uncommon among transgenders.

Health Care

It is a saddening fact that the social ostracism faced by the transgenders is extended even to the medical sector. Many doctors and other medical personnel, who allegedly should be aware of the true condition of transgenders, however shun them, often denying them their right to health. As many of the transgenders are engaged in the flesh trade there is a high prevalence of HIV/AIDS and other sexually transmitted diseases. As a result, the health of a good number of transgenders is in a pitiable state.

Navodaya Movement conducts medical camps in the community with the help of other NGOs. Our social workers take up the cases of those who require higher referrals, accompany them to the hospitals and facilitate their diagnosis and treatment. Navodaya also arranges for specialized medical camps for cancer, TB, hepatitis, STD, blood testing, etc. Sex Reassignment Surgery is a major need of the community and Navodaya guides them in this aspect.

Vocational Training and Livelihood

A good majority of the transgenders find their means of existence through begging, sex work or through *baddhai* (dancing during special occasions like marriage or birth of a child). Their lack of education, or the certificates to prove it, combined with the general aversion of the public to work side by side with the transgenders, prevents them from getting a good job.

Navodaya helps TGs who are interested to pursue their formal education. Navodaya realizing the scope and importance of independent vocational trades is therefore also involved in providing the required training to transgenders. Different institutes and government authorities are contacted for giving the TG Community skill training programmes. Regular meetings are held with the community members at the various *gheranas* to understand their needs and interests. Some of the areas for training which were identified through such sessions are driving, beautician course, bag stitching, goldsmith training, jewellery making, tailoring and embroidery. Several companies and agencies were contacted to induct the TGs in their training courses and provide employment. Cab services like Ola and Uber have also agreed to take in transgenders as drivers. Navodaya is thus facilitating driving classes for those interested in following that line of work. Talks are also underway with BPOs to employ those transgenders who are fluent in English and have basic computer skills. Navodaya thus provides Spoken English classes while also facilitating Computer classes. A beautician course for TGs has also been started. Through income generation programmes, TGs are facilitated to start their own livelihood ventures (small scale business) like textile selling, tea shop, vadapav stall, etc.

Awareness and Advocacy

A fundamental change in the situation of the transgenders would be possible only when society learns to look at them as human beings. The general fallacy that transgenders are sinners with deviant character and that their condition can be 'treated' through medicine, counseling or marriage needs to be dismantled. It has to be understood that the 'problem' is actually not with the transgenders, but rather with the societal understanding of the transgender.

Hence, the second arm of Navodaya's work with the transgenders is actually the work with the society. Navodaya conducts awareness progammes, seminars and workshops with the aim of breaking the ice between the public and the transgenders. Sensitization campaigns are conducted focusing on schools and colleges as well as hospitals and churches. Such programmes are presently being conducted in the states of Maharashtra and Kerala, and will be extended to other states as well. Navodaya has also partnered with the National Council of Churches in India (NCCI) to conduct awareness campaigns in the churches on a national scale. Navodaya also joins hands with the government offices and agencies to provide any help possible to the TG community.

Helpline

Navodaya Movement started a Transgender toll free helpline number (1800 3000 5110) in 2015. Counselors are always on line providing services in English, Hindi, Marathi and Malayalam. The Helpline continues to help transgenders and other family members by giving guidance and information as per their need.

Short Film

Through the effort and support of wellwishers, a short film in Malayalam, Karuna, was released to portray a positive image for the transgenders. The short film, produced by Mrs. Preethi Kuruvila and Mr. Vinod Kuruvila, while highlighting the plight of transgenders in daily life by showcasing the discrimination practiced by all sections of the society – men-women, young-old, educated-illiterate, rich-poor, etc., strove to share the message that transgenders too are human beings with humanity and compassion and all they yearn for is tolerance and acceptance by the society at large.

Birth Centenary Project

The Mar Thoma Church understanding the significance of the Navodaya Transgender Programme has decided to take this ministry on a bigger scale throughout all its dioceses in India. Thus, it has found its place as one of the two projects taken up by the Church as part of the Birth Centenary celebrations of H.G. The Most Rev. Dr. Philipose Mar Chrysostom Mar

Thoma Valiya Metropolitan (the Metropolitan Emeritus of the Church). Various programmes and schemes are being planned for the year for the welfare of the transgender community in addition to a series of seminars in Kerala. Land has been set apart for the transgender ministry both in Kerala as well as in Mumbai to initiate projects of Vocational Training as well as for a short stay shelter for the transgenders.

The Indian Orthodox/Malankara Orthodox Syrian Church

Immediately after the Delhi High Court Judgment of 2009, the late Metropolitan of Delhi, Dr Job Mar Philoxenos, sent out an open e mail stating " *Homosexuality is a criminal offense*"- although it was his personal view. This view was echoed by Ramban Skariah a few weeks later in an interfaith meeting in Delhi. However, in a more recent book "Church and Legal Literacy", a handbook for Orthodox Priests and Church Leaders, the Orthodox Metropolitan of Gujarat, Dr Geevarghese Mar Yulios, advocates for a softer stand and more inclusive language towards the gay community. This is also the stand taken in the Indian Orthodox e group called ICON in a letter by Dr Mar Nicholavos, Metropolitan of the North East Diocese of America, who currently serves as a Central Committee member of the World Council of Churches [WCC]. Meanwhile, the Metropolitan of Niranam, and till recently the President of the Orthodox Mission Board, HG Mar Chrysostomos, gave a report at the " *Church Leaders and KAP's*" Dialogue in New Delhi on August 27th, 2015. He spoke about his experience meeting with sexual minorities at a similar dialogue in Tiruvalla in June, 2015, organized by the Kerala Council of Churches, where he heard the voice of Gays and TG's crying against homophobia and transphobia, and recommended a more sensitive approach. 'We must love TG's and those with alternative sexualities, are they not human?" he asks. [Quoted in the *Malayala Manorama* of June 3, 2015].

[The above was compiled by **Fr Philip Kuruvilla**, NCCI]

In 2016, the Orthodox Seminary in Kottayam organized a one day Seminar – where the Mar Thoma and CSI seminary students were invited [see separate report under Theological College's response.] This was a path breaking step for the Orthodox Church.

[Report below by **Fr Jacob Mathew**, Lecturer at the Orthodox Seminary in Kottayam:]

Here are some of the initiatives after the we've taken in solidarity with the LGBTIQ during and after the "Dialogue on Church & Transphobia," held at the Orthodox Theological Seminary [OTS], in Kottayam in August, 2016.

Subsequently, we were able to motivate the editorial board of the Malankara Sabha, the official Magazine of the Malankara Orthodox Syrian Church/Indian Orthodox Church to bring out one volume with five articles and with the editorial write up highlighting LGBTIQ. We presume not less than one lakh people across denominations read and reflected on the contents of this official magazine from the Orthodox Church.

Metropolitan Dr Gabriel Mar Gregorios [Bishop of the Indian Orthodox Diocese of Thiruvananthapuram & former President, KCC] attended the Asian Consultation on Human Sexuality organized by the NCCI in Bangalore in February, 2017. Later, at the valedictory function of the FFRRC 2017, held in the Mar Thoma Seminary in Kottayam, and inaugurated by him, Dr Gabriel Mar Gregorios spoke on the theme, "The cause and urgency of the issues of LGBTIQ." Morever, some of the students both in the FFRRC and in the BD course have shown interest to write their term papers and even theses on these issues.

The Salvation Army: India Western Territory

Report of Seminar on Human Sexuality and Gender identity held from July 14 to 18, 2016 at three Venues: Anand, Mumbai and Ahmednagar.

The Salvation Army has always been in the forefront to fight for those who are in need. At present, the Third Gender is a burning issue globally. The seminars on human sexuality and gender identity was arranged at Anand, Mumbai and Ahmednagar by the Salvation Army India Western Territory with the support of National Council of Churches in India under the leadership of Commissioner M. C. James, Territorial Commander. The Territorial leaders, guests and the resource persons were welcomed with flowers. The Divisional Commanders, DDWMs, DYS & local officers from all the Divisions, Institutional heads with their delegates participated in this program. There were many resource persons including Gays, Lesbian and Transgender. Many hands were joined to give them welcome along with the Bouquets. Following are the resource persons:

1. Rev. Fr. Philip Kuruvilla – General Coordinator of NCCI- ESHA Program

2. Rev. Fr. Thomas Ninan-Associate General Coordinator-NCCI– ESHA.

3. Mx. Mallika - Transwoman

4. Daniel – Intersex person

5. Ms Poornima – Social Worker

6. The chief hijra of Mumbai joined for the Mumbai program

Commissioner M.C. James, Territorial Commander spoke about the services that Salvation Army had been started by the General William Booth without any cast, creed, religion and gender discrimination. At present, The Salvation Army is also working and thinking about this issue. The Commissioner in his speech said though it is a great issue it is not a new in this world it was in the world but we were not able to recognize it. The Commissioner explained the issue with illustrations like women who were stoned by the people because of her adultery, common sins Sodom and Gomorra and their end. He reminded the congregation about the verse recorded in the Holy Bible 1st Corinthians 6 which clears that people of various sinful behaviors and sexual immortality will not enter in the kingdom of God. The Commissioner also challenged with the illustration of Good Samaritan and the motto of The Salvation Army 'Heart to God and Hand to Man'. He made the congregation to understand that when we support the needy people who are facing problem whoever it may be (Gay, Lesbian, and Transgender etc.) we support the Christ. Lastly the Commissioner concluded his devotion with the word LOVE - God is love and love is God. Further the Commissioner mentioned that God has given 10 Commandments to Moses, but Christ has given us refined ones - only two - and reminded us we should love the sinners and those who we come across in our life.

Following this, Captain Andrews Christian, the Administrator of Emery Hospital Gujarat, shared the information about the services of NCCI and how Salvation Army is collaborating with them in the ministry. He shared the brief information of the previous seminar attended by him on this subject.

Following this we were able to hear the voices of the persons of the LGBTIQ community, who are facing the problems of being rejected, abused and hated by the community at large. One of them, Vijayaraj Malika, a transwoman said "I am neither a Ms or Mr. but I am 'Mx'. Vijayaraj Malika, who is well educated from Kerala and was at that time part of Marthoma church Mumbai's Navodaya Program. She shared about her feelings, how she felt like a rat in a cage, and a criminal in jail. Further Daniel — who is an intersex person - shared about the problems they face from their own family members, relatives, friends and colleagues. He had been through many dangers and difficulties and problems, which made him attempt suicide many times. He further shared that he praised God for the way he has been created in his mother's womb by God and liked to be always like that throughout his/her life. He is a Sunday school teacher in his church. Mr. Khushal Shrestha, who is originally from Siliguri, shared that after his coming out in his identity as a Gay, his family has not accepted him. However, with patience and strength that he has managed to live by himself. He has a challenge before him to work for his community, and give them courage to live life in his fullness.

Fr Philip Kuruvilla and Fr. Thomas Ninan, who are associated with NCCI – ESHA program shared the history of NCCI's human sexuality work and also provided biblical and theological inputs. In all the meetings, the delegates were divided into groups and they were given two questions. Each group listed the answers and presented them before the congregation. Here below are the 2 questions and some of the responses:

Q.1 What are some of the barriers we find in our Church today in making it a more inclusive Church?

Barriers:

1. Fundamentalism
2. Our culture does not allow us
3. Lack of education
4. Narrow mind
5. Lack of awareness
6. Church spirituality
7. Hiding their identity of T.G.
8. Husband and wife agenda
9. Splitting of the Church and Fear that Church loss their image
10. Social reasons
11. Inferiority complex
12. Shameful situation in the Church

13. Society have narrow mind

14. Misunderstanding

15. Shameful feelings

16. Lack of education

17. Lack of personal meetings/visitation/counseling

18. Being isolated from society

19. Their belief/behavior/rituals are different from society

20. Very difficult to convince fellow Church members about their acceptance

21. We do believe that according to Bible activities and behavior of Gay/Lesbian are sin

22. No TG has approached till date wanting to enter into Church

23. Hiding identity

24. Nobody in Church till date found and no barriers for them

25. Fear to show the reality to Church

Q.2 How can we as a pastors overcome these barriers and make our Church more inclusive?

Overcoming the barriers:

1. Community awareness

2. Bible teaching through seminar

3. Separate meetings for them

4. Visitation/ corps community

5. Respecting their identity

6. No criticism

7. Using their talents

8. Involvement in Church activity

9. Friendly relationship. Social help and breakthrough and seeking Government and Salvation Army support

10. We have to educate the Church. Bible based discussion

11. We have to pray for that to happen

12. Discussion with Society leaders

13. We have to make the people understanding in descriptive way

14. This subject to be added in education syllabus

15. More books to be written and awareness through films, drama

16. Through posters and newspapers awareness should be created

17. Live testimonies

18. Scientifically check up

19. Creating friendly atmosphere

20. Removing fear

21. We have to give place in Church

22. We have to love them

23. Awareness in Church through religious teaching

24. Understanding their feelings

25. Treat them with love and avoid abusive language

26. Prayers

27. Bible study

28. We have to arrange more awareness programme in Church

29. Church has to have black and white policy for such people's inclusions

30. We do need some trained people in this area so they can counsel to people

31. We have to prepare our people mentally

32. More and more individual and group counseling required

33. Encouraging to such people/individual to accept the reality

34. As an officer we have to visit them/love them and encouraging them through words of God

35. Officer should find such people and take care of them

36. We can help them by involving them in our meetings/worship

The time was so precious that we spent together, thinking and listening about the subject and the community. The said seminars made us alert and helped us to think that as God's servants, what can we do for the LGBTIQ community?

The Catholic Church's Response

His Holiness the Pope's positive statement regarding gays in 2014 has had some reverberation in India. Cardinal Gracias, who is also the Catholic Archbishop of Bombay, gave a statement in response to a letter from Queer Azaadi Mumbai (QAM), an LGBT group, about a sermon at St Thomas Church, Goregaon, where the priest allegedly described homosexuality as "a great sin" and opposed gay marriage. The Hindustan Times reported Cardinal Gracias said, "Going by the data in the letter, some of what the priest said is alright and some part is inappropriate. *The Church does not accept gay marriage because the Bible teaches us that God willed marriage to be between man and woman. On the other hand, to say that those with other sexual orientations are sinners is wrong. I do think we must be sensitive in our homilies [sermons] and how we speak in public, and I will so advise our priests.*" He added that the Church loved everybody, including those with different sexual orientations. In June, 2017, in Aluva, Kerala, Catholic nuns offered housing for the transpersons who have been given jobs in the Kochi Metro Rail Project. However the Catholic Bishops Conference of India [CBCI] does not seem to have shown much initiative in this field, and they have been unable to send representatives to any of the national- level Consultations organized by NCCI-ESHA in recent years.

Responses by the Senate of Serampore College and affiliated Theological Colleges

The Senate of Serampore College

The Senate has been extremely positive towards the LGBTI communities. It began by including HIV and AIDS in the curriculum for BD students in 2012. A Reader, 'Inclusive Communities", edited by Dr Wati Longchar and Fr Philip Kuruvilla, was released on February 4th, 2014, which encouraged greater inclusivity of Persons Living with AIDS [PLWA's], and the LGBTI or the "Rainbow" community as they were described by one theologian. In 2014 they also included an optional paper on 'Human Sexuality "in the curriculum for BD students. Meanwhile, the Board of Theological Education for the Senate of Serampore College [BTESSC] has been holding Consultations in various Theological Colleges. It even did a program highlighting this issue in Aizawl Theological College in January 2016. Subsequently, Rev Dr Patra was at the inauguration of the program in Leonard Theological College where NCCI's ESHA program began its work among several theological colleges. The NCCI's ESHA program is also working on a second Reader to supplement the one brought out by Dr Vincent Rajkumar of CSIRS and Dr George Zachariah. This Reader is Co-Edited by Rev Dr Roger Gaikwad and Fr Thomas Ninan, and is due to be released in August 2017. [For details of this Reader, see 'NCCI Publications on Allied Topics' in the *Addendum*].

Transphobia and Homophobia:
The Role of Theological Colleges
NCCI-ESHA and Bishop's College, Kolkata

The National Council of Churches in India has been a pioneering ecumenical Christian organisation boldly taking up issues that the weaker and the most vulnerable in our society face. Most of the time issues related to sexual minorities have been ignored and deliberately overlooked by the churches. A one day workshop was organised by the ESHA programme of the National Council of Churches in India jointly with Bishop's College on the theme "Transphobia and Homophobia in Churches: The Role of Theological Colleges" on 13th September 2016. This program gave the Bishop's College community a change to ponder upon the issues and challenges faced by sexual minorities. NCCI-ESHA program team consisting of Fr. Philip Kuruvilla and Fr. Thomas Ninan and Mr. Vijayan and from Bishop's College around 85 students and faculty members actively participated in the workshop.

The program started with the inauguration and welcome by Rev. Dr. Sunil Caleb, the Principal of Bishop's College, followed by Devotion and Bible Study on the theme "Embracing Diversity" by Mr. James Wesly S. Dean of Studies, Bishop's College. The Keynote Address on the theme Transphobia and Homophobia in Churches was given by Fr. Philip Kuruvilla, and Fr. Philip also briefed the participants about the joint venture that NCCI-ESHA has undertaken along with the Theological Colleges and Churches on this very pertinent Issue that church and society has to grapple with today. In order to understand the context and challenges faced by gender minorities. We had four friends namely Ms. Madhuja Nandi, Ms. Pompi Banerjee and Mr. Pawan Dhall and Anupam Sircar from the LGBTIQ community. The resource person challenged the audience by sharing their personal stories of struggle, pain and discrimination that they faced in their lives. Mr. Anupam Sircar shared few important points from legal perspective. This was followed by a session on 'The Church, Homophobia and Theology' by Dr Wati Longchar (Professor, Yushan Theological College and Seminary, Taiwan) and a session on 'Ministerial Perspectives on Human Sexuality and Gender Minorities' by Rev Philip V Peacock (Professor, Bishop's College, Kolkata). Thereafter ample time was given for group discussions, reporting and question and answer time. During the discussion and question answer session the following needs were identified. The need to re-read the scriptures from the perspective of gender minorities and the need to envision alternative theologies that are more inclusive in nature was deeply felt. Some of the key outcomes of the workshop are the reaffirmation about the importance and beauty of the diversity of God's creation. When confronted with diversity and differences the importance of being empathic, loving and the need for embracing diversity were highlighted during the workshop.

To say a few words about the impact of the workshop on Bishop's College; one can definitely say that the workshop has really challenged many of us by shaking our narrow uninformed parochial perspectives. Even after the end of workshop the discussions continued in our classrooms, dining hall and hostel corridors etc. In classroom discussions on human sexuality now students participate with more enthusiasm and with clarity of thought than before. One of the important fruits of the workshop is increased awareness, openness and interest in the area of gender diversity. This has resulted in one of our final year Bachelor of Divinity student undertaking research in the area of "Human Sexuality and Gender Diversity" and the thesis title is "A Theological Reflection on the Concept of Image of God in Relation with the Sexual Minorities." In the previous years we also had a final year student preparing and preaching his final year evaluation sermon and Eucharist worship highlighting the plights of Transgender by rereading the creation narratives. We have also started to offer the optional course

"Human Sexuality" for the final year BD Students at Bishop's College. For us at Bishop's College it was really a joy to work in partnership with NCCI. Bishop's College has always been open to issues faced by sexual minorities; in 2013 a debate was organised by the Middleton Society of Bishop's College on the title "The Church should bless Homosexual Marriages". The workshop has really helped us in continuing the debate and has paved the way for open discussion and has really challenged our narrow uninformed perspectives for which we are thankful to National Council of Churches in India.

Report of Activities and Programmes on Human Sexuality, Gender Equality and Sexual Minority at Eastern Theological College, Jorhat, Assam

The First Programme on Human Sexuality was organized at ETC, Jorhat under the initiative of ESHA Programme : A Workshop Jointly Organized by the ESHA Programme of the National Council of Churches in India (NCCI), and the Eastern Theological College, Jorhat, Assam.

1. Rev. Phanenmo Kath, Assist. Prof of Pastoral Counselling and Psychology presented a paper on the topic: "The Church, Transphobia and Homophobia: The Role of Theological College"

2. As a follow up programme, the Institute for Leadership Enhancement and Ministry Augmentation (ILEMA) of the Eastern Theological College organized and Seminar for BD Final Years and M.Th students in Four Disciplines (Christian Theology, History of Christianity, Christian Education (CM), and New Testament) on the Issues on Human Sexuality, Sexual Minorities, Gender Equality on November 2016. The resource persons were: 1. Rev. Dr. Razousalie Lasetso, Dean of ILEMA and Prof. of New Testament, Rev. Dr. Woba James HOD History of Christianity and Assist. Prof of History, and Rev. Phanenmo Kath, Chaplain and Assist. Prof. Pastoral Counselling and Psychology.

3. As a result of the two seminar Programmes held at Eastern Theological College, Jorhat, Assam a Bachelor of Divinity Student by name Ms. Imnanaro Longcher BD 2016-2017 batch wrote a

Thesis on Christian Response to LBGTIQ Community. She has already completed her BD. degree and now continuing her Master of Theology in Systemic Theology M.Th.

4. On 17th July 2017, The Christian Ministry Department (Post Graduate) **Eastern Theological College, Jorhat Assam** Organized a Seminar on Issues in Christian Ministry on the Topic: "Understanding Human Sexuality: Christian Response to LBGTIQ Community"

Presenter : Mr. Doukholien Hengna

Respondent Mr. Martin Zairem

Moderator : Rev. Phanenmo Kath

5. Eastern Theological College, Jorhat, Assam, being a premier theological college in North East India has a total enrolment of 280 students for two regular degree programmes, BD and M.Th in four disciplines, [Christian Theology, History of Christianity, Christian Education (CM), and New Testament].

Besides we also offers Master of Arts in Holistic Child Development (MA-HCD), also co-ordinates D.Min programmes of the Senate of Serampore college. Moreover we also guide 5 (five) D.Th students under Senate of Serampore College. Very soon we are planning to upgrade to Doctoral Research Centre in Three Disciplines Viz; Christian Theology, History of Christianity, Christian Education (CM), and New Testament. With all this development one of the major concern we emphasis is on the area of Human Sexual (Sexual Minority, and Gender Equality).

6. Very frequently the Faculty members of ETC, Jorhat actively participates in all NCCI programmes of Human Sexuality, gender Equality and sexual Minorities. Also participates in other Regional, National and International forum on such pertaining issues.

7. ETC, Jorhat also has a Women Study Centre, headed by a Dean and Committee members among the teaching Faculty. This caters to the needs and aspirations of the women concerns and issues. The

centre frequently organizes programmes related to women rights, gender equality and issues related to such subjects.

In brief, I can confidently conclude that Eastern Theological College, Jorhat, Assam, is one of the most happening colleges among Theological Seminaries in the country, in terms of its commitment and involvement on the Issues of Human Sexuality, Gender Equality and Sexual Minorities.

To God be the Glory!

The Gurukul Lutheran Theological College, Chennai – A brief report: Interventions in the field of Human Sexuality and Gender Diversity

The Gurukul Lutheran Theological College and Research Institute, Chennai is committed to issues related to Human Sexuality. At the NCCI-ESHA workshop held at the Ecumenical Resource Centre, United Theological College, Bangalore from April 19-20, 2016, the following future plans were suggested for Gurukul:

- Create awareness among the theological community —college faculty and students on Human Sexuality, through Faculty/Staff-Student workshops and seminars

- Invite persons of the sexually marginalized communities to address the college community on various occasions including during worship services

- Identify and encourage students to engage in ministry with the sexually marginalized during their Field Education and beyond

- Introduce courses on Human Sexuality and related issues in the BD/M.Th. curriculum. Encourage the faculty and students to do research on these topics and to avail of the limited scholarships available through the NCCI-ESHA.

Accordingly, the following programs were executed at Gurukul during the period 2016-2017.

1. The Women in Church and Society desk of UELCI organized a one day program on the theme, 'Towards Empowering People of All Genders: A Day with Transgender' on the 31st of May, 2017 at Ziegenbalg Auditorium, Gurukul Campus. This was attended by the Gurukul students, UELCI staff, and local pastors. It created a platform for the pastors and congregation members of local churches to establish relationship with the friends from transgender community in Chennai. Transgender friends shared their life experiences that brought out the hardships and challenges they encountered. The gathering also reflected on how church can become an inclusive community in welcoming transgender friends. Several pastors shared their willingness to work towards a church that treats transgender at par with others.

2. Some of the Gurukul students in the BD programme had personal interactions with the LGBTQ community during their Summer Field Education program.

3. Gurukul continues to offer a 2 credit course on Human Sexuality for M. Th. II students in the first semester. This course covers the Biblical, theological, ethical and ministerial perspectives on Human Sexuality. Students present seminar papers on the above areas which are responded to by their colleagues and faculty members from different departments.

I express my gratitude to the college administration especially the Director, Revd. Dr. A. G. Augustine Jeyakumar, the Principal, Revd. Dr. K. David Udayakumar, and the NCCI leadership for their continued support and encouragement for this partnership program. I hope that our college will be able to make substantial contribution in theory and praxis to the contextual issue of Human Sexuality thereby helping the students in their ministerial formation and providing theological guidelines to its participating churches and the Indian society at large.

'Homophobia and Transphobia: Role of Theological Colleges'
Report of the NCCI Seminar held at John Roberts Theological Seminary, Shillong

This seminar was held on the 7th September, 2017 at Rev. Kelvinel Memorial Chapel, John Roberts Theological Seminary, Mawklot Shillong. It is the first of its kind that the seminary could host. It is fortunate enough that NCCI, Nagpur could come to our college together with members of the LGBTIQ community representing some NGOs in Shillong and Assam. The discussion and face to face interaction with the members of the LGBTIQ community who have undergone series of discrimination, rejection, humiliation, physical and mental abuse, verbal abuse, was not only note worthy but an eye opener to all the members of JRTS community. The seminar also included lectures, slide show, testimony, interaction programme, and discussion and so on. The entire programme with different items and contents was well planned and organized in such a way that it could be beneficial and meaningful to the audience.

Some important comments by staff and students

1. The seminar was very helpful to our community as it was a new issue which is rarely discusses and deliberated within the church circles. To many among the entire audience this was the first time exposure to this type of programme and they had face to face interaction with the members of the LGBTIQ community.

2. It gives us profound knowledge and understanding about the plight and the experience of the member of the community in their journey in a society that does not count them as equals. The experience and ordeal they have to face throughout the journey is painful. Hence, it gives us new insights and new thoughts- not only about the seriousness of the issue but the urgent need how to accept and accommodate this section of population not only within the church but in the society as well.

3. It helps us to understand that human sexuality is a complicated issue and therefore need to have comprehensive understanding about it and other related issues connected with it. Our inherited and traditional understanding on this issue needs to be deconstructed so that we could able to see things with open mind and in a positive way.

4. It helps us to realise that we should not discriminate any individual on the basis of sexual orientation. This make us understand that we must not judge anything at face value without understanding the real reason what make people to do or live the way they are.

5. The Church need to be open on the issue and be accommodative so that no sections or groups be ignored or sidelines at any level. It should be place that gives room or space to all section of the population so that it will become the place where all sections of population have hope for a better life. Discrimination of any kind within the Church should not be encouraged nor tolerated. It entails that the Church need to reconsider its stands on this burning issue.

6. However, though the seminar has positively contributed to our knowledge it will be much better if we get some more information from medical perspective on this issue and a little more detail on legal perspective. In this seminar we have dealt at length on this issue from human rights perspective - therefore needs some more clarification.

Feedback collected from the students

1. The issue is very much helpful for them as it part of the curriculum prescribed by the Senate of Serampore. Most of the issues they are studying are mostly theoretical but it is good that this kind of programme gives them the opportunity to have practical involvement with this section of the population.

2. It was a wonderful experience to many of them to realize that these people are part of God's creation and created in God's image and need to be respected and accepted as they are. One cannot be ignored on the basis of sex or sexual orientation. For all these is part of the mystery of how things come into being and have to exist as they are.

3. The students felt that as we often talk about inclusivity so it is great opportunity for them to be with this community which till today was being ignored and isolated. Hence they take this as a first positive step in dealing with this group of people and how to be more accommodative and open towards this issue.

4. However this issue needs to be taken seriously so that it will not influence other young people who simply want to experience the other side of the fence. Awareness programmes for the same need to be taken into consideration as we are dealing with the issue.

5. Some answers were not so clear and convincing.

Suggestions

1. This kind of seminar needs to be conducted on a regular basis in our institutions so that the student can be benefitted and learn how to respond to this issue in a proper manner.

2. As they have to be involved in the practical ministry of the church the students wished that the seminar provided them with some tools on how to deal with it at a different level.

3. As theological students they wish that some text from the Bible related with the issue need to be taken into account.

4. If the organizers could bring educators or resource persons from different religious backgrounds it will be more informative and enriching.

5. It will be appreciated if steps are taken to make the church involved on this issue so that we can discuss this issue at different levels in the Church.

Outcome of the Seminary

This seminar helped us realise that we need to be open to different issues affecting human life and other creatures. No one should be discriminated on the basis of sex, gender, status, qualification, degree, economic status, etc. This is one of the optional courses prescribed by the Senate of Serampore College that the seminary considers of primary importance. The seminary is open to have more seminars that deal with different issues affecting Church and society.

Report of Leonard Theological College, Jabalpur to NCCI-ESHA

Greetings from Leonard Theological College.

Our college is privileged and honored by the opportunity given by NCCI- ESHA with yet another avenue in our theological venture to partner in God's ministry by conducting a one day workshop on 29th July, 2016 on the theme **Church and Homophobia**. Speakers from different specializations were invited to deliberate on the subject matter. For instance, Fr. Kuruvilla introduced the subject which provoked and aroused the curious minds of the audience. This was followed by presentations by Dr. O. P Raichandari HOD, psychiatry department Netaji Shubash Chandra Bose Medical College, Jabalpur, on the medical and psychological issues related to human sexuality, Advocate Arpan Pawar explicated on article 377 and Dr. George Zachariah enlightened the community on biblical and theological perspective on this issue. Another flavor was the voices from the LGBT Community- Rajneesh, Tapasya Verma and Sandhya Ghawri. It was in fact an eye opener as we began to theologically engage on the subject matter- Human Sexuality.

Simultaneously, the college sent two students to participate on a workshop on the theme **Religion and Sexuality for Seminary Students**, jointly organized by the ECC, Aneka-Trust and NCCI and National Ecumenical Forum of the Gender and Sexual Diversities. This was held on 26- 28 July, 2016 at ECC, Whitefield, Bangalore.

Eventually, both the Faculty and the student body took initiative in its own capacity in the form of participating, organizing, initiating and writing. Some of the follow-ups are mentioned as follows:

Following the workshop the School of Research committee of the college decided to concentrate its year long Staff Study Circle presentations on the theme: Partnership in God's Mission, affixing the theological area on Human Sexuality. This was approved by the Faculty Council and its outcome is the content from different perspectives in the College Journal "*Samskriti*" 2016-17 issue. A highlight of the content is mentioned as under:

1. Naveen Rao, "Partnership in God's Mission: Challenging of Interpreting Human Sexuality from the Biblical Texts."

2. Tekayaba Walling, "Diversity in Sexuality: Probing Eunuchs for an Inclusive Community."

3. David C. Scott, "Radha in the Erotic Play of the Universe."

4. Bendanglemla Longkumer, "Partnership in Mission: Inclusive and Accessible Mission."

5. Bendangtemjen, "Historiography of John Chrysostom's Concept on Homosexuality: Mapping the Partnership Trajectories."

6. Sulabha P Ahaley, "Methodist Infant Baptism and Christian Nurture."

The college also decided to open invitation to the students to take the Human Sexuality course to which few students responded and completed the course successfully. The college continues to offer the course successively. To this all the teachers came forward to teach from their respective departmental perspectives, which reflect the commitment of the college in contributing to this. For the course the students are asked to work on a project which will be helpful in having an indepth exploration on the subject matter in their BD level.

Leonard has different organizations under the Student Council. One of the organizations, Literary and Debating Society organized an inter-fellowship Debating on the Theme "Church and the LGBTQ Community" on 17th August 2016. This was an enriching time for the Leonard community as speakers deliberated on this theme both against and in favor.

Leonard is honored to have encouraged students to work on their BD thesis on this subject matter and in the 2016-2017 academic session we had one student who wrote on his thesis entitled: "Developing a New Missiological Model for Transgenders by Revisiting Salvation as Humanization by M. M Thomas." He was the recipient of **Scholarship for Students Pursuing Research in Human Sexuality and Gender Diversities**. For this year (2017-2018) we have another student writing thesis on the title, "Homosexuality, A Challenge to Christian Families: Theological Response."

The tie-ups between Leonard and NCCI-ESHA continues and hence, Dr. Bendanglemla Longkumer was invited to present a paper on "Biblical and Theological Perspectives on Human Sexuality and Gender Identities" at a Joint Program of NCCI and the CNI Bhopal Diocese at Indore, on 22nd March 2017.

The registrar will be representing the college for the National Consultation on Inclusivity related to Gender, Sexuality and Religion, scheduled to be held in Chennai from August 10-12, 2017.

Homophobia and Transphobia in Churches: Role of Theological Colleges
Brief Report of the Workshop from the Karnataka Theological College, Mangalore

Homophobia and Transphobia in Churches: Role of Theological Colleges was organised jointly by the ESHA Program of the National Council of Churches in India, and the Karnataka Theological College, Mangalore on 26th August 2016 at Bishop Jathanna Auditorium, KTC, Mangalore, which was a first attempt on the topic *Homophobia and Transphobia* at the college.

In the last academic year 2016-17, in the midst of a dilemma in offering the optional course in the syllabus for the BD students, we had decided to offer the course and two of us from the faculty opted to teach the subject in the second semester for the BD third years. And that was the perfect time when Fr. Philip Kuruvilla approached the college to find the possibilities of organising the workshop on the said theme, we gladly agreed to hold the workshop but limited the participation only to the faculty and the students, a closed circle, fearing the churches and the public negative responses, as it is yet to come to terms with Gender Diversity and Human Sexuality, and church does not speak anything openly on these issues.

However, the outcome of the workshop was very surprising and interesting. Under the main theme the topics covered were: *Ecumenical Accompaniment with Sexual and Gender Minorities*; *Christian Anthropology and*

Public theology for inclusivity to the LGBTIQ; and New Testament and Doctrinal Perspective. Apart from these, there were *Voices from the LGBT Community* and where people could discuss openly with the LGBTQ members, and another session with group discussion/workshop to come out with *Responses by Churches and Theological Colleges.*

Impact of the Workshop on the Students

The students were much enriched with all these inputs and their response to LGBTQ community and the issues related to were positive and motivating.

They expressed that:

* such topics should be part of the curriculum in the theological colleges.

* such workshops and seminars often be conducted for theological reflections, acceptance and solidarity.

* Theological colleges be a welcoming community to diverse gender identities

* Theological colleges could be a forum for initiating such dialogues with Church and the LGBTQ community as well with other faith communities.

* Church need to open its doors to include diverse gender identities and create open spaces for discussion and dialogue on Gender Identities and Human Sexuality.

* Be the agents to promote a just and inclusive community and society.

At the College

Soon after this workshop, we were at ease to teach the optional course on *Human Sexuality* in the second semester for the BD third year students. The syllabus was prepared by the senate of Serampore College, and two of us taught this course. This course focused on a critical study of theological and ethical interpretations of human sexuality within the Christian tradition, challenging the distorted and abusive interpretations that legitimize patriarchy, homophobia, sexual subjugation and abuse, etc. The study covered vast areas of Christian Sexual Ethics and doctrines of original sin, dualism, sexual morality, gender stereotypes, hetero-normative, and so on towards a liberative theology of human sexuality and inclusive community.

This opened space among the students for theological discussions and reflections on various issues concerned Gender diversity and human sexuality and opened up opportunities for a more liberative and inclusive understanding for a better society.

Further, students were encouraged to participate in the seminars and meetings at various occasions and meet the LGBTQ community to have greater understanding of their problems and issues.

One of the students came forward to write the thesis on Human Sexuality and we are encouraging her to go ahead with the proposal even with the limited reading materials.

The need for more reading materials and text books are felt greatly, and hence request ESHA program to make them available to the theological colleges.

Plan to organise a few workshops and seminars for church leaders and members at different areas in and around Mangalore to transform the faith communities into inclusive communities, with the help of ESHA Program!

Orthodox Theological Seminary, Kottayam

It was quite a pathbreaking event that was conducted by the Orthodox Church in August 2016. The program was to highlight the issues of the Transgender Community, and with them, to learn about the problems of other LGBTIQ. It was called the "Dialogue on Church & Transphobia," and was held at the Orthodox Theological Seminary [OTS], in Kottayam in August, 2016.

The OTS, along with the ESHA (NCCI) & the KCC, have organized this dialogue in the Smrithi auditorium of the OTS on Monday the 8th August 2016. This meeting was attended by 24 students from the Mar Thoma Theological Seminary, Kottayam, 17 students from the Kannamoola United Theological Seminary, [KUTS] Thiruvananthapuram, of the CSI Church, along with the 23 students of the MTh & DTh student community of the FFRRC of Senate of Serampore, and 174 students from OTS at the BD level.

The meeting was presided over by the principal of the Orthodox Theological Seminary [Fr. Dr. O. Thomas], and led by Fr Dr Reji Mathew [Secretary, KCC], Fr. Philip Kuruvila [ESHA-NCCI], Dr Varghese Punnoose [Dept of Psychiatry, Govt. MCH, Kottayam], Prof. George Zachariah [Dept.of Ethics, UTC, Bangalore] and by the representatives of the Transgender and Intersex communities viz. Mx. Mallika, Ms. Olga, Ms. Ananya and Daniel. Fr. Thomas Ninan [ESHA-NCCI] and Fr Dr Jacob Mathew [OTS] also spoke on the occasion. The meeting was an eye opener, not only to the student communities from the three seminaries of the three Episcopal

Churches in Kerala, but the ecumenical student body of FFRRC comprising of students from the Pentecostal, the Methodist, the Reformed Churches, and students as far from Mizoram, Assam, Meghalaya and Manipur also participated.

Subsequently, we were able to motivate the editorial board of the Malankara Sabha, the official Magazine of the Malankara Orthodox Syrian Church/Indian Orthodox Church to bring out one volume with five articles and with the editorial write up highlighting LGBTIQ. We presume not less than one lakh people across denominations read and reflected on the contents this official magazine from the Orthodox Church. Certain pages of the annual publication of the OTS viz. DEEPTHI 2016, was earmarked for articles for this cause.

Some of the students both in the FFRRC and in the BD course have shown interest to write their term papers and even theses on this issue. In short, the cause of LGBTIQ is getting into the minds of the student community of these seminaries in Kerala, and the involvement of students at the MTh-DTh levels could be increased in future.

[Excepts from the Report submitted to Bishop HG Dr Zacharias Mar Aprem, visiting professor, OTS, Kottayam, Kerala]

The United Theological College, Bengaluru

Initiatives on theological reflections on human sexuality

1. Organized a Seminar on Church and Homophobia in collaboration with ESHA NCCI on 6th August 2016. Dr. Wati Longchar, Dr. John Samuel Ponnusamy, Ms. Rosy Zoramthangi, Mr. Romal Laisram, Fr. Philip Kuruvilla and Fr. Thomas Ninan gave leadership to the Seminar. About fifty students and faculty members attended the Seminar.

2. As part of the concurrent field education program, several BD students got the opportunity to associate with sexuality and gender minorities and their organizations.

3. Mr. Karedi Silo did his senior sermon and worship on the theme human sexuality.

4. The course "Theological and Ethical Reflections on Human Sexuality" was offered for BD IV students in 2016-17. This year the same course is offered again for the BD students. The course "Sexual Ethics" is offered for MTh students this year.

5. Mr. Arvind Theodore did his MTh (Christian Ethics) thesis on the topic, "A Christian Ethical Response to Homosexuality with Special Reference to Homophobia in the Indian Christian Community." ESHA has awarded him the scholarship last year.

6. At present, the following students are doing theses on topics related to human sexuality:

a. Samuel Ragland Paul (BD) "Re-reading Incarnation through Queer Perspectives with Special Reference to Transgenders." Supervisor: George Zachariah

b. Priscilla Rawade (MTh Old Testament) "An Interpretation of the Holiness Code in Leviticus (17-26) from the Perspective of Homosexuality in the Present Context of Church in India." Supervisor: K. Jesurathnam

c. Shobha M (MTh Christian Ethics) "Church, A Moral Community of Disciples and Equals: Re-visioning Ecclesiology and Ethics from the Perspectives of Transgender Community." Supervisor: George Zachariah

d. Imnabenla Jamir (DTh Christian Ethics) "Towards a Relevant Sexual Ethics for India: Indian Church's Engagement with Homophobia with Special Reference to the Work of the National Council of Churches in India." Supervisor: George Zachariah

CHAPTER - 5

Documents, Reports and Statements: Helpful NGO's and Suggested Web Links/Books

Documents, Reports and Statements: Indian

An Epistle on Human Sexuality to the Churches in India

Outcome of NCCI'S 2nd Study Institute on Human Sexuality 24th to 26th of September, 2003 : Student Christian Movement of India (SCMI), Bangalore

Chapter 1: Greetings and Introductions

Dearly Beloved,

1. We who are called to be believers in the one Body of Christ address to you this epistle.

2. Grace and Peace to you! We the participants of the 2nd study Institute on Human Sexuality would like to address you in the name of God in and through whom we affirm our sexuality.

3. We have gathered here with the ecumenical affirmation that God is the source of all life and God affirms life in all its dimensions which includes human sexuality.

4. We know God also by knowing our sexuality.

5. On the invitation of the National Council of Churches in India, we the 70 participants sent by the member churches, organizations, institutions and other ecclesial communities, met here at the Student Christian Movement of India (SCMI), Bangalore from 24th to 26th of September, 2003 for the Second Study Institute on Human Sexuality. This was jointly organized by the SCMI, Indian Society for Promoting Christian Knowledge, United Evangelical Lutheran Church in India [HIV/ AIDS Desk] and the Church's Auxiliary for Social Action, with the assistance of International Services Association (INSA), Bangalore. We also received international guests representing Churches in Brazil and in Malawi sent by the World Council of Churches.

6. We struggled together with the issues of human sexuality. We listened to several theological presentations, Bible Studies and Devotions. We involved in group exercise, discussed in thematic tracks and participated in interactive games. We watched informative and educations films on human sexuality. We also visited People living with HIV/AIDS, and interacted with efforts at healing and caring for these people.

7. Our struggle through these processes led us to write this epistle to you.

8. We as the ecumenical movement are meeting here for the second time after the first attempt made in 2001 at Ooty when the First Study Institute on Human Sexuality was held. The results of that attempt was the First ever statement of the Indian ecumenical movement on Human Sexuality. The wider ecumenical movement in India however was reluctant to give it its due prominence.

9. We are also aware that we are meeting in a context that has changed since Ooty. We now observe openness in society with regard to sexuality discourses and the willingness to educate our children in the issues and concerns of human sexuality.

10. The new economic scenario of globalization has led to changing patterns in relationships, in family and in other social structures.

11. We also meet at a significant moment in time when the global churches are not only struggling with these issues, but are also expressing themselves differently. For example the issues surrounding the Consecration of a gay bishop, the ordination of gay/lesbian priests and pastors, and the solemnizing of same-sex marriages.

12. The rapid development in information technology has also enabled an openness and offered a new space in relation to human sexuality discourses.

13. This has led to the breaking of the 'culture of silence' with regard to human sexuality.

14. Furthermore, there have been advances in science and technology that are continuing to redefine our understanding of human sexuality in terms of genetic engineering to DNA mapping, cloning etc. These have brought to the fore the issues related to bio-ethics.

15. All these changes have dramatically affected and influenced the structures and configuration of relational patterns within and outside the family.

Chapter 2: "My sexuality is a gift from God".

1. Our theological quest in struggling with the issues of Human Sexuality helped us to affirm that, to be human is to be sexual.

2. We came to understand that knowing sexuality is knowing God.

3. We grappled with scriptural texts that would undergird our understanding of sexuality. To our surprise the scriptural understanding of the 'metaphor of the Body' led us to believe in the equality of all members of the body while affirming their diversity.

4. Diversity is not negated, while quality is affirmed.

5. Sexual minorities are affirmed as equal parts of the Body and therefore they cannot be discriminated against.

6. We now know that when one of us suffers "all of us suffer" (1 Cor. 12:12-27).

7. This has encouraged us to reject the dualistic understanding of the 'body' as sinful. We recognize that our understanding of body and sexuality as sinful, is also a result of cultural conditioning. For example, in an effort to reject the dualistic understanding of the body as sinful. We re-imaged our perspective of the sacrament of baptism as a celebration of the body.

8. We discussed the controversies surrounding the notions of what is natural and unnatural (heterosexuality and homosexuality), sex for pleasure and sex for procreation and the notions of right and wrong sexuality.

9. We humbly ask therefore "who decides what is natural, and what are the forces that legitimize this as natural?"

10. We looked at how the covenantal partnership within a marriage is no longer 'a given', and this leads us to assert that we need to reconstruct the structures of family and relationships.

11. We recognize the there are ambiguities in our acceptance of our bodies as being created in the image of God (Gen 2:11). This is because, within the Old Testament, there is a reluctance to give God a body.

12. In order to give God a body, we need to revalue our bodies as female and male.

13. When we can reclaim male and female sexuality in all its dimensions – from the barrenness to the fertility, from the potency to the impotency – then we can embody God in a holistic way, as being both responsive and reactive to us.

14. We were led to understand, that in the effort to revalue what has been devalued in our sexuality, we need to also re-image sexual minorities as people with a claim to their rightful place within the Body of Christ.

Chapter 3: Our Theological Quest

•   The journey into the realms of human sexuality led us to define human sexuality in its multiple dimensions.

- Human sexuality includes a range of feelings and behavior, expressing relationship through look, touch, word and action. It includes the identity and role of gender and sex (anatomy and physiology).

1. Human sexuality is also about power.

2. Sexuality could exist independently of marriage or the physical act. We affirm therefore, that human sexuality embraces all forms of human expression and is a function of our whole personality that is lifelong beginning from birth.

3. We reaffirm that human sexuality is God's gift.

4. Several issues that invade our social life distort this all-embracing understanding of human sexuality.

5. The issues of single parenthood and the lack of adequate understanding of adolescent sexuality have resulted in serious behavioral conflicts in society.

6. Distorted understanding of human sexuality has deeply affected the so-called traditional 'family'. And hence we addressed the related issues like drug addiction, rape (also within marriage), unwanted pregnancies, HIV/AIDS, STDs (sexually transmitted diseases), promiscuity and the like.

7. With the onslaught of the new age electronic/digital communications, there has been a progressive increase in the commoditization and commercialization of the human body.

8. These twisted understandings need to be addressed.

9. We recognize that sexual rights are also human rights. This understanding leads us to reject several forms of gender discrimination, stereo typing and exclusion.

10. There is a need to demystify the language related to human sexuality. This will facilitate the emergence of an alternative, inclusive, non-dualistic language that goes beyond cultural, religious and adopted conditions.

11. While dealing with issues of human sexuality, we identified the inescapable and intrinsic connection of human sexuality with the whole gamut of HIV/AIDS. While we acknowledge that this connection helps liberate us from the narrow and simplistic linking of 'sin' and HIV/AIDS.

12. We need to reject our judgmental prejudices towards commercial sex-work as a profession, and our attitude towards commercial sex workers as a community.

13. Our understanding of human sexuality is built on a strong commitment to a value system, which is based on love, justice, inclusiveness, healing, relationality, faithfulness and dignity. Therefore our ethical framework for relationships should also be based on these values.

Chapter 4: Actions and Approaches to communicating our understanding of human sexuality:

• Be receptive to people's levels of openness before broaching the topic of sexuality. Talk about embarrassing things related to sexuality in a way that people understand it as normal part of being a body. Be comfortable to talk about sexuality ourselves before we try to talk about it to others.

• "know your body' can be a helpful phrase to explain the entire dimension of sexuality but be careful in the implications that can be drawn from this.

• not taking the Bible literally.

• Rights and responsibilities go together.

• gender stereotypes can be unlearned.

• Human sexuality education should be encouraged in all levels – schools, colleges, etc.

• Pastors need to be given sexual education.

- Counselors in each church should be trained to effectively communicate the understanding of sexuality.

- Making liturgical language to be inclusive of all sexualities; include sexual minorities in intercessory prayers.

Chapter 5: Our Prophetic Discipleship

1. There is a prophetic responsibility for the faith community to participate in the 'exclusion experience' of the excluded and drawing from those experiences and resources in order to become a channel for the liberation of all parts of the Body of Christ.

2. When Moses was the adopted son of Pharaoh living in the Palace, he could not perceive the suffering or need for the liberation of the Israelite people. It was Moses who was a fugitive in the desert, who was hiding, who was able to discern the God of the burning bush, perceive the suffering of the Israelites and envision their liberation.

3. The Jesus experience also was drawn from the context of identifying with the struggles of the oppressed communities and thereby articulating and involving in a participatory liberation for all peoples.

4. Our prophetic discipleship places a similar demand on us on the faith community to participate in the struggles and from the side of the marginalized envision a liberation that is inclusive.

5. We should draw strength from the faith experiences of Tamar, Esther, and Ruth and Naomi, Rahab, Mary Magdalene – the woman caught in adultery, the Samaritan woman, the Eunuchs in the books of Esther and Acts in our effort to be prophetic.

Chapter 6: Commendation and Benediction

1. We affirm our human sexuality in all its dimensions as a gift of God.

2. We confess that as a Christian communion, we have rejected, excluded and ignored people who also have a rightful place in the same Body of Christ.

3. We acknowledge the there are diverse understandings of God and sexuality which are also unique.

4. We affirm our unity and our diversity in the Body of Christ.

5. Grace be with all those who love the Body of Christ.

AMEN.

[From NCCI Archives]

An Ecumenical Document on Human Sexuality

Created by the Commission on Justice, Peace and Creation, NCCI, and adopted by the Honorable General Body of the National Council of Churches in India, on 24th September, 2011, for implementation (vide Res. No.21/GB/2011) and first published by Dr. Roger Gaikwad, General Secretary, NCCI, in 2012.

Preamble

At the heart of Christian faith is the core spirituality which each Christian is called to follow: Love God and love your neighbour as yourself. Based on the foundational theological understanding that every human being is made in the image of God, we urge the Churches to review and affirm sexuality as a gift from God. While we celebrate this divine gift, we lament the loss of its sacred character in the way in which we perceive and practice sexuality, resulting in acts of sexual violence. Therefore we affirm:

1. Love in all its forms, 'agape', 'philea' and 'eros', is central to the Christian understanding of the divine and the consequent ordering of human communities

In essence, God is love. The Bible bears witness to this self-revealing God of love. It bears witness to a God who out of love reaches out to liberate creation. The New Testament suggests that the summary of God's Law is love. Accordingly, the Christian vocation is to love God and to love the neighbor as one's own self. The Christian faith tradition has understood love in three forms: 'Agape', 'Philea' and 'Eros'. All these three forms of love are integrated and interrelated. In 'agapeic' love God gives God-self away for creation. In 'phileal' love God comes to dwell with us and befriends us. At the heart of this self-giving and befriending love of God is a desire within the life of God to know and to be known. This 'erotic' desire of God to know and be known makes 'agape' and 'philea' possible. As God reaches out to us to know us, we are invited to enter into the triune life of God by "knowing" God. This "knowing" in the New Testament tradition is an 'erotic' knowing. It arises out of our "restless" quest for our life with and in God. At the heart of all our human relationships is the desire to know and to be known. This desire which is a gift from God as a consequence of being created in the image of God makes all human relationships possible.

2. Sexuality is characteristic of our being created in the image of God and has the potential to facilitate our becoming in God. At the foundational core of Christian theological anthropology is the belief that we are all created in the image of God

As being counterparts of God, we reflect God's longing and capacity to love. To be in the image of God, therefore, is to be in love as relational beings. Our desire to know and to be known by the other is characteristic of the love that binds human communities, a manifestation of which we see in the making of love in a covenantal relationship. This form of love expressed in mutual respect, consensus and tender care enables us to grow in the bond of love thus facilitating the sanctifying process of our becoming into the likeness of Christ which is love.

3. Sexuality is essentially relational and has pluriform expressions

Sexuality as an indispensable dimension of all human development and life is as complex and diverse as the human population, because each human experiences and expresses sexuality in different ways. Sexuality is pluriform, ambiguous and fluid. Sexuality is essentially relational and involves human relations with the self, the other and the divine.

4. Sexuality can however be distorted

Though human sexuality is an indispensible dimension of life, it is also experienced and expressed in a distorted way. The beauty, sacredness and transcendence of materiality of human sexuality is distorted by unequal power relations, violence, objectification and commodification of the body and sexual reductionism instead of a liberative sexuality. This distorted concept of sexuality is underpinned by culture, theology and the judgmental moralizing of the church.

5. We need to Re-read Sexuality in Scripture, Tradition and Liturgy

Readings of scripture, tradition and liturgy, with openness to sensuality, affirm sexuality. Scripture provides us with instances of deep love, sensuality and sexuality being expressed by biblical characters. The biblical vision of the future of the world is couched in a sensuous language of the union of the bride and the bridegroom. Christian tradition in its mystic spirituality and the consequent aesthetic expressions have embraced sexuality as a form of Christian love. Such awareness calls us to re-read the scripture and tradition to retrieve the sacred character of sexuality and its centrality in our spiritual pursuits.

The dichotomy between spirituality and physicality is blurred when sexuality is embraced within a horizon of human flourishing and covenantal love. Our popular imagination of reality and the consequent spiritual practice is conceived in dualistic terms of dichotomy between the "spiritual" and the "material." Such dichotomy often results in trivializing sexuality or relegating sexuality as being something profane. Such dichotomy and the consequent distortion of sexuality can be overcome by embracing sexuality as a gift from God and practiced with recognition that it facilitates human flourishing and deepens covenantal love.

7. The Church has to be an inclusive just community

A theological conversation on sexuality will further enable the church's self-understanding and witness as a welcoming and affirming community, making space within which the human rights and dignity of all will be upheld.

From An Ecumenical Document on Human Sexuality : Published by Rev Roger Gaikwad for NCCI

[From An Ecumenical Document on Human Sexuality : Published by Rev Roger Gaikwad for NCCI: Copyright: NCCI: 2012]

Senate of Serampore College's Course syllabus

'Human Sexuality: Theological and Ethical Reflections' 2 Credit hours, Optional Course, College Examined: Theology Cluster

Course Objectives

This course focuses on a critical study of theological and ethical interpretations of human sexuality within the Christian tradition to equip the students to enable the faith communities to celebrate human sexuality as a divine gift, challenging the distorted and abusive interpretations that legitimize patriarchy, homophobia, sexual repression and abuse, and negative attitudes towards pleasure and sensuality. The course provides the students the opportunity to grapple with issues of sexual ethics from South Asian context and to search for ethical discernment and praxis. The course is expected to equip the students to transform our faith communities into inclusive communities enabling the sexual well-being of all God's children without prejudice and discrimination.

Course Requirements

1. Informed, and active participation in the class **15%**

2. One Group Seminar presentation based on ethical issues (Unit 3) **25%**

3. Final examination or a research paper of approximate 20 pages **60%**

Course Outline

Unit 1: Church and Human Sexuality: A Critical Evaluation

Doctrine of Original Sin, Dualism, Body as evil, Women as property incubators and fallen Eves, Sensuality as concupiscence, Monasticism and suppression of body and sensuality, Patriarchal family and marriage as institutions to regulate sexuality, Marital fasting, Celibacy, Augustine, Aquinas, John Chrysostom, Luther and Calvin

Unit 2: Church and Sexual Morality: A Critical Evaluation

Sexuality and Natural law ethics, Procreation as the *telos* of sexuality, Chastity and Virtue ethics, Victorian morality and colonization of body and desire, Colonial and "Christian" perception of traditional understanding of sexuality as immoral, Sexual sins, Social construction of gender stereotypes, Hetero-normativity and homophobia

Unit 3: Towards a Liberative Christian Sexual Ethics

Sexuality as Social construct (Foucault), Rethinking body and gender, Rethinking sexuality and sexual difference, Queer ethics, Just love and Just sex, Re-visiting ethical issues—Sex and single person, Dating and Cohabitation, Marriage and Family, Contraception, Sexual abuse and Intimate violence, Women's control over their body and reproductive rights, Sexual differences and Same-sex Unions

Unit 4: Towards a Liberative Theology of Human Sexuality

Whose Sexuality, Whose Tradition, Whose Scripture: Perspectives from the excluded bodies, Theological reflections on *eros* and sensuality, A body-affirming spirituality, Redeemed Masculinities

Unit 5: Church: An "Erotic" Community of Friends and Lovers

Statement of the NCCI-ESHA Pre-Assembly:
Towards Just and Inclusive Communities
April 19-20, 2016:
United Theological College, Bengaluru

The NCCI-ESHA PRE-ASSEMBLY focusing on "Greater inclusivity in churches and theological education" brought together 60 delegates from various theological colleges and churches from various parts of India from April 19 – 20, 2016 at the United Theological College, Bengaluru, to engage in two days of exciting deliberations.

Indian society at large looks at the issue of sexuality with much suspicion and taboo, often influenced by the predominant notions within their communities and their religions. This has resulted in the marginalization of the communities of persons with diverse sexualities in India, who today are fighting for the repeal of Section 377 of the IPC, advocating for a dignified life in the society for their constitutional rights and much required space in society.

At the same time, diverse sexualities are today an acknowledged and open fact of Indian society. With changing societal norms, active and easily accessible social media and open discussions, an increasing number are coming out to share their journeys – their doubts and struggles – and are gradually finding peer, legal and civil society support.

The pre-assembly heard, and was deeply touched, by stories of the struggles of persons having diverse sexualities. Presently, except for a few stray voices, the Church in India is in denial about the magnitude and impact of this issue. It has only a limited idea of the extent to which its members and youth are faced with this within themselves and in their peer circles. Christian families are not able to find the support they need from the Church or from their personal faith. It is important to acknowledge that the present situation of the Church is our individual and collective failure, and not the fault of those with diverse sexualities. Our understanding of the biblical traditions and their administration in the church has certain limitations in attending to people with different sexualities.

The Pre-Assembly is convinced and recommends that the time has come for the Church to urgently respond and with deliberate purpose to their needs.

CHALLENGES

- There is widespread lack of clarity on the issues regarding persons with diverse sexualities such as :

  o definitions, and the implications of the differences within persons with diverse sexualities

  o understanding of their perspectives

  o separation of gender identity and sexual orientation

- The present response of churches and theological colleges:

  o The response ranges between ostracism and a reluctant acceptance

  o Most are judgmental; persons with diverse sexualities are stigmatised and discriminated against; Homophobia is common

  o Insensitivity to the perspectives of persons with diverse sexualities in their use of language and interpretation of scripture

  o Do not know how to respond to genuine struggles of individuals understanding their sexualities

- Difficult to get agreement by the Churches to accept / address different sexualities. This is a sensitive issue that can cause divisions within the church

- Creating awareness in churches

  o The task is mammoth - in size as well as to change long-entrenched beliefs and understandings

  o Difficulty of practically communicating the message to congregations

  o There is varying capacity of the local churches / congregations

- Wide gap between theological education and grassroots realities

  o Faculty have differing perspectives on human sexuality

  o Few theological colleges provide experiential learning experiences in this area

WAYS FORWARD

- The Church in India needs to accept that an increasing number of persons are expressing their diverse sexualities, and is happening in the Church community as well

- The Church in India should envision its mission as a journey alongside persons with diverse sexualities, offering respect and love, and accepting members who have diverse sexualities as fellow-believers

- Create clarity on the various aspects of diverse sexualities (definitions, perspectives, etc.)

- The NCCI member churches and theological colleges should take a decision to address the issues of human sexuality and homophobia

  o End the culture of silence in the Church around issues of human sexuality diverse sexualities

  o Actively build awareness and inclusive Christian perspective on human sexuality including diverse sexualities

  o Build capacity of the local churches / congregations / theological colleges

  o Eliminate the stigma and discrimination and contempt against those with diverse sexualities

- o   Develop compassionate responses to the struggles of individuals discovering their sexualities. This should be developed as a focused pastoral issue, providing appropriate care and counseling facilities and training

- o   Help affected persons to integrate with society through initiatives like Self Help groups, employment in Church bodies and agencies, etc.

- o   Engage in discussions with members of the extended Christian family, and in inter-faith and secular forums

- Theological colleges should be challenged:

  - o   to take a proactive stance, assimilate and interpret secular and other perspectives, and serve as thought leaders for their churches and as role-models to their students

  - o   discussions on human sexuality including diverse sexualities should be beyond the classroom – such as student forums, campus and church Bible studies, clergy and alumni refresher courses, publications in church and christian magazines

  - o   to go out and interact with society - interact with grassroots realities of sexuality (in integration with their other grassroots initiatives)

[Compiled by Fr Thomas Ninan and Fr Philip Kuruvilla]

Documents, Reports and Statements: International

Yogyakarta Principles [2006]

From the 'Introduction to the Yogyakarta Principles'

[For full text and details see: *http://www.yogyakartaprinciples.org/introduction*]

All human beings are born free and equal in dignity and rights. All human rights are universal, interdependent, indivisible and interrelated. Sexual orientation and gender identity are integral to every person's dignity and humanity and must not be the basis for discrimination or abuse. Nevertheless, human rights violations targeted toward persons because of their actual or perceived sexual orientation or gender identity constitute a global and entrenched pattern of serious concern. They include extra-judicial killings, torture and ill-treatment, sexual assault and rape, invasions of privacy, arbitrary detention, denial of employment and education opportunities, and serious discrimination in relation to the enjoyment of other human rights. These violations are often compounded by experiences of other forms of violence, hatred, discrimination and exclusion, such as those based on race, age, religion, disability, or economic, social or other status.

The International Commission of Jurists and the International Service for Human Rights, on behalf of a coalition of human rights organisations, have undertaken a project to develop a set of international legal principles on the application of international law to human rights violations based on sexual orientation and gender identity to bring greater clarity and coherence to States' human rights obligations. A distinguished group of human rights experts has drafted, developed, discussed and refined these Principles. Following an experts' meeting held at Gadjah Mada University in Yogyakarta, Indonesia from 6 to 9 November 2006, 29 distinguished experts from 25 countries with diverse backgrounds and expertise relevant to issues of human rights law unanimously adopted the Yogyakarta Principles on the Application of International Human Rights Law in relation to Sexual Orientation and Gender Identity.

The 29 Yogyakarta Principles address a broad range of human rights standards and their application to issues of sexual orientation and gender identity. The Principles affirm the primary obligation of States to implement human rights. Each Principle is accompanied by detailed recommendations to States. The experts agree that the Yogyakarta Principles reflect the existing state of international human rights law in relation to issues of sexual orientation and gender identity. They also recognise that States may incur additional obligations as human rights law continues to evolve.

The Yogyakarta Principles affirm binding international legal standards with which all States must comply. They promise a different future where all people born free and equal in dignity and rights can fulfil that precious birthright.

Statement:
Jakarta Statement on
Church and Homophobia
Venue: Jakarta Theological Seminary
from 23rd to 26th November, 2014

We, the participants of the International Consultation on Church and Homophobia held at Jakarta Theological Seminary, believe that each person is created in the image of God, and each person is precious to God.

We affirm that sexuality is a divine gift, and hence God intends us to celebrate this divine gift in life-giving, consensual, and loving relationships. It is in such celebrations of our sexuality that we grow into the fullness of our humanity, and experience God in a special way.

We believe that our negative attitudes towards sexuality and our body-denying spirituality stem from distorted understandings of God's purpose for us. The embodied God who embraced flesh in Jesus Christ is the ground for us to love our bodies and to celebrate life and sexuality without abuse and misuse. So God invites us to experience sexual fulfillment in our relationships of justice-love with the commitment to be vulnerable, compassionate, and responsible.

We recognize that there are people with diverse sexual orientations, gender identities and gender expressions. The very faith affirmation that the whole human community is created in the image of God irrespective of our sexual orientations, gender identities and gender expressions makes it imperative for us to reject systemic and personal attitudes of homophobia, transphobia and any kind of discrimination against persons of diverse sexual orientations, gender identities and gender expressions.

We believe that the Church as 'Just and Inclusive Community' is called to become a community without walls to reach out to people who are stigmatised and demonised, and be a listening community to understand their pains, desires, and hopes.

We envision Church as a sanctuary to the ostracised who thirst for understanding, friendship, love, compassion and solidarity, and as the Body of Christ that joins in their struggles to live out their God-given lives. So we appeal to the Christian communities to sojourn with people with diverse sexual orientations, gender identities and gender expressions and their families without prejudice and discrimination, to provide them with ministries of love, compassionate care, and justice.

We implore Christian communities to begin to engage in dialogue – not debate – with persons with diverse sexual orientations, gender identities and gender expressions and listen to their stories and struggles as acts of love.

We urge churches, seminaries and Christian communities to engage diverse voices and perspectives in theological reflections, particularly persons of diverse sexual orientations, gender identities and gender expressions. We encourage more research to be undertaken on issues pertaining to human sexuality in their respective socio-cultural context.

We hope and pray that the embodied God will bless our endeavours to grow into the fullness of life, and to transform our faith communities into communities of dignity, respect, egalitarianism, justice and love.

Report of the Asian Consultation on Church Responses to Human Sexuality and Gender Minorities

Feb 7-9, 2017 Venue: Ecumenical Christian Centre, Bengaluru

An Asian level consultation on Church Responses to Human Sexuality and Gender Minorities was held at the Ecumenical Christian Centre, Bengaluru from Feb 7 – 9, 2017. The consultation was organized by the National Council of Churches in India in collaboration with Kerk in Actie, the Ecumenical Christian Centre and the Bread for the World, bringing together delegates from the South and South East Asian countries. 50 delegates took part in the consultation, consisting of theologians, queer theologians, church leaders and Christian representatives from the LGBTIQ communities from the region.

Background of the Consultation

Through the last few decades, while the Western world has at large been comparatively liberal in integrating the sexual and gender minorities (LGBTIQ) within the mainstream society, the East, particularly the Asian countries have handled it with much suspicion, trepidation and caution, in spite of the very positive stand of health agencies like the WHO in this regard. A significant number of school drop outs, the resulting illiteracy and inability to get jobs, result in a high number of LGBTIQs engaging in sex work and begging to make a living, facing increasing stigma and discrimination from all sections of the society. This continues to affect the key affected people [KAP's], especially LGBTIQ communities in Asia, who are unable to live a life of dignity in the margins.

In the Asian context, while faith engagement in this area has been limited, there has been a few churches and theological colleges which have gone ahead to do unique ministries among the sexual minorities. The National Council of Churches in India [NCCI] has, since 2001, engaged the churches in India in the area of Human sexuality and Gender identities. Besides the "Document on Human Sexuality" accepted by the NCCI Member churches in 2009, it has – in this last year - engaged with five member churches and eight theological colleges in India, bringing about awareness and a compassionate and pastoral response from them.

In such a context, there is a need to consolidate the faith responses and learning from an Asian point of view, which in turn will go a long way in contributing towards faith responses to human sexuality all over the world.

Aims and objectives

i.   To bring together church responses and engagement with sexual minorities from this region of Asia to consolidate networking and key learning, and to decrease the stigma of the Church towards these communities.

ii. To identify relevant ways of church and theological engagement with the sexual minorities in three specific areas, namely a) Contextual Bible Reading, b) Sermon methodologies, c) Theology of life.

Outcomes

i.   A broad directory of church responses to human sexuality and gender minorities in South and South East Asia.

ii. Develop interest among theologians and churches from South & SE Asia and bring out resources in contextual bible reading, sermon methodologies and theology of life for church engagement with sexual and gender minorities, in the geographical context.

iii. Raise key issues that need attention from communities and government agencies and identify further role for church engagement.

Key points shared

Inaugural

In the inaugural address, Dr Manoj Kurian from the WCC stressed that sexuality is a part of our being, and our experience of it is defined by our religious, social and political context. Sexuality invokes powerful and contradictory binaries:

- it can embody a loving relationship but also ignorance and hatred;

- it can empower and also subjugate/control.

- The faith context is important, but can also promote violence

Therefore, we need to have safe spaces of grace to accompany each other in understanding our sexualities, and cannot afford to continue ignoring it. If we as a faith community keep shut, we deprive the young from understanding this from faith perspective. The features of safe spaces, and how they operate at different levels was explained, relating to: Governance and leadership, Ethical and theological, Community, Congregation and Family.

Plenary 1: Church Engagement in Human Sexuality – The Kairos framework

Moderator: Dr Manoj Kurian, WCC, Geneva

Presentation by Prof Gerald O. West, **School of Religion, Theology and Classics, University of KwaZulu-Natal, Pietermaritzburg, South Africa**

Prof. West described the Kairos Framework as a way for Christians to work on issues of human sexuality. The inherited church theology does not have the capacity to engage with emerging struggles. The Kairos process advocates for a People's Theology from among such struggling communities, such as the LGBTI people of faith, though it may be "rough". People's theology is important as it precedes Prophetic Theology, and socially engaged biblical scholars and theologians should come alongside LGBTI forms of People's theology, facilitating forms of Prophetic Theology within the Church.

Panel Discussion 1: Church engagement in Human Sexuality: Scope and Impact of Contextual Theology related to Human Sexuality

Moderator: Metropolitan Dr Geevarghese Mar Coorilos, Syrian Orthodox Church (India) & Moderator, Council for World Mission and Evangelism

Panelists: Prof Gerald West **(South Africa)**, Ms Pearl Wong **(Hong Kong)**, Prof George Zachariah **(India)**, Bishop Arichea Daniel **(Philippines)**, Rev Miak Siew **(Singapore)**

Presentation 1: Queer theologies in the Asian context – scope for church engagement, by Ms Pearl Wong, Queer Theology Academy, Hong Kong

Ms Wong discussed doing queer theologies in the context of Hong Kong and in collaboration with queer Christians from other Asian countries. Highlighting that shame and stigmatisation lead to hiding of sexual identities, she spoke of the need to challenge the hetero-patriarchal normative, and the need for a theology that liberates queers from heterosexist domination and stigmatisation. Queer Theology empowers queer Christians. Queer Theology Academy offers, among other things

- Courses on Sexuality and Ethics

- Workshop offering resources with a queer theological perspective:

  o Counter fundamentalist churches and Christians with homophobia

  o Minister more effectively to LGBTIQ congregations

- Theological articulation of LGBTIQ concerns and perspectives through publication

Presentation 2: The impact of doing Contextual Theology in Human Sexuality with church engagement – the South African experience, by Prof Gerald West, South Africa

Prof West discussed three examples of Contextual Theology in South Africa, each of which drew on its own "People's" theology:

- South African Contextual theology

- South African Black Theology

- South African Feminist / Women's Theology

Each offers its own resources:

- South African Contextual theology offers "the church as a site of struggle" and "theology as a site of struggle"

- South African Black Theology offers "the Bible as a site of a struggle"

- South African Feminist / Women's Theology offers "culture as a site of a struggle"

Together they offer a way of doing theology from below

The institutional church has failed to embrace this opportunity. It remains mired in theology of retribution, and constitutional and legal framework are perceived as threats to the status quo. The Church, which was at the forefront of other struggles for liberation, is lagging behind in this struggle for LGBTI – it is retreating and objecting, constrained by the theology it has received.

Theology needs to happen at the margins, by those marginalized by the churches and by those working with LGBTI sectors outside the church (places like Ujamaa Centre). And this needs Church leaders willing to take a stance, and act as a bridge between the Church and the LGBTQI community

The other aspect to keep in focus the need for systemic impact, as the rights of LGBTI is a justice issue, not a moral issue. Contextual theology focuses on systems and structures (particular social systems eg heteropatriarchy)

Contextual Bible theologies deconstruct dominant theologies and give voice to the less dominant ones. They move these from the margins to the Centre and increase the social, ecclesial and theological space to do theology in the context of diverse sexualities. It is important that the Centre is willing to participate in this theological work with the margins, and needs to be shown the way.

Response 1: Prof George Zachariah, United Theological College, Bengaluru

Prof Zachariah raised the questions of whether the methodology of contextual theology is adequate to develop a queer theology and whether queer theology is capable of developing an inter-sectional approach in the Indian context, since it has to take into account caste, class, ethnicity and multiple religious belonging. Moreover, it still remains a solidarity theology because the discrimination against LGBTIQs constrains participation of theologians who are queer. He emphasized that the Church in India needs to initiate dialogue with the queer movements.

Response 2: Rev Miak Siew, Free Community Church, Singapore

Rev Miak started with this striking statement, "Being here and hearing you all talking about this is healing to me", as a reference to the gap between the Church and the Academia when it comes to doing Contextual theology. He recounted how the Free Church in Singapore started as group to do Bible studies, and then formed as a church after a member was excommunicated from his mega church.

The brokenness that LGBT persons feel is often caused by the church which, rather than being a place for reconciliation and healing, is a place for condemnation and discrimination. An LGBTQI person has many more identities apart from his or her sexuality. Yet, when one hears the statement, "Love the sinner, hate the sin", it is difficult because it feels as though he/she being identified only as a sexual object, whereas sexuality is only a small part of his/her identity. They are not acknowledged or allowed to express the many talents they have in music, art, singing, teaching Sunday school, etc.

Healing of the brokenness is like *Kintsugi* , the Japanese art of repairing broken pottery with lacquer dusted or mixed with powdered gold, silver, or platinum. As a philosophy, it treats breakage and repair as part of the history of an object, rather than something to disguise. Rev Miak has found that he is better able to take sides with people who have been marginalised; "my brokenness is the site of God's action". He also emphasized that the challenge is to respond to the needs of all those who are oppressed (not just the LGBTQI community) and help them to put their pieces back together.

Response 3: Bishop Arichea Daniel, United Methodist Church, Philippines

Bishop Arichea observed, "Listening to these presentations gives me a sense of guilt. I have not done enough, I didn't do things right enough. I must confess, that more than not, I have advocated for LGBTQI communities without their involvement. I thought I was doing well, until I got here." He admitted that he has not dealt with hetero-patriarchy or hetero-sexism, which he felt were the real issues that need to be dealt with. It is an easy temptation to involve with LGBTIQ issues without their involvement. It needs to be pondered how much good such a process has done to the marginalized, in the name of contextual bible studies through all these years.

PLENARY 2: Church Responses from the Region
Moderator: Rev Michael Scheunemeyer, United Church of Christ, Ohio, US

Country presentations were made about church responses from their respective countries on issues related to human sexuality. The following presentations were made:-

i. India, Fr Philip Kuruvilla
ii. Indonesia, Rev Juswantori Ichwan
iii. Hong Kong, Ms Lai Shan Teresa Yip
iv. Philippines, Ms Darlene Caramanzana
v. Singapore, Rev Miak Siew

PANEL DISCUSSION 2: CHRISTIANITY, SEXUAL DIVERSITY AND ACCESS TO HEALTH SERVICES

Moderator: Dr Vijay Aruldas, Former General Secretary, Christiam Medical Association of India, Delhi

Panelists: Dr De'de' Oetomo (Indonesia), Dr L Ramakrishnan (India), Rev Philip V Peacock (India), Dr Manoj Kurian (Geneva)

Presentation: Christianity, Sexual Diversity and Access to Health Services, by Dr De'de' Oetomo, APCOM

Dr De'de' Oetomo shared the two principles and 10 practical steps to ensure access to health services:

Principles:

1. Love seeking understanding: This requires a willingness to learn more about gender, sexuality and sex without prejudice and a service desire to really understand the issues, needs and concerns of sexually diverse, gender variant, and HIV-positive Christians

2. Listening from the heart: forge sincere friendships, dialogue as equal partners, set aside pre-conceived ideas of authority, truth claims and fixed ideas.

Practical steps: 10 steps..

1. More balanced and non-discriminatory education

2. Create spaces where Christian churches and communities can dialogue

3. Spirit of listening

4. Journeying with and supporting MSM, TG and PHLIV

5. Increase official church statements denouncing discrimination and violence against them

6. Collaborate with schools, colleges, universities on bullying of gender variant and sexually diverse children, teens and young adults

7. Include more MSM, TG and PHLIV in church ministries

8. Encourage greater collaboration in human rights and social justice initiatives

9. Promote greater collaboration on HIV awareness, care and treatment

10. Identify experts who can facilitate discussions on alternative biblical and theological interpretations.

Response 1: Theological perspectives - Rev Philip V Peacock, Bishop's College, Kolkata

Rev Peacock highlighted the following points:-

1. For those who want to be faithful to Christ and are queer lifestyle, an alliance that can be built, of "faithful Christian" and "faithful queer person"

2. Shifts in Christianity have resulted in seeing Sin is now seen more as an individual act, rather than as a result of the matrix in which we are embedded. This leads to blaming of the victim for the victimization and constrains the understanding that salvation is through grace.

3. Listening – theology is always about us speaking and talking ... what we need to do is to listen. Allies may have created the space, but the voices must be those of the vulnerable.

4. Changing the furniture – the use of different imagery helps to open up the issues to newer understanding and exploration.

There is the danger of reducing all discourse on legal, social, political, sexual rights to HIV and AIDS, and further the HIV AIDS discourse being reduced to gays.

Response 2: Medical perspectives - Dr L Ramakrishan, SAATHI, Chennai

Dr Ramakrishnan highlighted the Medical aspects in the Indian/Asian context:

Highlighting how even currently used medical text books have inappropriate definitions that cause harm (gave examples), he explained that among medical professionals too, there is stigma, lack of knowledge, inability to diagnose, poor understanding of the context. Their knowledge and beliefs mirror that in general society, rather than being scientifically validated.

His recommendations included:

— LGBTIQ – friendly services should be included as one criteria of defining min quality std of care. Not look at it as something compassionate etc...

— Pre-service and in-service training need to include sensitisation in medical colleges

— Can CMAI etc offer community affirming helpline, position papers opposing conversion therapy that can be shared in religious and health and family circles- is vitally important.

— Medical service providers should know NALSA and Court Koushal (2013) i.e.

  o they are not aiding and abetting becos of 377 – they need to be told this is not so.

  o legal gender identity is by self definition not by legal, medical grounds- docs find it hard to digest they aren't the final word on a person's gender.

Response 3: Global perspectives, Dr Manoj Kurian, WCC, Geneva

Dr Manoj said that the situation in South Asia is no different from other parts of the world. With youth getting their information from the internet and their peers, wrong notions of sexuality, patriarchy etc will only be reinforced. It is incumbent for medical professionals to take up, as a self-regulation effort, to equip themselves.

Plenary 3: Church engagement with Human Sexuality in Asia: The Jakarta Consultation & Statement
Moderator – Fr Philip Kuruvilla, NCCI – ESHA, Nagpur

Presenters: Ms Pearl Wong, Rev Miak Siew and Rev Philip V Peacock

Ms Wong took us through the background, participants and structure of the Jakarta statement and how it had been taken forward in Hong Kong (translated into Chinese, put up on many websites, discussed on a forum on sexual minorities in Hong Kong.

Rev Miak Siew raised key questions:

• how do we enter into the conversation without creating schism in my church? Or causing harm?

• Queer people bring gifts to the church as well. (Question is: How radical is God's love?)

• How do we experience God's radical love and grace?

Rev Philip Peacock emphasized that:

1. We must begin to embrace QT as a politically subversive enterprise. Theology still have the imaginative ability to stand at margins and subvert systems of dominance

2. Epistemology —we must understand that the expression of God that LGBTQIs have tells us something of the divine that we don't have access to otherwise — something to be learned from and saved

3. QT has to transgress the categories of Christian theology in our discourses on love..agape,

4. The Jakarta meeting seemed to convey that we had reached an impasse in the ecumenical world- between justice and unity – we are losing out on justice for the sake of unity

5. Homosexuality is not just a western issue.... It is an issue of justice unity emerging from our third world context.

In closing, Fr Philip Kuruvilla pointed out that in India, between 2009 (when the NCCI statement invited harsh criticism from member churches) and 2015 (when there is acceptance), and explained that this is because the public context has changed.

Panel Discussion 3: Indian Christian Responses- Showing the way

Moderator: Rev Asir Ebenezer, Church of South India, Synod

Panelists: Rev Abin Abraham (Mumbai), Bishop Timothy Ravinder (Coimbatore), Capt. Andrews Christian (Anand), Ms Olga Aaron (Chennai), Dr Jijo Kuriakose (Kochi), Daniel Mendonca (Mumbai), Ms Anshi Zachariah (Bengaluru), Ms Edwina Pereira (Bengaluru),

Rev Abin Abraham, Director of Navodaya Movement, Mumbai and from the Marthoma Church described their work with the transgender communities in Mumbai, which included giving practical assistance in facilitating documentation, accessing education and skill development, and accessing appropriate health facilities.

Bishop Timothy Ravinder from the CSI Diocese of Coimbatore shared about their strong focus on working with pastors so that congregations can be reached, and on sensitising educational institutions, particularly with respect to a ministry related to Transgender communities.

Captain Andrews Christian from the Salvation Army Western Territory described how they are building awareness and understanding of their church leaders, identifying barriers and solutions for the greater involvement of LGBTQI in the churches in their region.

The discussion identified that in general the churches in India are relatively more comfortable to work with TGs compared to working with LGBQIs.

Ms Olga Aaron, a Christian Transgender, talked about the situation with TGs in Tamil Nadu. She explained from her personal experiences how as children, transgender men have more difficulty because of social masculinity norms, while TG women (girls) will not stand out as much. Highlighting that children and youth discovering their sexual identity are especially vulnerable, she empathised the importance of focusing on this area through sensitization among media, schools and legal systems, and the need for child rights policies for gender non-conforming children (to include it in special children category).

Dr Jijo Kuraikose from the Queerla movement in Kerala, discussed the Kerala queer movement, and the many initiatives it has taken to raise the public profile of gay and lesbian communities in Kerala – Pride Marches, Art Exhibition, Research paper, articles in media. A study of 155 Christians who were gay or lesbian, during 2016 showed that church and faith questions had been a major cause of 'damage', that some were still in the faith while others had abandoned it. *(Mr Romal Singh from Bengaluru, explained later how the abandonment by the faith community often caused negative reactions, a desire for revenge and to hit out at others, and a loss of accountability resulting in negative moral and ethical behaviours.*

Mr Daniel Mendonca, as an intersex person from Mumbai, talked of the discrimination he faced personally, and how he was labelled a sinner for no fault of his. He asked, "Church talks about compassion, love and mercy to all; where does it disappear when LGBTQIs appear?" and urged the church to "accept us the way we are", without letting gender be in front of humanity.

The two NGOs, Aneka (Ms Anshi Zachariah) and INSA India (Ms Edwina Periera) described their focus on capacity building, and their work with Churches including NCCI and Senate of Serampore. Aneka also supports two collectives, Karnataka Sexual Minorities Forum and Karnataka Sex Workers Union, has undertaken action research studies, and is active in advocacy. As Ms Edwina mentioned, there are many LBGTIQs in the congregations, who are not able to come out. She raised two key questions, namely, would there be a way we could also support children and adolescents to see their sexuality as a God given gift to be valued? Can the Church be a protective space with protective systems for inclusion, reaching out and empowering the marginalised, irrespective of the gender or sexual orientations?

Panel Discussion 4: Church engagement in Human Sexuality: Pastoral responses

Moderator: Bishop Arichea Daniel, Philippines

Panelists: Pastor Pauline Ong (Singapore), Mr Lifter Tua Marbun (Netherlands) Rev Michael Scheunemeyer (USA), Mr Romal Laisram (India)

Presentation 1: Journeys of faith - Pastor Pauline Ong, Free Community Church, Singapore

Pastor Pauline shared, she always felt herself strange and different. Living in a Christian family, she could find no one to talk to, even in times of break-up, as her Church would not find her lesbianism as acceptable. There was extremely loneliness; often felt like running away from God. Despite all these, God reached out to you; a small voice to her: "I love you". In response to her friends, mostly pastors and missionaries regarding a signature campaign initiated vocal anti-gay Christians in Singapore to support continual criminalization of gay sex, Pauline came out, with a feeling of a deep division that "I am both 'we' and 'them'. Friends have never met any gay Christians before, but an urge to know more; offered respect and support. Owing to the difficulty in openly expressing political stands, "Pink Dot" event was launched in 2009 to allow people to show their support to LGBTQ people in a form of a funfair; number of participants grew exponentially from 2000 in 2009 to 27,000 in 2016. Gayness becomes a gift, no need to be fixed, but to be loved àbecomes a blessed brokenness.

Presentation 2: Journeys of faith - Mr Lifter Tua Marbun, Indonesia / Netherlands

Agony with own sexual contacts with men since young: seeing own body as sinful, felt disgusted and shameful, fearful of death, wished for suicide: no one he could talk to; loneliness; continually suppressed own homoerotic desire. During his seminary years, the more he urged for healing his own homosexuality, the more he got sick àfinally accepted own homosexuality. He created own imagery of homosexuality: brokenness. To love and to be loved are good thingsà toward the wholeness, self-fulfilment and self-acceptance. His sister thought that he had chosen a sinful life and worried that he had no children to take care of him when he gets old; Family is the first priority in his own tribe.

He went on to co-author with Ruard Ganzevoort, "ADAM & WAWAN" about pastoral counseling with gay men. He found that sex with men does not make one gay and he may still get married with a woman; they could not tell clearly about their own sexuality. It is easy for us to stigmatize something beyond our beliefs and vision, such as homosexual having sickness, being pedophiles, those victims of abuse àthey cannot live with dignity. Most gay men aspire for relationships of equality and respect. Jesus says that neither parents of the man born blind have sinned. Nouwen: the wounded and the sick can become the healer. The LGBTIQ people are not object of mission: condemn them, then save them; they are not sinful nor sick: reach out and bring them close to church, so they continually live with Christian values and make contributions

→ Missiodei: should be from the perspective of God; Learn from LGBTQ experiences

→ Theology of Reverse Mission: LGBTIQ people speak freely about their faith

His homosexuality is a gift of God; his sexuality opensnew ways to work for God; An imagery of homosexuality: Being authentic or being who you are, as God knows you. Jesus was faithful to himself and his calling; LGBTQ people can be the same.

Presentation 3: Sermon methodologies - Rev. Michael Schuenemeyer, United Church of Christ, Ohio

God accompanies them when in exile (testimonies of LGBTIQ). A sermon should be to the ground, the most local level. A key question to ask ourselves is, what is the lens we use? Church tradition: negative messages about sex.

→ We need to see sex as a good gift, love, life, pleasure, celebrating with joy and holiness

We need a curriculum: Sex is healthy and pleasurable and people find it natural to express sexual feelings. Life is a sexually transmitted mode of living; Sexuality and spirituality inseparable. Gender and sexual identities are respected. Sexual relationships are grounded in values such as healthy; should be consensual, mutually pleasurable, appropriate to their age, with rights and responsibilities to choices, no double standards, no human rights violations. Methodologies of Jesus: meet with sinner and eat with them; he broke the Jewish purity law, which causes separation with others; never meant to recruit the most virtuous. Heresy is NOT to preach inclusion.

→ Rubric of inclusion → lens of Jesus, Gospel to those vulnerable → To create spaces

Welcoming resources: Human Rights Campaign published, "OUT and Scripture". In the Gospel story of the lost child, Nouwen identifies with these 3 characters: → We don't know why the youngest son leaves and what made him return (Maybe the parenting); the parent go out to meet him with open arms — completely, no stigma

> → The elder brother works so hard to do good things (like religious institution)

> → Father responds with affirmation and invitation; Will the elder son learn to call this brother again and join the celebration?

Jesus and Samaritan woman: Women as property at that time; she did not feel shameful with Jesus; Zachariah, the tax collector, was invited to eat with Jesus. We should take courage to take the text in such a way that helps people to find empathy.

Presentation 4: Church Life Engagement – Queer Churches, Rev. Miak Siew, Free Community Church, Singapore

Not all LGBTQ people survive, but die of suicide. Abomination; God hates you àrealities for many LGBTQ persons. LGBTQ persons are "positive examples" of Christians. If the focus is on church (structure), then they miss to reconcile sexuality and spirituality. He saw himself as the Samaritan woman with five husbands; living a double life; not healthy; continued to struggle.

Churches only speak about the six passages related to homosexuality and beyond that; and then, what? What is sexual ethics? Healing is not just the biblical knowledge; rather, seeing other gay men's pieces of healing; a community for them to share their struggles. The Free Community Church set up the Lesbian United for Self Help. Use of substance (meth or ice) is common among gay men to run away from their struggles, so they set up the 12-step support group. Jesus tells the leper to go to the religious authority and he is only healed on his way. Identities are marked; yet, healing rests in the resistance against being marked. Creating spaces is a step-by-step process; small things first. Transgendered persons are more hidden in Singapore. He stressed that let the LGBTQ people own the process.

Presentation 5: Church Life Engagement – Queer churches, Mr Romal Laisram, Human Rights Law Network, Bengaluru

In a recent Pride event across a campus, 50 students marched; A slogan by a student was striking, it said, "Has Jesus said about gay people?" and below that, there was nothing as the answer. He was very positive about Christianity's stand on homosexuality. Established a faith-based self-help group of gay Christians. Since condemned and abandoned by own churches, gay Christians do not look back to their faith as inspiration for relationship. Do not know what same-sex relationship should look like as only wife-and-husband model is the norm; so what we have today is, do whatever one wants, drug abuse and breakdown on social morality. Hence, one would become a sinner just by identifying as gay, whereby there is impending guilt, it's hard to start a relationship and there is much isolation: their lives as sinful judgement à isolation. Therefore, it is a big challenge for this group is to find a positive, loving church community, where one can find from talking about the idea as sinner to talking about loving a person of same sex. It is easy to have sex with men and reduce to sex, putting sex = sexuality. There is a need for healthier sex. If one was a bottom, then accept oneself as bottom without striving to prove one's masculinity through sex. There should be equality in relationships. It is more vulnerable for those who have gone through lots of abuses.

What can the Church do?

→ Encourage gay people to search for the one suitable partner, engaged in committed relationship

→ Provide a support system

→ Encourage the possibility for single persons to be happier persons

Workshop: Methodologies of doing Contextual Bible Studies in Human Sexuality

Moderator: Metropolitan Dr Gabriel Mar Gregorios, Indian Orthodox Church

Presenter: Prof Gerald West, South Africa

Contextual Bible Studies evolved after 30 yrs of work in South Africa, particularly in KwaZulu-Natal. The context has been to respond to the needs of the vulnerable and exploited from their reality.

The Core values included the **6 Cs, namely Community, Criticality, Collaboration, Change, Context and Contestation. There is much value in the process of** learning from collaboration.

The process involves:

a) small groups sharing, large group reporting, small group sharing alternately

b) Scripture gets more time than preaching time.

c) Slows down the process, takes you back to the text. ..again and again…rereading…noticing things that have been neglected…as its food for margins

d) Remains faithful to the core values

e) Everything every person says is written down on flip charts, not erased (persons inputs is valued – empowering for the disempowered)

f) No final answer or closing summary. Each takes away their own reflections.

Prof West then shared 3 examples:

1. Gen 19:1-13: Story of Sodom

2. Gen 2:18-23: Choose your own partner

3. Mark 12:18-27: Confrontation by Sadducees

During the process of facilitation it is crucial to keep in mind the following principles:-

1. Enter with an attitude of learning, not teaching

2. Spend most of the time on scripture reading and group

3. "Shut up and listen"

4. It is an expression and exploration of "People's theology"

Group Discussion Reports

1. For each country to take an inventory of resources.

    — what materials we can share (online / offline)
    — what is already available
    — whitelists of professionals (doctors, lawyers, psychiatrists, psychologists)

2. et up facebook group

3. Resources pooling

    — what are the existing organisations

    — identify strategic partners (NGOs, businesses, allies)

4. Set up and/or connect to national networks and regional networks

5. Conduct research on how discrimination from church impact LGBTQ lives and use it as a platform/ framework for dialogue

    — eg. stigmaindex.org (HIV/AIDS related)

    — eg. frameworkfordialogue.org

Publicise - startup - linkup

Standing in solidarity with other minorities eg interfaith issues, death penalty, etc

Timeline - complete 1 & 2 by May 2017.

Group Report from Indian participants

How can we affirm and encourage these ministries of LGBTIQ peoples/gross root ministries?

- Be with the ministries, in what they are doing (like Bravoh Movement/ Qic/APCOMetc). We need to create awareness among our churches first, then we have to bring in resource people from these groups to give awareness to deacons/pastors.

- Our efforts should not fail because of the resistance of the congregations so first we need to give clear biblical insights.

- Care & support to PLHIV – for that individual experiences will help but beyond inclusion in worship we need to get into their family, community, life and accompany each in their real needs.

- Identify gaps in laws & raise voice as faith groups

- Services should not be charity based but integral

- How many churches will welcome TGs etc in worships? Leaders/bishops should break-in congregations regarding the existence of these groups; for example Visitation- when there are TGs do we do house visits? Or do we speak about them in sermons? We need to create space to talk about family as being more than heterosexual.

- Can we make 'ally-groups' in churches, and within these groups can we give them competency based training i.e. about LGBT realities, terms => basically understand their understanding before any campaign – this needs strategic plans to find if there are allies within the congregations

- Meeting of parents of LGBT who've come out recently and many of whom go through conflict of having traditional faith that speaks against their realities- how to document such personal issues/family issues? Data collection is necessary.

- How to circulate this meeting's statement to more audiences (via translations into vernaculars, sharing on social media etc)- and creation of more such statements from recognised faith groups.

- Write about LGBTIQ people/issues in church newsletters, magazines etc - of their life stories and in their testimonies sections.

How do we strengthen the LGBTIQs in our regions (persp/persons/ resources)?

If we keep queer as 'other' as 'marginalised' then the discussions are different but what we need is a "positive sexuality for all" approach and theology should be able to create that; sexual orientation should not be defining this discourse but a holistic positive approach to positive sexuality for all.

How to strengthen theology in our regions? We don't have much material for teaching (human sexuality) and these needs to be created; How to produce and make accessible teaching material to relevant institution? We need to create from the people.

Equip the trainers i.e. we learn together with students on the subject;

Relook at the curriculum in theological colleges;

Church counselors don't have skills to attend to LGBT so make that part of curriculum; Have exposure/internship with persons from different orientations for example with TG's etc.

In seminaries Human sexuality course is optional and/or one paper on Feminist Theology is compulsory and &sexuality is part of it; However the recommendation from this group is that we don't make courses compulsory as it's not helpful when students come into the course with resistance. Instead how we theological colleges generate interest in such courses (ie) through field education and work with queer communities etc- then students begin to own the cause and take it forward.

— Material on Human sexuality is there but its expensive so access and contextualisation of available material is what is needed.

— We need to write at several levels-all needed i.e. academic, popular writing, Bible studies, short reflections, material for youth, kids (Sunday school material that raises gender questions and strategic material calling for solidarity.

— Do theology: We can't replace theology with social analysis that's too superficial; we need to talk about serious new ways about God, Christ etc. not that we have answers but that we are finding our salvation from the margins as its "we"/"I" that needs saving not the approach that says "they need saving".

— Culture of inclusion creates a problem in the sense that all need positive sexuality; Kids need to know about safe sex; Youth groups don't talk about positive sexuality rather its prescriptive directives like abstention that are not helpful.

— Ministry is not satisfaction of the church but for church to "Be" a church and move from compassionate to wholesome intentional inclusively to become the church. Problem is not out there -we are all part of the problem, not that its charity for 'others'; We are the last place people come to! How do we challenge Catholic church statements that nullify statements like ours KCCD(response)?

What can we do about services and ministries that surround/ intersect with these ministries? how to strengthen them? (Education, health, etc)?

— All churches have schools: we need to intro this into moral education in schools: Understanding of body, ability/disability, sexuality etc.; we need to Move away from ethics to of right/wrong to consensual/non consensual; Invite LGBT persons to share their experiences; Educational systems need open courses on sexuality

— It's a struggle in churches/institutions to know i.e. how many of us know in our institutions that there are LGBT children? In some regions like NEI we don't even like to discuss these issues like sexuality. But we have to look out for them/welcome them then we will really see them; Also our institutions need to take seriously the stand that some non-religious institutions like colleges takes when they have an open non-discriminatory policy that says whoever you are you will be treated equally Vs saying we need to identify such students and care for them in a special way -as this may draw undue attention to them and make them targets of bullying etc and as institutions we should not pressure such people to come out instead we make a policies and spaces that will protect them. In the sense make this a policy decision of institutions rather than labelling them and remove the word "different"/ "crooked" etc from our perspective.

Inclusively should be redefined and councils in mainstream should have place for LGBTIQ persons. Core values of church need to be redefined; When inclusion of LGBT is not a core value then we need to change policies. Change in policies then makes it a crime is necessary their human rights are protected as their right not as charity; then the policy enables them to fight for their rights as human beings rather than by explicitly uplifting their sexual orientation.

— Health services: there needs to be more job opportunities created; there needs to be Sensitization of all levels; Policies @all levels by churches and institutions for example Can church institutions at +2 level be welcoming of TG drop outs so that they are enabled to become employable — sort of like an open school system that will help them compete for mainstream jobs as well.

Statement from the Consultation

The delegates of the Consultation discussed and submitted a statement as a common resolution, which is attached separately.

Process at the Consultation

The programme schedule of the Consultation included the following process:-

Date/Time	Programme Details	Names of Speakers	Details
06 Feb '17		Arrival	
07 Feb '17		Day 1	
8.00am	Breakfast		
9.00am	Registration		
	Inaugural Session		
	Inaugural Prayer and worship	Organised by Rev Dr John Samuel	Secretary, ISET, ECC
	Welcome	Prof Dr Mathews Chandrankunnel	Director, ECC
	Inaugural Address	Dr Manoj Kurian	Ecumenical Advocacy Alliance, WCC
11.00am	Introduction to the Consultation	Rev Dr Roger Gaikwad	General Secretary, NCC India
	Felicitations	1. Metropolitan Dr Geevarghese Mor Coorilos	Moderator, Council for World Mission & Evangelism
		2. Ms Mousumi Sarangi	Program Manager, ICCo & kerk in actie
		3. Dr Dédé Oetomo	APCOM
		4. Ms Nandini Kapoor-Dhingra	UNAIDS India
		5. Dr L Ramakrishnan	Vice President, SAATHI

2.00pm	**Plenary 1: Church Engagement in Human Sexuality – The Kairos framework**		
		Prof Gerald West	University of KwaZulu – Natal, Pietermaritzburg, South Africa
	Moderator	Dr Manoj Kurian	Ecumenical Advocacy Alliance, WCC
	Plenary 2: Church Responses from the Region		
2.30pm	Moderator	Rev Michael Schuenemeyer	United Church of Christ, Ohio
	India	Fr Philip Kuruvilla	NCC India
	Indonesia	Rev Juswantori Ichwan	Indonesian Dutch Reformed Church
	Hong Kong	Ms Teresa Yip	Hong Kong
	Philippines	Ms Darlene Caramanzana	NCC Philippines
	Singapore	Rev Miak Siew	Free Community Church, Singapore
4.00pm	**Tea**		

	Panel Discussion 1: Church Engagement in Human Sexuality: Scope and Impact of Contextual Theology related to Human Sexuality		
	Moderator	Metropolitan Dr Geevarghese Mor Coorilos	Syrian Orthodox Church, Niranam Diocese & Moderator, CWME
	Panelists:-		
4.30pm	1. Queer theologies in the Asian context – scope for church engagement	Ms Pearl Wong	Executive Director, Queer Theology Academy, Hong Kong
	2. The impact of doing Contextual Theology in Human Sexuality with church engagement – the South African experience	Prof Gerald West	University of KwaZulu-Natal, Pietermaritzburg, South Africa
	3. Responses : i. Academia	Prof George Zachariah	Dept of Ethics, UTC, Bangalore
	ii. Church Life	Rev Miak Siew	Free Community Church, Singapore
		Bishop Arichea Daniel	United Methodist Church, Philippines
6.30pm	**Break**		
7.00pm	**Dinner**		

08 Feb, '17	Day 2	
8.00am	**Breakfast**	
9.00am	**Prayer**	Led by Foreign delegates	Indonesia and Sri Lanka
	Panel Discussion 2: Christianity, Sexual Diversity and Access to Health Services		
	Moderator	Dr Vijay Aruldas	Former General Secretary, Christian Medical Association of India, New Delhi
	Responses:		
9.30am	Paper Presentation	Dr Dédé Oetomo	GAYa NUSANTARA, Indonesia
	Theological perspective	Prof Philip V Peacock	Bishops College, Kolkata
	Medical perspective	Dr L Ramakrishnan	Vice President, SAATHI
	Global perspective	Dr Manoj Kurian	EAA-WCC, Geneva
	Plenary 3: Church engagement with Human Sexuality in Asia: The Jakarta Consultation and Statement		
11.00am	**Moderator**	Fr Philip Kuruvilla	NCC India
	Presentation 1	Ms Pearl Wong	Laity, Queer Theological Academy, Hong Kong
	Presentation 2	Rev Philip V Peacock	Bishops College, Kolkata

Panel Discussion 3: Indian Christian Responses - Showing the way		
Moderator	Rev Asir Ebenezer	Church of South India Synod, Chennai
Response of the Indian Churches :	Capt Andrews Christian	Salvation Army, Western Territory
	Rev Abin Abraham	Navodaya, Marthoma Church, Mumbai
	Bishop Timothy Ravinder	Church of South India, Coimbatore Diocese
11.30am Response of the LGBTI Community representatives	Ms Olga Aaron Dr Jijo Kuriakose	Bravo Movement, Chennai Queerla, Kochi
Response from NGOs	Mr Daniel Mendonca	College of Social Work, Nirmala Niketan, Mumbai
	Ms Anshi Zachariah	ANEKA, Bengaluru
	Ms Edwina Pereira	INSA, Bengaluru
1.00pm	**Lunch**	

	Panel Discussion 4: Church Engagement in Human Sexuality: Pastoral responses	
	Moderator	Bishop Arichea Daniel	United Methodist Church, Philippines
2.00pm	Journeys of faith	Pastor Pauline Ong Mr Lifter Tua Marbun	Free Community Church, Singapore Netherlands
	Sermon methodologies	Rev Michael Schuenemeyer	United Church of Christ, Ohio
		Mr Romal Laisram	Human Rights Law Network, India
4.00pm	**Tea**		
	Workshop: Methodologies of doing Contextual Bible Studies in Human Sexuality		
4.30pm	**Moderator**	Prof Gerald West	UKZN, South Africa
		Metropolitan Dr Gabriel Mar Gregorios	Indian Orthodox Church, Diocese of Trivandrum, India
6.00pm	**Break**		
7.00pm	**Cultural Program**		
8.00pm	**Dinner**		

09 Feb '17	Day 3		
8.00am	**Breakfast**		
9.00am	**Prayer**	Led by Foreign delegates	Singapore, Philippines and Hong Kong
	Consultation Report	Dr Vijay Aruldas	Chief Rapporteur
	Draft Statement of the Consultation		
	Moderator	Dr Manoj Kurian	EAA-WCC, Geneva
		Rev Dr Roger Gaikwad	General Secretary, NCCI
9.30am	Panelists	Dr Manoj Kurian	EAA-WCC, Geneva
		Ms Darlene Caramanzana	NCC Philippines
		Dr Dédé Oetomo	APCOM
		Fr Thomas Ninan	NCCI – ESHA, Nagpur
	Plenary 4: Group Discussion Reports		
11.30am	**Moderator**	Rev Dr Roger Gaikwad	NCC India
1.00pm	Concluding program and Vote of Thanks	Dr John Samuel	ECC, Bengaluru
	Lunch		
1.30pm	**Departure**		

Statement: South and South-East Asian Responses to Human Sexuality and Gender Diversities

Ecumenical Christian Centre, Bengaluru: February 9th, 2017.
An invitation to Churches and Theological Institutions:
Reflection, Repentance and Redemption

We are fifty church leaders and church representatives, theologians and members of the civil society, from diverse sexual orientations, gender identities and expressions and sex characteristics from India, Indonesia, Hong Kong, Malaysia, Netherlands, Philippines, Singapore, South Africa and the USA.

We gathered for a consultation on *'South & South East Asian Church Responses to Human Sexuality and Gender Identities',* convened by the National Council of Churches in India (NCCI), supported by Ecumenical partners, from the 7th to the 9th of February 2017 at the Ecumenical Christian Centre in Bangalore, India.

We affirm that sexuality is a divine gift, which is to be celebrated in life-affirming, consensual, and loving relationships. We recognize that we are people with diverse sexual orientations, gender identities and gender expressions and sex characteristics and that all are created in the image of God.

We reviewed and reflected on the various facets of churches' engagements in India and other Asian countries from 2001 in dealing with Human Sexuality. Having listened to the stories of Christians with diverse sexual orientations, gender identities and gender expressions and sex characteristics, and the work of inclusive churches and theologians, who have struggled to preserve the dignity and the rights of marginalised communities.

We reject systemic and personal attitudes of homophobia, transphobia and any kind of discrimination against persons of diverse sexual orientations, gender identities and gender expressions and sex characteristics.

We also acknowledged the need for greater inclusion of people with diverse sexual orientations, gender identities and gender expressions and sex characteristics. in the life and work of faith communities.

We acknowledged the achievements of many churches and communities, and celebrated the progress that has been made in addressing Human Sexuality. It is a journey of hope and we have come a long way, but we realised that we have still much to do!

We repent for our lack of adequate engagement with issues related to Human Sexuality, which is contributing to ignorance and silence, increasing the vulnerability of individuals and communities.

We studied the Bible, prayed, and worshipped together. We recognised that it is only a theology of the people from the margins of society, which carries their cries, aspirations and passions that lead us to a Prophetic Theology. The scriptures take new life in its encounter with reality. We acknowledged the role of the Bible in pastoral accompaniment and the need to wrestle with the Holy Scriptures, seeking redemptive messages over the retributive. We also became aware of the need to revisit some of the existing imagery and symbolism and the necessity to introduce challenging new ways of encountering Human Sexuality in our faith contexts.

We listened to stories of brokenness that people with diverse sexual orientations, gender identities and gender expressions are experiencing. We acknowledged that some of this brokenness has been inflicted by the church. In the midst of their yearning for God and the church, often, they experienced rejection and exclusion. But we also saw the resilience of those communities, inspired by the radical love of God. We were reminded of 'Kintsugi' a Japanese method for repairing broken ceramics with a special lacquer mixed with gold, silver, or platinum. The philosophy behind the technique is to recognize the history of the object and to visibly incorporate the repair into the new piece instead of disguising the cracks. The repaired object is more beautiful than the original. This is a beautiful metaphor for how our brokenness is mended (re-membered) by the love and Spirit of God that holds us together, both as individuals and as the Body of Christ. In our brokenness and fragility, we also collectively represent the 'Wounded healer', Jesus Christ.

We are convinced that the way we perceive and experience Human Sexuality and our level of inclusion of people with diverse sexual orientations, gender identities and gender expressions and sex characteristics within faith communities contributes to who we are and what we become. It also influences as to how we relate to each other and transforms our communities and nations.

From this gathering, where we experienced friendship, healing and redemption, we extend our invitation to all our churches and people of Faith. Let us journey together as one people with diverse sexual orientations, gender identities and gender expressions and sex characteristics. Let it be a journey of Love, Faith and Hope, a pilgrimage of Justice and Peace!

Hence we call on our churches and people of Faith to:-

• Become sanctuaries of love, which are just and inclusive.

• Be listening communities that are empathetic and responsive to the pains, desires, and hopes of people.

• Be transformed as Safe and Sacred Spaces of Grace, which are trustworthy, affirming, accompanying and healing environments that promote friendship, acceptance and solidarity.

- Become informed, competent and open spaces, where people are able to discuss issues related to Human sexuality in the context of their faith.

- Transform their institutions- be it providing health services, education or other services, to be welcoming and competent in providing holistic and adequate services and care.

- To engage in dialogue with persons with diverse sexual orientations, gender identities and gender expressions and sex characteristics and listen to their stories and struggles as acts of love.

- Embrace the diversity in humanity, and be in solidarity with people with diverse sexual orientations, gender identities and gender expressions and sex characteristics and their families, without prejudice and discrimination, to provide them with ministries of love, compassionate care, and justice.

- Engage diverse voices and perspectives in theological reflections, particularly persons of diverse sexual orientations, gender identities and gender expressions and sex characteristics. Also respecting and responding to the inter-sectionality of issues in different socio-cultural contexts, and not to see any issue in isolation.

- Work across different Faiths, to work together, to promote a just and inclusive society.

- Advocate with governments and civil society to ensure that people with diverse sexual orientations, gender identities and gender expressions and sex characteristics enjoy a social, economic, cultural and political environment, for the their wellbeing.

May God bless our endeavours to be transformed and to grow into the fullness of life. May we transform our faith communities into communities of dignity, respect, egalitarianism, justice and love.

Helpful NGO's and
Suggested Web Links/Books

Indian NGO's that work for the
LGBTI Communities

AmaNA

AmaNA [All Manipur Nupi Manbi Association]

AmaNA Development Project: Livelihood support for Transgender Communities

All Manipur Nupi Maanbi Association (AMANA) is a coalition body and was initially formed by three CBOs working in different districts in Manipur, viz., Maruploi Foundation, AASHA, and SAVE. From July 2012 onwards, it expanded its network and now has six CBOs altogether. AMANA has established itself as a network of CBOs of Men who have Sex with Men (MSM) and Transgender (TG) communities in Manipur.

LGBTI people in Manipur– and elsewhere in the Northeast - are extremely vulnerable to harassment, discrimination, violence and sexual assault. AmaNA (a state-wide community network of LGBT people) has been working to document and address human rights violations against LGBT communities, and strengthen community-led initiatives and institutions. These include support to establish ETA, the first state collective of transgender men, lesbian and bi women. We raise awareness of Education, legal, social and health issues impacting the well-being of LGBTI communities among media, government and civil society stakeholders. We have initiated dialogue with the Manipur Branch of the Indian Psychiatric Society (IPS), to take a public stand on homosexuality in line with the stand taken by Indian Psychiatric Society - which has officially acknowledged that homosexuality is not considered a psychiatric disorder, and that attempts to change it are unethical and unscientific. We have also commenced discussions with religious leaders to generate their support on LGBTI issues.

AmaNA strives to provide technical support for, and to serve as, a resource for MSM/TG issues in the entire northeast. This projects works to strengthen the network as an association, to help identify issues, and to build up the capacities of its members.

Contact Email: nupimanbi@gmail.com

Aneka

Aneka (which means diverse or plural) is a human rights organization initiated in Jan 2007 and was formally registered in January 2008. Aneka aims to foster social justice and to enhance, promote and protect rights of marginalised communities especially sexual minorities (LGBTIQ communities) and sex workers. Aneka does this through capacity building of sexual minorities and sex workers in Karnataka, action research on LGBTQI issues and policies, and initiating and hosting dialogues of sexuality and religion. We primarily focus our work on capacity building and collectivisation in Bangalore and in Karnataka – though much of our work has implications at the national and international level.

Vision

Aneka envisions a just society where the voices of marginalised communities, especially Sex Workers and Gender and Sexuality Minorities have created space for life with dignity and freedom of choice. Aneka has involved as a support to LGBTIQ communities and collective of sex workers for the past decade.

Initiatives

1. Organised capacity building of community leaders

2. Engaged in policy level advocacy for these groups

   3. Aneka has undertaken action research with Jogappas, an undocumented and little known trans identity, and documented the unique identity and culture,and also highlighted the needs and challenges of the Jogappa community to live with a rightful and

respectful life. [,'Jogappa: Gender, Identity and the Politics of Exclusion' and "Three Journeys: Cameos of the Jogappa Community in Karnataka"(Kannada & English versions) published in 2014.]

4. Initiates sexuality dialogues with various stakeholders including faith groups through dialogue. In this, Aneka has initiated interfaith as well as intra-faith discussions on the intersectionality of Religion, Gender and sexuality

5. Networking with likeminded organizations and other marginalized movements[like dalits, women etc], is also involvement of the organisation.

[Website: https://www.facebook.com/anekaindia/]

The Humsafar Trust

The Humsafar Trust (HST), founded by Ashok Row Kavi, one of the leading LGBTQ organizations that covers a spectrum of sexual minorities in India. HST has a familial vibe, it has been a home for the people in the community who have found great support here.

HST is a convener member of Integrated Network For Sexual Minorities (INFOSEM). INFOSEM is a national level network for sexual minorities in India since 2003. HST has been actively involved in some of their initiatives. *Yaariyan* (friendships) is an LGBT group, *Umang* (joy) is for LBT persons, *KinnarAsmita* represents the transgender persons and *Sanjeevani* was set up for the MSM and TG persons living with HIV. HST also has set up, CONNECT, which is a National Online Resource Center, that connects LGBTQ community worldwide.

There are 4 verticals in HST: Health, Advocacy, Capacity Building, & Research.

HST's **health department** aims to reduce the HIV/STI prevalence among the men who have sex with men (MSM) and the TG/ Hijra community by promoting safer sex practices. Another focus of the health department in HST is to make accessible to the community people the health care services with much ease and without stigma.

The **advocacy department** in HST is involved in sensitizing corporates and educational institutions and media. They advocate with direct influencers such as doctors, police, lawyers, pharmacists, job recruiters and indirect influencers such as municipal corporators, political parties and policy makers.

HST mentors and **provides capacity building** to community based organizations (CBOs). Capacity building support is provided to HIV intervention teams of HST which is specific to the needs of MSM and TG outreach programmes to ensure provision of quality services in physical sites and internet reach.

The **research team** in HST has played an important role in informing, designing and guiding interventions pertaining to the HIV related risk behaviours of men having sex with men. HST has collaborated with Sion hospital and medical college to study the mental health issues of MSM persons.

Contact Us at the Drop In Centre: 3rd floor, Manthan Plaza, Nehru Road, Vakola, Santacruz (east), Mumbai 400055, India.

Telephone number:022-26673800/26650547

Website: *www.humsfar.org*: Email: *info@humsafar.org*

Social Media: @HumsafarTrust on Twitter, @TheHumsafarTrust on Facebook

The Naz Foundation [India] Trust

1.   About Naz

The Naz Foundation (India) Trust has pioneered rights based service delivery, advocacy and policy change for people living with and affected by HIV. Since 1994 Naz's work has shaped the HIV/AIDS sector to respond to the most pressing needs of communities who are multiply marginalized, owing to their socio-economic circumstances. Their pioneering programmes and services have centered a nationwide movement, legacy and leadership in building a culture of rights and agency; shaping inclusive communities, institutions and policies that re-inforce the constitutional framework of equality and citizenship for all.

This ethos is encapsulated in the programme outcomes of improving health, reducing stigma and empowering families. These goals are achieved through workshops and training with community members from the LGBTI sector, judicial sector, healthcare institutions and directly with young people from low income urban communities.

Naz enables these community members, one individual at a time, through their flagship programmes covering direct service delivery and capacity building of individuals managing child care institutions based on the national standards of child protection policies, providing care to children living and affected by HIV and socio-economic marginalization.

2.   Vision

To create a just and equitable society by transforming individuals from socially and economically excluded communities into agents of change.

3.   Mission

The mission of Naz is to build vibrant ecosystems that:

- o   Energise and enable individuals from excluded communities to realize their potential and act as change makers/agents of change.

- o   Build partnerships, networks and linkages to catalyse a critical mass of such leaders.

- o   Engage and influence governments, businesses and other stakeholders to take this movement to scale.

4.   Naz's Flagship programs

a.   Naz's Care Home:

Naz established a care home for HIV positive children in 2001 after a positive orphan child was abandoned at our doorstep. The Care Home was founded on the belief that all children have a fundamental right to a loving, fun-filled childhood with access to health, education, and a safe, stigma-free environment. In 2009, National AIDS Controlled Organization designated Naz India as Community Care Centre for Children. Naz has since maintained a care home for HIV-infected children by providing educational, nutritional, medical, recreational, and psychosocial support. The children are primarily from Delhi, Maharashtra, Manipur, Uttar Pradesh, and Bihar, and were referred from childcare institutions, hospitals, and other NGOs. The care home currently sustains 25 children aged between 4 and 19 years.

b.   Naz's Sport for development (S4d) programme – Goal

Naz's preventive initiative focuses on women's empowerment through the Goal program; its a sports based development initiative targeted at young girls and women from economically disadvantaged backgrounds. The program uses the dynamic medium of sports (Netball) along with training on critical issues of life such as gender equality, sexual and reproductive health, HIV, financial literacy and rights that will empower them and enable them to make healthy & informed life-choices. Since 2006, program has directly reached out to more than 40,000 girls and young women.

c.   Training

Naz India's training are focused at raising awareness on issues related to HIV, gender, sex and sexuality for prevention and protection, improving the rights of children and people living with HIV, promoting proper care and support of people and children living with HIV/AIDS and reducing the stigma and discrimination against them. We have reached out to care homes, Child Welfare Committees, doctors, nurses and other institutions, organizations, agencies and groups (both, governmental and non-governmental) across India.

d.   Advocacy

Naz India was a pioneer in providing services to the MSM and LGBT community in India, and continues that important work. Naz India is an active supporter of the LGBT community in India. We, at Naz, believe that LGBT people should have equal rights to social inclusion, sexual health education, and career opportunities. We aim to be a strong support system for LGBT people in times of need through our involvement.

Contact us: The Naz Foundation [India] Trust , A-86, East of Kailash, New Delhi-110065

Email: naz@nazindia.org : Website: www.nazindia.org

Queerala:
An organization for Kerala LGBTIQ

All human beings are born free and equal in dignity and rights. They are endowed with reason and conscience and should act towards one another in a spirit of brotherhood- Article 1, The Universal Declaration of Human Rights.[1]

It is this notion of Equality that motivated a few Malayali gay men who were friends from the cyber world, to form a formal support group to address lively concerns pertaining to Sexual Orientation and Gender Diversity. Queerala,[2] an organization for Kerala LGBTIQ community originated in 2013 June, and after few years of online operations, is now connected with at least 3500 Malayali[3] belonging to the sexual minority. Queerala primarily focuses on extending awareness on various facets of LGBTIQ lives and related issues on the same, in the state we dwell in. The support group of Queerala conducts bimonthly meetings - each with a specific topic or focus - for LGBT people and their allies, to build and expand their support system, besides including healthy discussions on recent media reports on community issues and queer scenario at the state, national and international levels. We also take necessary actions to intervene in cases and crises[4] occurring to openly gay[5] or transgender people .

A few of our initiatives, which had got wide reception, include *Free Hugs* campaign,[6] which was organized in three major cities in Kerala and *Wiki Loves Pride* in association with the Wikimedia India Chapter. While Free hugs[7] was more a public event where our members and allies presented 'warm hugs' to the public which was kind of new in the state, Wiki Loves Pride[8] could inspire more young minds utilize their sharp writing skills to add *n* number of articles on homosexuality and LGBT rights to Wikipedia Malayalam pages. Another pivotal area we look into is providing peer support for sexual health and HIV awareness with support from related testing and counseling centers in the state. Queerala, as a Queer support group, always holds the Queer Pride March in Kerala, which is organized by the alliance. Our volunteers are in forefront to work for the annual Pride event, raise funds and networking with allies in promoting the event. An art initiative from us was Homomorphism,[9] which was an Art project, to pinpoint notions on same gender intimacy, which are often mis-represented in our State. The art exhibition, which got wide response, inspired us to take it further and reproduce it in other major cities in India. Another crucial facet we are looking into in recent months, is helping our less-privileged Trans friends to get permanent jobs, and to accompany advocacy and awareness for the city police forces - who recently has gone wild, threatening the dignity of a few Transgender friends in the city.

Having seen the improved reception we achieved in Kerala, we believe all these events/activities/campaigns regarding the LGBT community issues need to be taken to a higher level of panel discussions on policy making and work place inclusions, which can inspire the govt./public sector to initiate support systems for the cause, and cater to further workshops, etc. Such events would definitely motivate other groups working for various social causes to take up leadership and to come up with such events in the near future. Foreseeing the above said our latest academic intervention was a research conference[10], 'Quest – 2016' - *two day national seminar on queer discourses and social dialogues* aimed to bring forward the least discussed facets[11] of queer lives in Kerala. The two day national conference witnessed three plenary sessions, four panel discussion and around 22 paper presentations by scholars from around the nation. Rev Fr Philip Kuruvilla, from the ESHA Program of NCCI, was an invited guest for the program, who gave a presentation on NCCI's involvements for the sexual minorities in India. A major outcome of the two day program- and we are still working on it - would be a detailed report on the possibility of educational level inclusion, workplace non- discrimination, research initiatives etc. The ultimate aim of our group is to fuel further healthy media-academic-political discussions regarding alternate sexuality and related topics. We have formed several coalitions, and one such was the alliance with National Council of Churches in India, who had organised a seminar[12] on *'Envisioning an Inclusive Church: Dialogue on Homophobia and Transphobia'*. Considering the contemporary possibilities in the context of expanding the scope of the State's transgender education and related State-level interventions, we have been trying options to broaden existing syllabi to be more Sexual Orientation and Gender Identity (SOGI) inclusive. Certain core areas of social science studies like political science, teacher education, mass communication, legal education, etc., which have information on gender diversity, human rights and sexuality, have been identified and decision makers from respective board of studies were contacted to discuss possibly more inclusive curriculum. National Council of Churches in India in its recent South Asian Consultation on Church Responses to Human Sexuality [February, 2017], released a path-breaking statement[13] in solidarity with the sexual minorities. We truly feel that such strategic and practical actions shall certainly encourage further dialogues and inclusive interventions,from other faiths as well, to have dynamic plans based on a humanitarian approach..

Above all we keep our prime focus area as the mental health issues of community friends, who very often stay in agony owing to lack of proper support from family members, friends and society. Homosexuality, which is still a taboo topic in Kerala, needs closer as a humanitarian topic and the human rights associated with the same. Moving beyond rage and disbelief, Queerala will focus on how to channelize the youth' energy into productive policy and effective strategy, with the advantage that we can focus on leadership development that prioritizes building alliances through campus-based training programs. We hope to develop young leaders with the potential of effecting positive change, and to organize a coalition which combines forces - viz., various minority human rights, women's rights, health and LGBTIQ rights - in order to direct the Movement towards a society which has respect for sexual diversity. As we cross into our fourth year of being operational in Kerala, and work towards second-line leadership training, peer exchange, documentation of violence faced by community, and educational level alliances etc., we are ready with a physical working space, to create sustainable modes of income and skill development, document community issues as records for future references, and have knowledge - exchange to mould an academic hub pertaining to gender and sexuality topics in the Kerala context, and to facilitate actual research in the area of queer studies.

End Notes

1 *http://www.un.org/en/universal-declaration-human-rights/*

2 *http://queerala.org/*

3 *http://www.deccanchronicle.com/nation/in-other-news/310517/forced-marriage-haunts-gays.html*

4 *http://www.thenewsminute.com/article/claustrophobic-when-inside-abused-when-outside-lgbt-community-kerala-38332*

5 *http://timesofindia.indiatimes.com/india/Why-are-we-afraid-of-gays/articleshow/48043973.cms*

6 *http://timesofindia.indiatimes.com/life-style/people/Kochi-youth-hugging-their-way-to-happiness/articleshow/36350999.cms*

7 *http://www.newindianexpress.com/cities/thiruvananthapuram/A-Gathering-with-Much-Difference/2014/09/01/article2408172.ece*

8 *http://www.thehindu.com/news/cities/Kochi/wikipedia-to-hold-editathon-on-lgbt-issues-in-kochi/article6606781.ece*

9 *http://www.deccanchronicle.com/151130/lifestyle-offbeat/article/art-coming-out*

10 *http://quest.queerala.org/*

11 *http://www.thehindu.com/news/cities/Thiruvananthapuram/Seminar-flags-off-dialogue-on-queer-issues/article16895172.ece*

12 *http://queerala.org/envisioning-an-inclusive-church-dialogue-on-homophobia-and-transphobia/*

13 *http://queerala.org/asian-consultation-on-church-responses-to-human-sexuality-and-gender-minorities/*

Email: queerala2014@gmail.com: Website: www.queerala.org

SAATHII
Solidarity and Action Against
the HIV Infection in India

SAATHII is a national NGO working on access to health, justice and social welfare for marginalized communities, including lesbian, gay, bi, trans, intersex and other (LGBT+), and communities impacted by HIV/AIDS. It engages in advocacy for LGBTI+ inclusion with legal services authorities, health care institutions, educational institutions, and faith communities.

SAATHII- Chennai : Ph: (+91) 44 2440-3663/947 :Email: info@saathii.org

SAATHII- Hyderabad : Phone: (+91) 40 2767-4757 :Email: info@saathii.org

SAATHII - Delhi : Phone: (+91) 11 4100-7035 : Email: info@saathii.org

SAATHII – Bhubaneswar : Phone: (+91) 674 255-2845 : Email: info@saathii.org

SAATHII -Kolkata :Ph: (+91) 33 2416-4836 : Email: info@saathii.org

SAATHII : Jaipur :Phone: (+91) 141 405-2682 : Email: info@saathii.org

SAATHII -Imphal : Email: info@saathii.org

Suggested Web Links/Books

Suggested LGBTI Web Links

Here one can find a list of LGBTIQ+ - friendly resources including counselors, community groups, websites, and mailing lists for LGBTIQ+ communities of Indian and South Asian origin. Please note that this page is an attempt to aggregate potentially useful resources for greater awareness and networking, but inclusion of an organization or list on this page does not constitute an endorsement of its services.

o   http://orinam.net/
o   http://www.humsafar.org/
o   http://www.projectbolo.com/
o   http://mingle.org.in/
o   http://www.bombaydost.co.in/
o   http://pink-pages.co.in/
o   http://www.gaylaxymag.com/
o   http://gaysifamily.com/
o   http://saathii.org/
o   http://nazindia.org/
o   http://www.allianceindia.org/
o   http://fiftyshadesofgay.co.in/

Lists of LGBT+ groups and mailing lists in India:

• *http://orinam.net/resources-for/lgbt/groups-and-lists/*

Lists of university and college LGBT+ groups in India:

• *http://orinam.net/resources-for/lgbt/campus-initiatives/*

For other responses:

➢ For the response of an ex- Catholic Priest, see: http://orinam.net/ ancy-and-andy/

➢ For a monthly magazine, see www.vartagensex.org- a website which includes the monthly issues of Varta in webzine format

➢ Other Studies:

• Pew Global Attitudes Research has studies on social attitudes on sexuality issues in various countries, including many in Asia: see *www.pewglobal.org.*

• The International Lesbian and Gay Association publishes an annual State Sponsored Homophobia, State SponsoredTransphobia set of maps, charts and essays. See www. ilga.org.

• The UN Development Programme has published 'Being LGBT in Asia' reports specifically on Cambodia, China, Indonesia, Mongolia, Nepal, Philippines, Thailand and Vietnam. See www. asia-pacific.undp.org.

• The Asia Pacific Forum of National Institutions for the Promotion and Protection of Human Rights in 2016 published a major study on issues and best practices: Promoting and Protecting Human Rights: Sexual Orientation, Gender Identity and Sexual Characteristics: A Manual for National Human Rights Institutions, 244 pages. See *www.asiapacificforum.net.*

Suggested Books

A. Books recommended by the Senate of Serampore College as part of their syllabus

'Human Sexuality: Theological and Ethical Reflections'

2   Credit hours, Optional Course, College Examined: Theology Cluster

1.   Required Readings by the Syllabus

Anderson-Rajkumar, Evangeline, "Significance of the Body in Feminist Theological Discourse" in *Bangalore Theological Forum*, vol. xxxiii, no.2, Dec. 2001

An Ecumenical Document on Human Sexuality (Nagpur: CJPC-NCCI, 2012)

Cahill, Lisa Sowle, *Sex, Gender, and Christian Ethics* (Cambridge: Cambridge University Press, 1996)

Cheng, Patrick S, *Radical Love: An Introduction to Queer Theology* (New York: Seabury Books, 2011)

De La Torres, Miguel A., *A Lily among the Thorns: Imagining a New Christian Sexuality* (San Francisco: John Wiley & Sons, 2007)

Ellison, Marvin M, *Making Love Just: Sexual Ethics for Perplexing Time* (Minneapolis: Fortress Press, 2012)

Ellison, Marvin M and Sylvia Thorson-Smith (eds.), *Body and Soul: Rethinking Sexuality in Justice-Love* (Cleveland: The Pilgrim Press, 2003)

Ellison, Marvin M and Kelly Brown Douglass (eds.), *Sexuality and the Sacred: Sources for Theological Reflection* (Louisville: Westminster John Knox Press, 2010)

Farley, Margaret A., *Just Love: A Framework for Christian Sexual Ethics* (New York: Continuum, 2006)

Foucault, Michel and Robert Hurley *History of Sexuality, Vol. 1: An Introduction* (New York, Vintage Books, 1976)

"Human Sexuality: Theological and Biblical Reflections," *Gurukul Journal of Theological Studies*, Vol. XXIII, No. 2, June 2012

Lebacqz, Karen (ed.), *Sexuality: A Reader* (Cleveland: The Pilgrim Press, 1999)

Menon, Nivedita (ed.), *Sexualities* (New Delhi: Women Unlimited, 2007)

Rajkumar, Christopher (ed.), *Public and Sensual: Exploring Solutions: Bible Studies on Human Sexuality* (Nagpur: NCCI, 2012)

Sheerattan-Bisnauth, Patricia and Philip Vinod Peacock, *Created in God's Image: From Hegemony to Partnership: A Church Manual on Men as Partners Promoting Positive Masculinities* (Geneva: WCRC/WCC, 2010)

Varghese, Winnie, *Christian Response to Homophobia* (Bangalore: BTESSC, 2014)

Zachariah, George (ed.), *Church and Homophobia* (Bangalore/Delhi: CISRS/ISPCK, 2014)

2.   Suggested Readings by the Syllabus

Althaus-Reid, Marcella, *Indecent Theology: Theological Perversions in Sex, Gender and Politics* (London: Routledge, 2000)

Althaus-Reid, Marcella, *The Queer God* (London: Routledge, 2003)

Amirtham, Metti, *Women in India: Negotiating Body, Reclaiming Agency* (Delhi: ISPCK, 2011)

Brock, Rita Nakshima, *Journeys By Heart. A Christology of the Erotic Power* (New York: Crossroad, 1988)

Butler, Judith, *Undoing Gender* (London: Routledge, 2004)

Carden, Michael, *Sodomy: A History of a Christian Biblical Myth* (London: Equinox, 2004)

Chakraverty, Radha, (ed.), *Bodymaps: Stories by South Asian Women* (New Delhi: Zubaan, 2007)

Cheng, Patrick S, *From Sin to Amazing Grace: Discovering the Queer Christ* (New York: Seabury Books, 2012)

Clark, Elizabeth (ed.), *St. Augustine on Marriage and Sexuality* (Washington, D.C.: The Catholic University of America Press, 1996)

Countryman, William, *Dirt, Greed, and Sex: Sexual Ethics in the New Testament and Their Implications for Today* (Minneapolis: Fortress Press, 2007)

Evdokimov, Paul, *The Sacraments of Love: The Nuptial Mystery in the Light of the Orthodox Tradition* (New York: St Vladimir's Seminary Press, 1985)

Fuchs, Eric, *Sexual Desire and Love: Origins and History of the Christian Ethic of Sexuality and Marriage* (New York: The Seabury Press, 1983)

Garton, Stephen, *Histories of Sexuality: Antiquity to Sexual Revolution* (London: Equinox, 2004)

Thatcher, Adrian, *God, Sex, Gender: An Introduction* (Hoboken: Wiley-Blackwell, 2011)

Gilson, Anne B., *The Battle for America's Families: A Feminist Response to the Religious Right* (Cleveland: The Pilgrim Press, 1999)

Gross, Robert E., *Queering Christ: Beyond Jesus Acted Up* (Cleveland: The Pilgrim Press, 2002)

Gross, Robert E and Mona West (eds.), *Take Back the Word: A Queer Reading of the Bible* (Cleveland: The Pilgrim Press, 2000)

Heyward, Carter, *Staying Power: Reflections on Gender, Justice and Compassion* (Cleveland: The Pilgrim Press, 1995)

Isherwood, Lisa and Elizabeth Stuart, *Introducing Body Theology* (Cleveland: Pilgrim Press, 1998)

Jennings, Theodore W, *An Ethic of Queer Sex: Principles and Improvisations* (Chicago: Exploration Press, 2013)

Jensen, David H., *God, Desire, and a Theology of Human Sexuality* (Louisville: Westminster John Knox Press, 2013)

Kosambi, Meera, *Crossing Thresholds: Feminist Essay in Social History* (New Delhi: Permanent Black, 2011)

Koshy, Vineeth, and Philip Kuruvilla, (eds,), *Positive Readings: Biblical Reflections on HIV & AIDS for Young People* (Nagpur: NCCI, 2011)

Kuruvilla, Philip, and Wati Longchar (eds.), *HIV & AIDS, Towards Inclusive Communities: A Theological Reader* (Delhi/Nagpur: ISPCK/NCCI, 2014)

Nelson, James, *Between Two Gardens: Reflections on Sexuality and Religious Experience* (Cleveland: The Pilgrim Press, 1983)

Nelson, James B., *Body Theology* (Westminster: John Knox Press, 1992)

Policy on HIV & AIDS, A Guide to Churches in India (Nagpur: ESHA - NCCI, 2009 and 2011)

Puri, Jyoti, *Woman, Body, Desire in Postcolonial India: Narratives of Gender and Sexuality* (New York: Routledge, 1999)

Rogers, Eugene F., (ed.), *Theology and Sexuality: Classic and Contemporary Readings* (Oxford: Blackwell, 2002)

Stone, Ken (ed.), *Queer Commentary and the Hebrew Bible* (Cleveland: The Pilgrim Press, 2001)

B.   Books [and websites where they are available] recommended by members of the LGBTIQ+ community for reading. Please note that this is an attempt to aggregate potentially useful reading resources for greater knowledge, but their inclusion does not constitute an endorsement of their content.

*   Because I Have A Voice, Edited by Arvind Narrain and Gautam Bhan
    http://www.amazon.in/Because-Have-Voice-Queer-Politics/dp/819022722X

- Same Sex Love In India, Edited by Ruth Vanita and Saleem Kidwai, *http://www.amazon.in/Same-Sex-Love-India-Readings-Literature/dp/0312293240*

- Law Like Love Edited by Arvind Narrain and Alok Gupta, *http://www.amazon.in/Law-Like-Love-Queer-Perspectives/dp/9380403143*

- Queer: Law and Despised Sexualities in India by Arvind Narrain (Old book but relevant nevertheless): *http://altlawforum.org/publications/queer-law-and-despised-sexualities-in-india/*

- This Alien Legacy, Human Rights Watch Report by Alok Gupta, *https://www.hrw.org/sites/default/files/reports/lgbt1208_webwcover.pdf*

- Human Rights Violations Against Sexual Minorities in India but PUCL-K

- Human Rights Violations against the Transgender Community, *http://www.pucl.in/reports/human-rights-violations-against-transgender-community*

- A Report on Human Rights Violation of Transgenders in Karnataka, 2014, *http://orinam.net/content/wp-content/uploads/2015/08/FINAL-REPORT-ON-HUMAN-RIGHTS-VIOLATIONS-OF-TRANSGENDER-PERSONS.pdf*

Comprehensive Sexuality Education Books – highly recommended for children and teenagers – from TARSHI

Talking About Reproductive and Sexual Health Issues [TARSHI] believes that all people have the right to sexual well being and to a self-affirming and enjoyable sexuality. TARSHI works towards expanding sexual and reproductive choices in people's lives in an effort to enable them to enjoy lives of dgnity, freedom from fear, infection and, reproductive and sexual health problems.

The Red Book: For children aged: 10-14 years

The Blue Book: For children and teenagers aged 15+

The Yellow Book: A Parents Guide to Sexuality Education

The Orange Book: A Teachers Workbook on Sexuality Education

Website: *www.tarshi.net*; Facebook: *www.facebook.com/tarshi.ngo*; Twitter: twitter.com/tarshingo

TARSHI

Address: C-29 Basement, East of Kailash, New Delhi 110065

Addendum

Contributors (in order of writing)

Sam Killerman, better known as the person who created the 'Genderbread Person' at http://itspronouncedmetrosexual.com/2013/01/a-comprehensive-list-of-lgbtq-term-definitions.

Dr. George Zachariah - An Adjunct Professor of Ethics at the United Theological College, Bangalore, and one of the foremost theologians in Asia working on issues around human sexuality and gender diversity.

Dr. Aruna Gnanadason has worked for long with the World Council of Churches based in Geneva, and has written extensively on Gender issues and feminism. Currently an independent Consultant.

Mr. John Lalnuntluanga is a Faculty of History of Christianity at the Leonard Theological College, Jabalpur. He is currently working on his PhD.

Dr. Geevarghese Mor Coorilos is Metropolitan of Malankara Jacobite Syrian Church and an esteemed Theologian. He is a visiting Professor at various theological colleges across the globe. He has held several positions with the NCCI and the World Council of Churches.

Dr. Joseph N. Goh is a Lecturer in Gender Studies at the School of Arts and Social Sciences, Monash University Malaysia, and an ordained clergyperson with the Old Catholic Movement. He holds a PhD in gender, sexuality and theology, and his research interests include queer and LGBTI studies, human rights and sexual health issues, diverse theological and religious studies, and qualitative research.

Dr. Varghese Punnoose MD, is Professor and Head of Department of Psychiatry, Government Medical College, Kottayam, Kerala.

Dr. Ronald Lalthanmawia is Head of the Community Health Department, Christian Medical Association of India [CMAI], Delhi.

Dr. T. S. Sathyanarayana Rao, is from the Department of Psychiatry, JSS Medical College, Mysore, Karnataka.

Dr. K. S. Jacob is from the Christian Medical College, Vellore, Tamil Nadu.

Sanchit Saluja is a 4th Year law student of B.A., L.L.B. (Honours) course at the National Law University, Delhi.

Ms. Anjali Gopalan is the Executive Director of the Naz Foundation [India] Trust.

Ms. Rebina Subba is a Lawyer and Founder-Chairperson of Shamakami, an NGO dealing with sexual minority issues based in Shillong, Meghalaya.

Rev. Fr. Thomas Ninan serves the National Council of Churches in India as the General Coordinator of the ESHA Program. He is an ordained minister of the Indian Orthodox Church. He is a Post Graduate in Theology and Development from the University of KwaZulu-Natal, South Africa.

Shruti Ambast and Namrata Mukherjee are Research Fellows at Vidhi Centre for Legal Policy, New Delhi.

Maya Ann Joseph, model, and transwoman, lives in Kerala.

Daniel Francies Mary Mendonca is currently working for YUVA as a community organisor in Mumbai. Daniel is often called upon as a resource person during work with sexual minorities.

Mr. Lifter Tua Marbun is originally from Indonesia and is now residing in the Netherlands.

L. Romal M Singh is a 30-year-old writer, editor, activist, and performer, who calls Bangalore home.

Payana is a Community Owned-Managed Organization which was formed by Alternative Sexuality Minority Community Members in 2009 in Bangalore.

Deepak Kashyap is a counseling psychologist and a certified life-skills trainer with a private practice in Mumbai, India. He holds a Master's Degree in Psychology of Education from the University of Bristol, UK, and has been trained in New York and Oxford. He is author of *The Pink Booklet*.

Rev. Fr. Philip Kuruvilla is an ordained minister of the Indian Orthodox Church and was earlier Dean of the St Thomas Orthodox Theological Seminary in Nagpur. He holds several degrees, including a Master of Theology from the University of Oxford. He has been working with the National Council of Churches in India since 2000. He has been the General Coordinator of the NCCI's ESHA Program and is now its Consultant. [For more details see: About the Editor]

Arcot Lutheran Church: Rt. Rev. G. Raja Socrates, Bishop/Chairperson ALC, and Rev. V. Murali Christian, Director, Dept. of Gender Issues. Church of North India: Compiled by Philip Kuruvilla with inputs from Dr Alma Ram and Rev. Deepak Yohan.

Church of South India: Rev. Asir Ebenezer, Director, CSI-SEVA, CSI Synod, Chennai.

The Mar Thoma Syrian Church: Rev. Abin Srambickal, Director, Navodaya Project.

Malankara Orthodox Syrian Church: Fr Jacob Mathew is Lecturer at the Orthodox Theological Seminary in Kottayam.

The Salvation Army: Captain Andrews D. Christian, Administrator, Salvation Army, Emery Hospital, Anand.

Rev. James Wesly S., Dean of Studies, Bishop's College.

Rev. Phanenmo Kath, Assist. Prof. Pastoral Counselling & Psychology, Eastern Theological College, Jorhat Assam.

Rev. Fr. George Varughese, is a Lecturer at Gurukul Lutheran Theological College, [GLTC], Chennai

Rev. Dr. S. Hayong is a Lecturer at John Roberts Theological Seminary [JRTS], Mawklot, Shillong.

Dr. Bendanglemla Longkumer, is Faculty in the Christian Theology Department, Leonard Theological College, Jabalpur.

Rev. Dr. R. Annie Watson is part of the Faculty of Karnataka Theological College, Mangalore.

Rev. Fr Jacob Mathew is Lecturer, Orthodox Theological Seminary [OTS], Kottayam.

Prof. Douglas Sanders is Professor Emeritus, University of British Columbia, Vancouver, Canada; former Visiting Professor, LL.M., Chulalongkorn University, Bangkok; Academic Associate, Institute for Human Rights and Peace Studies, Mahidol University, Bangkok; resident in Thailand since 2003.

Pearl Wong, is Director of Queer Theological Academy, Hong Kong.

About the Editor

Philip Kuruvilla has a wide range of experience, and when taken together with his Indian Orthodox Church background, it forms a rainbow hue which exemplifies his colourful personality. Born in Kolkata, he received his education at some of the finest institutions -he completed his schooling from La Martiniere, Kolkata, graduated with Political Science Honours from Hindu College, Delhi University; took a Bachelor of Divinity degree from the Senate of Serampore, a Masters degree in Social Work from Nagpur University, and was awarded a Master of Theology Degree from Oxford, through Westminster College. At 21, after graduating from Delhi, he joined the family business, manufacturing rubber dock fenders for Indian sea-ports. A keen sportsman, he played rugby at international levels, and captained a Kolkata First Division Hockey XI; he rode horses, winning races as an amateur jockey. By the age of 26 he had hitchhiked over 25 countries in Asia, Europe, North America, Australia and New Zealand – no mean feat in the 70's - before setting up *Pan Asian Tours,* his own travel agency in Kolkata, mentioned in the *Lonely Planet's* 'Travel Guide to India'. As a young entrepreneur, a sportsman, and a socialite - he was an integral part of Kolkata's high life - he was least expected to turn a spiritual *seeker.*

In 1983, aged 32, a very personal decision to search for God and a more spiritual life led him to Kerala and a monastery set among rolling hills and secluded waterfalls. After a year here, the 4 year Divinity degree from the Orthodox Seminary in Kottayam seemed a logical step. His subsequent work as a Youth facilitator for the Orthodox Church all over India, remains legendary even today. After his ordination as a priest in 1995, he was appointed Dean of the new and historic St. Thomas Orthodox Theological

Seminary set up in Nagpur. In June 2000 he was nominated by his church to the post of Executive Secretary of the India Watch Desk of the NCCI, which worked for Human Rights and took on the pandemic of HIV & AIDS through the Churches. His work forced the mostly reluctant Indian churches to take up issues related to AIDS, which is probably why, in March 2006, he was selected by the Christian Conference of Asia (CCA) based in Chiang Mai, as their *first* Consultant on HIV and AIDS. In April 2011, he was invited by the General Secretary of National Council of Churches in India to rejoin NCCI as the General Coordinator of ESHA's [AIDS] program, which took a new direction as of August 2015, when it forayed into the arena of human sexuality and gender diversity. He has since been working towards greater inclusivity for the LGBTQI communities among NCCI's member churches, *and* among the theological colleges all over India. With his experience in this rare field, and his dynamism, he is perfectly suited to bring out such a publication which will positively affect the lives of many who are ostracized by society for their sexual preferences.

In the last 3 decades, he has created 5 video documentary films, and several audio productions. He has several books to his credit, some as author, others as editor or co-editor, all of which leave footprints showing the direction and the experiences of his life's journey. During his tenure in the CCA, he helped to draft its *"Church Policy on HIV & AIDS"* for all the Asian Churches. His work with HIV/AIDS has transcended the barriers of religion - during the last 10 years he has partnered with HH Sri Sri Ravi Shankar, Swami Agnivesh, Pujya Chidananda Swamy of Parmarth Ashram in Rishikesh, and with Jamia Millia Islamia University in Delhi, to name a few. Meanwhile he also continues to hold honorary international positions, eg., Secretary of the Asian Interfaith Network on AIDS (AINA), and Honorary Member of the International Network of Religious Leaders Living with HIV/AIDS [INERELA +, Asia Pacific Region]. He has attended and given presentations at many international conferences.

In 1992 he married Bibi, a counselor and mentor for German social work volunteers in India. They have two children - Maria is a journalist in Chennai, and David is assisting a cyber-security start up while simultaneously arranging adventure tours in Nagaland. Fr. Philip continues to be Consultant for NCCI's ESHA program, while serving in the Holy Trinity Chapel set in the serene surroundings of Soukya: an integrated healing centre in Whitefield, in Bangalore. He can be reached at frpkuruvilla@hotmail.com.

NCCI Publications on Allied Topics

2004: *HIV/AIDS: A Handbook for the Church in India*: ©NCCI Editor: Kuruvilla, Philip

2009: *Policy on HIV/AIDS: a Guide to the Churches in India*: ©NCCI

2011: *Positive Readings: Biblical Reflections on HIV & AIDS for Young People*; ©NCCI Editors: Kuruvilla, Philip and Koshy, Vineeth

2012: *An Ecumenical Document on Human Sexuality*: ©NCCI

2012: *Public and Sensual: Exploring Solution: Bible Studies on Human Sexuality*: (C) NCCI Editor: Rajkumar, Christopher.

2014: *HIV/AIDS: Towards Inclusive Communities*: ©NCCI Editors: Kuruvilla, Philip and Longchar, Wati

2017: *Christian Responses to issues of Human Sexuality and Gender Diversity: A Handbook for the Churches in India*: ©NCCI Editor: Kuruvilla, Philip

2017: *A Theological Reader on Human Sexuality and Gender Diversities: Envisioning Inclusivity*: ©NCCI: Editors: Gaikwad, Roger and Ninan, Thomas

About the Theological Reader: This Reader has been developed based on the syllabus of the Senate of Serampore College on Human Sexuality and Gender Diversities for B.D. graduates. Written [by eminent theologians from all over India] from a context where churches and religious communities at large have considered the issues related to gender diversities and sexuality as taboo, the book is a relevant starting point for any serious theological engagement on the topic. It requires courage to embark on a theological journey which discerns the human understanding on this issue, and this book has taken that, pastoral, pro-life and transforming journey. The National Council of Churches in India has striven since 2001 to promote life, justice and peace, taking a prophetic stance to engage churches and theological colleges in this regard.

www.ingramcontent.com/pod-product-compliance
Lightning Source LLC
Chambersburg PA
CBHW081141020726
47504CB00009B/1954